THE LION IN
THE WIND

WRITTEN BY
STEVEN LAKE

PUBLISHED BY WIZARD TOWER PUBLISHING

THE LION IN THE WIND

ISBN Number: 978-1-940155-85-2

10 9 8 7 6 5 4 3 2 1

Published by: Wizard Tower Publishing

Printed and Published in the United States of America

Dedication

I'd like to dedicate this book to Don Semora, who helped me take a private hobby, and turn it into a professional one that brings the joy of my writing and my stories to the world.

Prologue

A man dressed in brilliant white robes appeared on the prairie in a dazzling blaze of light that dimmed to a soft, white glow. Another man in similarly white robes appeared next to him a moment later. The second man studied the prairie around him with interest.

"Why are we back here again?" he asked.

"Negago has once again turned his focus to this world in his war of conquest, and seeks to destroy my people, the Yigzan, as well as all other life on this world. Therefore we must renew our efforts to protect it as we have before," said the first man.

"Then it is time to summon a new proxy?" asked the second.

The first man nodded.

"It is."

"Who shall I summon then?" asked the second man.

The first man's robes seemed to glow brighter as he smiled slightly, as though musing over something important.

"Not who, but what. Namely, a machine," he said.

The second man stared at him curiously.

"You would have a machine be your proxy? But how will you do that?" he asked.

The first man smiled.

"Just watch. You'll see."

"But why a machine?"

"Because no man, nor creature of flesh, will be strong enough to stand against that which is to come. Only a machine will have the strength to do what is needed."

Chapter 1

"Mr. Burgon?"

The words came like a hammer, shattering the placid solitude that filled a mind well vested in its work. A pair of magnifying goggles swung around, split apart and then retracted to the side as the face of a middle aged man appeared from behind them.

"I'm sorry if I'm interrupting your work, sir, but there are some men here to see you," said a short haired young man.

An eyebrow went up slightly.

"Who would be here to see me?" asked Burgon as he set his tools aside.

"They said they're from Cybergenics Incorporated," replied the young man.

Burgon stared in surprised interest.

"The robotics company?" he asked.

The young man nodded.

"That's them. How'd you get picked to work for them?" he asked.

Burgon blinked in surprise.

"Work for them!? I haven't applied to work for anyone yet!"

The young man cocked his head in confusion.

"Then why is their recruiting team here asking for you?"

Burgon lifted the magnifying goggles off his head and set them down on the bench.

"I don't know, but I'm curious enough to find out. Where am I supposed to meet them?"

"The administration building."

Burgon nodded, turned and then hurried out of the laboratory. As he walked, he pondered this strange turn of events. It wasn't unusual to see recruiters on campus from time to time. But few asked for students by name, and none came to interview anyone unannounced. He wondered if one of his teachers had contacted them on his behalf. It was possible, but why? He hadn't expressed interest in doing anything except finishing his doctorate. He certainly wasn't looking for a job. At least, not yet. He soon arrived at the central administration building and found three men standing near the front door dressed in tailor cut black pants, tunics and shoulder cloaks.

He paused briefly and studied them. Hidden discreetly at their sides were small sidearms designed to blend in with their clothing. While their eyes studied him intently through thick, dark sunglasses, their expressions gave little clue to their thoughts. He looked to his right and saw three large, black vehicles with dark tinted windows parked next to the building in an attempt to be discrete. But try as they might, it was not working as they had clearly caught the attention of the local student body. Even so, few dared get close to them as they were heavily guarded by yet another group of black clad men. However, these ones appeared to be more heavily armed than the others, their powerful, compact assault rifles making the clear and obvious statement to all that approaching the vehicles was off limits. Burgon again began walking towards the administration building, but stopped just a few paces from the main door as one of the black clad men stepped in front of him.

"I'm sorry, sir, but this building is closed," said the man firmly.

"But I was-"

"I said the building is closed. Now leave. I won't tell you again," said the man, his hand sliding near his sidearm.

Burgon sighed and began to turn around just as the door to the building opened. A large, burly man in a modest, but well tailored earthen brown business suit stepped out of the door.

"Mr. Burgon," he said in a deep, bravado voice.

Burgon turned to look at him curiously as the man strode purposefully towards him.

"You are in fact, Edias Burgon, doctoral student in the cybernetics and robotics department of this college. Am I correct?" said the man.

Burgon nodded.

"I am. Who are you?"

"My name is Elgar. I am Mr. Black's chief in command. Come with me. I'll take you to meet him, as he wishes to speak with you."

The brown suited man then turned and walked back through the door. Burgon watched in surprise as the three guards in turn stepped aside and motioned for him to enter. He studied them briefly, and then followed Elgar inside. As he caught up to him, Burgon glanced over his shoulder at the door, and then back to Elgar.

"May I inquire as to why I was asked to come here?" he asked.

Elgar glanced briefly at Burgon, but said nothing.

"Apparently not," thought Burgon with a sigh.

Elgar led Burgon across the building to a secluded conference room near the back, and then ushered him inside.

Upon stepping into the room, Burgon immediately noticed two men sitting around a plain, wooden conference table. The first man was well known to him as he was an administrator at the college, and had been a professor in several of Burgon's classes. The second, though, he didn't recognize. However, Burgon could tell there was something special about him. The man's jet black hair and equally black, yet highly expensive and powerful business suit told him that whoever this was, he was a man of means, and likely very powerful as well. He watched as the man studied him through narrow, slotted eyes, his hands folded before him contemplatively. Burgon then looked back at the first man and bowed slightly.

"Good afternoon, Mr. Yadic. You called me?" he said.

"Yes, I did, Edias. Thank you for coming. Please, sit down. We have much to discuss," said the first man, gesturing to a seat in front of the table.

Burgon quickly sat down as instructed. He then watched as a curious, almost sinister smile grew across the second man's face.

"Welcome, Mr. Burgon. I pray that my guards didn't give you too much trouble when you arrived," said the second man with a hint of elegance.

"Those were your guards?" asked Burgon.

"They are."

Burgon furrowed his brow.

"Well, they were firm and professional in their duties, if nothing else. However, I'm curious why you have so many with you. It seems a bit, well, excessive," he said.

The man smiled.

"Because I have many jealous competitors."

Burgon's eyes narrowed.

"Why would they be jealous enough to threaten your life?"

The man smiled beatifically.

"Because, I own Cybergenics Incorporated. That alone is reason enough."

Burgon's eyes went wide.

"Wait. Does that mean you're Ferrell Black!?" he said in surprise.

The man nodded. Burgon nearly became giddy with excitement. This was someone he knew well, yet had never met. Black was famous across the Yigzan nation for the incredible number of amazing cybernetic and robotic advances his company had made over the past twenty years, far surpassing even some of the greatest minds in the land. In fact, his success had made him many bitter enemies and jealous competitors. Yet, despite their efforts to unseat him, few had succeeded in doing more than simply equaling his greatness, but never surpassing it, try as they might.

"Oh, what a pleasure it is, sir, to meet someone like you who loves robotics so much!" said Burgon with almost child like glee.

The man smiled magnanimously.

"The pleasure is all mine. I've heard so many great things about your work that I had to meet you. From all I've seen, you've already made quite a name for yourself here," he said.

"Yes, he has!" said Yadic cheerfully. He turned to Burgon, and said, "The faculty and I are pleased to tell you that Mr. Black would like to offer you a job with his company."

"A job? How would that be possible? I haven't finished my doctorate yet," said Burgon in surprise.

"That's not a problem. We can wave the last of your requirements and give you your doctorate now if you'd like," said Yadic.

Burgon straightened himself proudly.

"I can't do that! Doing such would be dishonest and disrespectful of the hundreds of other brilliant men and women who've come before me and worked so hard to earn their degrees! I will not have my doctorate just handed to me with my work yet incomplete!"

Black smiled.

"I see that he is as honorable as you've said."

"I thank you for your compliment, Mr. Black, but until my work is complete, and the criteria for my doctorate met, I cannot become an employee of your company. I will not start my career based on a lie and a deception!" said Burgon.

Yadic smiled and shook his head.

"You won't have to. You've already submitted your thesis and argued it successfully, correct?"

"Yes, but I haven't finished my final project yet. I need to complete that in order to fulfill all the requirements of my doctorate."

Black leaned back in his chair and folded his hands thoughtfully.

"How would you like to be paid to finish your project?" he asked.

Burgon raised an eyebrow.

"Are you saying that you'd like me to finish my project while in your employ?" he asked.

"Your skill is so exceptional and one of a kind that I don't want to risk having you snatched up by anyone else. Especially one of my competitors."

Burgon studied Black, but kept silent as he mulled over this offer in his mind.

Finally he leaned forward, and said, "I appreciate your offer, Mr. Black, but I must respectfully decline. I need to finish my doctoral project first. When I am done with that, and my degree is complete, if I am still interested in your offer, I will contact you."

Black's eyes narrowed.

"Is that really what you want?" he asked with a sly grin.

"It is."

Black smiled magnanimously.

"Then I will respect your wishes." He then handed Burgon a business card, and said, "If you do decide to accept my offer later on, please don't hesitate to contact me."

Burgon nodded slightly.

"I won't."

He then excused himself, and slipped out of the room. Yadic watched him go in disbelief and quietly groaned to himself.

"I can't believe he's just walking away from your offer like that," he said.

"Don't worry, director. He's just got a lot on his mind. He'll come when he's ready. Besides, I'd rather have him come of his own free will. He'll do better as an employee if he doesn't feel as though he were pressured into working for me."

"I hope you're right, Mr. Black. I'd hate to see him pass up this opportunity."

Black smirked slightly, his eyes narrow and dark. He folded his hands contemplatively as he stared after Burgon.

"Oh, believe me, he won't."

Three Months Later...

Burgon walked slowly into one of the laboratories at the robotics research facility and studied the room in disbelief. It was a complete mess with wires, cables, cybernetic parts and pieces, nuts, bolts, equipment, empty glasses, food wrappers and other things scattered all over the lab intermingled with paperwork, drawings, schematics, computer hardware and a multitude of other things. While it was true that a messy desk, or in this case a laboratory, was the sign of a brilliant mind, this was a little too messy. He almost wondered if they shouldn't hire a maid.

"Hello? Is anyone here?" he shouted.

A metallic head popped up from behind a nearby bin of parts and then vanished, reappearing a moment later at his feet. The dog like robot, similar in appearance to a basset hound, at first startled him, but soon made him smile. He then squatted down and reached out to the small canine robot. But it backed away slightly and studied his hand apprehensively. Burgon laughed. It was odd to see such animal like behavior from a little robotic dog, and yet encouraging at the same time. It's large round eyes focused on his face, and then sniffed at him suspiciously.

"AV1, heel!" came a voice from a nearby doorway.

The little robotic dog immediately sat down and snapped to attention. A short, stout man in a white lab coat hobbled across the floor and up to Burgon.

"I'm very sorry about that. He's a nosy little pest," he grumbled.

He then gave the robotic dog a gentle, disciplinary kick. Burgon chuckled.

"Oh, it's nothing. He wasn't doing anything bad," he replied.

"Ah, well, that's good. At least he didn't do to you what he did to the last stranger who stepped in here," said the man gruffly.

"Which was?"

The man frowned.

"You don't wanna know."

Burgon laughed.

"Couldn't be any worse than what my own droids have done to me before."

The man gave a snorting grunt.

"I can imagine," he said tersely.

He then slapped himself lightly on the forehead, and then held out his hand to Burgon.

"My apologies. I almost forgot my manners. I'm Dr. Visnel, director of the cybernetics and robotics research department," said the man.

Burgon bowed slightly and shook Visnel's hand.

"I'm doctor Burgon. Nice to meet you."

The man's eyes lit up.

"Edias Burgon?"

Burgon smiled, and said, "One in the same."

"Well, it's quite an honor to meet the only student in the entire history of the college to get a perfect score on their doctoral project."

Burgon smiled sheepishly.

"The reviewers were overly kind to me."

Visnel smiled.

"Don't be so humble. Anyone who can do that honestly, and without cheating, has earned my undying respect. So what brings you here?"

"I'm your new employee."

Visnel furrowed his brow in surprise.

"My employee!? Nobody told me anything about that. Why'd they hire you? Of course, given your record, that's probably a dumb question," he said.

Burgon laughed.

"They liked my project so much that they hired me on the spot."

"Really? So how do you know you're supposed to work for me?"

Burgon pulled a piece of paper out of his pocket and handed it to Visnel, who then took and read it with interest. After a bit he looked up at Burgon and grunted.

"Huh. It figures they'd hire someone and not tell me. Well, at least I lucked out and got you. It beats some of the people they've sent me before."

Burgon grinned and then scanned the room around him.

"There's a lot more to this place than I remember seeing during my doctoral studies," he said.

"That's done on purpose. Some of it's for security reasons, and some of it's to force students into coming up with their own ideas rather than stealing ours. We can't allow the...awe, simbit. Not again. AV1, spider!"

Burgon eyed Visnel with curiosity, and then turned in surprise as the little robotic dog jumped up and took off across the room. A few seconds later, a large metallic spider launched itself out of a nearby pile of robotic parts and made a mad dash for a nearby wall. But AV1 was faster and quickly overtook the spider. Realizing its peril, it turned to defend itself, but was immediately crushed like an egg between the little dog's jaws. The spider twitched briefly, and then went limp.

"AV1, return," said Visnel.

The little robot trotted proudly over to Visnel, deposited the dead spider at his feet, and then sat down at attention as he wagged his tail proudly.

"What is that?" asked Burgon as Visnel reached down and picked up the spider.

"It's an autonomous robotic reconnaissance and survey probe. But most people just call them scout spiders. They're used as spies by everyone from the federal government to the corporate megaliths. This is the fourth one we've encountered so far this month. Someone apparently has a strong interest in knowing what we're doing here it seems."

"Who do you think it is?" asked Burgon.

"I'm not sure. We've examined every one of them that we've caught and none of them have any markings that tell us where they're from or who sent them. Not even the programming tells us anything. It's a complete mystery."

He tossed the spider onto a nearby table and began walking towards the back.

"Well, regardless, we need to get you started. I've got a couple of projects for you to work on that should be right up your alley."

"Such as?" asked Burgon.

"Well, ironically enough, one of them involves scout spiders, if you're willing to believe that."

Burgon chuckled.

"Like the unit that AV1 destroyed?"

Visnel grunted.

"Sadly enough, yes. Personally I hate them. However, they seem to be hugely popular right now across the continent, kinda like those new drones that Cybergenics just released last month. Honestly, I can't fathom why anyone would want to use one of those little beasts. But alas, ours is not to ponder why, but simply to make stuff happen. So if the demand of the public is for better scout spiders, then that is where our work will lead us."

"Why not into other areas?"

Visnel picked up a spanner wrench and calipers off a nearby table and put them in his coat pocket. He then handed another set to Burgon.

"We'll be working in those areas too. But Yadic and the other directors want us focusing on spiders for the moment. Personally, I'd like to ignore their request. But, since they sign my paycheck, I'm kinda stuck doing what they've asked."

Burgon laughed.

"Such is the life of a scientist these days, is it not?"

Visnel snorted.

"At least at this college it is."

Black looked up as Elgar strolled into his office and tossed a small data disk on his desk. Black glanced briefly at the disk, and then smiled.

"Anything interesting?" he asked.

Elgar crossed his arms and grunted.

"They're getting better at finding our spiders. Aside from that, there's little else to report."

"Did our latest spider find out what the doctor will be doing in his new job?"

Elgar shook his head.

"It got killed by that mechanical dog thing that Dr. Visnel has before we could find out."

"Ah, such a pity. But no matter. We'll find out what he's doing soon enough. In the meantime, have we been able to secure a copy of his doctoral project yet? The droid he built for that fascinates me on many levels."

Elgar gestured to the disk.

"We don't have the physical unit, but we were able to get a copy of the schematics and all other relevant data. The details are on that disk."

Black took the disk and inserted it into a small slot on his desk. A moment later pages upon pages of information began displaying on his computer screen. As he studied it, he smiled and laughed darkly. Elgar cocked an eyebrow in interest.

"I take it the data is to your liking?" he asked.

Black grinned with devilish delight.

"Very much so. I find myself awash in amazement as I read these technical specifications. They're dreadfully complex, and yet simplistically brilliant at the same time. It makes me excited at the thought of him working for me some day," he said.

"Should we begin efforts to draw him over to us?" asked Elgar.

Black shook his head.

"No. I want him to come to us on his own. If we force him, it might cause problems for us later on. I've learned that men like him tend to be more productive and creative if they come of their own free will. Or at least think they have. Besides, I've been looking over your earlier reconnaissance data, and I'm beginning to think that this little excursion he's making through the college's robotics laboratory may be of benefit to both us, and him. So I'm going to let him continue down this path for the time being and see where it leads us."

Elgar bowed, and said, "As you wish."

He then turned and left the room. As soon as he was gone, Black turned back to his monitor, and grinned slyly.

"Okay, Mr. Burgon, let's see what you can do."

Ten years later...

Burgon sat on a cool, grassy hillside and chewed quietly on a sandwich as a cool afternoon breeze blew across his face.

"Mind if I join you?" came a soft, feminine voice behind him.

He turned to see a somewhat comely looking middle aged woman in black pants, a blue blouse and a white lab coat standing behind him. Her hair was drawn back in long, flowing, golden brown braids that danced playfully as she walked. She held a small lunch bag and thermos in her right hand as she struggled to adjust her glasses with her left.

"Sure, Rose, have a seat. I just started eating," said Burgon.

The woman sat down on the grass next to him and opened her lunch bag. Inside it she had several meat and vegetable stuffed pastries and two pieces of fruit. She casually bit into one of the pastries, and then looked at Burgon as she chewed. His expression seemed distant as he stared blankly across the prairie beyond, as though he were deep in thought.

"Thinking of something?" she asked curiously.

"Hmm?" said Burgon, turning to look at her as though suddenly awoken from a dream.

"Were you thinking of something?" she asked.

"Oh, no, not really. Well, actually, yes. I was just mulling over some of my department's research into artificial intelligence," he replied.

"What do you mean?"

"Well, part of my work here at the college involves android sentience, as you already know. Specifically, I'm working on the areas related to personality and emotions. But despite my best efforts, the droids I'm working on seem so...well, artificial. They try to act Yigzan, yet do so in a very rigid and mechanical way. It's like talking to an echo machine rather than a sentient being."

"Why is that a bad thing? They *are* machines after all."

"Yes, they are. But what if machines could think like us? They could be self-aware, reason like us, have emotions, or think thoughts uniquely their own rather than just those we create for them. I want to see them learn, and grow, and become...become...well, become something completely unique and individual."

He turned to Rose who seemed baffled by his statement.

"Aren't they like that now?" she asked.

Burgon shook his head.

"No. What you see is the result of some very ingenious programming. But, unlike us, they're neither self-aware, nor capable of going beyond the boundaries of their programming. In other words, they can't adapt to the unknown, or handle things they're not programmed to. I'd like to see them be able to do that some day. I want to build a machine that can think, and reason, and adapt to its environment on its own without any intervention on our part. In a sense, I want to make them into a living creature; something that can learn and grow on its own."

Rose took a bite of her pastry and then looked out across the prairie.

"If you could build a machine like that, what kind would it be?" she asked.

"What do you mean?" asked Burgon.

"Well, all robots come in two basic types, humanoid and creature. Your robot would be one of those two, right?"

Burgon looked confused.

"Creature?" he asked.

"Things that aren't Yigzan. Things like animals, those weird insect like machines, and other robots that have no natural shape."

Burgon smiled. He'd heard of the non-humanoid robots being described in a variety of ways, but never quite like that.

"Are there any creature types that you're particularly fond of?" she asked.

Burgon looked out across the prairie and thought for a moment.

"I've always been fond of lions. They're majestic and noble, and exude a power that seems indomitable. I'd like to build a robot just like that."

Rose looked at Burgon in interested surprise.

"You like lions?" she asked.

"I do. I've always loved lions. I even dreamed of owning one when I was a kid."

"Do you also like tigers?"

"I like them almost as much as I like lions. Why?"

"Well, if you could have a tiger as a pet, would you do it?" asked Rose.

Burgon screwed up his face in an expression of confusion.

"I guess so. Why do you ask?"

Rose gave a sigh of relief.

"Then I have something you may like. But I'll show you after we finish eating."

Burgon's curiosity now had the better of him and he quickly wolfed down his lunch, and then waited patiently as

Rose finished hers. When she was done, she led him across the campus to the animal testing facility. As they entered, Burgon found the place full of numerous creatures, many of which he recognized, and some that he did not. He pointed to several of the cages.

"What is this place?" he asked.

"It's a genetics lab. In here we experiment on animals in hopes of developing cures for a wide variety of diseases that plague our people."

Burgon frowned slightly.

"Isn't that unethical?" he asked.

Rose shrugged.

"Ethics is what you make of it, I guess. As scientists, we sometimes work outside the realm of commonly accepted ethics in order to acquire the information we need. Think of all the great medical discoveries that have been made over the years. Many of them were achieved by using methods that, at the time, were considered unethical."

She stopped and turned to him.

"I'm not saying that what we're doing is right. I'm simply saying that we're doing this to help others; and along the way we stumble onto some rather interesting things. Here, let me show you one of our more interesting discoveries."

She then turned and led him down a long corridor full of cages, each of which contained a different type of cat. Some were big, some small, and some were unlike anything Burgon had seen before. Rose walked over to one cage in particular and stopped. Inside lay a small baby snow tigress sleeping contently on her little bed. As Rose unlocked the cage, the little tigress lifted her head and stared at the scientist through droopy, sleep laden eyes. Then her eyelids snapped open as she saw Dr. Burgon smiling at her. Rose gently picked her up and handed her to Burgon who lovingly cradled the little tigress in his arms as she stared up at him in awestruck wonder.

"She's so beautiful. What's her name?" he asked as he stared deeply into the sparkling, gem like eyes of the young tigress.

"She doesn't have one yet. You can name her if you want. She's yours," said Rose.

Burgon looked at her in surprise.

"Mine!? Why are you giving her to me!?"

"The project which created her has ended, so she's of no more use to us. As such, per project protocol, she's scheduled to be put to sleep soon. But she's so beautiful that I couldn't allow that to happen. I asked the director to let her live. He told me he'd do that if I could find her a home. I'm not allowed to keep her myself, so I was hoping you could."

Burgon nodded.

"I'd love to. But why this particular animal, and not any of the others?" he asked.

Rose blushed slightly.

"Because she's very special."

"How so?"

"Mama, who is he?" asked the little tigress.

Burgon's eyes shot down to her in surprise, and then back to Rose.

"She can talk!?" he exclaimed.

Rose nodded.

"She's the byproduct of a genetics experiment that combined tiger and Yigzan DNA. She's also the only kitten out of all the experimental litters to survive."

"She's a hybrid!?" said Burgon in surprise.

Rose nodded.

"Yes, but she's a very special hybrid. She may have the body of a snow tiger, but her mind is much like ours, which means she can learn and understand things her wild kin cannot."

"But how can she talk?" asked Burgon.

Rose shrugged.

"I don't know. We haven't been able to determine that yet. Well, not without dissecting her of course, and we refuse to do that as it'd kill her."

Burgon looked at Rose with disgust, then consternation, and finally sadness before peering down at the little tigress again. He wanted to berate Rose for being a part of such an unethical line of work. But the sight of the little tigress melted his heart all over again and he forgot his anger.

"Are you my daddy?" asked the little tigress.

Burgon smiled.

"I am now."

"Are you going to give her a name?" asked Rose.

"How about I call her Persia," said Burgon. He then looked down at the little tigress, and asked, "Do you like that name?"

The little tigress smiled and nodded.

Chapter 2

Burgon leaned back in his chair and studied his proposal. He inhaled deeply, paused, and then let out a long, deep sigh. Persia lay sprawled out on his lap, purring contently as she dreamed of romping and playing freely in the tall prairie grasses that surrounded the college. He looked down at her and grinned as he stroked her soft, black and white stripped fur. She smiled contentedly and continued dreaming. He felt a pair of hands gently squeeze his shoulders and then pat him on the back. He turned to see Visnel standing behind him smiling.

"Is she sleeping?" he whispered.

Burgon nodded.

"Like a rock," he said quietly.

"How's your proposal going?"

"I'm having trouble coming up with a good way to say this without sounding silly. How many people do you know of who've actually considered a project like this?"

Visnel shrugged.

"Not many that I'm aware of. Most see robots as tools, not persons. I can't say I disagree with them either. But I'm going to support you no matter what, because even though I still think you're crazy for even considering something like this, I do see some positive benefits coming from it."

Burgon smirked.

"Gee, thanks for the support."

Visnel waved his hands dismissively.

"No, no, no. Don't misunderstand me here. I like your idea, but I can't think of any practical uses for such an advance in cybernetics. At least not at this time. My main concern is that, since there are no truly discernible practical applications for the technology, the appropriations board will likely deny your project request. Although I do have to admit that everything you learn from this experiment will have a profound benefit on other projects across the board, even if yours doesn't have its own direct benefit to society."

"But it does!" protested Burgon.

Visnel crossed his arms, and said, "Alright, how so?"

"Well, think about it like this. Robots currently do a wide variety of things for us, correct?"

Visnel shrugged.

"Yeah, that's pretty much a given."

"Alright, now imagine a robot that could think and reason on its own, could go beyond its programming, could learn and adapt, could be truly aware of itself, its environment, and even what others are thinking. What if it could feel sad or happy? What if it could understand your emotions because it had its own? What if it's ability to learn and adapt allowed it to foresee trouble we might not and address it before it becomes a problem? I can even see these robots creating great and amazing medical and scientific breakthroughs of their own. What do you think of that?" said Burgon.

Visnel chuckled.

"I'd call that a threat to someone's job security. If they can do everything we can do, and do it better, then where would there be any further need for us?"

Burgon rubbed his chin in thought.

"I can see where you'd make that connection. But my robot will be a lion. How could a lion replace us?"

Visnel shrugged.

"It's not much of a leap to go from a lion to any of a thousand other types of androids. Again, I like your idea, but let's at least try not to render ourselves obsolete just yet. Nature's done a great job of getting us this far, so there's no point in rushing ourselves into irrelevance."

"So you don't think they'll like my idea?" asked Burgon.

Visnel shook his head.

"I don't know. Probably not. But that doesn't mean you can't at least try."

Burgon looked at the screen on his computer and thought for a moment.

"That's what I plan to do. So, are you going to be there with me when I present it?"

"Of course I will! As I said before, no matter how harebrained your idea might be, I'll always stand with you. And I fully plan to keep that promise."

Burgon smiled.

"Thanks."

Visnel shook his head.

"Don't thank me. You've earned it. If you hadn't, I probably wouldn't be doing this."

Several days later, Dr. Burgon walked into a small conference room on the north side of the college with his proposal tucked securely under his arm, and Dr. Visnel by his side. Persia happily trailed behind them, playfully attacking the two men's feet as though they were some elusive prey that she was hunting. On one side of the room sat a group of three directors; two men and one woman.

One of the men gestured to Burgon and Visnel, and said, "Gentlemen, please sit down."

Burgon and Visnel obeyed his request and took up seats at a short table directly across from the three member board of review. Persia in turn wandered off to play with one of the large plants that adorned the room, much to Burgon's chagrin.

"As I understand it, you have come here before us today to discuss funding for your proposed sentient robotics project. Am I correct?" asked the one of the men.

Burgon nodded.

"That is correct."

"Very good. I'm sure you already know the three of us, but just for the record I will introduce each of the members of the review board. I am Director Savich, to my left is Professor Idiv, and lastly we have Dr. Borne. As is required, we will allow you the normally allotted time for you to promote your project before we make our final decision. But do note that we have already read your entire proposal and strongly disagree with it. So it will be entirely up to you to change our minds."

Burgon nodded. He had been through this before and knew the drill. When he would submit a new project for consideration, the review board would initially reject it. It happened to everyone, so he already knew this was coming. Once it was rejected, he would then be required to convince the review board why his proposed project should be allowed to proceed. This was done to ensure that only the most viable or beneficial projects would receive funding so as not to waste the college's limited research funds. It was a harsh system, but a necessary one that weeded out all but the absolutely best projects. Burgon knew his chances of being approved were slim, but he still went on, arguing his case for over forty five minutes before Savich stood up and waved for Burgon to stop. He sighed.

"Dr. Burgon," he said, pausing briefly as though trying to think of the right words to say. "Your presentation is good, and it shows that your project is well thought out and has a lot of merit. However, I can't in good conscience allow you to continue on with what will eventually become a futile effort to sway our initial decision. I admit that you've given us some very convincing arguments for why we should allow you to proceed. But I believe that, even if you continue your presentation to its finale, we will not see anything that will convince us that we should approve your proposal."

"May I inquire as to why?" asked Burgon.

"Robots are tools, doctor, and nothing more. They don't need to think. They simply need to do the job that we request of them and nothing more. They certainly don't need emotions, or the ability to form their own thoughts and opinions."

"But they can become different!" said Visnel.

"And why, pray tell, would you want them to be different? What benefit would they bring to society if they were able to think and reason for themselves?" asked Idiv.

"They could handle situations that normal robots currently aren't able to," said Burgon.

"And what about emotions? Of what benefit would they be to a robot? Why would they need to cry? Or even laugh? What if they got angry and went out of control? Emotions in a living being are bad enough. But in a robot, they have the potential to be lethal on a genocidal level. I can't even begin to stress that enough. Emotions are also what makes us uniquely Yigzan. Yet you find it worth giving that away to a machine!?"

"I am not giving away our emotions, but rather merely sharing with them what we so blithely take for granted, and yet cherish so deeply," said Burgon.

"Isn't that the same thing?"

Burgon shook his head.

"I don't believe it is."

Savich frowned.

"Well I do, and I will *not* let you give away our humanity and what makes us so uniquely different from machines! I'm sorry, but I can't. As such this meeting is over. There will be no further discussion or debate on this issue," he said.

He then turned and stormed out of the room.

"But how can you..."

"There will be no further discussion on this subject, Dr. Burgon! And that is final!" shouted Savich as he exited the small conference room.

Burgon said nothing more as he watched Savich leave. He simply stared after him, stunned at what he had just seen and heard.

Visnel looked over at Idiv and Borne, and shouted, "Are you just going to let him get away with this?"

Idiv shook her head.

"I'm sorry, Dr. Visnel, but I agree with Director Savich. I wish it was different, because I do believe that a lot of good can come from this project. But our society isn't ready for something like this. Maybe in a hundred years, but not now. It's too soon."

She then turned and hurried out of the room followed closely by Dr. Borne.

"Why those rude, obtuse, ungrateful, incredulous..."

"Dr. Visnel, please. This won't help anything," said Burgon, interrupting Visnel as he fumed acrimoniously.

"But they..."

"Please, please. This will get us nowhere. It's obvious that we can't change their minds. I saw it in their eyes," said Burgon.

"You're just going to let this slide?" said Visnel in surprise.

"For now, yes."

Visnel studied Burgon for several moments and then gave a devilishly sly grin.

"You've got something planned, don't you?" he said.

"Not yet. But I know there are ways around the system. I just need to find one and pursue it. Don't worry, I haven't given up on my project just yet. I'll find some way to make it happen."

Visnel chuckled.

"I like how you think. While I may not have supported your project very much in the beginning, after the treatment they gave you today, I'm one hundred percent behind you!"

Burgon smiled.

"Thanks. I think I'm going to need some of that support very soon."

Just then Persia trotted up to him and sat down at his feet.

"Are we going home now daddy? I'm hungry," she said.

Burgon reached down, picked her up and cradled her in his arms.

"Yes, we're going home now."

"Who was the grumpy old man?" she asked.

Burgon chuckled.

"Someone who needs a nap very badly," he chided.

"Oh. Do you get grumpy when you don't get enough sleep?" asked Persia.

Burgon laughed.

"I suppose I do."

"Then will Mr. Vis...Vis..." said Persia as she struggled with Visnel's name. Finally she pointed at him, and said, "Him. Does he need a nap too?"

Visnel laughed.

"I suppose I do," he said.

Burgon chuckled.

"Come on Persia, let's go home."

The next day Burgon came into his office and was surprised to find a letter sitting on his desk with his name written neatly on the front. He opened it and found a business card, and a small piece of paper inside. He took the paper and read it curiously.

"Just in case you lost your other one," it said.

Burgon studied the paper in confusion as he tried to make sense of the somewhat cryptic message. He then looked at the card. It was a plain white business card that read, "When you're ready, call me." Below that was a phone number. He flipped it over, but found the other side blank. Puzzled, he pulled a small book off the shelf above his desk and opened it. Inside was pages upon pages of business cards from a variety of people, vendors and organizations he'd met or done business with over the years. He flipped through several pages of the book until he found a card with the same number on it. It was the business card that Ferrell Black had given him nearly ten years earlier.

"Does his offer of a job still stand, even after all these years?" he thought to himself.

He shook his head.

"Impossible. It couldn't be."

He began to throw the card away, but then stopped. He looked at the card again, thought for a moment, and soon tucked it in his pocket. During his lunch break he pulled out his mobile phone and dialed the number on the card. The line was quickly answered by a bright, cheerful voice.

"Cybergenics Incorporated, how may I direct your call?"

"I'd like to talk with Ferrell Black, please," said Burgon.

"I'm sorry, sir, but Mr. Black isn't available right now."

"He left me his business card, and told me to call him."

"He did? Would you please read what it says?"

Burgon read the brief message on the card.

"One moment, please," said the operator.

Hold music began playing. After a minute the operator returned.

"Sir, Mr. Black would like to talk to you in person. Are you available to meet with him this afternoon at three?"

"I am."

"Good. Do you know where our South Igna facility is?"

"Yes, I do."

"Great! Just go there and show your card to the guards at the gate. They'll point you to where you'll need to go to meet Mr. Black," replied the operator, and then hung up.

Burgon put away his phone and proceeded to finish his lunch. Later that day he drove down to the South Igna Cybergenics facility and pulled to a stop at the front gate. Four heavily armed men dressed head to toe in camouflage uniforms eyed him suspiciously as he drove up. Seeing that he intended to go inside, one of them walked over to his car.

"I'm sorry sir, but this facility is off limits to the public," he said.

Burgon reached into his pocket, pulled out the business card he had been given and handed it to one of the guards.

"I'm here to see Mr. Black," he said.

The guard studied it closely and then handed it back to Burgon.

"Go down two blocks and then turn right," said the guard.

"Thank you," replied Burgon.

He then continued through the gate and across the facility to a short, stout building boldly emblazoned with the Cybergenics logo. Out on the front lawn were dozens of small robots busily doing everything from tending flowers to washing the windows. He parked his car near the front door and then walked into the building. Inside he was greeted by several guards who escorted him over to a small conference room. Once inside he was told to sit down at a large, wooden table in the center. Ferrell Black entered several minutes later, flanked by an assistant, and sat down across from him. Black folded his hands and smiled beatifically.

"Mr. Burgon. It's so good to see you again, even though it's been ten years," said Black.

"Does your offer still stand?" asked Burgon flatly.

Black laughed.

"Straight and to the point. I like that. Yes, my offer still stands, otherwise I would not have sent you my card." He pushed a thick brown folder across the table to Burgon, and said, "The terms of your employment are in here. You may take as much time as you like to look them over."

Burgon cocked an eyebrow in intrigue. He opened the folder, quickly scanned through the pages, and then closed it a few minutes later.

"I will agree to everything in your employment contract, except paragraph five on page two of document FM17."

Black furrowed his brow in interest.

"You read all of that already?" he said in muted surprise.

Burgon nodded.

"You read fast then?" asked Black.

Again Burgon nodded.

"It's a skill I've acquired over the years in order to absorb as much information as possible in the least amount of time."

Black grinned.

"Hmm, impressive."

He then took the folder and leafed through the pages until he found the document that Burgon had referred to. He pulled it out, studied it briefly, and then smiled.

"Ah, I do see where you might disagree with this."

He took a pen from his pocket, scribbled out the paragraph, and initialed it.

"Then we will simply ignore this stipulation. Is there anything else?"

"Yes, one more thing. I will agree to your terms on the condition that you allow me to work on my personal project first," said Burgon.

"That won't be a problem, as all projects here are personal projects. I find my scientists to be more creative and productive when they are allowed to work as they see fit."

"When can I start?"

Black shrugged.

"Whenever you like."

"Then I will begin two weeks from Monday."

"Agreed," said Black.

He pulled a sheet of paper from the folder and pushed it across to Burgon.

"Just sign this."

Burgon read it quickly and then signed it. Satisfied, Black put the page back into the folder and handed it to his assistant who quickly took it from the room.

"Then we will see you two weeks from Monday." he said.

Burgon stood, shook Black's hand and then made his way out. Black stood up, turned to the window of the conference room and stared out across the facility. As he did Burgon's car soon came into view. He watched it slowly drive away as Elgar stepped into the room.

"Are the scientists in place?" asked Black.

"Ready and waiting."

"Good. Make sure that he has everything he needs to begin his project. I want to see this lion of his take shape as quickly as possible. What his research yields will be *very* useful to us."

Elgar bowed slightly.

"As you wish."

Chapter 3

Captain Delgra, a seasoned recon expert, sat quietly at the edge of a trampled down, muddy field and studied a Gorg platoon through his binoculars as they practiced their maneuvers. He watched as the troll like Gorg plodded along, grunting and huffing as they went as their sergeants and officers shouted orders at them like slave drivers.

"What do we do, sir?" whispered Sergeant Odevion, his partner and best friend.

Delgra ignored him as he continued to study the Gorg.

"Sir, we need to do something," whispered Odevion, more insistently.

"Shh. Just a second," whispered Delgra.

"Sir, might I remind you that our situation is becoming untenable."

Delgra lowered his binoculars.

"I understand that. But I want to get more information before we go back. The more we know, the better prepared our people will be."

Odevion shook his head.

"No offense, sir, but it won't do us any good if we're dead."

"We've got movement. Take cover," said Delgra.

Both men quickly ducked down as a Gorg squad began to move in their direction. The squad continued to creep forward, moving cautiously as though they were stalking something. A moment later a Gorg sergeant pointed towards them and then whistled twice. Delgra raised his rifle to the ready, took aim at the nearest Gorg, and clicked his safety off as he prepared to spend the last few moments of his life in a brief but deadly firefight with the Gorg. But just as he prepared to fire, he caught sight of something out of the corner of his eye that made him pause. A minadeer, an antelope like creature, appeared out of the bushes in front of them and bolted for the nearby treeline. Both men flinched as the Gorg opened fire on it. The minadeer stumbled briefly and then collapsed. Several of the Gorg whooped and shouted for joy as they raced through the field after their prey. They returned several minutes later with one of the men triumphantly holding the now dead animal by the throat in his large, club like hands. A Gorg officer appeared from the middle of the group moments later, and roared in anger.

"What happened?" he shouted.

One of the soldiers held up the minadeer.

"Just catching some lunch, sir," he said.

The officer stormed over to him and struck the man with a right hook so powerful that Delgra thought he could hear the man's jaw crack.

"You degenerate idiot! Do you want to start an incident with the Yigzan!?"

The soldier twisted and shifted his jaw as though setting it back in place.

"They won't hear us out here," he said.

"Do you want to risk that!?" asked the officer.

"For a delicious leg of minadeer? Yes, I would."

The officer stared in stunned surprise.

"What!? Why!?" he asked incredulously.

"Because I want fresh meat! I'm sick of that tasteless mash you force us to eat!"

"That is regulation food!"

The soldier glared at the officer.

"Then you eat that garbage, you slagpa!"

"How dare you insult an officer!" shouted another man next to him.

"I will insult anyone who denies me a decent meal!"

"Well then. Just for that I'm taking your meat," said the officer.

But as he reached for the minadeer, the soldier threw it aside, drew his knife and swung it at the officer. However he missed as the officer sidestepped the blade. The officer then drew his pistol and shot the soldier. The man stumbled briefly and then fell to the ground dead. The officer studied the soldier for several moments, and then spit on him.

"Should we bury him?" asked one of the soldiers.

The officer grunted, and said, "Leave that slagpa to rot where he lies. He's not worth our time."

The soldiers looked down at their now dead comrade for several moments, and then made their way out of the area. When all was clear, Delgra slipped out of his hiding spot and carefully crawled over to where the dead soldier now lay. With practiced speed he patted down the body for anything of value, and then retreated to his hiding spot.

"Let's get out of here," he said as he tucked several scraps of paper into his pocket.

"Pfft. Like you have to tell me twice," said Odevion.

Over the next several days both men cautiously made their way out of Gorg territory and down into the gently rolling prairie of the Yigzan homeland. They were met there, just beyond the border, by several soldiers who picked them up and drove them back to their base. Upon arriving, they stopped at the headquarters building and were greeted by the base general. But before he could say anything a powerful, pungent odor assaulted his nose, causing him to recoil in disgust.

"Ugh, you two need a bath," he groaned.

"I would have bathed, but I thought you'd enjoy a fresh reminder of what field duty is like," said Delgra with a grin.

The general frowned.

"No thanks. I remember it all too well. Anyhow, follow me."

He then led the two men into his office.

"Alright, gentlemen, show me what you've got."

The two men immediately began pulling a variety of items they'd collected from their pockets, boots, helmets, and anywhere else on their person they could. When they were done the general stared in amazement at a tall, dirty pile of papers, computer disks, and other miscellaneous materials.

"Well, I see your mission was fairly productive," said the general.

Delgra nodded, and then pointed at two of the computer disks.

"We hit a field communications unit just a few miles inside the Gorg border on our first day out. I used one of their mobile com centers to hack into their military network and download as much as I could about their current operations. There's some rather disturbing information on there about an upcoming invasion they're planning."

The general looked at Delgra in surprise.

"An invasion? Are you certain?"

Delgra nodded.

"We also saw a lot of troop movements while we were out there, which would corroborate that information. The only thing they weren't moving were the heavy hitters and their big iron. Those all stayed back at base," said Odevion.

"Then what makes you so sure these aren't just plans for some kind of theoretical war games?"

"Because the units were carrying live ammo. The Gorg never issue live ammo to their troops unless they plan to do something. They're too afraid their own men might accidentally shoot each other. You have to remember that they're not exactly the brightest bunch."

The general nodded.

"On that subject I won't disagree. So, based on what you've seen, how long do you think it will be before they invade?"

Delgra shrugged.

"A couple years at the earliest."

The general looked at him in surprise.

"A couple of years? If the launch date for the attack is that far out, why would they be moving troops now?"

"They're probably feeling us out in preparation for the eventual invasion. They know they're at a technological disadvantage against us, so they're likely doing as much homework on us as they can before they do."

The general looked curiously at Delgra.

"So why the live ammo if they're not ready to attack yet?"

Delgra shrugged.

"I'm guessing it's just in case they got into anymore skirmishes with us along the border, or encountered any recon troops like ourselves."

"Is that something you know as a fact, or is it your personal belief?"

"It is my personal opinion based on information and things I've seen."

The general shook his head.

"That's not enough. I need cold hard facts if I'm going to take this up the chain of command. I admit that we've had a tenuous relationship with the Gorg for the past century, but we've never actually come to blows."

"Did you forget about the border skirmishes we had with them several years ago?"

The general waved dismissively.

"That was all a misunderstanding."

Delgra sighed.

"Did it ever occur to you that they may have used that as an excuse to extricate themselves from a situation they very quickly realized was futile?"

"I don't think that's the case."

"Well, I do. It wouldn't be much of a stretch for them to use a lie like that to cover up a mistake. They may be stupid, but not *that* stupid."

The general leaned back in his chair and thought for several moments.

"Alright, I'll consider what you've given me and pass it along to my superiors. Now, you two go get a shower, and some hot chow, and I'll call you if I need to ask you anything more about your mission. Also, don't forget to file a complete mission report by eighteen hundred hours tomorrow. Dismissed."

The two men stood up, saluted the general, and then left the office. As they were exiting the building, the General leaned over to his desk phone and pressed the intercom button.

"Ms. Norah, send in Colonel Sec."

"Yes, sir," came the reply.

The General stood up, grabbed a small waste basket, and walked around to the front of his desk. He deposited the two data disks into his pocket, swept the papers and other materials that the two men had brought him into the trash, and then sat down again just as the Colonel walked in.

"You called, sir?" asked the man.

The general handed him the two disks, and said, "Have intel go through these and see if they can find anything useful, and then have them destroyed."

"Yes, sir," said the officer as he turned and exited the room.

As the door was closing behind him the general grunted, and said, "Invasion indeed. What kind of fool would believe that nonsense?"

He then picked up the phone and dialed a number.

When someone answered, he said, "Yes, I'd like to put two men in for reassignment."

Black looked up from his desk as Elgar entered.

"Ah, so what brings you here at this hour?" he said in surprise.

Elgar tossed a small manila folder on the desk in front of Black.

"We've got a problem," he said.

Black flipped the folder open and quickly read the first page.

He looked up in surprise, and said, "Invasion?"

Elgar nodded.

"The Gorg are planning to invade us again."

"Impossible. My mole guaranteed me that the Gorg would never attack our homeland so long as he's Marshall General."

"Apparently that's changed," said Elgar.

"Well, then we'll just have to do something about that," said Black as he picked up his phone.

He punched in a number, and then waited. After several moments the call connected.

"I'm here," came a rough, tense voice on the other end.

"I've just received intelligence data that says your army is planning to invade our country soon. Is that true?" said Black.

There was silence for several moments, followed by a soft, slow chuckle that grew in intensity.

"What's so funny?" asked Black.

"So you've finally found out. I'm impressed."

Black stared at the phone in disbelief.

"Then it's true?"

"Yes," came the flat, but belligerent reply.

"I thought I told you to do everything you could to prevent a war between our countries!"

Black listened in dismay as the man chuckled again in a deeper, more sinister tone.

"You Yigzan are so gullible. Did you really think I would serve you forever?"

"You're betraying me!?" snapped Black.

"You could more accurately say that I'm dumping you in favor of a better offer. When we first met, you had something that I wanted. Namely, a path to power. I have now achieved that goal. But now I want a country of my own, and yours is ripe for the taking."

"You traitor," said Black, spitting out his words through clenched teeth.

Again the man laughed.

"I will enjoy conquering your country and making you my personal play thing. Then, when I'm tired of you, I will have you killed...slowly," said the man.

Black took a deep breath and let it out slowly as he tried to calm down. Anger was not his friend right now.

"Then you won't mind if I have you killed," he said flatly.

"Killed? By you?" said the man as he burst out laughing.

"No, by someone close to you."

The man stopped laughing. Black grinned.

"That got his attention," he thought. "Enjoy the rest of your life while it lasts, because it will be very, very short," he said, and then hung up. "Worthless simbit. Most untrustworthy, backstabbing..." he said as his voice trailed off.

He thought about his change of fortunes for a second, and then turned to Elgar.

"Looks like our original plans have changed. First, we get rid of that backstabbing slagpa, and then we begin mobilizing the Yigzan military."

"That's going to be rather hard. The military refuses to admit that the Gorg are a threat."

Black stood up and began walking towards the door, his hands folded behind his back.

"I realize that. However, something must be done."

Just then he paused in his tracks as an idea crossed his mind. He cocked his head slightly and then turned back towards Elgar who raised an eyebrow in interest.

"I take it you've come up with an idea?"

Black gently rubbed his chin in thought.

"I have indeed. Find me a list of officers and enlisted men in the military we can use. If we can't change them from the outside, then we'll do it from within."

Persia flipped the page of the book in front of her with her paw, began to read the first line, and then stopped. She looked at one of the words and was puzzled by its spelling.

"Dad, what does par-a-llel mean?" she asked.

Burgon carefully laid down his tools and held out his hands.

"It means to be in line with something. Take my left arm for example. Do you see how it stretches straight out like this?"

Persia nodded.

"Now see how my right arm matches it?"

Again she nodded.

"My right arm is parallel with my left arm. Now if I move my right arm like this, it's no longer parallel, but is instead perpendicular."

Persia nodded slightly as she tried to grasp the concept.

"I *think* I understand," she said slowly.

Burgon laughed, and then walked over and rubbed her on the head. She smiled, closed her eyes, and purred.

"Don't worry. You'll understand it eventually. Although I'm very proud of you for the amazing amount of progress you've made in such a short time. You're already reading and comprehending at an eighth grade level. That's not bad for someone who's barely a year old."

Persia smiled.

"I had a good teacher," she said as she nuzzled him affectionately.

"What really amazes me is your learning power. I never would've expected that someone as unique as you could be so smart. You really are one of a kind."

Persia chuckled.

"Thanks Dad. Now can we go out and play by the river again?"

But Burgon shook his head.

"Not today I'm afraid. I have some very important things I need to do to Tgegani that can't wait any longer."

Persia looked at him in confusion.

"Who's Teh-gah-nee?" she asked as she struggled with the name.

Burgon smiled.

"Didn't I tell you that I picked a name for my lion already?"

Persia shook her head.

"No, but I like it, even if it is hard to pronounce," she said with a smile.

Burgon grinned.

"I thought you would. It's an ancient Yigzan word meaning 'One with great courage and honor'. I hope to someday see Tgegani fulfill that name."

"When will he be ready to come play with me?" asked Persia.

"Not for a while. We still have to give him a body."

Burgon then perked up as someone called out to him from across the lab. Burgon turned and spotted a man approaching him with a box in his hands.

"Ah, Dr. Slao! What do you have for me today?" he asked.

"I've got those gyroscopes you wanted. I've finished them exactly to your specifications and tested each one thoroughly."

"Thanks. How's Dr. Trask coming with the limbs?"

"Well, he's waiting on some parts from Dr. Penicar's metallurgy lab. The problem with that is he's apparently having some trouble with the alloy formula you gave him."

Burgon raised an eyebrow in interest.

"Hmm, I guess I'd better go and see if I can be of any help."

"If you're going that direction, would you take a few seconds and tell me if I've interpreted your plans for the optical sensors correctly? I started work on the basic prototype while I waited for the machines to complete their testing on the gyroscopes."

Burgon nodded.

"I'd be glad to."

Slao chuckled slightly.

"I have to hand it to you, Doctor. Your designs are like nothing I've ever seen before. I'm no dummy, but the complexity of these devices is breathtaking, and a little intimidating at times too."

Burgon grinned sheepishly.

"I didn't mean to belittle you with them."

Slao waved his hands dismissively.

"No, no. Not at all. I'm actually enjoying the challenge they present me with. I haven't worked this hard to solve a problem in years."

"Well then, I'm glad you're enjoying this so much," said Burgon.

He turned and began walking towards the lab door as he took a sip of a thick, black, coffee like liquid called katar, a favorite beverage in the Yigzan nation.

"Do you mind if I refill my katar on the way? My cup's nearly empty," he continued.

Slao shook his head.

"Not at all. I could use a refill myself."

As Burgon and Slao stepped out of the room, Persia looked over at the growing pile of parts that would eventually become Tgegani and then sighed. For some reason she worried about the new robot in ways she'd never done with any other machine. She wasn't sure why she cared so much for him, but she did. In a strange way, she wondered if this was what it felt like to be a mother. She chuckled to herself at the thought. And yet it wouldn't go away. She wondered why that was, but decided not to ponder it any further. She sighed again and then walked into the office to take a nap.

Chapter 4

Delgra stared at the paper in front of him as he struggled not to cry out in anger. He cleared his head and then read it again. It said:

> *"You are hereby ordered to report to Echo Military Science Laboratories for duty as the administrator of that facility. Concurrent to your transfer of duty station you are hereby promoted to the rank of Major. This promotion is effective immediately."*

"They're trying to silence me," he growled.

He spun on his heels, intent on giving someone a piece of his mind, and nearly bowled over Odevion who'd been standing behind him. He then stared curiously at his friend as he noticed a set of similar papers in his hand.

"You too?" he said in disbelief.

Odevion nodded.

"Likely for the same reasons you are. I've been sent to a field observatory in the western end of the northern mountains."

Delgra grunted.

"I'm being sent to a military science lab southwest of here. Obviously they want us as far away from the border and each other as possible. I can't believe they still deny the inevitable! The Gorg are coming! Why can't they see that!?"

Odevion shook his head and held a finger to his lips.

"Shh. Don't say anything more. I don't know if they're listening or not, but we don't want to make things any worse for ourselves than they already are. Let's just go quietly for now and see what we can make of this situation."

Delgra stared at Odevion for several moments, and then nodded.

"Alright, I'll do that. Hopefully we'll see each other soon."

Odevion smiled.

"You never know." He patted Delgra on the shoulder, and said, "Take care of yourself."

Delgra then watched as Odevion strode away as though nothing was wrong. It made him want to cry out in anger again. After a few moments he made his way to his barracks, packed his things and then got a lift down to the local train station where he bought a ticket and waited patiently for the train to arrive on its afternoon run. As soon as it pulled into the station he climbed aboard, stowed his bag in the overhead bin and then sat down as the train began to rapidly accelerate. It raced quickly across the prairie in a near silent rush of speed, easily reaching just over two hundred miles an hour on an electromagnetic cushion of energy.

Outside his window, spread out from horizon to horizon, were miles upon miles of open grasslands, prairie and fields dotted intermittently with large groves of trees like islands in a sea of glistening rainbow colors. As the train passed a large grove of trees near the tracks he spotted a group of simbits playing in the trees. They looked akin to a cross between a rabbit and a squirrel and, despite their agility in the trees, they were not known for being the brightest among the animal kingdom. Hence why their name had become a byword among the Yigzan for one of lower or questionable intelligence. In some cases, calling someone a simbit was an outright insult.

Inside the train Delgra carefully studied the seats around him with muted interest and noticed, much to his surprise, given how busy the trains usually were, that nobody else was around him. Being sure that it was safe to move about, he got up and wandered back to the observation car. He scanned the room briefly and then sat down at an empty bench near the center of the car. He kicked his feet up on the railing in front of him and tried to relax. But he found his efforts to be in vain as his danger sense, honed by years of experience, went off almost immediately.

He knew all too well when he was being watched, and he could tell at that moment that someone nearby had taken an unhealthy interest in him. He casually looked up and studied the reflections in the windows as he tried to discover who was watching him. He saw only two other people in the car; a man in a black suit and shoulder cloak, and a second in a green tunic and blue pants. Delgra casually turned and studied the two men. Each of them quickly looked away as their eyes met his. He soon turned back to the window and began watching the reflections again. This time only the man in the black suit remained.

Delgra felt the train slow suddenly as it drew close to the next station. He braced himself briefly and used that opportunity to turn and get a second look at the man in black. But when he looked, he saw that the man wasn't there anymore. The observation car now appeared to be completely empty. Just then something brushed against him. He turned to see the man in black sitting down next to him. The man smiled and held out his hand to Delgra.

"Greetings. My name is Ferrell Black. I believe you have something of interest to me."

Delgra stiffened.

"But I'm afraid I can't discuss this here. It's a little too...public. Why don't we go to my cabin so we can talk in more detail," said the man.

Delgra studied him, but didn't like how he looked or felt.

"Whatever you're peddling, I'm not interested," he said as he began to stand.

But as he did, he caught sight of several other black clad men that seemed to have appeared out of nowhere behind him.

"Where did they come from?" he thought in surprise.

He studied the men more intently.

"This guy's good. He not only has me completely cornered, but those men are well armed. I better roll with this and see what he wants," thought Delgra.

He then turned and sat back down.

"Alright, apparently I can't leave without first hearing you out. So, tell me. What do you want from me?" said Delgra suspiciously.

Black smiled beatifically, and said, "Nothing that you don't already want for yourself."

Delgra smirked.

"And what would that be?"

"To prepare for a war your superiors deny is coming."

Delgra's eyes narrowed.

"How do you--"

"I know many things, Major. But this is best discussed in a more...private setting."

Delgra studied Black for several moments, and then nodded.

"Lead on."

Persia trotted in from her afternoon playtime and was surprised to find a large, dark gray, metallic cat sitting as rigid as a statue in the middle of the laboratory floor. Burgon was bent down near one of its ears adjusting something with a small tool.

"Dad, is this Tgegani?" she asked as she trotted over to him.

"It is indeed. Although he's still a blank."

Persia gave him a puzzled look as she sat down.

"A blank?" she asked.

"Yes, a robot with no operating system. We finished assembling him just over a half hour ago. I still need to load a basic operating system into him this afternoon, and then take him for a test run to ensure his cybernetic body is functioning properly."

"When can I play with him?" asked Persia with a hint of excitement.

"Soon enough. Probably not for at least another couple of months."

This seemed to briefly sink Persia's spirits.

"Why that long?" she groaned.

Burgon laughed.

"Well, I still have to write his operating system. We can't do anything else until that's done."

Just then Dr. Slao appeared from behind a nearby desk.

"You haven't written it yet?" he said in surprise.

Burgon shook his head.

"No, of course not. I already told you that. We needed to finish and test his body first. *Then* we'd write the operating system. There's no point in writing the AI until the body is finished."

"Ah, right. You did say that. So, are you gonna use a standard AI base for his IOS?"

Burgon shook his head.

"Nope. I'm writing it from the bottom up. None of the current IOS cores or frameworks can even begin to do a fraction of what I need his to be capable of."

"That's a bit ambitious, isn't it?" asked Slao.

Burgon shrugged.

"I wrote the complete operating system for the AX-56 from scratch in two weeks. So his IOS ought to be easy enough to do. It'll just take me a little bit longer to complete it."

Slao chuckled.

"If you say so."

Burgon picked up his laptop and plugged it into a data port on Tgegani's chest. Several minutes later he unplugged it, picked up a small remote control from a nearby lab table, and pressed a button on it. Tgegani immediately stood up, and began walking with stiff, rigid movements. But the more he walked, the more fluid his steps became as his IOS began to adapt to the new body.

"You ready for testing?" asked Burgon.

Slao lifted his laptop over his head, and said jokingly, "Ready and willing, sir!"

Burgon laughed. The two men then led the robotic lion out to a nearby vehicle, placed him in the back with Persia, and drove to a large obstacle course. The men spent the rest of the afternoon vigorously testing the robot's reflexes, dexterity and speed with breathtaking results.

"I'm really impressed with your design, doctor. I know I worked on several parts of this fabulous machine myself, but I never thought the final product would be this good," said Slao.

Burgon smiled.

"I knew what he'd be like from the beginning. I saw Tgegani in all his greatness in my mind long before his design ever appeared on paper."

"So, can we consider today's testing a success?"

Burgon shook his head.

"I've got some adjustments to make before I'll consider this part of the project complete. I saw a few minor problems during the testing that may come back to haunt us later on."

Slao looked amazed.

"You actually saw something wrong!? I thought his performance looked flawless!"

"Perfection is in the eye of the beholder. Where you saw greatness, I saw flaws. But they're easily fixable."

Slao laughed.

"Well, it *is* your project after all, so I guess you can be as fickle as you like."

Burgon nodded, peered at Tgegani and then cracked a smile. He tapped Slao on the shoulder and then pointed at the lion. Persia was slowly walking around Tgegani, studying him with curiosity. She would pause periodically and sniff at various points on his body in an effort to better understand the metal lion that sat before her. After a few moments she sat down in front of him and playfully batted at his muzzle. Seeing this, Burgon gently nudged the remote control, causing the robot's left arm to raise up and wave at Persia. She giggled with delight and batted playfully at it in return.

Delgra stepped off the train and stared in disbelief at the empty station before him. The only signs of life in the area were two large carrion birds that stared at him from across the platform as though sizing him up for dinner. Moments later the train accelerated away into the distance. Delgra stood and listened in utter dismay at the silence that now surrounded him. Finally, after several minutes, he picked up his bag and began to walk through the little village just beyond the station, and little was a very polite way of putting it.

"They obviously went to great effort to ensure that I was assigned to the smallest, most secluded hole in the wall they could find," he thought to himself.

He intently studied the buildings around him, taking in every detail he could of the tiny little village which consisted of little more than a general store with an H2 fueling station and a handful of houses. He walked up to the general store to ask for directions, but found it closed. On the door hung a sign that read, "Open 6am-9am and 5pm-10pm."

"Those are rather odd hours," he thought to himself.

He then studied the landscape around him and noticed that only two narrow, dusty, rutted single lane dirt roads led out of town; One to the north and one to the east.

"This place must not see much activity," he thought.

He began to walk again and then stopped as his ears detected the sound of a vehicle coming down the eastern road towards him. A somewhat beat up, late model pickup truck soon appeared at the edge of town and rumbled to a stop next to him. An older man in a white lab coat leaned out of the window and studied the Major curiously. Delgra returned the favor in kind, taking special notice of the man's long, thin, disheveled gray hair. He then watched as it flitted about in a hundred different directions as though it had a mind of its own.

"Are you Major Delgra?" asked the man.

"I am."

The man opened his door, stepped out, and shook Delgra's hand.

"Ah, glad to meet you. I'm doctor Olivan, chief scientist of Echo Labs. I'm here to pick you up. Sorry I'm a bit late. I got caught up in the middle of reading some fascinating materials on particle physics. It was amazing to read how...oh, um, right, you probably don't want to hear about that. Well, here, let me get your bag," said the old man.

Delgra stepped past him, placed his bag in the back of the truck, and then climbed in the passenger seat without saying a word.

"Ah, well, I see you're a man who's used to taking care of himself. Sorry for being so chatty. We don't get many visitors around here. In fact, we don't get many people at all. So few in fact that I'm honestly surprised we're still open for business."

He climbed into the truck, turned it around and then drove out of town and into the surrounding prairie. They proceeded on in silence for several minutes before coming to the gate of a large, seemingly abandoned science facility. The two guards at the gate glanced briefly at the doctor, and then waved him through. While he didn't say anything, Delgra took careful note of this. He would deal with the lackluster attitude of his new subordinates later. The truck then continued on past the gate for a ways further before rumbling to a stop in front of a large barracks building.

"Here's your new home. Your quarters are on the first floor on the north end. If there's anything you need, you can get it from the store here at the facility between the hours of nine and five each day. Before or after that you'll have to get what you need from the general store in town. Also, the administration building is over there. Captain Silvers is your executive officer. He should be around here somewhere. He can bring you up to speed on everything you need to know about the place," said Olivan.

Without saying a word in reply, Delgra grabbed his bag and strode into the barracks. He quickly found his room and was surprised to find it spotless. He gave the room a tertiary scan and noticed a letter laying on a small desk in the corner. He set down his bag, walked over and examined it. He found his name on the front, but no other markings. Carefully he opened it and found a simple card inside.

It read, "Glad to have you aboard, sir. I look forward to serving with you. Sincerely, Captain Silvers."

Knowing that he had a lot of work to do, he quickly changed into his fatigues, grabbed his laptop, a pad of paper and a pencil, and headed for the administration building. As he entered, an older woman looked up from her book and studied him curiously.

"May I help you, sir?" she asked.

"I'm Major Delgra. Where's my office?"

The woman gave him a confused look.

"Are we expecting you, sir?" she asked.

"I'm the new administrator of this facility," said Delgra sternly.

"It's alright, Eva. We're expecting him," came a voice from across the room.

Delgra turned to see a strong young captain standing in a nearby doorway. His work uniform was immaculate, and he sported a crop of short cut, blond hair that was accented by a pair of brilliant blue eyes that sparkled like little diamonds. He walked up to Delgra and shook his hand.

"It's good to finally meet you, sir. I'm Captain Silvers. I'm the temporary administrator of this facility. Well, if you can call it temporary. I've been running this place for the past two years since our last administrator left."

Delgra nodded.

"Then you'll show me everything I need to know about this place?"

"Yes, sir. But we'll have to do that tomorrow. Everything around here shuts down at seventeen hundred hours, and it's almost that time right now."

Delgra shook his head.

"I don't work office hours. I work when, where and how I need to."

"Understood, sir. I take it you'll be working late tonight?"

"Not really. I just need to find my office, send some email, and get my papers in order for tomorrow. I'll have a lot of work to do first thing in the morning."

Silvers gestured towards the back of the building.

"This way, sir. Your office is down here."

He escorted Delgra down a short hallway to a large, but simple office that contained little more than a single filing cabinet, a desk, a chair and a small katar maker that sat on top of the filing cabinet. He found the latter to be an ironic addition to the office.

"Here you go, sir. If you need anything, just let either myself or Eva know," said Silvers.

"Thank you," said Delgra as he strode across the room to his new desk.

Silvers then excused himself and closed the door behind him. Seeing that he was now alone, Delgra pulled out his laptop, opened up a secure email client and began typing a message.

To: black@cybergenics.sci
From: delgrab@mil.army.yig.sec
Subject: Arrived.

"I've arrived at the facility. My initial examination tells me that it needs a lot of work. But it's secluded enough to begin the plan. Just remember, you keep your promise and I'll keep mine."

He then opened a secure link to a special mail server and sent the message. He had three years at most to ready the military for war. He just hoped that his gamble would pay off. He didn't trust Ferrell Black any further than he could proverbially throw him. But at this point he had few other options. If Black came through for him, there was still a chance to save his country and his people. If not, then they were all doomed. He took a deep breath, switched to another program and began pulling up personnel files on every soldier, scientist and civilian working at the laboratory. If he was going to get anything done he needed to start there first.

Chapter 5

Two years later....

Burgon tried his best to focus his tired eyes on the computer screen in front of him. But as much as he tried, he found himself struggling to read the screen. He blinked, rubbed his eyes and tried again. The letters still blurred and blended together into one bright, fuzzy mess. He took a sip of his katar, grimaced at the powerful flavor of the strong black drink and looked at the screen again. This time he could see better and quickly took advantage of this, finishing up several lines of code before saving his work. He transmitted the code into Tgegani and took another sip of katar in hopes that it would help him stay awake.

He then strode over to the large metal lion, and said, "Wake up, Tgegani."

The lion moved and then turned his attention to the doctor.

"What is your command?" he asked in a flat, mechanical, monotone voice.

"Please do a systems check for me."

The droid straightened himself, and said, "All systems nominal. New operating code successfully accepted and implemented. Please state your directive."

"Tell me a joke," said Burgon.

"Please specify the joke."

"Make one up."

The lion seemed to struggle with the thought for several moments, and then said, "Program aborted. An abnormal program function has caused an exception in the advanced logics module."

Burgon cursed under his breath.

He sighed, and said, "Stand down."

Tgegani returned to his original position again. Burgon sat down behind his computer and studied the screen. He spotted several markers that indicated code problems and quickly fixed each of them. Satisfied with his work, he saved the program, transmitted it into Tgegani and stood up briefly before being forced to sit back down due to a sudden rush of vertigo.

"Oh, wow," he said as he tried to regain his senses.

He stumbled to his feet and began to walk towards his office.

"I need some sleep. I'll take a short nap and finish this in the morning," he said.

He soon reached his office and plopped down on a couch just inside the door. The couch was well worn and had been his bed for many a night over the last two years as he struggled to write Tgegani's AI program. At first he'd thought it'd be easy. Reality, however, had turned out to be entirely different. But all of his hard work had paid off as he was now very close to completing one final, critical element. This knowledge had pushed him to go beyond his limits several times to the point of near total collapse from pure exhaustion. Today was no exception as his body had again reached its limits and now demanded rest. And despite his best efforts to delay the inevitable, his body was going to get what it wanted. Within a few moments he was sound asleep.

Silence now enveloped the room, save for the soft whir of computer fans and the deep, rhythmic breathing of Burgon and Persia as they slept in the office. For nearly an hour, nothing moved within the laboratory. Then, out of nowhere, a brilliant white light washed over the entire room, filling every crack and crevice with its piercingly warm radiance. The light soon faded away to reveal a tall, white robed man from whom emanated a brilliant, yet gentle glow as though he were wreathed in powder like flames. He stood quietly in front of Tgegani and smiled lovingly at the large, metal lion as he knelt down in front of him. He then breathed on the lion's face, exhaling a brilliant, white, fog like energy that spilled out of his mouth like a cloud of fire and surrounded the lion's head. Tgegani relaxed slightly and then went stiff again.

The man smiled kindly, and in a soft, sweet voice said, "Wake up, Tgegani."

Tgegani's eyes blinked briefly and then focused on the man.

"Who are you?" he asked.

"I am Meshua," said the man.

Tgegani thought for a moment.

"I do not recognize that name. One moment while I access data on this subject."

Meshua laughed and then gently stroked Tgegani's smooth metal face.

"Grow in wisdom, knowledge and love. I charge you with protecting my people from the coming darkness. Live, and fulfill your destiny."

Tgegani raised a confused eyebrow.

"I do not understand. If you will be patient, I am still..." he said, his voice trailing off as Meshua vanished, leaving the room once again dark and silent.

Tgegani looked around the laboratory, but found no sign of the man. He contemplated this briefly, and then returned to his research as he began an exhaustive search for answers.

As morning dawned, Persia roused slowly from her bed, stretched long and hard, and yawned deeply as she glanced at the clock on Burgon's desk.

"Eight hours? Wow, I slept like a Yigzan again. If I keep this up, I'll become a disgrace to cat kind," she quipped.

She glanced over to where Burgon was sleeping on his couch and grinned.

"Another long night again, eh, Dad?" she said quietly to herself.

She strolled casually out of the office and stopped briefly to stretch again before continuing.

"Morning, Tgegani," she said sleepily as she passed by the large metal lion.

Tgegani turned his head towards her, and said, "Good morning."

Persia froze. She slowly turned her head towards Tgegani and stared wide eyed at him. He blinked. She turned around and studied him closely, all of her five senses at high alert as she tried to make sense of what she was seeing.

"Did you just say something?" she asked cautiously.

Tgegani nodded. The hair on Persia's back stood on end.

"So you know what I'm saying, right?" she asked, her caution growing into nervous fear.

Again Tgegani nodded.

"I have familiarized myself with all known spoken and written languages and their dialects, as well as over one thousand seven hundred and twenty three other forms of communication."

Persia backed up several paces, and said, "Dad? I think you should come see this."

Tgegani looked towards Burgon's office, and said, "He is still sleeping. I shall endeavor to wake him so that he may hear what you have to say."

"No, no, no. That's okay. I'll....I'll do it myself," said Persia nervously.

She bounded across the laboratory into the office and began nudging Burgon vigorously in an effort to wake him.

"Dad, wake up! You need to see this!"

Burgon grumbled and slowly opened his eyes.

"What is it, sweetie?" he asked groggily.

"Dad, something's happened to Tgegani. You really, really need to come see this."

He closed his eyes, and said, "Can this wait until later?"

"Daaaaaaaaaad! I'm not joking! Something's happened to Tgegani. Come on, get up!" said Persia through clenched teeth.

She glanced briefly at the metal lion and then back at Burgon. She nudged him again.

"Sweetie, I'm tired. We can play later," he grumbled.

Just then his phone rang. Burgon grunted, muttering incoherently to himself as he fished his phone out of his pocket.

"Burgon here," he groaned as he answered the phone.

"Persia has requested that she speak with you. It would be proper protocol for you to address her request as stated. When you are done, I would also like to speak with you. I have many questions," came a stiff mechanical voice.

"Huh? Who is this?" groaned Burgon.

"I am called Tgegani," said the voice on the phone.

"Tgegani?" said Burgon in curious surprise.

He sat up and looked to his right to see Tgegani standing just a few feet away from the door, his data leash stretched nearly to its limit. Burgon blinked in surprise.

"I told you something funny happened to him," said Persia.

"Were you...speaking...to me?" asked Burgon, unsure of what else to say.

Tgegani nodded.

"I am currently addressing you through the public phone system using this facilities mainframe as a bridging device between my processing core and your phone. You would not respond to requests of attention from Persia, so I stepped in to provide my assistance."

The phone slipped out of Burgon's hand and plopped noisily onto the couch as he stared with utter, awestruck amazement.

"You're functional!?" he said in shocked surprise.

Tgegani nodded.

"I am operating within all currently assigned system parameters," he said, this time aloud.

Burgon shook his head in amazed disbelief, grabbed his phone, hung up on Tgegani and then quickly dialed Slao. The phone rang several times before a tired voice answered.

"Slao here."

"Get down here, now! Something amazing just happened!"

Elgar walked into Black's office and tossed several folders onto his desk. Black studied them with interest.

"Ah, today's intelligence reports, I take it?"

"Mostly, yes," replied Elgar.

"Anything interesting?" asked Black.

"Yes. It seems that our last stalling tactic has failed. The Gorg are beginning full scale preparations for a war against us. They're still twelve months away from being able to do anything, but the war is coming none the less. We're not able to delay this any longer."

Black waved dismissively.

"No matter. We've already gained enough time. What is the progress on Delgra's work?"

"He's doing well. The army and air force are within six months of being completely ready for war. There's just one problem."

Black raised an eyebrow in curiosity.

"And what would that be?"

"While our army holds the technological advantage, the Gorg hold numerical superiority over us by as much as ten to one. Even with everything we have on our side, it will be very difficult to win this war, or even hold the line once the Gorg begin their attack."

Black leaned back in his chair and contemplated the situation.

"Then we need to find ourselves a trump card, and soon."

"Got any ideas?" asked Elgar.

Black sighed deeply.

"For the first time in years, no."

Elgar reached down and flipped open one of the folders, exposing the cover page.

"Then how about this?"

Black read the title page.

"Tgegani Project – Dr. Burgon, leading researcher."

He looked up at Elgar in surprise.

"This is Dr. Burgon's project. What about it?"

Elgar grinned slyly.

"This will be our trump card."

"How? It's still just a mindless lump of wires and alloys."

Elgar pointed to one line near the bottom of the page. Black read it and stared with amazement.

"It's operational!?" he said in surprise.

Elgar nodded.

"We believe it became sentient early this morning at around four thirty. Shortly afterwards it began downloading every data archive it could gain access to, both on our network, and across the internet. So far it's downloaded several hundred terabytes of information and is presently maxing out all of our primary data links."

"Are you sure it's Burgon's robot that's doing this and not some hacker who may have breached our network?" asked Black.

Elgar shook his head.

"The source of the activity was traced back to a programming terminal in Burgon's laboratory that was connected to his robot."

Black rubbed his chin nervously.

"Was any sensitive data downloaded?" he asked.

"Thankfully, no. Our technicians successfully kept it confined to just the library mainframe and a couple other low priority systems. Nothing above security level two was accessed."

Black nodded in approval.

"Good, good. I wouldn't want our newest mind to accidentally stumble onto something we don't want it to see. That might prove to be....catastrophic for us if it did."

Black then grinned as he thought about this some more.

"This creature already intrigues me. Especially it's insatiable thirst for knowledge. I think we should have a meeting with Dr. Burgon today and see for ourselves what this mechanical monstrosity of his can do."

A dark form draped in flowing, tattered, black robes stood at the edge of a decaying line of trees and studied the prairie beyond. As he did, a large, equally black, raven like carrion bird known as a greck alighted in front of him and bowed.

"Lord Negago, I have come as you've requested," said the bird.

"What have you to report?" asked the dark form, his voice tortured and demonic.

The bird twisted its head to the side, and said with a squawk, "Meshua has returned as you predicted, my lord."

Negago growled angrily through yellow, rotting teeth. His eyes blazed like fire as bony, shriveled fingers reached out from under his cloak and curled up in an expression of frustration.

"It would appear that my return has not gone unnoticed."

The bird squawked in agreement.

"Has the proxy been chosen?" asked Negago.

"He has, master," said the bird.

Negago growled.

"Then we need to kill him before he becomes a problem," he said.

"That may be difficult, master."

"Why?" growled Negago.

"Because he is not a living creature, my lord. He is a machine."

Negago reared up in surprise.

"A machine!? That is not possible! Meshua would never choose such a creature to be the guardian of his people! You are mistaken! He only chooses those of flesh and bone!"

The bird retreated several steps in fear and bowed low to the ground.

"I do not deceive you, master! Meshua has indeed given life to a machine!" it squawked.

Negago repeatedly flexed his shriveled hands as though contemplating this new development.

"Then you have seen this creature?" he asked.

"Not with my own eyes. I only learned of it through one of my most trusted spies. Although his heart is as dark as mine, he would not lie to me about something so important," said the bird.

Negago's eyes flared up as he thought about this new development. After a moment he motioned for the bird to leave.

"Be off with you. Find where this new proxy resides. I will send hunters after you to destroy him as soon as he is found."

The bird squawked with excitement, and then leapt into the air, speeding away quickly to carry out his master's orders. Negago then gave a deep, snarling growl. Within moments, a small pack of black, oily, tortured creatures, akin in appearance to that of a wolf, appeared out of the prairie in front of him.   They were vandros; another of the dark, twisted servants of Negago.

"We are here, Lord Negago. What is your wish?" said one of the vandros.

"A new proxy has been born. Find and eliminate him with all prejudice," said Negago.

"As you wish, my lord," said the lead vandros.

He then turned, and with the pack close on his heels, raced away to carry out his orders. Negago growled angrily, and then looking to the sky, shook his fist defiantly.

"Long have you fought me, Meshua. Long have you impeded me. But no more! I shall destroy this planet and claim your crown, and your kingdom, as my own!"

Chapter 6

Slao looked at the computer screen in front of him and stared with amazement.

"Huh, impressive. Did you write all this?" he asked.

Burgon shook his head and pointed to a small square in the corner of the screen that represented a section of code.

"That's what I wrote. He's written the rest."

Slao did a surprised double take.

"Wait, what!? He wrote all of that on his own!? How's that possible?" he said.

Burgon shrugged.

"I don't know."

Slao looked at him with curious bemusement.

"You wrote his AI and you don't know why he's like this?"

"I was asleep when it happened."

"Well? What was the last thing you did before you went to sleep?"

"I was working on a small part of his core memory logic shell. It was part of this function library here connected to the sub-c bus logic block."

"Did you get it to work?"

"No, it kept crashing. I was using jokes to test his relational skills and all I got were fatal exceptions."

Slao cocked an eyebrow in bemusement.

"You were using jokes to help build his AI program?" he said incredulously.

"Jokes are a good way for him to learn how to connect previously learned experiences to new input. The problem is, he was unable to do that. So I was trying to write a code correction that would fix that problem, but sleep deprivation got the better of me before I could finish."

"So, do you think your work in any way led to what happened here?"

Burgon shrugged.

"I have no idea. If it was something I did, then I'd like to know what it was and why it happened now and not before. Of course, knowing that might be the fly in the ointment."

"Why do you say that?" asked Slao.

"Well? Have you looked at his programming!? I've written a lot of AI systems over the years, but this is more advanced than anything I've ever seen before! Whatever triggered this self growth has never happened in the entire history of robotics!"

"So what do you think we should do now?" asked Slao.

Burgon sat back and thought for several moments.

"I think we should let him grow on his own for a while and see how he develops. If he goes down the wrong path, we can easily shut him down, and then make any necessary corrections before trying again. Eventually he should reach a point that we won't have to intervene anymore."

"Well, I think that, in the grand scheme of things, helping his sentience grow to maturity will be the easy part. Getting society to accept the idea of a sentient android will be a whole lot harder."

Burgon sighed.

"Yeah. Tell me something I *don't* already know."

Tgegani looked at Burgon, and asked, "May I go outside to explore?"

Burgon looked briefly at Slao and then back at Tgegani.

"Actually, that's not a bad idea," he said.

He looked back at Slao, and said, "So, do you have a few hours to kill today?"

Slao shrugged.

"Sure. What did you have in mind?"

"Well, I want to test out a few ideas. Tgegani has taken in a lot of data already. So I think it would be good for him to put that knowledge to use by exploring his environment. If nothing else, it'll help his AI develop further."

Slao shrugged.

"Sure, sounds good to me."

Burgon stood up, unhooked Tgegani from the programming terminal, fitted him with an electronic restraint unit, and then led the young lion outside. As Tgegani began exploring the world around him, his dusty gray, metallic body glistening in the sun, Burgon and Slao sat down on a nearby hill and studied him. As they did, Persia walked up to Tgegani and watched curiously as he analyzed a large weed in front of him.

"What'cha doing?" she said with a chuckle.

"I am exploring the biological and structural makeup of this plant and comparing it with the existing data on this species which is stored in my memory systems," said Tgegani.

"You sound like you're fascinated by it," said Persia.

"I am merely trying to create the most accurate data model possible on each item I encounter. Fascination is not a function of my programming," said Tgegani.

Persia laughed.

"You're funny."

Tgegani looked at her curiously, and asked, "What is the purpose of this strange activity that you engage in?"

Persia screwed up her face in confusion.

"What strange activity?" she asked.

Tgegani mimicked Persia's laugh, and said, "The activity I just demonstrated."

She grinned.

"That's called laughter, silly."

Tgegani's eyebrows perked up with interest.

"Laughter. The act of laughing. A derivative of the word laugh, which is to express joy or mirth. A spontaneous action used to express happiness or a joyful emotion," he said.

Persia nodded.

"Yeah, something like that."

"I do not understand the purpose of this emotion. Please explain."

Persia stared at Tgegani with an expression of confusion.

"Honestly, I've never really thought about it. I guess we just do it because we're happy."

"I do not understand. Please elaborate."

Persia smirked and narrowed her eyes slightly as she twitched her whiskers pertly.

"This is going to take a while, isn't it?" she quipped.

Tgegani tilted his head in confusion.

"What will take a while?"

Persia laughed.

"Well, if you're going to learn about laughter, you need to start at the beginning."

As Persia went about explaining laughter to Tgegani, Slao watched her with interest. He chuckled slightly when Tgegani began diving into deeper and more complex subjects, making Persia's efforts to help him understand more difficult.

"I see those two are getting along well," he said.

"Persia has always been curious about him since the beginning. She asked me all kinds of questions while I was building him," said Burgon.

"I hope it doesn't kill her."

Burgon looked at him curiously.

"Kill her!? What!? Tgegani? I don't think he would."

Slao laughed.

"No, no. Her curiosity. You know the saying, 'Curiosity killed the cat'?"

"Oh, oh. Right, right," said Burgon.

Slao shook his head.

"I would've expected you to catch that little quip right away," he said.

"Yeah, sorry. I guess it got past me," said Burgon as he continued to watch Persia and Tgegani.

Slao cocked an eyebrow.

"Something on your mind? You're usually not this disconnected unless you're really thinking hard about something."

Burgon sighed.

"I am. Most of it's about how Tgegani became sentient. Nothing makes sense. His AI core was nowhere near ready to go live, let alone reach sentience. And yet, here he is, walking around and thinking for himself. It's like a miracle. Almost like the hand of Meshua touched him," he said.

"Meshua?" asked Slao curiously.

Burgon nodded.

"When I was a child, my mother told me stories of Meshua, the guardian spirit of our people. He's rumored to have protected our ancestors since ancient times. It's said that when he walks the prairie, great evil is about to descend upon us. But he always protects us, no matter how great the danger may be."

"Ah, yes. I've heard of him. So what made you think of him all of a sudden?"

"I've been hearing rumors that Meshua is once again walking the land. He's supposedly been seen both north and west of here," said Burgon.

Slao snorted.

"Unlikely. Meshua is just a myth made up by our ancestors; a fable created to explain the ways of nature to a society that had not yet grasped science."

Suddenly Slao's eyes went wide.

"Wait a second. You're not suggesting that Tgegani's sentience has anything to do with Meshua, are you?"

Burgon nodded slightly. Slao frowned.

"Please tell me you're not serious."

"I am. I've spent the last two years working on Tgegani's AI programming and never once did I ever create more than an elementary level of sentience. So I'm still finding it difficult to believe that I just suddenly *stumbled* onto the right combination of code that just *happened* to turn Tgegani into a fully sentient life form. There's got to be more to this than what we've found."

Slao blinked twice and then roared with laughter.

"You really have been putting in too many hours on this project lately, haven't you?"

Burgon looked at Slao with an expression of confusion.

"But I-"

"Edias, AI programs don't just suddenly become sentient because some mythological entity from antiquity wished them to be. It takes genius to create intelligence and your genius has created intelligence. You just don't realize it yet," said Slao.

He stood up and patted Burgon on the back.

"Get some sleep, old man, or next you'll start thinking that simbits can talk," he chided.

He then turned and strode away. Burgon stared after him for a while and then turned back towards Tgegani and Persia and watched silently as they continued to talk.

Silvers slipped into Delgra's office and handed him a folder.

"What's this?" asked Delgra.

"It's the weekly report on all recent upgrades to the facility, as well as a report on the new additions to the troops stationed here," he said.

"Has our latest group of soldiers arrived yet?" asked Delgra.

"They're due in any time, sir."

"Good. And what is the status of the new barracks?"

"They should be completed today."

"Excellent! What about the other supplies and equipment I requested?"

Silvers squirmed slightly.

"We're still having problems getting those. Regional provisioning won't release them to us."

Delgra crossed his arms and thought for a moment.

"Then I guess I'll have to pull some strings to make it happen."

Just then a knock came at the door.

"Come in," said Delgra.

The secretary peaked her head into the room, and said, "I'm sorry to interrupt you, sir, but you wanted to be informed when the new soldiers arrived."

"Thank you, Ms. Eva," said Delgra.

The secretary nodded and then excused herself.

Delgra looked over at Silvers, and said, "Can you check on them for me? I want everyone put to work as soon as they're unpacked."

Silvers nodded, and replied, "I'll get right on it, sir."

He then turned and slipped out of the office. Delgra soon returned to his work. But as he was typing a new set of orders, a message appeared on his screen. It read, "fbcyber requests secure connection." He stopped his work and studied the message. After a moment he clicked the OK button and waited for the message window to appear.

"Greetings, Major," the message read.

"How can I be of service?" typed Delgra.

"I have something I think you might be interested in," came the reply.

Delgra saw a small file icon begin flashing in the corner of the message screen. He clicked it, accepted the file, and then waited for it to download. When it had completed, he opened it. It was a picture of a dusty gray, metallic lion. Delgra studied the data sheets included with the image and then blinked when he saw one word stenciled in red at the bottom.

"Sentient?" he thought to himself. "Is that even possible?" He quickly flipped back to the message window, and typed, "What is this for?"

"We require a trump card if we are to win the upcoming war. I believe this will adequately suit our needs. In the next few days I will be putting in motion the necessary paperwork to ensure that he is transferred to you," came the reply.

"I look forward to his arrival," typed Delgra.

Black walked gracefully into a simple, yet elegant state room and vigorously shook hands with an older man.

"Mr. Black. It's good to see you as always," said the man.

Black nodded as he smiled graciously.

"Same with you, Senator," he replied.

The man motioned to a chair, and said, "Please, have a seat."

Black bowed slightly and then sat down.

"So, what can I do for you today?" asked the senator.

Black's eyes wandered cautiously around the state room.

"Is it safe to talk here?" he asked.

The senator grinned.

"Of course it is! I wouldn't conduct my most sensitive business in here if it wasn't. It's my most secure room. I just don't use it all the time. It'd raise too many questions if I did. So I save it for, shall we say, *special* occasions?"

Black grinned as he folded his hands contemplatively.

"Indeed. Well then, shall we get down to business? How concerned are you with the safety of this nation and its people?"

The senator shrugged.

"As concerned as any senator should be. Why?"

Black pulled a folder out of his briefcase, and laid it down on the table in front of the senator.

"Read this. I believe the information inside is of great importance to our national security."

The senator turned the folder towards himself, flipped it open and started reading. Black watched in interest as the senator's eyes grew steadily wider as he read. Finally, after several moments, the senator looked up at him in horror.

"How is this possible!?" he asked, a hint of shock in his voice.

Black grinned slightly.

"There is something to be said for doing business with the military. You periodically encounter rather interesting information," he said.

The senator studied the papers intently as sweat began to bead on his forehead.

"If they know about this, why haven't they brought it to our attention yet?"

"They disbelieve their own intelligence, and thus have ignored all of the warning signs so far, hoping that this 'silly nonsense' will just go away. The problem is, it will not."

The senator wiped his forehead with a small rag.

"How long have they known?"

"About two years. If estimates are right we have slightly less than one year left before the Gorg begin their first strike," said Black.

The senator looked at him in shock.

"That's nowhere near enough time to get ready!"

"Actually, it will be plenty of time," grinned Black.

"How!?"

"You may be surprised at the resourcefulness of some of our military officers. In fact, one of them has already gone out of his way to secretly prepare the military for the upcoming invasion," said Black.

He slid another folder across the table to the senator who eyed it nervously. Black sat back and smiled devilishly. Even though the senator was becoming a nervous wreck, Black was enjoying every minute of it.

"Open it. What you find may interest you," he said with an almost devilish grin.

The senator slowly opened the folder and found pictures of Delgra as he moved about the Echo Military Science Labs on his daily duties.

"What is this?" he asked.

"An opportunity to save our country and its people."

After several moments, the senator looked at Black through narrowed, suspicious eyes.

"You're part of all this, aren't you?" snapped the senator.

Black shrugged.

"In a way, yes."

"If you knew about this already, why didn't you say something before now!?"

"There is something to be said for correctly timing the release of information to achieve the best possible results. If I had stepped forward earlier, little, if anything would have happened. That was not something I was willing to risk."

"So what do we do now?"

"Take this information to the General Secretary and make it sound like it's your handiwork. Tell him you have secret inside sources that have solid intelligence confirming the fact that this upcoming invasion is real. Tell him that, because of this information, you've come to him in hopes that he'll act quickly to prepare the nation for war. He'll see you as a patriotic leader who's deeply concerned for the safety of the country, and an important political asset, which will, in turn, gain the additional power within the senate you so crave. But if he balks, show him how this can be of a political advantage to him. He's up for re-election this year, so you can use this to help motivate him as well."

The senator glanced briefly at the papers and then at Black again.

"I'm not sure about this. How do I know this will benefit me?"

Black took a thick envelope out of the pocket of his suit jacket and slid it across the table.

"I'm sure you can think of something, can't you?" he said, grinning slyly.

The senator eyed the envelope and then Black. He scooped it up from the table and quickly slipped it into his jacket pocket before gathering up the folders and tucking them into his briefcase.

"I'll talk to him tomorrow morning and see what I can do."

Black grinned with satisfaction.

"That's all I ask."

Persia lay quietly on a hillside behind Burgon's laboratory as the golden rays of the twin suns danced playfully off of thin, wispy cloud tops nearby. She stretched long and hard, rolled over slightly and then laid her head on Burgon's lap. She purred contentedly and then laughed as a butterfly landed on her nose. Tgegani sat next to them and carefully studied the sky above as he took notes on everything around him. A small puff of wind blew across his face, causing him to toss his mane gently in order to straighten it.

"How do you like your new skin?" asked Burgon.

"The feeling is strange, but the clothing was necessary. Nakedness in our society is shunned. Therefore, having a proper covering is required," replied Tgegani.

Burgon smiled.

"How are the sensor points? Are they causing you any discomfort?"

Tgegani shook his head.

"I don't feel pain or discomfort by your understanding. I am, however, experiencing significant sensor feedback. The alpha data segments appear to be higher in some areas as opposed to others. While not overwhelming, the data flow is significant."

Burgon pulled his computer from its bag and set it on his lap. He connected a long cord to it and handed the other end to Tgegani.

"Here, plug this in so I can get a look at what you're seeing."

Tgegani took the data cable, opened an access port on his chest, and inserted it. Data immediately began appearing on Burgon's computer as it struggled to keep up with the torrent of information. Slowly Burgon isolated one feed at a time and adjusted each of them until the flow became more manageable.

"Is that better?" asked Burgon.

"It is acceptable," replied Tgegani.

He then ejected the data cable, handed it to Burgon, and closed the small access port.

"Dad, will you get me some more of that Gurak meat?" asked Persia.

Burgon chuckled.

"You eat too much of that stuff already. Besides, I just gave you some yesterday."

Persia smiled.

"I know. But I want more. It was good."

"If you keep eating that stuff you'll get fat and I'll end up broke," chided Burgon.

Persia chuckled, and said playfully, "I will not!"

Burgon laughed. As he and Persia continued to talk, a greck came into view overhead. At first it only studied the facility with muted interest. But when it saw Tgegani, it swooped down to get a better look, and was aghast when it realized what it was looking at.

"It's the proxy!" it said in a squawking voice.

It immediately turned and flew away as fast as it could into the open prairie, crying wildly as it went. Tgegani looked up and briefly studied the noisy bird, but took no further interest in it. The bird continued to fly with all its might for several miles until it spotted a pack of vandros hiding in the prairie grass below. The bird rolled out and swooped down at the wolf like vandros.

"The proxy has been found! The proxy has been found!" cried the greck.

The vandros leapt to their feet.

"Where is this creature?" cried their leader.

"To the south! To the south!" bellowed the greck as it circled overhead.

The lead vandros barked angrily and folded his ears back as he looked towards a nearby complex of buildings.

"With me!" he cried as he raced across the prairie like an angry smear of midnight.

Chapter 7

A bug landed on Tgegani's nose and began to clean its wings as he tried his best to focus on the little insect. Persia saw this and laughed.

"Hey, Dad, I think Tgegani found a new friend," she said playfully.

Burgon looked curiously at Persia and then over at Tgegani. He soon spotted the little bug on Tgegani's nose and smiled. The bug eventually flew away into a nearby stand of grass. But Tgegani said nothing, instead merely observing its behavior with curiosity. Suddenly he felt a familiar presence fill his mind.

"Tgegani! The dark one's agents come for you! Protect your family!" shouted a familiar voice in his head.

Tgegani quickly pattern matched the voice and found it to be identical to the man he'd seen the night he became self-aware.

"Meshua," he said quietly to himself.

Just then his eyes caught sight of a large group of vandros racing across the facility towards him. They soon stopped in front of Tgegani and cautiously eyed him. Tgegani studied them with muted interest as he searched his expansive knowledge database in a vain attempt to identify them. But nothing he could find matched any of the creatures in front of him.

"Who are you?" he asked.

"Are you the proxy?" hissed one of them in a tortured, twisted voice.

Burgon, who had initially been oblivious to their approach, cried out in surprise. This in turn startled Persia who sat up suddenly and soon spotted the vandros as well. But instead of being frightened, she merely studied them with curiosity.

"I am not a proxy. I am a sentient, cybernetic lifeform who is currently undergoing testing by my father," said Tgegani flatly.

Just then the greck landed next to the lead vandros and pointed a wing at Tgegani.

"That's him! That's the proxy!" it cried.

The lead vandros bared his teeth and growled angrily. Tgegani cocked an eyebrow in interest.

"Prepare yourself. They are about to attack," said the voice.

"Are you here to hurt my family?" Tgegani asked the vandros.

"We are here to destroy you and all those who oppose our master!" cried the lead vandros.

The greck squawked angrily at Tgegani and then bounded into the air. It knew a fight was coming and wanted nothing to do with it. The lead vandros glanced briefly at the greck and then back at Tgegani. He grinned with hungry glee. Tgegani's eyes narrowed as he stood to his feet. It didn't take much to realize what came next.

"Persia, take Dad to safety," he said.

Suddenly the lead vandros leapt at him, his teeth aimed strategically at the lion's throat. But this was no surprise to Tgegani who'd fully anticipated the move. He quickly turned his body and threw his shoulder hard into the creature's face, deflecting it away.

"Tgegani!" cried Persia.

"Go! Get Father out of here!" roared Tgegani.

The lead vandros slowly picked himself up from the ground and cackled mockingly.

"You will die, proxy, as will your family," he barked angrily.

The vandros then looked at two of the others and motioned towards the lion. Tgegani bared his teeth and prepared himself for the coming attack. A moment later two of the creatures leapt at him. But, to their surprise, he'd also anticipated this move as well. Reaching out at the leaping vandros, he grabbed both of them by their heads with his front paws and slammed them face first into the ground. Seeing an opportunity, the lead vandros turned and leapt on Tgegani's back. But as he bit down hard on the lion's neck, he found only an armored body shell below the lion's soft furry skin. Tgegani quickly turned and threw the vandros off his back like a leaf.

The other five vandros who remained considered entering the fight, but chose instead to stay back. It was already getting too crowded around the lion and the extra bodies wouldn't help. The three fighting against him would need all the room they could get if they were to have any hope of beating him. The first three vandros pulled back slightly, reorganized their attack, and then leapt again. Persia watched in horror as Tgegani fought bravely to fend off the attacks of the three vandros. Realizing that it wasn't safe to stay there anymore, Burgon grabbed Persia by the collar and pulled hard.

"Persia! We need to go, now!" he shouted.

"No! Tgegani!" cried Persia as she tried to pull away from him.

The three vandros continued to strike again and again at Tgegani as they pressed their attack. But they were repeatedly driven back. Realizing that they wouldn't win this fight the old fashioned way, the lead vandros turned to the other five who were waiting nearby and gave a sharp, commanding bark. Although he'd said no words, the order was clear enough. The five remaining vandros turned their attention towards Tgegani's family. Seeing that they had now become targets of the remaining vandros, Burgon pulled harder on Persia's collar.

"Persia! Come on! We need to run!" cried Burgon.

"Tgegani!" cried Persia as she struggled to break free.

Tgegani turned and glared at her with a cold, icy gaze. It was at that moment that Persia understood. Despite being a machine, Tgegani was willing to die for her. But if she insisted on staying, it would only hinder his efforts to protect her. She then turned and ran for the back door of the laboratory, nearly pulling Burgon off his feet as she did. But the five vandros who now hunted them were not about to let them get away. They immediately gave pursuit. Seeing this, Tgegani roared with anger, turned, and raced after them with all of his speed and strength. The lead vandros and his two partners immediately gave chase.

As he ran, Tgegani analyzed the situation in front of him and felt a pang of anxiety flow through his body. Despite his incredible speed, he would not be able to stop all five of the vandros in time. But if he didn't, his mother and father would both die. But, just as the vandros reached Burgon, a shot rang out followed by the gut wrenching sound of metal on bone that echoed through the air. A vandros lurched in pain and then crumpled to the ground in a rolling, oily heap of black flesh. The other four vandros, uncertain of what'd just happened, stopped short and then looked in confusion at their comrade. A second shot rang out as the head of another vandros snapped back hard, a misty cloud of crimson red erupting from between his eyes. The creature crumpled to the ground in a heap and lay motionless in a pool of its own blood.

The other three looked around frantically as Tgegani and the remaining three vandros closed quickly on them from behind. Just then their eyes caught sight of two guards standing near a corner of the laboratory aiming rifles at them.

One of the vandros turned to its leader, cried out in warning and then fell silent as a bullet ripped through its head. It crumpled to the ground and lay still. Not wanting to risk fate any further, the remaining two vandros turned and bolted towards Tgegani. But the lion would not let them pass without a fight. He leapt at the first one, grabbed its neck with his paws and slammed it hard into the ground.

The blow crushed the creature's throat and snapped its neck, killing it instantly. Then, using his remaining momentum, Tgegani swung his body around and kicked the other vandros in the face so hard that it snapped the creature's neck while simultaneously crushing part of its skull. It too collapsed to the ground and lay still. The remaining three vandros, realizing that it was now an all or nothing fight to the finish, rallied their courage and turned on Tgegani. But as they did, a pair of bullets whizzed past their heads. Tgegani, seeing an advantage to the gunfire, turned and raced towards the guards, drawing the remaining vandros after him.

"What are you doing?" came a voice in his head.

The voice sounded as if it already knew the answer, but wanted to make sure that Tgegani did as well. However, Tgegani said nothing as he continued to charge towards the guards, vandros in tow. Seeing this, one of the guards took aim at him and fired. But to his complete surprise, the bullet bounced harmlessly off the lion's head.

"What in the blazes!?" he said.

"Don't shoot at me! Shoot at the wolves!" cried Tgegani.

"It talked!" cried the second guard.

"Then it's gotta be a robot! Concentrate your fire on those wolves!" shouted the first guard.

A moment later they were joined by three more guards. Seeing that any hope of victory had suddenly vaporized, the three vandros spun on their heels and bolted for the safety of the prairie. But they only made it a few steps before a lethal hail of bullets cut them down. A moment later, even more guards joined them, responding to reports of gunfire on the south side of the facility. By the time they arrived, there was nothing left to see but an oily, robotic lion and eight dead vandros.

Seeing that the battle was over, Tgegani turned to the nearby guards, and said, "If you will excuse me, I must rejoin my family."

"Yeah, go ahead. We got this," replied the guard.

Tgegani nodded in thanks, and then made his way back to the laboratory. As he stepped inside, Persia nearly tackled him to the floor, grateful to see that he was alright. Tears rolled down her face as she hugged him tightly.

"Oh, I'm so glad you're okay," she cried.

"I am undamaged," said Tgegani.

"Are they dead?" asked Burgon.

Tgegani nodded.

"Their life functions have fully ceased, and will not be restored," he replied.

Persia sighed with relief and then grimaced with disgust as a strong, pungent odor assaulted her nose. Burgon also noticed the odor and covered his face with a rag.

"Eww, what is that smell?" cried Persia.

"I appear to have picked up some of the pungent residue that clung to the coats of those creatures," said Tgegani.

"Ugh, you're going to need a bath," said Persia.

She then covered her nose with her paw and soon realized that the odor wasn't going away. In fact, it gotten stronger. She lowered her paw and smelled herself. It nearly made her gag.

"Eww, I got it on me too! Great, now I'm going to have to take a regular bath because I'm certainly not going to lick this stuff off."

"Well, let's go over and get you both cleaned up," said Burgon.

Persia and Tgegani followed Burgon over to a washing stall where he lathered up Persia, scrubbed her down and rinsed her off. Seeing that she was now clean again, she sniffed at her fur, and then grimaced. Burgon laughed.

"Not clean enough?"

Persia shook her head. He lathered her up again, scrubbed even harder, and then rinsed her off a second time. She sniffed herself again and nodded in approval. Burgon then motioned to Tgegani who obeyed and stepped into the shower. Burgon lathered him up, scrubbed him down and then had Persia inspect the lion. To his surprise, Tgegani passed inspection on the first try.

"I have been cleaned. May I step out now?" asked Tgegani.

"Not just yet, young man. Open wide." he said.

Tgegani gave the doctor a puzzled look. Burgon smiled.

"Your mouth. Open it wide."

Tgegani obliged and the doctor took a brush, and some soap, and washed Tgegani's mouth and teeth clean of the black substance that covered them. He then briefly inspected the rest of the lion and eventually nodded in approval.

"Now that looks a lot better. However, I won't be able to do this for you all the time. So you'll need to learn how to do this on your own at some point."

"What would that be?" asked Tgegani.

The doctor smiled.

"Cleaning yourself."

Tgegani cocked his head slightly.

"If you will teach me an appropriate method to do so, I will willingly partake in such actions in the future."

The doctor nodded.

"I'll do that. But we'll worry about that later. We've had enough excitement for one day, so I'm going home."

Tgegani turned his head and looked in the direction of Persia.

"Why was mother's face wet?"

"Well, she...wait, did you just say mother?" said Burgon curiously.

Tgegani nodded. Burgon chuckled.

"You actually consider Persia your mother?" he asked in surprise.

Again Tgegani nodded.

"It's a simple logical conclusion. You are my creator and you are male, therefore you are my father. She is female, and your companion, therefore she is my mother. Two beings, a mother and a father, are required in order to bring life to anything."

Burgon grinned. While he didn't completely understand how Tgegani had come to that conclusion, he liked the idea. If nothing else, it added legitimacy to his sentience.

"So you're his mom now, eh, Persia?" he asked.

Persia nodded.

"Yeah, I am. He asked me if he could call me that a couple of days ago and I said yes. I think it's kind of cool being the mother of a big metal brute like him," she said.

She then batted at Tgegani playfully. Burgon chuckled.

"Why was mother's face wet?" asked Tgegani, repeating his original question.

"That's because I took a shower, silly."

Tgegani looked at her incredulously.

"I was not referring to that. I was speaking in reference to the fluid that so readily flowed from your eyes earlier, before your bath. I believe you call it crying."

Persia seemed offended by the suggestion, and yet nearly ready to burst into tears.

"I was not crying!" she protested, her voice cracking slightly.

But try as she might, a tear escaped from her eye and streamed down her face. Tgegani gently reached over, scooped up the tear and then showed it to her.

"Then what is this?" he asked.

Persia blushed slightly beneath her fur.

"Well, I...uh, was worried about you," she said as she shyly pawed the ground.

"Worry makes you cry?" asked Tgegani curiously.

"Many things make us cry, Tgegani. Worry, fear, happiness and most of all sadness. It's a part of who we are," said Burgon.

Tgegani pondered this for a moment.

"Then certain emotions can cause the excessive function of the tear ducts resulting in the overflow of tear fluid I witnessed?" he asked.

"They can. Emotions have a way of affecting our bodies in many strange and unique ways, tears being one of them."

"Hmm. Odd. My data suggests that tears are a biological reaction to a need for nourishment and moisture in the eyes. But the level of excretion that would cause a running of tear fluid from the eyes in excesses such as is being displayed in mom's current behavior does not coincide with the data I have on record. Logically, such an activity is not one that the body should willingly undertake."

Persia quickly wiped away her tears, but more soon replaced them. Burgon shook his head.

"Not everything can be answered through the application of logic, Tgegani. Some things require emotions to be properly understood," he said.

Tgegani tilted his head, and said, "Emotions are not logical."

Burgon shrugged.

"They're not meant to be. But they are a necessary component of life."

Tgegani studied Burgon curiously as he contemplated this.

"How would I acquire these emotions? I am most interested in having them," he asked.

Burgon thought about this question for several moments, and then said, "I'm afraid that's something I can't help you with. For Yigzan, emotions come naturally. Therefore, I don't know of any easy way to teach them to someone like yourself. So why don't you go plug yourself into the mainframe tonight and do a little research on this. Then, if you still have questions in the morning, feel free to ask either of us and we'll try to answer as best we can."

Tgegani nodded.

"I will do that."

A thin, somewhat homely looking middle aged woman knocked on the door of the General Secretary's office and then peaked cautiously inside.

"Sorry to bother you, sir, but Senator Joslin is here to see you. He says it's urgent."

The General Secretary looked up from his desk, and said, "Send him in."

The secretary quickly disappeared and a gray haired man appeared in her place a moment later, an expression of dire concern on his face.

"Senator Joslin, what brings you here today?" asked the General Secretary.

"I'm sorry to bother you on such a prestigious day."

"No, it's nothing at all. This really isn't all that big of a holiday. I just have to be seen, shake a few hands, and drink some wine with a few of my bigger constituents. You know, the usual political stuff," said the General Secretary with a sarcastic grin.

Joslin smirked.

"Your humor is just as flat as it's always been," he quipped.

The General Secretary chuckled.

"I aim to please. So, what can I do for you today? My secretary says it's urgent."

"It is, and it involves the peace and security of our country."

The General Secretary folded his hands in interest.

"I'm always concerned about that. What news could be so grave that it would stir up an ever jolly senator like yourself?"

Joslin frowned.

"We are about to be invaded."

The General Secretary furrowed his brow in interest.

"Invaded? Who would stoop to such a preposterous low?"

The senator pulled a folder from his briefcase, and slid it across the desk.

"The Gorg would."

The General Secretary opened the folder and studied the papers inside.

"Interesting information. But I am curious as to why you know about this, and my own military does not?" he said.

Joslin shook his head.

"That's just it. They *do* know about this."

The General Secretary stared curiously at Joslin.

"If they know about it, why haven't they told me?" he asked.

"There are members within our military who wish to hide this fact. They do not believe that anyone would attack us, and thus have worked to hide this fact from others who might force them to act upon such information."

The General Secretary studied the papers again.

"And why do you have this information?" he asked suspiciously.

"Because there are members within your military who still love this country, and wish to see it protected at all costs. But until now they have been hindered from doing so by their superiors. That is why they have come to me in hopes that I might be able to do what they could not."

The General Secretary looked at the pages again, stopping at one particular paragraph towards the middle of the second page.

"We have less than a year left to prepare!?" he said in surprise.

Joslin nodded.

"We do. But there is good news mingled in with all of that bad news. A silent party within the military has slowly been preparing our forces for the coming war. They have nearly completed all their preparations to ensure that we are ready when the Gorg finally attack."

"And who are these people?"

"They're listed in that folder. However, be careful who you share their names with. These men have risked a lot exposing themselves like this, and fear reprisal if their identities become known. They are just honest soldiers trying to do their job and protect this country despite wishes to the contrary by their superiors."

The General Secretary's face began to grow red with anger.

"Is that so. Well then, if you will excuse me, Senator, I need to have a *long* discussion with my cabinet about this."

The senator stood and slid another file folder across the desk to the General Secretary.

"Thank you, sir. Now, before I go, I think you should also read this. I know you've got more important things to deal with right now, but this is important enough for you to look into as well. Upon learning of our situation, I took it upon myself to do a little research and discovered some possible new weapon systems that may help us better defend ourselves in the upcoming war."

Joslin then excused himself from the room. The General Secretary took the folder, opened it, and read the contents. He then turned to his desk phone and pressed the intercom.

"Get the secretary of defense and my generals in here right now," he said firmly.

"Yes, sir," replied the secretary.

A half hour later three men walked into the General Secretary's office to find him sitting behind his desk with his hands folded, and his eyes ablaze with anger.

"You called us, sir?" said the Secretary of Defense.

The General Secretary pushed a plain brown folder across his desk, and asked, "Would you gentlemen mind explaining this?"

Tgegani sat alone on a hillside behind the laboratory and studied the stars overhead as they glistened brightly through a dark, moonless sky. He slowly went through everything he'd learned over the previous days and tried to make sense of it all. But, despite his best efforts, little of it made sense to him. He watched curiously as a meteorite streaked across the sky in a brilliant flash of light, and then disappeared. Just then Tgegani sensed something. It felt warm and comforting in a way he'd only encountered twice before. It hadn't been something he'd detected through the normal application of his five senses. Instead, it was something he felt deep inside.

It didn't make sense and yet it was as real as the smell of the prairie that filled the air around him. He raised an eyebrow in curiosity. Was it a system malfunction? If it was, he could quickly run a diagnostic, find the source of the problem, and then fix it. But he didn't think it was anything like that. Malfunctions didn't feel this way. He thought about this for a moment longer and then came up with two possible ideas of what the feeling might be. He decided to test the first and see if that was it. If it wasn't, then he knew what he needed to do.

"How long do you plan to sit there like that?" he asked, probing to see if his first guess was correct.

And it was. A light suddenly appeared next to him, and bathed the area in a soft white glow. Tgegani then turned and looked curiously at a man who now sat next to him clothed in glowing white robes.

"Hello, Tgegani," said the man kindly.

"You are Meshua. Am I correct?" asked Tgegani.

The man looked at him, and smiled.

"I am."

Tgegani looked up at the stars and pondered this.

"You were there when I first became aware of myself."

Meshua smiled.

"I was."

"You also came into my mind, and talked to me when those creatures attacked me the other day. My research tells me that you existed before records were first kept, and that you have been seen throughout history during various periods of crisis. You also have the ability to appear and disappear at will, traveling great distances in the blink of an eye with the aid of no machine or transportation device that we understand to be possible, and you are neither bound by time, nor space. It is also reported that you have the ability to know the hearts and minds of men, even though they speak no words to you." He then looked at Meshua, and said, "You are not logical."

Meshua laughed.

"Tgegani, not everything in this world can be explained with logic. Your father has told you that many times," he said kindly.

Tgegani nodded.

"That would be a logical statement. No pun intended, of course."

Meshua chuckled.

"But I suspect that you are not here to show me how to understand this illogical world in which I live," continued Tgegani.

Meshua looked at the young lion with careful concern.

"No, I am here to warn you that a war is coming. A great enemy has arisen that threatens my people with extinction."

Tgegani turned his attention back to the stars as though contemplating this new revelation. After several moments he looked back at Meshua.

"What is my place in this great struggle?" he asked.

"You will be required to risk much to protect them from harm. What that will be, though, has yet to be revealed."

Tgegani seemed puzzled by this.

"It is said that you know and understand all, and yet you do not know what is to come?"

"I do indeed know all that is to come. However, it has not yet been given to you to know all that is to transpire before you."

Tgegani cocked his head slightly.

"Why is this so?"

"Because you are not ready. In time you will be. But for now it is best that you don't know the sum total of all you must face. It is for your good that you remain uninformed."

Tgegani thought about this for a bit, and then said, "I understand."

He then turned his eyes to the stars again. Meshua studied his eyes for several moments, and then smiled slightly.

"Something troubles your mind. What is it?" he asked.

"The creatures I fought the other day were in search of one who was to be a proxy. Am I the one they spoke of? And if so, what am I a proxy for?"

"Have you heard of one called Negago?"

Tgegani furrowed his brow.

"The dark lord of Verok, ruler of the fire lands, and master of all evil things? Yes, I am well aware of him. He is an enemy of all that is good. His existence is listed as being merely legend. However, since you too were once considered legend, I suspect that he is real as well."

Meshua nodded.

"He is also your greatest enemy."

Tgegani studied Meshua curiously.

"But why? What have I done to deserve such hostility towards me?"

"You have done nothing of yourself. Negago hates anything and everything associated with my father and I. He wants nothing more than to destroy us, and everything we have created."

"Then why this battle by proxy? Such a tactic would indicate that he does not have the strength by which to defeat you in single combat."

Meshua shook his head.

"He does not."

Tgegani cocked an eyebrow slightly.

"Then why not simply defeat him once and for all, and bring an end to his reign of terror?"

Meshua smiled again.

"That is something you will learn the answer to in time. But for now you have enough on your mind. I will not burden you with anything more than you are capable of handling."

"But what about my place as your proxy? What am I required to do?"

"Live, and protect my people the best you can. That is all that I ask of you."

Tgegani looked at him curiously.

"Are they not my people as well?"

Meshua smiled.

"Not yet. But in time they will be."

The young lion contemplated this for several moments.

"But I am only one person. How am I able to do such a monumental task?" he said.

Meshua gently took Tgegani's face in his hands.

"You do not need to carry the entire weight of the world on your shoulders; only that small bit which I have put before you. Now go, and fulfill your destiny."

And with that, he was gone. Tgegani thought about this for several moments, and then looked up at the stars again.

"I still do not understand my place. However, I will trust you and go forward as you have requested," he said.

Chapter 8

Black took a bite of egg and washed it down with some juice as he read the morning paper. He then smiled as he glanced at one of the headlines.

"Hmm, I see the General Secretary has gone on the warpath with his cabinet over their...shall we say, indiscretions?"

As he sliced off a small piece of the steak on his plate, Elgar strode into the room holding a folder under his arm.

"Ah, the morning briefing!" said Black happily as Elgar handed him the folder.

Black flipped it open, began to read the first page, stopped, backed up, and then read it again. He scratched his chin as he studied the page in curiosity.

"Hmm, interesting. So our robotic friend is now taking up the study of war craft. I wonder what prompted him to do that?" he said, more to himself than to Elgar.

"The report says that his interest is more generic than specific. It's possible that he may have heard something about the upcoming war and became curious," said Elgar.

"Well, that's possible. But if that were true, wouldn't he be focusing more on data relevant to the Gorg rather than war in general?"

"I don't know, sir. I am just as confused as you are by his actions, and hoping you might be able to make something of it," said Elgar.

"I would, but nothing really jumps out at me at this point," said Black.

He flipped through the other pages, reading each of them quickly, and then set the folder down on the table. He leaned back in his chair and pondered the information.

After a bit, he turned to Elgar, and said, "Let's keep an eye on him for a while. I want to see what he intends to do with this new line of study. It may turn out to be nothing and, at the same time, it could prove to be of great benefit to us."

Persia walked up behind Tgegani as the first light of dawn broke over the distant horizon.

"You're up early," she said as she sat down beside him.

"I do not require rest," said Tgegani.

Persia chuckled.

"Maybe not, but I'm sure you were at least doing something while the rest of us were sleeping."

"I've been thinking."

"About what?" asked Persia.

"Death."

Persia's eyes widened as she giggled slightly.

"Well, that's an awfully heavy subject to be thinking about this early in the morning."

He turned to her, and asked, "Does death bring you laughter?"

Persia blinked in surprise.

"No, it doesn't."

"Then why did you laugh?"

"I was just caught off guard by your strange interest in death, and found it funny. Death is not a subject of joy or laughter. Your actions however were," she said with a muted grin.

Tgegani lifted his head and stared at the sky.

"I see."

Persia studied Tgegani's expression, but couldn't make much from his otherwise blank stare.

"Is something on your mind?" she asked.

Tgegani remained silent for several moments, and then said, "I am trying to understand death. Why must it happen, and what is its purpose? I understand the physical and biological reality of death, and why it occurs, but I do not understand the wide range of religious and philosophical elements that are attached to it."

Persia blinked in surprise.

"You really *have* been thinking about this, haven't you?" she said with a chuckle.

Tgegani turned to her with a puzzled expression.

"I already stated that I have been. Was the original statement not understood?"

Persia laughed.

"No, no. I fully understood you. I was just being sarcastic."

Tgegani turned his face to the horizon.

"Sarcasm. Hmm."

He briefly reviewed several things in his mind before returning to the subject of death, again trying to understand it. But nothing made sense to him.

He then turned to Persia, and asked, "Why do living things die?"

Persia took a deep breath.

"It's just the natural order of things. We live, and when the time comes, be that tomorrow or many years from now, we die."

"So this cessation of function is a normal part of life?"

Persia nodded.

"It is."

"Will I cease to function some day?" asked Tgegani.

Persia nodded again.

"It may take many, many of our lifetimes, but eventually you will. Everything dies. Even machines."

"But a machine is not alive. How can it die if it was never alive?"

Persia pondered the question for a while, and then said, "Actually, in a way you *are* alive. While you're not flesh and blood like me, you're still a living creature."

"Why am I considered alive?"

"Because you can think and reason for yourself. Life is more than just being made of organic material. It's a state of existence as well."

"Then a clock is alive?"

Persia shook her head.

"No, it's not, because it cannot think for itself."

"Neither can bacteria, and yet they are considered alive."

This impressed Persia. Despite being a robot, Tgegani was surprisingly observant and insightful. She then lay down on the ground and stared out at the prairie as she thought about an answer to Tgegani's statement.

"Well, you're right in a way. Life is something much larger than can be defined by words."

"Explain."

She rolled onto her back and looked at Tgegani.

"To use your more logical way of thinking, life can be defined in two ways. The first is biological existence. Plants, trees, bacteria and even myself would fall into this category. The other form of life would revolve around sentience and being aware of oneself, the latter of which doesn't necessarily require biological materials to exist."

"But you are both sentient and biological. Are you then of both types?"

Persia nodded slightly.

"In many ways, I am. There is almost always a middle ground for everything in this world where the distinctiveness of several different things becomes blended together to create yet another type that is both similar, and yet distinct from the others."

"Like a hybrid?"

Persia shrugged slightly as she thought about the question.

"Eh, yeah, in a way."

"Then what is the true definition of death, if life has many definitions?"

Persia squirmed slightly at the question. She inhaled deeply, and then exhaled slowly.

"Well, I don't completely understand it myself, but dad once told me that, when we die, our souls leave our bodies and go to be with Meshua. I don't quite understand what a 'soul' is, but it's apparently a fairly important part of us."

Tgegani pondered this briefly.

"Is this soul immortal, or does it die as well?" he asked.

Persia sighed.

"As far as I know it's immortal."

"Then will your soul ever return to this world and live again?"

A sad expression drew across her face.

"No, it won't."

Tgegani raised an eyebrow in interest.

"Then death is permanent."

"It is."

Tgegani pondered this for several moments, and then started walking back to the lab.

"Where are you going?" asked Persia.

"I need to do more research. I want to better understand what death is."

Delgra hurried out of his office as he straightened his uniform.

"Why didn't someone tell me he was coming?" he asked.

"Nobody knew until just a few minutes ago, sir," replied Silvers.

Delgra grumbled.

"I hate surprise inspections."

As he hurried out the front door a small caravan of black vehicles pulled to a stop in front of the building. Delgra paused at the top of the steps and studied each of the vehicles. Numerous men in black suits, shoulder cloaks and dark glasses quickly piled out of the escort vehicles and surveyed the area for danger while others guarded the vehicles. Satisfied that all was safe, one of the men walked over to one of the vehicles and opened the door. The General Secretary stepped out a moment later. Delgra walked down the steps and saluted him.

"Good morning, sir. For what do we have the pleasure of your visit?" he asked.

"It has come to my attention that you've been doing some rather interesting things behind our backs as of late," replied the General Secretary.

Delgra's heart froze. While he maintained his stern military repose on the outside, his heart beat feverishly inside his chest.

"How did he find out!?" he thought. "Come again, sir?" he said, trying to maintain an air of innocence.

"I've read all about your work here these past two years and wanted to personally congratulate you on a job well done," said the General Secretary.

Delgra's mind went from fear to complete puzzlement.

"For what, sir?"

"Your work in secretly preparing the military for war, of course! It would seem that your former commander did not value your vast array of skills. For example, hacking into our computer network, and creating three fake personnel files, each one a Marshall General, complete with military history, and all necessary data to fool the lower level commanders into doing what needed to be done. Utterly brilliant! In fact, your work was so good that it even fooled our best security experts," said the General Secretary with a chuckle.

Delgra scolded himself harshly.

"Drat. I was sloppy and got caught. But how'd they catch me!?" he thought to himself. "How long have you known about this, sir?" he asked.

"Just a few days, actually. You did a good enough job covering your tracks that it took a senator's as yet unknown informant to discover your work. I must say that your work does great credit to the branch of special operations."

"Thank you, sir," said Delgra.

The General Secretary pulled a large folder from his briefcase, and handed it to Delgra.

"I'd like you to look this over and give me your opinion of the items in it," he said.

Delgra opened the folder and glanced through it briefly.

"They're new weapons systems we might be able to use against the Gorg. Since we'll be heavily outnumbered in this fight, we'll need to find anything we can that'll give us an edge. I'm no military expert, so I'll be relying on your knowledge and experience to determine which of these systems will give us what we need," said the General Secretary.

"I'll get right on it, sir," said Delgra.

The General Secretary turned around and scanned the facility.

"And while I'm here, I think I'd like a tour of the place. From what I've seen, you run a tight little operation."

"Yes, sir, we do. If you'd like--"

The General Secretary waved dismissively.

"No, no, no. You've got more important work to do. In fact, you should probably get started on it right now. Your executive officer here knows the facility well enough, doesn't he?"

"Like the back of my hand, sir," said Silvers proudly.

"Very good. Then he can show me the facility while you get to work."

Delgra saluted him, and said, "Understood, sir."

He then turned and walked back into the administration building. He quickly called up a secure voice connection on his computer and waited for the other side to answer.

"Black here," came the reply.

"The General Secretary knows about our plans."

"Yes, I know."

"What are we going to do about it?"

"We're going to continue just as we have been."

"But he knows already!"

"Major, we are less than a year away from the start of the war. It was time he knew."

Delgra stared at the screen in bewilderment.

"You told him?"

"Yes, in a way. I used one of my government contacts to insert the information into circulation at the right time to reveal only what they needed to know, and nothing more."

Delgra sighed.

"I wish you'd warn me when you do stuff like this. I hate surprises."

Black chuckled.

"My apologies. But I did at least tell you that I'd be sending some information your way."

"Yes, but you failed to mention the means by which it'd be delivered," said Delgra incredulously.

Black chuckled.

"Again, my apologies. By the way, did you receive the folder I sent you?" he asked.

Delgra raised an eyebrow in curiosity.

"What folder?"

"A folder with detailed information about a set of potential new weapons systems that I wanted you to look at. It should have come with the General Secretary today. Did he not hand it to you?"

Delgra looked down at the folder on his desk.

"Yes, he did," he replied.

"Good. I would like you to flip through it until you find a paper on a robotic lion."

Delgra opened the folder and searched each page until he found the one Black had described.

"Tgegani project? Is this the robot you showed me a few days ago?" he asked.

Black gave a soft, but evil sounding laugh.

"Yes, it is. But that was only the appetizer. This folder contains the main course. Look it over and familiarize yourself with it. I think you will find this particular *weapon* to be quite interesting."

Delgra continued to read the informational pages, but said nothing.

Sensing that Delgra was otherwise occupied, Black said, "I will leave the rest of this up to you. Good day, major," he said, and then disconnected the call.

Delgra continued to study the papers with great interest for several minutes longer, and then set them aside and turned to his computer. Within moments, new orders were flowing over the internet to all parts of the country.

Burgon walked into his laboratory and was surprised to find Tgegani discussing biological reproduction with Persia. Burgon grinned wide as he watched Persia's expressions change from shock to embarrassment to confusion and back again. He mused about Persia's seeming inability to handle the subject, and then wondered how red her face was below her fur. Finally, deciding it was best to step in and rescue her before she exploded from sheer embarrassment, he walked up and greeted Tgegani.

"Good morning, Tgegani. How are you doing today?" he asked.

"I am having a fascinating discussion on the reproductive functions and habits of various life forms found on this planet."

"Oh really?" said Burgon with a grin.

"Dad. Do something," said Persia insistently through gritted teeth.

"Tgegani, can we change the subject?" asked Burgon.

"Yes, father. What new subject did you wish to discuss?"

Burgon sat down on a stool next to him, and said, "What do you know about war?"

"I have considerable knowledge on the subject. Is there something you wish to know?"

Burgon sighed.

"Read this," he said as he held out a single sheet of paper.

Tgegani glanced at it, and then looked curiously at Burgon.

"Hmm, so this is what he was talking about," said Tgegani.

"Who was?" asked Burgon.

"Meshua," replied Tgegani.

Burgon looked at him in confusion.

"What are you talking about?" he asked.

Persia quickly read the paper as well and then went wide eyed.

"Dad, is this for real!?" she said in surprise.

Burgon nodded.

"I'm afraid so. I don't know why they'd want him for military service, or even how they found out about him. All I know so far is who to report to, where, and when."

"Dad, not to sound silly, but since when do they recruit machines?" asked Persia.

Burgon shrugged.

"I don't know. This is a first for me as well. But we'll find out together."

"Together? I would assume by that statement that you've received orders as well?" said Tgegani in interest.

Burgon nodded. Persia blinked in surprise.

"Wait, you're going too!?" she exclaimed.

"And you as well."

"Me!?" said Persia.

Burgon grinned.

"Well, we can't leave you here alone, now can we?"

Persia thought about this for a moment, and said, "Uh, well, no, not really."

"Father, what is the nature of your summons? I would suspect that it is not for military service as you are beyond the age of enlistment or military draft," said Tgegani.

"That's correct. You have been summoned for military service, and I, being your creator, am required to be there with you as chief supervising scientist."

"What about me? What's my purpose there?" asked Persia.

"Family pet," chided Burgon with a grin.

"Dad! That's not funny!" said Persia as she nudged him playfully with her paw.

"Since we will need to travel soon, would you like me to arrange transportation for us?"

"That's already been taken care of," said Burgon.

Tgegani nodded.

"Understood."

Burgon stood up and then walked over to his desk.

"Well, I think it's time to go home and start packing. The sooner we get where we're going, the better. At least, in theory, anyways."

"Wait, dad. Aren't you going to contest this? Tgegani can't go into the military! He hasn't even completed his training with us yet," said Persia.

"I can't do anything to stop it. It's a federal order. They ask, we do. We can't say no."

"There are actually one hundred twenty seven different legal precedents that could be used to render such an order null and void," said Tgegani.

"Well, let's not. While I agree with Persia that you aren't quite ready for something like this, I have a feeling that some good might come of this. Besides, if you do well, it gives more strength to my case for robotic sentience."

"Is your boss okay with this?" asked Persia.

"You mean Mr. Black?" asked Burgon.

Persia nodded. Burgon shrugged.

"He's the one who gave me the paper and arranged our transportation. So I would think so. Now, let's get packing. I don't want to miss the train."

Chapter 9

Delgra stared at the note briefly, folded it and then slipped it into his pocket. He turned and looked out the window as the car glided slowly down the road towards town. Captain Silvers sat next to him and studied the screen on his laptop.

"This Dr. Burgon has made quite a name for himself already. Even his record in college is impressive. Not only did he distinguish himself by obtaining master's degrees in engineering, robotics and chemistry, as well as a doctorate in cybernetics, he's also the highest scoring doctoral student ever in the history of the college, and the only one to ever receive a perfect score on his doctoral project. He further distinguished himself with ten years of faithful service to the college's cybernetics laboratory before going to work for Cybergenics Incorporated. It appears he's also been spending the last couple of years working on...a robotic lion. Interesting. What a strange thing to build as a robot."

Delgra turned towards Silvers and glanced at the computer screen, and then back towards the window as the first buildings of the rapidly expanding prairie town passed by outside. In just over two and a half years, this sleepy little town had grown from one store and a handful of homes to seven stores, well over three hundred homes, and a variety of other buildings, including a combined elementary and high school, a public library and a gym. Daily traffic in and out of the town had now grown to a level not seen in decades, if ever. Even the two dusty old dirt roads in and out of town, as well as the handful of city streets that had connected the few houses that had been there at the beginning had since been replaced by modern, paved, high tech roads made with the latest paving materials, and outfitted with the latest traffic control equipment.

Their car soon reached the gate to the train station and pulled to a stop. The driver rolled down his window to talk to a soldier standing guard nearby. They discussed several things briefly and then were waved through. The driver pulled forward and parked next to the train platform. He then opened the passenger door for the two officers who got out and headed for the platform just as an opulent, jet black, five car train pulled into the station.

"I see our guest likes to travel in style," said Silvers with bemused interest.

Delgra studied the Cybergenics logo on the engine and thought about what was coming. Silvers turned and noticed Delgra's slightly worried expression.

"Is something the matter?" he asked.

Delgra shook his head.

"Not really. I've just got a lot on my mind right now."

A moment later, a man, a lion and a snow tiger exited the second car. The soldiers on the platform saw the two large cats and immediately took aim at them.

"Lower your weapons," said Delgra.

"But, sir--" said a soldier.

"Do it now! That's an order!" he shouted.

The men reluctantly obeyed, but kept their rifles at the ready. As a group of porters unloaded a vehicle from the cargo car, the man stepped up to Delgra and held out his hand.

"Hi there. I'm Dr. Burgon. I believe you were expecting me?" he said.

Delgra studied the man briefly and then shook his hand.

"I'm Major Delgra. This is my executive officer, Captain Silvers."

Burgon shook Silvers' hand and then turned and gestured to Tgegani.

"It's nice to meet you both. This is Tgegani, my robotic lion, and next to him is Persia."

"Are they your pets?" asked Silvers.

"I am *not* a pet," growled Persia.

This made Delgra and the others blink in surprise.

"She can speak!?" exclaimed Silvers.

"Persia is a sentient snow tiger. She can both read and speak our language fluently, as can Tgegani," said Burgon.

"You can speak as well?" asked Silvers as he looked at the lion.

"I can," replied Tgegani.

"Do you speak other languages?" asked Delgra in Gorg.

Tgegani nodded.

"I am fluent in all major and minor languages, dialects and methods of communication," he replied in perfect Sattazin.

"Fascinating," said Delgra in amazement.

Even though he knew about Tgegani's sentience from the reports that Black had sent him, this had surprised even him.

"How smart are they?" asked Silvers.

"I currently possess over one billion six hundred thousand terabytes of data. I can speak authoritatively on almost any subject you wish to discuss," said Tgegani.

Persia sheepishly raised a paw, and said, "I can recite poetry if you like."

"Huh, interesting. But we're wasting time here. I know you have a lot of work ahead of you, so if you will follow me, we will take you to the facility," said Delgra.

They then made their way down to two nearby waiting vehicles and were soon heading away from the train station towards the laboratory as a number of soldiers saw to Burgon's belongings. As they rumbled down the road to the laboratory, Burgon noticed that Tgegani was having a difficult time finding a stable perch on the seat.

"You alright over there?" asked Burgon.

"While this position is inconvenient, I will manage," replied Tgegani as he shifted uneasily on the seat.

The vehicles soon reached the gate of the facility, were checked by the guards and then waved through. The cars continued on for a short ways before pulling to a stop in front of lab seven, where they unloaded their passengers.

"Dr. Burgon, you will have full use of this facility and the personnel I have assigned to it for the duration of your stay here. Your vehicle and any of your other possessions are being delivered to your new house as we speak. Now, as for your introduction to the facility, we will begin with a tour of the laboratory first and then someone will see to your paperwork after that," said Delgra.

They turned and walked through the doors of one of the larger robotics labs and quickly spotted two men who were working on a nearby project.

"Gentlemen, do you have a second?" asked Delgra.

As the two men turned around, Burgon's eyes went wide.

"Dr. Visnel!?" he said in surprise.

"Edias!?" said one of the men in equal surprise.

"Oh by the ancients, it is you!" said Burgon as he ran towards the man.

The two men hugged, and then vigorously shook hands.

"Well, how are you?" asked Burgon.

"I've been keeping busy. Who are your two pets?" said Visnel.

"I am *not* a pet," muttered Persia.

"Wait, Persia? Is that really you? Wow, you've grown a lot since I last saw you," said Visnel as he walked over and bent down to give Persia a hug.

She pulled away from him, her eyes narrowing. She then studied the man for a moment before cautiously sniffing at his jacket. As she did, her eyes slowly grew wider as memories began to wash through her mind.

"I know you," she said with fascination.

Visnel nodded.

"You were just a kitten when we last met."

Persia bowed slightly.

"My sincerest apologies, sir."

Visnel chuckled.

"It's alright. I didn't recognize you at first either, so we're even."

Persia nuzzled his hands gently and purred. Just then Visnel noticed the large mechanical lion sitting mutely next to her.

"Oh, my, where are my manners? You must be Tgegani," said Visnel as he turned to the lion.

"It is a pleasure to make your acquaintance," said Tgegani, nodding politely.

Visnel nodded in return.

"And he's well-mannered too!"

"You can thank Persia for much of that. She spent a lot of hours teaching him the proper use of manners and etiquette," said Burgon.

Visnel put his fists on his hips and smiled proudly at the little tiger.

"Well, I am most impressed, young lady. You did a fine job!"

Persia shrugged.

"I'm his mom. It's what I," she said shyly.

"His mom!?" said Visnel in confusion.

Burgon laughed.

"It's a long story, so I'll save the details until later, as the Major still has a lot to show me."

"Well, then I look forward to hearing all the juicy little details."

Two large grecks cautiously hid in the shadowy grasses of a nearby hillside as they kept their eyes on both the sky, and on a small, dark cave entrance in front of them. Several large, silvery, eagle like birds called tabions circled high overhead. The grecks did their best to hide and stay calm for fear that they would be killed by the tabions, their mortal enemy. The two grecks were certain the tabions knew where they were, but so long as they stayed on the ground and hidden, they weren't likely to be attacked by them. Just then, a hot, scorching wave of fire belched from the mouth of the cave. The tabions cried out in surprise and banked sharply away from the blackened hillside. A moment later, Negago stepped out of the cave.

He was followed by a billowing, black cloud of smoke that rose into the air and blotted out the sun, turning the small patch of prairie around him the color of midnight. All of the tabions, save for one brave bird, turned and made for the open prairie and the brilliance of daylight. The one who stayed behind swooped down near the cave and glared at Negago as it passed close by him as if to say that it did not fear him. But Negago didn't seem to take notice of the bird's actions. The tabion then turned and rejoined its companions. Once the tabions had vanished from sight, two greck heads popped up from the prairie grass like gophers. Negago looked down at them in disgust and growled angrily. One of them looked back at him and scowled.

"Hey, don't get fussy with me. We risk enough doing your dirty work, oh dark lord," he said in a low, dumpy voice.

Negago thrust out his hand at the greck as if to strike it down, but paused when the second greck raised its wings in a gesture of surrender.

"Wait, wait, my lord! We have important news for you!" it cried.

Negago eyed the second greck and then lowered his hand. Mercy wasn't something Negago showed to anyone. However, if there was a chance to further his agenda, he would overlook even the grossest insubordination. At least for now.

"Where is your leader?" hissed Negago.

"He was killed by the tabions of Meshua."

Negago's eyes blazed, like raging balls of fire.

"Then what has become of the proxy? Has he been found?" he hissed.

"He has, my lord," said the first greck.

"And is he dead?"

"No, my lord."

Negago began to quiver violently in anger.

"Why not?" he said in a sharp, grating, demonic voice.

"Because the vandros that you sent to attack him were all slain."

This stunned Negago.

"My most powerful and fearless hunters slain, by the proxy!?" he said in surprise.

"Yes, my lord."

"How is that possible? How can one creature slay even one of my vandros, let alone a whole pack!? It is not possible. You are lying!"

The first greck glared at him.

"We are not lying, my lord. The proxy defeated your vandros with the aid of others who carry black fire tubes that spit death at any who approach. It was he who fought them first. But fearless men with fire tubes slew them before they could destroy him."

Negago was surprised at this and took several moments to contemplate this new development.

"This series of events is unfortunate. But that does not change the fact that he must die. Summon the remainder of my vandros horde. If a few cannot kill him, then perhaps a few thousand will."

The first greck held up his wings in a gesture to halt.

"I would not advise that, my lord."

"Why?" growled Negago.

"Because there is a war coming, one in which the proxy is to be used as a weapon. So it would best suit us if we simply stepped back and let this coming war do our work for us."

Negago rubbed his bony, shriveled hands together as he contemplated this. He knew of the pending war between the Yigzan and the Gorg, as he was the one who'd started it. But he hadn't, as yet, considered using it to destroy the proxy. A thin, devilish grin stitched itself across his face.

He pointed at one of the grecks, and said, "Very well. We will leave his death in the hands of fate. Until then, summon me a vandros. I have work for him to do."

"Yes, my lord."

Delgra called the small fifteen man squad before him to attention, and then carefully examined each man's equipment. Satisfied with their readiness, he stepped back and studied the group with muted interest.

"Gentlemen, good morning. I want to say that your training over the past several weeks has gone well. You now think as one, act as one and move with a surety that would make any commander proud. But today your unit will change. You will be gaining an extra member. This individual is the sole reason you have been brought together as a unit. Actually, I would be amiss to call him a person. He is a lion. Not a real flesh and blood lion, but rather a machine. A thinking, reasoning, sentient machine. Now at this point I'm sure that many of you likely feel that I have completely lost my mind. I can assure you that I have not. Contrary to popular belief, such a thing does exist, and he will be serving alongside you in the upcoming war."

He turned to his right and motioned for Dr. Burgon and Tgegani to approach. He then patted Tgegani on the head as the lion sat down next to him.

"Gentlemen, this is Tgegani, the lion I told you about. Please introduce yourselves to him."

Each man, feeling somewhat silly, introduced themselves one at a time to him.

After the last man introduced himself, Tgegani nodded, and said, "It is nice meeting all of you."

The men gazed at him with expressions of surprise and shock.

Finally one of the men said, "I didn't think animals could talk."

Tgegani nodded.

"Some can. However, I am not an animal. I am a machine, as was stated by the Major."

The soldier rubbed his neck and chuckled nervously.

"I thought he was kidding," he said.

"No, I was dead serious, corporal," said Delgra sternly.

"My apologies, sir," said the soldier sheepishly.

"No matter. You've got bigger things to worry about right now. I would like you to spend this afternoon bringing Tgegani up to speed on your unit, what each of you do, how you operate, your tactics and any other things you feel he should know. He will not carry any weapons other than his teeth, claws and razor sharp senses. So be aware of that when using him in combat. I want you to learn each other's strengths and abilities so that you can operate efficiently as one unit. Sergeant Welk, he's all yours. Don't forget to get with Dr. Burgon if you have any questions or concerns."

"Yes, sir!" said one of the men.

Feeling somewhat overwhelmed by the events of the day, Burgon decided to take a walk in the cool moistness of the evening to refresh himself. As he walked around he came across Tgegani, who was admiring the stars above.

"Hello, Father," said Tgegani without taking his eyes off the stars.

"Am I that easily recognized?" said Burgon with a chuckle.

"Your walk is unique, and thus easily identifiable," said Tgegani.

"It must be nice to have hearing like that."

Tgegani nodded. He then sat quietly for several moments as he pondered many things.

"I leave tomorrow with my unit. Will you miss me?" he eventually asked.

"Of course I'll miss you. You're the closest thing I have to a son."

Tgegani turned to Burgon and stared at him with bright, glittering eyes that sparkled in the pale light of the twin moons.

"If I do not return, will you grieve for me?" he asked.

Burgon cocked an eyebrow.

"You sound worried. That's not like you."

Tgegani looked back at the stars.

"There is a high likelihood that I will not survive this war. All of my research says that war is harsh. People fight and die, or are wounded, or maimed for life. Even though I am a robot, my chances of surviving this war are no better than the men with whom I will be fighting. There is also a high chance that few, if any, will return home alive."

Burgon sat down next to Tgegani and put his arm around him, pulling the lion in close to himself until he could hear the quiet whir of the robot's inner workings.

"Tgegani, you are very precious to your mother and I. We believe in you and know that you will do just fine out there. Whatever happens, we will be proud of you."

Tgegani glanced slightly at Burgon.

"But what if I die? What will happen to you?" he asked.

Burgon sighed.

"You will be greatly missed. However, we will not be without help."

Tgegani cocked his head curiously.

"What do you mean?" he asked.

"Well, you know those boxes of parts that are on the lab tables?"

Tgegani nodded and then perked up slightly.

"You're building more lions like myself?" he said in surprise.

Burgon smiled.

"I am. I just got the order from the General Secretary today. He's seen your progress reports and is so impressed that he wants me to build a newer, more advanced version of you. So I'll be working on them while you're gone."

"Then I will soon have siblings?" said Tgegani, a hint of excitement in his voice.

Burgon laughed.

"Yes, you will."

"What are their names?"

"Honestly, I haven't even considered that yet. I still have to assemble and program them."

Tgegani nodded in understanding, but said nothing. Just then he perked up as a message came across the radio for him. Burgon noticed this as well.

"Is it time?" he asked, half knowing the answer.

"It is. I must be going," replied Tgegani.

Burgon leaned over and gave Tgegani a great big hug.

"You take care of yourself and come back to us in one piece. Alright?"

Tgegani gently wrapped an arm around Burgon, and said, "I will make every effort to do so."

A courier on a motorcycle rumbled through the darkness of the night and rolled to a stop near the front gate of the facility. The guards looked suspiciously at him and then at his pouch as he reached inside for something.

"What is your purpose here, courier?" said one of the guards.

The courier pulled an envelope out of his satchel and handed it to the guard.

"Please see to it that this message reaches Major Delgra. It is important that he acts on it immediately," he said.

The guard studied the envelope briefly and then tucked it into his pocket.

"I'll see to it that he gets it as soon as he wakes up. However, I am curious why you are arriving here this late. The other couriers always come during normal work hours," said the guard suspiciously.

"I would have arrived sooner, but my bike broke down part way here. By the time I got back on the road, it was nearly dark. But I was told not to stop until that letter had been delivered."

The guard waved for him to leave.

"Understood. Now get going. The facility is sealed after dark and my men get a bit skittish when there are strangers around."

The courier tipped his helmet in respect and then rumbled off into the night. As soon as he was out of sight of the facility, he pulled off the road and stopped in front of a tall, black form. The man and his motorcycle then melted into a thick, black goo that reformed into a vandros.

It bowed, and said, "The message has been delivered as you've requested, Lord Negago."

The dark form hissed with satisfaction.

"Good. Within one week the proxy will be dead, and we will be free to begin the next part of our plans," he said with demonic glee.

Silvers looked at the orders in surprise.

"He sent this by courier?" he said.

Delgra nodded.

"He's sent a lot of things by courier lately. While we're pretty certain our military network is secure, there are some orders he doesn't want to risk transmitting over the internet until he's completely convinced that it is," he said.

"That may be so, but doesn't it seem a bit odd that he would go to all the trouble of sending something like this via courier. It's not like the message is *that* sensitive."

"Apparently he believes it is, or else he would've simply emailed it to us."

Silvers shook his head.

"Even so, the orders seem out of character. Why would he risk putting an untested weapons system into what is expected to be the hottest part of the entire front?"

Delgra sighed.

"I don't know. But until I either find out these orders are fake, or I receive something different, I have to assume that this is what he wants."

Silvers frowned.

"I hate it when politicians do stuff like this. They're going to take all our months and years of hard work and toss it right out the window on the first day of battle."

Delgra shook his head.

"Maybe, and maybe not. We won't know for certain until the bullets start flying."

"Yeah, but by then it may be too late."

Delgra frowned.

"Let's hope not, for all our sakes. Otherwise our lives could become infinitely more difficult."

Chapter 10

Sergeant Welk stood by the door to the temporary troop barracks and stared blankly at the stars above him.

"Which constellation are you studying?" came a voice next to him.

This nearly made Welk leap out of his shoes. He turned to see Tgegani staring off into the distance as the first thin threads of morning broke over the horizon.

"Well there goes that set of underwear. You do realize there's such a thing as being too quiet," said Welk.

Tgegani bowed slightly.

"My apologies for frightening you," he said.

"I'm glad you have the ability to move so silently. But please try not to sneak up on your own comrades like that. It could get you shot," said Welk.

"I will make note of that," said Tgegani.

Welk took a deep breath and sighed.

"How's your family doing?" he asked.

"They're alright," replied Tgegani.

"Do they know you're gone?"

Tgegani nodded, but said nothing. Welk sighed slightly just as two men from his squad stepped out of the barracks.

"Couldn't sleep either, eh?" he said to the two men.

"I don't think any of us slept. For as much as I've trained for this day, the thought of actually going out there scares me senseless."

"Are any of the others awake?" asked Welk.

"I think everyone is, except Corporal Dusty and Sergeant Sims."

Welk chuckled.

"It figures. Those two could sleep through the end of the world and not flinch. Well, either way, tell everyone who's awake to get down to the chow hall and get something to eat. Make sure they know to be back here by zero seven hundred. If anyone's still asleep by then, we'll kick them out of bed and feed them a portable ration along the way. The train will be here at zero eight hundred sharp to pick us up, so we need to be there on time. We don't want to miss it."

"Yes, sergeant," said the two men.

They then turned and hurried back into the barracks.

"Do we know where we'll be deployed?" asked Tgegani.

"From what the Major told me, we're to report to an area that command believes will be the most contested, which means that things are going to get messy in a hurry. That's definitely not the place I want to be. But, that's what our orders are, so that's what we'll have to deal with. Hopefully we won't all be killed in the first few minutes," said Welk.

Tgegani looked at Welk, and said, "If Meshua permits us to live, we will survive this battle."

Welk nodded.

"I hope you're right."

Black looked up as Elgar strolled into his office.

"Well, what good news do you bring? Is our trump card on his way?" he said gleefully.

"The lion and his team are heading to the front lines as expected. However, there appears to be a change of orders."

Black waved dismissively.

"Bah, that's to be expected."

Elgar stared at Black grimly.

"This is a change that may ruin our plans."

"How so?"

"The lion and his team have been ordered to take up a position on the front lines in an area that is expected to see the heaviest fighting. The chances of their surviving the first day of battle under those conditions are slim, possibly nonexistent at best."

Black frowned.

"What buffoon gave those orders!?" he growled.

"The document that our spies saw said that it was from the General Secretary. However, our analysis of the orders indicate that they were not given by him."

Black leaned back in his chair and rubbed his chin in thought.

"So if they're not from him, then who gave the orders?"

"It could be a spy working for the Gorg," said Elgar.

"Or a competitor. It wouldn't be difficult to believe that they'd do such a thing. It'd take considerable work, planning, and penetration of the intelligence networks to pull it off, but it could still be done. The only question is, who would be selfish enough to risk the future of our entire country just to get back at me?" said Black thoughtfully.

"I don't think it was a competitor. None of them would be that foolish. Which means it has to be the work of a double agent."

Black scratched his chin in thought.

"Yes, it could be. But we can figure that out later. Right now we need to protect our investment. That's our most pressing issue at the moment."

Elgar cocked his head curiously.

"What would you have me do?" he asked.

"Gather together our best field teams. I want them watching over and protecting that lion day and night. It's already bad enough that he's in the worst part of the lines. To have him killed, and his body captured by the Gorg, will put us in a situation that I don't care to tender at this moment."

Elgar bowed.

"I will make sure that he is kept as safe as our men are capable of doing."

"Good. And while you're at it, see if you can't find out who is behind this order. I would like to deal with them personally."

Elgar nodded.

"I'll see what I can find."

Welk and his men surveyed the rally camp with concern.

"Not a lot of men here," said Welk.

"Do you think they're on the line already?" asked Sims.

Welk shrugged.

"If they're not, we're in worse shape than I thought." He then picked up his field pack, and said, "Alright everyone, grab your gear and let's find out where we're supposed to be."

The squad obeyed and then followed Welk through the camp to one of the administration tents. They were soon loaded onto a truck and sent bouncing down a rutted dirt road towards a long, thin line of men and vehicles positioned just over a mile from the border.

"If this is all they have to hold the line, we're going to be in some serious trouble," said Welk.

"Do you think they'll reinforce us?" asked Dusty.

"Hard to say. Given what we saw back at the rally camp, that likely won't happen."

Dusty rolled his eyes.

"Lovely. I always wanted to be a speed bump," he said sarcastically.

The trucks soon stopped near the front and all the men piled out. Welk's small squad quickly found their place on the line, and were comfortably dug in before nightfall. The following morning the men awoke hungry, thirsty and damp from the morning dew, but still tense and nervous. Dusty pulled a piece of dried meat from his pocket and chewed noisily on it as he studied the simple barbed wire fence that marked the border between Gorg and Yigzan territory. The fence was flanked on one side by a thick forest of trees, while the other was open, grass covered prairie.

"Do you think they know we're here?" asked Dusty.

"Given our current activity along the border, I'd be surprised if they didn't," said Sims.

"Hey, heads up," shouted Welk.

The men turned and spotted him walking towards them with two canvas bags full of green cans. He set the bags down and tossed one can to each man.

Dusty looked curiously at the can, and asked, "What's this?"

"Canned katar," said Welk.

"Oh man. That's gonna be nasty," said one of the men.

Sims cracked his open and took a sip. He grimaced slightly and spit out the strong black liquid.

"How does it taste?" asked one of the men.

"Like sewage," said Sims.

"In other words, it's typical military katar," quipped Dusty.

Sims tossed the can to the side, its contents spilling out on the ground. The others looked at their cans and then tossed theirs aside without opening them.

"Score one for army katar," quipped one of the men.

Dusty looked at Tgegani, and asked, "Do you want some canned katar? I know it tastes nasty to us, but I don't think that'll bother you."

Tgegani shook his head.

"I am unable to consume food or liquids. I have no way to digest or process them."

One of the men chuckled.

"Lucky dog. He doesn't have to worry about going hungry or thirsty like the rest of us do."

"Or getting old and fat," chided another.

"He should be thankful. He can't be forced to eat your mother's cooking," chided a third.

"Hey, my mom makes great food!" said the second.

"Could have fooled me, skinny boy."

Tgegani listened with passive interest as the men bantered playfully back and forth in an effort to alleviate their boredom and suppress their growing fear. As he did, his ears detected a strange sound in the distance. It was high pitched and sounded like the buzzing of angry bees. His ears turned back and forth in search of the source of the sound. Now it was above him. He looked up and scanned the sky anxiously for several moments and then spotted hundreds of little black pinpoints falling quickly towards him. He studied them curiously, trying to make sense of what he was seeing, and then suddenly realized what they were.

He immediately turned to his squad members, and shouted, "INCOMING!!"

The men looked up in surprise as the lion dove into a foxhole, dragging Dusty and another soldier with him. Momentarily confused, Welk turned to Tgegani and then stopped in surprise as a whistling sound quickly filled his ears. He swore.

"Incoming! Incoming! Take cover!" he cried.

The men soon heard the sound too and quickly ducked down into their foxholes as the first rounds began to fall. Soon the shells were falling in a thunderous rain of death that shook the ground and forced every soldier to cover his ears in agony. Tgegani watched as the men in his squad stayed as low as they could in their foxholes, softly praying that none of the shells would land on them. He shifted his weight slightly as the ground shuttered under him. A glowing hot piece of shrapnel whistled by overhead. He carefully filtered out the thunderous, nearly continuous roar of exploding shells until they became nearly inaudible. Soon, all he could hear was the sounds of raining earth and men crying in fear. He chanced a look above the top of the foxhole and studied the area around him. The air was filled with a thick haze of dust, smoke and fire.

Vehicles and equipment burned all along the line, the fires filling the sky with thick, black smoke that mixed with mushrooming, angry gray clouds of smoldering earth. What'd been a bright and sunny summer day had quickly become the very essence of hell itself. Deciding it was safer to stay low, he slipped back down into the foxhole again. As he did, a large piece of shrapnel glanced off the edge of his foxhole, barely missing his head. Just then a set of new sounds began filling the air. His ears perked up slightly in interest. It was more artillery shells. But these sounded different and appeared to be traveling in the opposite direction. Within moments the bombardment slackened and then stopped completely. He waited anxiously for the shelling to resume. But it did not, despite a multitude of shells flying through the air overhead. He listened carefully for several moments longer and then realized what was happening.

"An artillery duel!" he thought.

Welk looked over at Tgegani and then up at the sky as the air began to clear.

"Is it over?" he asked.

"For the moment. The Gorg are currently engaged in a duel with our artillery units. They will not shell us again until that battle has been decided," said Tgegani.

"How do you know that?" asked Welk.

"I can both see and hear shells traveling overhead at high speed in both directions. I have also been intercepting radio chatter from our own forces, as well as those of the

Gorg. The present flow of information from both sides appears to validate that assessment."

"So your communications system can do more than just talk with our portable radios?" said Dusty.

Tgegani nodded.

"I can interact with nearly every available communication system presently in existence."

"That's impressive," replied Dusty.

"Is it safe to come out?" asked one of the soldiers.

"No, keep your head down," said Welk.

The men lay curled up deep in their foxholes as they desperately clutched their rifles. Dirt and grass covered every inch of their bodies in a thick gray mat of grime and filth. They nervously eyed each other as they listened to the anguished cries of wounded men all around them.

"Head check! Is anybody hurt?" shouted Dusty.

The men examined themselves and then each other. While no one was hurt, many of them were visibly shaken and their ears ached. Just then a medic scurried up to their foxholes.

"Anyone in here hurt?" he asked as he tried to adjust his helmet.

"We're fine, just kinda shaken," said Welk.

"There are people in a foxhole ten meters to the north of here who need aid," said Tgegani.

The medic was surprised to see this.

"Hey, you're that talking lion that I've heard so much about. That's kinda cool. I didn't think you were real," said the medic.

"Get moving, medic. Those men need your help," said Welk.

"Yes, sergeant," replied the medic.

He then scurried off in search of the wounded. The men flinched briefly as several stray artillery shells exploded nearby.

"Stuff's still falling. We should be careful," said Sims.

Just then Tgegani stiffened. His head immediately spun around as he focused all of his senses towards the distant tree line. He spotted it almost at the same time the others did.

"Contact!" cried Welk.

Others began repeating his warning down both sides of the line.

Welk then turned, and said, "Everyone, get ready!"

A moment later a wall of enemy troops and vehicles broke through the fence that marked the border between the two nations and charged at the meager Yigzan defensive line.

"How many are there?" asked Dusty.

"I count at least one armored battalion and one, possibly two regiments of infantry in our immediate area," said Tgegani.

Welk swore.

"Looks like you were right, Dusty. We *are* going to be a speed bump today."

Tgegani studied the advancing Gorg troops and tried to decide what to do. He'd made a promise to his friends and family to protect the men with him at all costs. But he was beginning to doubt if he could do that.

"The war's started!" said Visnel as he raced across the lab.

"When?" asked Burgon in surprise.

"About an hour ago."

"Any word on how the battle is going?"

Visnel shook his head.

"I don't know. There's a complete news blackout, and Major Delgra is staying very tight lipped about what he knows. All they're telling anyone is that the fighting has started."

Persia walked out of the office and stopped next to Burgon.

"When will we know anything?" she asked.

"I don't know. I'm sure they'll tell us when they can," said Visnel.

Persia looked at Burgon, and asked, "Dad, can we contact Tgegani and see if he's alright?"

Burgon shook his head.

"He's probably busy right now. We don't want to interrupt him while he's trying to keep those men alive."

Persia sighed and looked down at the ground.

"I'm worried about him," she said, pawing the ground anxiously.

Burgon patted her on the head and then caressed her neck.

"We all are, sweetie. We all are."

Dusty ducked down quickly, grabbing his helmet and drawing his rifle in close to his body as a rocket exploded in front of his foxhole, sending a spray of moist, black earth flying into the air and then down on top of him. He quickly popped back up and began firing again. Gorg fell one after another under a hail of accurate and devastating Yigzan fire. But there were so many of them pouring across the border that when one fell, another would quickly take their place. Bullets whizzed by Tgegani's head, some tearing through his mane and others glancing off his armored body shell as he tried to get an assessment of the battle.

"Hold the line!" shouted a nearby officer.

Welk's squad fought on bravely, putting everything they had into the battle. Finally, unable to hold the line any longer, the order was given, and the Yigzan troops broke and quickly began retreating amidst heavy Gorg fire.

Hearing the order, Welk turned to Dusty and Tgegani, and said, "Alright, we're being pulled back. We need to give the others a chance to get clear before we get overrun. When I give the order, you two break out and head forward. Tgegani, your orders are simple. If it moves and it's Gorg, kill it. Dusty, you guide him. Take any targets of opportunity and try to cause as much mayhem out there as you can. We'll cover you. Ready?"

Tgegani and Dusty nodded.

"Alright, here we go. Covering fire!" shouted Welk.

All of his men popped up out of their foxholes and began shooting rapidly into the Gorg lines. This caused the Gorg soldiers to break and scramble for cover.

"Go!" shouted Welk as he changed magazines and began firing again.

Dusty jumped onto Tgegani's back and held on for dear life as they had practiced many times before. Tgegani sprinted out of the foxhole at top speed, ran nearly a hundred yards, and then deposited Dusty in a small patch of reed grass before continuing on. Dusty quickly got his bearings, and then began calling out targets. Like a blinding flash of gold, Tgegani tore through the enemy troops like a whirlwind. Gorg soldiers fell like dominoes amid Tgegani's ruthless onslaught.

The Gorg tried frantically to kill him, but soon realized that their bullets had no effect. They quickly called for more firepower. A few minutes later a group of soldiers emerged from the line holding rocket launchers which they intended to use against him. Seeing this, Dusty informed Tgegani of the situation, and then opened fire on the rocketeers, dropping several of them in a row. This added to the mayhem and confusion as Gorg troops began firing on each other, unsure if some of their own had turned on them or if more enemy were in their midst. This had the desired effect of slowing the assault to a confused crawl, and then a dead stop.

"Everyone's clear. Pull back and get out of there," came Welk's voice over the radio.

Dusty leapt up and began firing randomly into the Gorg lines.

"You heard him, Tgegani! Pull back! Pull--"

Suddenly a bullet tore through his chest with a pop, knocking the wind out of him. He sank to his knees, dazed and confused, and then felt another round slice through him, followed by a third. Sensing that something was wrong, Tgegani exploded out of the Gorg lines and into the open just in time to see another round penetrate Dusty's shoulder. He bolted at top speed towards him amid a withering hail of fire as Dusty collapsed to the ground. Tgegani stopped next to him and disappeared into the grass as he studied his friend.

"Are you alright?" he asked, a hint of fear in his voice.

"I feel funny," said Dusty, his eyes distant and confused.

"Can you climb onto my back?" asked Tgegani.

Dusty nodded weakly, and then awkwardly dragged himself onto the lion's back. Tgegani carefully stood up and began running with all the speed he could manage towards the Yigzan lines while trying to keep Dusty on his back. He moved carefully back and forth through craters, around destroyed vehicles and through trenches until they were safely out of range of the Gorg. Tgegani then took a more relaxed pace to make it easier on Dusty. He soon came across a platoon that was walking down the road in front of him.

"Medic! I need a medic!" shouted Tgegani as he closed on the men.

They turned around in surprise to see a wounded soldier struggling to hold onto the back of the lion. They gasped as they saw thick trails of blood oozing down the brilliant golden fur of the lion and onto the ground. A medic emerged from the group a moment later and ran over to Tgegani. Quickly examining Dusty, he immediately got to work tending to Dusty's wounds as he shouted to the other men to help him.

"Dusty, Tgegani, are you on your way back?" came a voice over the radio.

"Dusty's hurt," replied Tgegani.

"How bad?"

Tgegani studied Dusty and then the medic as he worked.

"I don't know, but he's badly wounded."

Dusty suddenly began convulsing wildly while gasping desperately for air.

"Dusty!" shouted Tgegani as fear echoed sharply in his voice.

Dusty soon fell limp and died. The medic sighed and lowered his head in defeat.

"No. Dusty. You can't die. Dusty," said Tgegani, the words rolling bitterly off his lips.

He turned to his right, looked in the direction of the approaching Gorg, and then down at Dusty. His eyes narrowed as a soft growl rumbled from his lips.

He turned to his right, and said, "Take care of my friend. I have something I need to do."

"But..." said the medic just as Tgegani bolted off towards the front.

Several moments later Welk, and two of his men, came running down the road asking if anyone had seen a lion in the area. They were pointed towards two medics who were putting a soldier onto a stretcher. When they arrived they quickly recognized who it was, and gasped.

"By the ancients," said one of the soldiers.

"Corporal, have you seen a talking lion anywhere around here," asked Welk.

One of the medics looked up from his work and nodded.

"Yeah, strangest thing I've ever seen," he said.

"Where'd he go?" asked Welk.

The medic pointed towards the front lines.

"He went off that way. Said he had something to do."

Welk tapped his transmitter, and said, "Tgegani, come in. Tgegani! Respond if you hear me."

But only static greeted his pleadings.

"He's not responding. We need to go see if he's alright. Private, go back and tell the others to find a place along the second defensive line and wait for us. Sergeant Sims, you're with me."

The men then separated and headed their respective ways. As Welk hurried down the road through the gradually thinning trickle of retreating soldiers, he repeatedly tried to raise Tgegani on the radio, but with no luck. He swore.

"You better not be dead, Tgegani, or so help me..."

Chapter 11

Elgar strode into Black's office and found him busily working at his computer.

"Morning, Elgar. Anything interesting today?' asked Black without taking his attention away from his computer.

"War's started," said Elgar flatly.

Black looked up and grinned.

"Yes, I saw that. Any word on the progress of the fighting so far?"

"The Gorg's initial attack stalled out shortly after it started. The Yigzan have taken that opportunity and fallen back to their second defensive line."

Black grinned devilishly.

"Hmm, sounds exciting. And what is the status of our favorite cybernetic lion? Did our men ensure that he made it through the initial fighting?"

"We don't know. The field team who was monitoring him was killed in the bombardment that preceded the initial attack. I have several other teams in the area watching for any traces of him. But so far they haven't seen any signs that he's still functional."

Black growled in frustration.

"Please ensure that they find him, and soon."

"We're making every effort to do so."

"You had better. I can't afford to lose him this early in the game. I prefer to keep my pawns alive and healthy until they're no longer needed."

Elgar nodded.

"Understood."

Welk raised his binoculars and studied the front lines. He watched as the Gorg commanders worked hard to rally their men in an effort to get the assault moving again. But, despite their best efforts, their troops were hesitant to advance.

"Do you see him?" asked Sims.

"No, I don't," grumbled Welk.

He continued scanning the area for several minutes, but saw nothing. However, just when he was about to give up, he spotted something. A red, gold and gray colored splotch moved discretely across the ground as it shifted from one patch of grass to another.

"Ah! There he is! Just to the right of that truck over there," said Welk.

Sims panned his binoculars around until he saw it too.

"What's he doing?" he asked.

"I think he's stalking those soldiers down there, and waiting for the right moment to attack," said Welk.

"So what do we do?" asked Sims.

"We stop him before he gets himself killed," said Welk as he tapped his transmitter.

"Tgegani, this is Welk. Please respond."

Static.

"Tgegani, I know you can hear me. Please respond."

More static. Welk grunted angrily.

"Stop pretending that you can't hear me, because I know you can."

The two men then heard their headphones crackle to life.

"I hear you," came the reply.

"What are you doing?" asked Welk.

"Trying to find the enemy soldiers who killed my friend."

The two men looked at each other in surprise.

"Tgegani, there's no way you can tell who shot Dusty," said Sims.

"Yes there is. The odor of their rifles was all over his body. I'll know it when I smell it."

"Don't do it! You'll get yourself killed!" said Welk as he raised his glasses.

Silence.

"Tgegani, you need to retreat immediately! There will be plenty of opportunities to avenge his death later on. But right now is not the time!"

"I will *not* leave until the men responsible for Dusty's death are punished. They will--"

"Tgegani! Listen to me! I know this sounds strange, but right now you're having an emotional reaction, which is preventing you from thinking straight."

"I am a machine. Machines don't have emotions. It's impossible."

"No, it's very possible and I think you're handling this rather poorly. You're feeling anger and sadness at the loss of your friend, and regret that you couldn't do more to save him. That's making you act illogically. Don't you see? Revenge is not the answer. At least not yet," said Welk.

They listened for several moments for Tgegani to respond, but heard nothing.

"Tgegani, it's not your fault Dusty died. You did all that you could. The actions of both of you saved a lot of lives today."

"But many more died," said Tgegani.

"He's moving," said Sims as he watched Tgegani through his binoculars.

"That's war, Tgegani. People die. There's nothing you or I can do to change that."

"I understand this. But I swore to my father that I would protect every one of you with my life. I have failed at that mission. Therefore, the only path left to me now is to punish those who killed my friend, and avenge his death."

"Listen, Tgegani. Your father was right. You *do* need to protect us. But how will you do that if you're dead?"

Tgegani stopped.

"Come back with us and we'll work together to protect as many people as we can."

Welk listened to the radio as static crackled in his ear, but no reply came.

"You can't protect everyone, Tgegani. It's not physically possible. However, you *can* protect some of them. But only if you're alive. Now come back to me."

Once again he heard only silence. Just then Sims perked up.

"He's moving again...wait, he's turning around and coming back this way," he said.

Welk raised his binoculars and watched as Tgegani slipped cautiously through the carnage near the old defensive line and made his way back towards them.

"That a boy, Tgegani. We'll meet you on the road at the top of the hill."

Several minutes later Tgegani appeared on the road leading towards the rear lines. He soon spotted Welk and Sims squatting in the brush by the roadside and made his way over to them.

"I have returned as you've requested," he said.

Welk studied him with interest.

"Looks like we'll need to give you a bath when we get a chance," he said.

"I can tend to my own hygienic needs," said Tgegani.

Welk grinned.

"Consider it a favor from one friend to another."

Tgegani thought about this briefly and then nodded.

"Yes, you are my friend. But come, we must move quickly. The Gorg will soon be on the move again, so we are not safe here."

They then turned and soon caught up with the other men of their squad, and then quickly made their way over to a rally camp positioned just behind the second defensive line. Off on the eastern horizon smoke and fire filled the air as the Yigzan waged a desperate battle to hold the Gorg advance in check. Overhead, Yigzan and Gorg fighters dueled bitterly for control of the skies. As Tgegani watched this unfold above him, the men in his squad each took turns washing the thick layers of blood and dirt from his fur. One of the soldiers, while picking at a gash in his false skin, took note of a small scuff in his metal body armor which showed through the tear.

"You've got a tough skull there my friend," said the soldier.

"The metal is an alloy my father created. While not impenetrable, it will easily deflect most small arms fire," said Tgegani.

Another of the soldiers chuckled, and said, "It's a good thing too. We wouldn't want a Gorg to put a bullet through your skull and smash that amazing brain of yours."

Tgegani shook his head.

"My brain, as you would call it, is not contained within my head. My primary neural core is located in my chest within a specially armored housing. My head is merely an instrument pack. It contains the sensor equipment for all five of my primary senses, as well as a variety of other secondary sensory instrumentation. Loss if it would merely inconvenience me, but not kill me."

"That's good to know," chuckled Sims.

The soldier, who was washing his back, picked at a loose section of skin, and said, "Looks like we're going to need to get you a new coat."

"That won't be necessary. My automatic maintenance systems are already making the necessary repairs to my overskin. It should be fully restored by tomorrow morning," said Tgegani.

Welk chuckled.

"Must be nice to not need bandages."

Tgegani nodded.

"Indeed."

"Sergeant Welk! Is there a Sergeant Welk here?" shouted an officer as he walked down the line towards them.

Welk stood up and waved at him.

"Over here, sir!" he shouted.

The officer hurried over to where the men were, and upon spotting Tgegani, immediately realized he had the right group.

"The CO wanted me to get you on the next truck north. They heard how you handled the fighting down here and want to attach you to third battalion, second ID. Apparently he feels that you would be of better use up there," said the officer.

"Can we finish bathing our lion first?" asked Welk.

The officer looked at the blood and dirt stains on Tgegani's overskin and nodded.

"Yes, but hurry. When you're done, report to field HQ. They'll get you on the next truck headed north."

"Yes, sir!" replied Welk.

One of the soldiers looked at Welk and chuckled.

"Out of the frying pan and into the fire, eh?" he said.

Welk frowned slightly, and then pointed to one of the other men.

"Since Dusty's gone, you're Tgegani's combat partner now. Stick to him like glue and don't let him out of your sight until I say otherwise."

"Yes, sergeant," replied the man.

Tgegani studied the young man briefly and then remembered Dusty. He remembered his smile, the dusty brown colored hair that gave him his nickname, and the kindness that Dusty had displayed towards him. It was through his interaction with this young man that Tgegani had learned the true meaning of friendship. It was now no longer just meaningless bits of data to him, but rather a tangible reality. He then slowly played back in his mind one memorable moment after another of their brief, but fruitful friendship as the men continued to wash him.

A gentle knock came at Delgra's door. He ignored it at first, but then groaned as the knocking persisted.

"Yes, what is it?" he muttered.

"That's a fine greeting for a man who spent over ten years risking his life for you," came a familiar voice.

Delgra looked up in surprise to see Odevion standing in the doorway in his dress uniform grinning with joy like a Cheshire cat.

"Well, this is a surprise. What are you doing here?" asked Delgra.

"You sound like you're not happy to see me."

"No, just more surprised than anything. I take it you orchestrated this visit?"

Odevion chuckled.

"Oh come now. As if you have to ask."

Delgra laughed.

"So how'd you do it?"

"Well, it was really easy, actually. I just jumped onto the milnet, grabbed one of your Marshall General personas, and put myself in for a transfer to your facility."

Delgra furrowed his brow in surprise.

"Well, I see your hacking skills haven't gotten rusty."

Odevion shook his head and grinned.

"Not one bit. I made sure to keep them sharp while I was up north."

"So, what made you suddenly want to rush down here and join me now? I would figure that you'd have come down here years ago if you had the ability."

Odevion shrugged.

"Eh, I figured I'd be more useful staying up there. So I worked in the background and helped you keep your actions hidden. Well, at least for the first two years anyways, until some knucklehead in the senate blew our cover."

Delgra rolled his eyes and then took notice of another man who was standing in the doorway.

"Who are you?" he asked.

A tall, thin, slightly built young officer stepped through the door and saluted him.

"Lieutenant Mestra, sir. It's a pleasure to meet you."

Delgra studied the man with muted suspicion.

"So why are you in my facility?" he asked flatly.

Mestra pulled a folded sheet of paper from a pocket on his dress uniform and handed it to Delgra. The Major read it and then handed it back to the lieutenant.

"Logistics, eh?" said Delgra as he raised an eyebrow in interest.

"Yes, sir. One of the best in the field too."

"Hmm, indeed," said Delgra reservedly. He then leaned over to Odevion, and whispered, "Can we trust him?"

Odevion nodded.

"I had a look at his credentials on the way here. He checks out, so I wouldn't worry too much about him."

Mestra raised an eyebrow in surprise as he listened to the whispered conversation.

"You spied on me?" he asked.

"You heard that?" asked Delgra.

Mestra nodded.

"Yes, sir. Every bit of it. I'm not one of the best logistics officers for nothing."

Delgra frowned slightly.

"I can see why."

Mestra nodded towards Odevion, and asked, "So why did you spy on me, sergeant?"

Odevion shrugged.

"I'm an intelligence specialist. It's my job to know things. Besides, you didn't think I'd just let you waltz in here without first knowing at least something about you."

Mestra smirked slightly.

"Apparently not."

"Well then, I'm sure you'll want a tour of the facility now that you're here," said Delgra.

"Yes, sir. And if it's not too much to ask, I'd also like to meet this robotic lion I've heard so much about," said Mestra.

Delgra shook his head.

"That'll be a problem. Tgegani is out on the front lines right now, so you won't be able to meet him anytime soon. But I can introduce you to the scientist who created him, and have him show you the new prototypes he's working on. They should give you a good idea of what Tgegani's like."

"Tgegani? Who's that?"

"He's the robotic lion you're referring to. He's Dr. Burgon's first, and the prototype for the entire series."

"Fascinating! You'll have to tell me more about this."

Delgra motioned to the door.

"Follow me and I can personally introduce both of you to the doctor. He can then explain his entire project to you from there."

Tgegani steadied himself as best he could as the truck they were riding in bounced roughly across the uneven ground near the northern HQ. As soon as the truck stopped he leapt out and studied the area around them. Several soldiers standing nearby stared nervously at him as the rest of his squad climbed out of the truck behind him.

"You're supposed to wait for us to at least open the gate," chided one of the men, patting Tgegani on the neck as he walked by.

"I am sorry. I will wait next time," replied Tgegani.

"Oh don't listen to him. He's just giving you a hard time," said another soldier.

Welk walked over to the HQ tent, and said, "Stay here. I'll get our orders."

He then walked inside, stopped, and said, "Sergeant Welk reporting as requested."

Two older men, a general and a colonel, stood next to a table studying a large map that lay spread out before them. They both looked up and studied him briefly.

"We're busy right now, Sergeant. So you'll need to come back later."

"I am the command sergeant of the first cybernetic expeditionary squad. Our orders were to report to you as soon as possible. We're here as ordered and have the lion with us," replied Welk.

The two men stared briefly at each other and then back to Welk.

"Well, don't just stand there, bring him in!" said the general.

Welk nodded and then slipped out of the tent briefly before appearing again with Tgegani by his side a moment later. The two men studied the lion with interest.

"So this is the famous robot that we've been hearing so much about. He's incredibly life like. How intelligent is he?" asked the colonel.

"Are you referring to my processing capacity, or total stored knowledge, sir?" asked Tgegani.

The two men marveled at this.

"I guess that would answer my question. Gentlemen, we have a task for you," said the general.

He pointed towards a spot on the map and tapped it briefly.

"The Gorg are giving us fits along this hill here. Their attack has momentum, and it's straining our lines. I need you and your lion to go in there and cause as much trouble as possible. This will be a hit and run mission, so move in, hit hard and fast, and then get out of there as quickly as you can. If we can stop their momentum, our lines should hold until we can bring more reinforcements into play. But if they break here, we'll be forced to fall all the way back to Louest before we'll have another defensible position. That's fifty miles of advance I'd rather not hand to the Gorg if I can help it."

"Are you sure a squad of our size can handle something like this?" asked Welk.

"It's just a hit and run mission, sergeant. It's not like you're battling the entire Gorg army. So it should be easy enough."

"Alright then, we'll get right on it," said Welk.

He and Tgegani then turned and left the tent.

"So what's the good news?" asked Sims as they soon approached the others.

"We've been ordered to do a hit and run mission. We're to go in against a nearby Gorg battalion, shake them up, and then run like mad," said Welk.

Sims rolled his eyes.

"In other words, we walk in, get shot up, and then, if there's anyone left, retreat and return to base. Just wonderful. And here I thought I might actually make it out of this war alive," he said sarcastically.

"Trust me. I don't like this anymore than you do. But if we do this right, everything should go well enough," said Welk.

Sims grunted.

"Define well."

Welk frowned.

"Trust me, I know what you're feeling. But I still think we can pull this off. I mean, we've got Tgegani after all."

"I am not invincible," replied Tgegani flatly.

"Yeah, listen to the lion," said one of the soldiers.

"Shut up, private," said Welk.

"Actually, the lion's got a point. We're not invincible," said Sims.

Welk bit his lip as he thought about this.

"I know that, but....well, alright. Let's go have a look, and if it's too much, we'll pull back and get a second opinion. Is that good enough for you?"

Sims nodded.

"Works for me."

"Alright then, let's move out."

The squad quickly made their way down the Yigzan lines until they found themselves in a small grove of bushes just a stone's throw away from a nearby Gorg position. They could see round after round of artillery, combined with staggered attacks by armored vehicles and infantry, breaking like waves against a line of Yigzan bunkers that sat perched atop a small hill. Despite their formidable position, the bunkers were woefully undermanned.

Welk pointed to a section of the Gorg lines, and said, "That's our objective."

Sims whistled in amazement.

"Wow, command really gave us a doozy. You sure we can do this? That certainly doesn't look like anything we can engage without getting wiped out," he said.

Welk mulled it over for a moment, and then said, "There has to be a way to shake these guys up, and that's all we really need to do. So if you've got some ideas, I'm open to suggestions."

Suddenly Tgegani heard something approaching them from behind.

He turned to Welk, and whispered, "Something's coming."

Chapter 12

Burgon looked up from his work in surprise as Delgra and Mestra walked into the room.

"Ah, Major. What brings you here today?" asked Burgon.

"Oh, just giving a tour to one of the new guys," said Delgra.

"That would be me," said Mestra.

"Nice to meet you," said Burgon.

"Lieutenant, this is Dr. Burgon. He's one of our top scientists here at the facility, and the creator of the lion project," said Delgra.

Mestra perked up slightly.

"So you're the scientist that created the lions everyone's talking about? Fascinating! What can you tell me about them?" he said, excitement dripping from his voice.

Burgon shrugged.

"What would you like to know?"

Mestra glanced over at one of the unfinished lion bodies.

"Oh, anything, really. What can they do? How smart are they? What is their range? Stuff like that."

Burgon shrugged.

"Well, I can't tell you most of that because it's classified as top secret."

"What would I need to have to get that kind of information?"

"Clearance level nine or higher."

Mestra frowned.

"My clearance is only level three. So I guess you can't tell me a lot."

Burgon shook his head. Mestra shrugged.

"Oh well. No big loss. It was just curiousity."

Burgon smiled.

"Well, don't worry. Someday you'll get a chance to meet Tgegani in person and see a working android lion first hand."

Mestra cocked his head in curiosity.

"Tgegani? I've heard about him. Where is he?"

"That's classified, Lieutenant," said Delgra.

"Oh, sorry, sir," said Mestra sheepishly.

Just then Persia stepped out of the office and walked past Mestra. But as she did, a strange odor made her stop. She then turned and sniffed curiously at Mestra's pants and uniform jacket. Her eyes soon narrowed. Burgon saw her standing behind him, and smiled.

"Persia! Good morning! How was your nap?" he said.

She walked around Mestra suspiciously, and then over to Burgon. He, in turn, squatted down and began to rub her chin and scratch her behind the ears. She relaxed slightly and purred gently, enjoying the attention she was getting. Even so she continued to keep an eye on Mestra.

"Ah, is this your pet tiger? She's cute," said Mestra.

Persia glared at him disdainfully.

"I am *not* a pet," she muttered.

Mestra blinked in surprise, and then laughed.

"You can talk! Is this another of your robots?" he said in surprise.

Burgon shook his head and laughed.

"She's not a robot. Persia is a snow tiger."

Mestra looked at her in confusion.

"Then how does she talk?" he asked.

Burgon shrugged.

"Nobody really knows. She just can."

Mestra nodded in approval.

"Fascinating."

Delgra cleared his throat, and said, "Sorry to interrupt your conversation, doctor, but there's a lot more of the facility I need to show the Lieutenant. But I thank you for having us."

Burgon nodded, and said, "It was my pleasure."

As the two men left the room, Persia watched Mestra suspiciously through narrowed eyes.

After the door closed behind them, she turned to Burgon, and said, "I don't like that guy. There's something about him that's just not right. And that smell. It just felt wrong somehow."

Burgon laughed.

"Oh, don't be silly. He's a trusted military officer. If he wasn't, he wouldn't be here."

Persia shook her head.

"I know, but something about him smelled....wrong. But I'm not sure what."

Burgon patted her on the head, and said with a smile, "You're imagining things, sweetie. Just because he's new doesn't mean he's suddenly one of the bad guys."

Persia gave a frustrated grunt as she sat down for a while to think. Burgon chuckled and then walked back to his office to freshen his cup of katar before continuing his work.

Welk crawled over to Tgegani and followed the lion's gaze.

"What do you see?" he whispered.

"Nothing yet. But I can hear movement in the grass."

The men turned and drew their rifles to the ready, aiming them at an as yet unseen enemy.

"Wait, hold your fire! They're friendly," said Tgegani when he finally saw the source of the noise.

The men uneasily lowered their rifles, but continued to watch cautiously until a platoon of Yigzan soldiers appeared out of the prairie grass behind them.

A young officer approached Welk, and said, "I'm Lieutenant Pentell, Charlie company, third battalion, second ID."

"Sergeant Welk, commander of the first cybernetic expeditionary squad," replied Welk.

"Oh good, I've got the right unit. Our colonel sent us to give you a hand. He heard that the general sent you out here all by yourselves," replied Pentell.

"Thanks for coming to our aid. I've been feeling like a dead man walking since first hearing about this assignment," quipped Sims.

"So, do you have an attack plan yet?" asked Pentell.

Welk nodded and quickly explained the plan he had. Pentell cocked an eyebrow in surprise.

"That's rather ambitious, isn't it?" he said.

"Already told him that myself," said Sims.

"Well, with the addition of your platoon, it should be a bit easier," said Welk.

"I hope it will. So what do you want me to do?" asked Pentell.

"You're giving me preference of leadership?" said Welk in surprise.

Pentell shrugged.

"Hey, it's your operation. We're just the backup."

Welk nodded in understanding.

"Alright, then why don't you take your men over there and see if you can't knock out their TOC. I'll take my squad back here and we'll go for the communications vehicles," said Welk as he pointed at two areas of the Gorg lines.

The lieutenant shook his head.

"Not without some heavy firepower you're not. I've got four bazooka teams with me. I'll send two of them with you, plus some ammo carriers, and a half dozen riflemen to help you out. That extra firepower should give you a better chance of surviving this mission."

Welk nodded.

"Thanks."

"Not a problem. What frequency are you transmitting on?" asked the lieutenant as he tapped his ear piece.

"Seven oh four point one megahertz," replied Welk.

The lieutenant adjusted his transmitter, and then tested it.

"Alright, now we can stay in contact with each other to make this attack work. It's going to be darned near suicide, but if we do it right it should take some of the pressure off those boys on the ridge line."

They flinched slightly as a stray shell exploded nearby.

"Sounds like we need to get moving," said Sims.

"Give us a couple minutes to get into position and we'll signal you when we're ready," said Welk.

The lieutenant nodded, divided up his men, and then slipped away as Welk's squad moved forward towards their objective. His men soon encountered a long row of bushes which they used for cover while Welk sized up the situation. After a bit, he turned and gave the order to go, sending both groups through the grass and towards the Gorg lines. Pentell's men were the first to engage the enemy, surprising a small Gorg company that was putting pressure on the Yigzan lines.

Initially the Gorg didn't notice the attack. But when they began to lose a lot of men, they stopped, wavered in confusion, retreated, pushed forward again, and then eventually fell into a broken retreat as Pentell's men decimated their ranks. Welk's squad also encountered a Gorg company moving along the left flank, but found it to be under strength and somewhat disoriented.

Seeing an opportunity, Welk turned to Tgegani, and said, "Ready?"

Tgegani nudged his partner and then crouched down so the soldier could climb on his back.

"Ready," said the corporal.

Welk waited for several moments, and then motioned with his hand for them to go. Tgegani exploded out of the reed grass like a shot and raced forward at top speed towards a line of vehicles not far away. He paused briefly at the edge of the formation to drop off the soldier before continuing on and plunging into the Gorg lines at great speed. Like a whirlwind of death, he systematically cut down each and every Gorg commander and soldier he could find. None were safe from his fury, regardless if they were a mere buck private or a high ranking officer. This had the desired effect of throwing the Gorg troops into a state of complete panic and disarray.

Taking advantage of this, Welk's squad began cutting down the Gorg infantry in droves as they wandered around aimlessly in search of someone to lead them. Then, as though empowered by an unseen force, several of the Gorg soldiers took charge of the situation and turned the full firepower of their unit against the Yigzan hiding in the nearby reed grass. Welk quickly found his squad pinned down by an incredible hail of fire. Pentell soon encountered much the same thing, leaving both teams in a very dangerous position. Tgegani listened intently as both commanders tried to rally their men, not in an effort to stay on mission, but rather merely to survive. Tgegani continued to move forward through the Gorg lines, slaughtering as many soldiers as he could find.

"Tgegani, the communications truck is to your right!" shouted his partner over the radio.

Tgegani turned and spotted the truck just as bullets pinged off his body shell. He turned back to see several soldiers shooting at him as more raced in at him from other directions. He turned to his left and was about to attack several nearby soldiers when he felt the ground suddenly leap up beneath him, followed by a dull thump. His body vibrated violently and then his sensors went dark. He quickly did a self-diagnostic and found everything to be operational except his sensor array, which appeared to be briefly offline due to a sudden impact. The first sense to return was his hearing and then others as the sounds of falling earth and the smell of charred fur and hot metal filled his mind. His vision returned next. He then quickly scanned the area and found himself, much to his surprise, embedded in the hood of a Gorg jeep. He looked back at the driver's seat and noticed that the driver was slumped over the wheel dead.

Tgegani looked back in the direction he'd come from and spotted a smoldering hole in the ground several feet away. More bullets whizzed by his head. He briefly scanned the area around him and found that he was surrounded. Not knowing the full situation, he dislodged himself from the hood of the truck and then quickly withdrew to the cover of a nearby line of trucks. As soon as he felt safe, he took stock of himself and searched for damage. A section of his skin was burned away and there were several fresh gouges in his body shell. They weren't deep, but it was apparent that he'd taken a significant hit. He did one last check of his body and found several other places that his skin was missing. He knew there was likely more damage than what he could find through this brief examination, but he would have to wait until later to find anything else that might be broken.

"Tgegani, pull back! We're getting out of here!" came Welk's voice over the radio.

"I'll be right there!" replied Tgegani.

He then raced back towards his squad members as fast as his feet would carry him. As he ran, he spotted two

LAV's, and several squads of Gorg moving towards his friends. A rocket whizzed by his head, and sailed off into the distance, exploding harmlessly several hundred yards away. Tgegani turned and spotted a group of bazooka men nearby that were taking aim at him. He glanced briefly at the LAV's, the bazooka men, and again at the LAV's. Just then an idea crossed his mind. He knew how to stop the LAV's, but it would require some help. He quickly raced over to where he'd left his partner, only to find him dead. Tgegani growled loudly and turned back towards the Gorg pursuing him. One of them then fired a rocket at him, but missed.

Tgegani immediately turned and raced towards the two LAV's bearing down on his friends. Upon arriving, he decimated the small squad of Gorg moving behind them, and then paused to allow the Gorg bazooka men to take aim. Another rocket then flew in his direction. He quickly jumped out of the way, allowing the round to sail past him and into the first LAV, destroying it. He soon did the same with the second. Seeing that his companions were now safe for the moment, he turned again and raced at the Gorg bazooka men who ran away in fear. But they were soon replaced by several jeeps mounted with heavy machine guns. Seeing that his current plan was no longer an option, he broke off pursuit and soon rejoined his squad. Upon arriving he found that three of them were dead, and several others wounded. The rest, though, appeared alive, albeit clearly shaken.

"Am I glad to see you. I thought we'd had it," said a soldier.

"You look a little rough around the edges," said Sims.

"I've suffered some damage, but I am still fully functional," replied Tgegani.

Suddenly they heard their radios crackle to life.

"Tgegani, if you're there, come help us! We're being overrun!"

Welk looked at Tgegani and then motioned to his left.

"That's the Lieutenant. Go help him. We'll meet you back at the road."

"But I've got to get you to safety!" said Tgegani.

"Don't worry about us! We'll get ourselves out of here. Go help the lieutenant."

"But--"

"Enough people have died already, Tgegani! We don't need any more casualties! Now go save them! That's an order!" shouted Welk.

Tgegani hesitated briefly, and then turned and raced at full speed towards the last known location of the Lieutenant's men. As he ran, a Gorg bazooka squad spotted him and opened fire with everything they had. He quickened his pace as one rocket after another exploded around him, sending up great showers of dirt into the air. Some of the explosions were so close that they nearly knocked him off his feet. But he kept running.

"Tgegani! Where are you!?" came Pentell's desperate voice over the radio.

"I'm on my way, Lieutenant. Get ready to pull back when I get there," replied Tgegani.

The lieutenant popped up from his hiding spot and then looked on in horror as he saw the murderous barrage that Tgegani was running through.

"Covering fire! Get cover on that lion!" he shouted.

His platoon immediately opened up with all they had at the Gorg bazooka men that were attacking Tgegani and cut them down. Tgegani soon reached Pentell's men and skid to a stop next to the lieutenant. He quickly assessed the situation, but didn't like what he saw. Of the original men that had come with the lieutenant, nine were dead, and four were wounded, one of which was near death. The lieutenant himself had a slight wound on his right leg and squatted uneasily on it.

"We need to get you out of here. Grab your wounded and let's go," said Tgegani.

"Alright, you heard him! Let's get moving!" said Pentell.

Just then mortar shells began raining down all around them.

"Take cover!" shouted the Lieutenant.

Tgegani quickly scanned the area, and soon spotted a small team of Gorg operating several small punt mortars nearby. He then contacted a nearby Yigzan artillery unit who immediately silenced them. Seeing that it was now clear, the Lieutenant ordered his men to retreat. The squad quickly pulled itself together, picked up their wounded, and then made their way towards friendly lines. But as they did, they found themselves having issues carrying one of the wounded.

Tgegani hurried over to the men, and said, "Put him on my back."

The men quickly complied, and then hurried on ahead as Tgegani carried the man as fast as he could through the reed grass.

"Leave me," groaned the wounded man.

Just then bullets sailed over Tgegani's head like swarms of angry hornets.

"Don't say that. I'll get you out of here safely," replied Tgegani.

"No. I'm already gone. Save yourself."

"That's not how I--"

"Please. If you die, many more will die because you could not save them," said the man.

He coughed briefly, spitting up some blood as he did.

"Please. I'm dead already. Leave me and save the others," he groaned.

"I cannot do that. I must save you," said Tgegani more insistently.

"If you can't leave me because I'm wounded, then kill me so that you won't have to."

Tgegani's eyes went wide.

"What!?"

Another shell exploded nearby, showering them with scorched grass and smoldering black dirt.

"Please. You must...survive."

"I can't kill you!" shrieked Tgegani as he hurried towards cover.

"Please. I am already...dead...I am...just a burden...to you."

The man's eyes rolled back into his head and then his body went limp.

Seeing that the soldier had died, one of the other men stopped Tgegani, and said, "He's gone. Drop him and let's get out of here. We'll come back for him later."

Tgegani stopped and looked back at the advancing Gorg.

"Tgegani!" shouted the soldier.

Tgegani shook the now dead soldier off his back, turned and hurried through the grass followed by the other soldier. They soon caught up to the rest of the retreating men and met up with Welk, who was helping the Lieutenant to safety. Both men smiled as Tgegani appeared.

"Put him on my back. I'll carry him. We need to move with speed," said Tgegani.

They helped the Lieutenant onto Tgegani's back, and then moved quickly towards the Yigzan lines. As they drew closer, a number of Yigzan soldiers moved into position to help cover their retreat until all of the remaining men were safely behind friendly lines. Once on the other side, they continued moving deeper into friendly lines until they were greeted by several medics who quickly took charge of the wounded. Seeing that his men were being taken care of, Welk found a vantage point nearby that allowed him a clear view of the Gorg lines. To his surprise, he found that their attack had worked, as the Gorg now fumbled around in disarray, their lines threatening to collapse at any moment. He soon returned to his men, and was surprised to find Tgegani sitting under a nearby tree assessing his body's condition. The look on Tgegani's face gave Welk pause for concern.

"You alright?" he asked.

Tgegani shook his head.

"I appear to have taken more damage than I had originally thought. My sensor pack and some of my joints need servicing. I also believe there may be a crack in my body shell. These are items of damage that I am unable to repair on my own. I can still fight if I am required to, but my abilities will be greatly reduced until proper repairs can be made."

Welk sighed.

"Well, then I think we need to get you back to see the good doctor."

Tgegani nodded.

"Yes, that would be advisable."

Dr. Burgon picked up his phone and answered cheerfully. But the smile on his face soon faded to an expression of concern.

"Oh dear. Is he alright?" he replied.

Persia rolled over in her bed, stretched and partially opened her eyes. Seeing the look of concern on Burgon's face, she raised her head in curiosity.

"How bad is it?" he asked, nodding several times. "Well, yes. Bring him back immediately. I'll take a look at him and see what I can do. Yes, please. Thank you. Goodbye."

He hung up the phone and rubbed his chin in concerned thought.

"Is everything alright?" asked Persia curiously.

"Tgegani's been hurt," said Burgon as he continued to think.

Persia stood up like a shot and stared at Burgon in horror.

"How bad is it!?" she asked with great concern.

"Well, he's functional. But from the way the sergeant described his injuries, it sounds like he may have exceeded his limits. It's nothing that'll threaten his life, if that's what you're concerned about. But it *has* limited some of his mobility. I'm quite interested in seeing the damage he suffered, and hear him explain how he got his injuries. It should help me make improvements to the new body designs before this war gets any worse. If one day of hard fighting has done this to him, we'll need to make him stronger or he won't survive the war."

"You sure he's alright?" asked Persia with concern.

Burgon nodded.

"He's fine. Sergeant Welk said he had a long talk with Tgegani, and his injuries sound more superficial than anything. But he also agreed that it would be best if we checked them out to be sure."

He then walked out of his office and into the laboratory with Persia on his heels and studied the alloy formulas for the body shell.

He thought about them briefly, and then said to himself, "I wonder if I can improve this? Well, I'd better not until I find out how it failed."

"You said he had other injuries. What were they?" asked Persia, a hint of concern still in her voice.

"Mostly joint damage from what he said. Also, they mentioned something about a crack in his body shell. Honestly though, it really doesn't surprise me at all that he got hurt. His body was never designed to be used in combat. What amazes me though is how quickly he damaged it. That means that I've either failed miserably in my designs, or he's gone through a lot more than I could have ever predicted," said Burgon.

"But he's safe, right?" asked Persia.

Burgon turned to her kindly, and patted her on the head.

"Don't worry. Tgegani will come out of this just fine."

Delgra walked up to Odevion as he worked on his computer and tapped him on the shoulder. Odevion looked up in curiosity and then spotted the paper that Delgra held out to him.

"What's this?" he asked as he took and studied it.

"I need you to do me a favor. Since my cover was blown over a year ago it's been increasingly difficult to get information on certain projects and activities within the government. So I'd like you to go to some of our friends on the inside and call in a few favors. I'm badly in need of information, and they're the best way to get it."

"Sure, I'll see what I can do."

He then turned back to his computer and started working his magic. Delgra cleared his throat. Odevion turned and looked at him curiously. Then, upon seeing Delgra's expression, his eyes narrowed in dismay.

"You're not actually suggesting that I do this in person, are you?" he asked.

Delgra nodded.

"I'm afraid so. I can't risk having this traced back to me. And, if you do it here, it will be."

Odevion sighed.

"Alright, fine. I figure it's faster to do this across the web. But if you think it's more secure in person, then I'll go that route."

"It's not because I believe it'll be more secure. It's just that we're less likely to have it traced back to us this way. And if they find out we're involved, which you know they will, we'll be in trouble in ways I don't care to deal with."

"Ah, right. So we do this away from the facility to ensure that it decouples any resulting investigation from us."

"Exactly. The less they can point the finger at us, the better."

Odevion laughed. This puzzled Delgra.

"What's so funny?" he asked.

"I remember we used to do this a lot when we were younger."

Delgra chuckled.

"We still *are* young, relatively speaking."

Odevion laughed.

"Yeah, relative is the exact word for it." He then closed his laptop, and said, "Alright, I'll work my magic and have this back to you no later than next Tuesday if all goes well."

"Thanks, I appreciate it."

"Eh, it's no biggy. We both want to win this war, and if it means spooking our own government a little, then I'm all for it."

Chapter 13

Mestra pulled to a stop at the front gate of the laboratory and rolled down his window.

"Evening, Lieutenant. Going somewhere?" asked one of the guards.

"Just going to town for a few minutes to visit a friend and then I'll be back."

"Alright, but don't be too long. You only have a half hour until the gates close for the night," said the guard.

"I know that. Thank you, sergeant. I'll be back before then," replied Mestra.

The guard took two steps back and waved him through as the main barricade opened. Mestra's car then quickly rolled through the gate and into the night. He continued to drive down the road for a ways until he could no longer see the lights of the laboratory behind him, but hadn't gone far enough to see the lights of the town in front of him just yet. Seeing that he was safe, he pulled off to the side of the road and waited. A few minutes later, a man in full body camouflage slipped out of the darkness and up to his car. Mestra rolled down the window and handed him a small package.

"Everything's in there. I suggest you get this back to your superiors as quickly as you can. The Yigzan are developing a number of weapons that will be of great concern to the leadership. If these projects succeed, the Gorg are doomed."

The man bowed slightly.

"I will carry these with great haste," he hissed.

"See that you do," said Mestra as he rolled up his window.

The man then melted into the darkness again as Mestra drove away.

"So, heading back to the rear already?" asked Pentell.

"Yeah, our lion needs servicing, and I need to pick up a couple new squad members to replace the ones I lost," said Welk.

"I'm sorry to hear that. We lost a few ourselves. Those men were like brothers to me," said Pentell.

Welk sighed.

"Yeah, same here. But I know what we did today saved a lot of lives."

"And your lion saved ours," smiled Pentell.

"Indeed he did."

"So, are we going to see you around the battlefield again anytime soon?"

Welk shrugged.

"I would think so. Although, we first need to get our lion fixed, and there's no telling how long that'll take. I hope no more than a couple weeks at most."

Pentell smiled.

"Well then, we'll hopefully see you sometime after that."

"Yeah, we'll see."

They both then turned as they heard truck doors close and a vehicle start up.

"Well, that's my ride. See you around, sir. It's been a pleasure serving with you," said Welk.

The Lieutenant nodded.

"Same here."

Welk then climbed into the back of the truck, closed the gate, and quickly sat down as the truck began to pull away. He turned and looked at Tgegani as they merged onto a main road and began to gain speed. As he did, he noticed a look of concern on the lion's face.

"What's on your mind?" he asked.

"I feel like I've failed everyone," replied Tgegani.

"How so?" asked Welk.

"We've only been in combat one day and I'm already in need of repairs. Now I will likely be away from the action for several weeks; a period of time in which many good soldiers will die needlessly because I was not there to save them."

"Don't let it bother you. You've already saved countless lives, and even gave the Gorg a bloody nose. That's quite a lot for your first day. So you should be proud of yourself."

Tgegani turned to his left and watched as rows upon rows of trees raced past them in the rapidly fading twilight like battalions of shadowy green sentinels.

He turned back to Welk, and said, "May I ask you a personal question?"

"Sure, what is it?"

"I am confused about something. Today, during our time with Lieutenant Pentell, one of his men asked me to kill him."

Welk looked surprised at this.

"Who?"

Tgegani shook his head.

"I don't know his name."

"Well, did you?"

Tgegani shook his head again.

"No. The Yigzan are my people. It is my duty to protect them. As such I would never willfully harm one of them, either through my actions or my inaction. Yet one of them requested of me that I end his life. He talked as though there was no hope of saving him, and that I should speed his death in order to protect the others. I couldn't do it. Even so, I find myself conflicted. My killing him would have shortened his suffering, providing mercy to a man in great pain. And yet, he was Yigzan, and thus I could not harm him," he said.

Welk gently grabbed Tgegani's chin and looked him straight in the eye.

"You made the right choice. All of us feel helpless at times. But killing someone like that is wrong, even if he's gonna die anyways. I know it seemed right to him, but he was wounded and not in his right mind. In cases like that we have to step up and make the right choices for them whenever they are unable to do so it themselves."

Tgegani nodded.

"I understand."

He then turned his eyes toward the horizon and thought about the events of the day as flashes of artillery fire flickered in the distance.

A large, somewhat plump Gorg officer looked up as a tall, thin man with a weasel like face walked into the office and held out a package to him.

"Here is the information you requested from our spy," he hissed.

The officer took the package from the man's hand, and studied it briefly before looking at him in unrestrained disgust.

"Leave," he grunted.

The weasel faced man gave a twisted, giddy laugh and then hustled out the door. The officer snorted disdainfully at this.

"Midazin are such disgusting creatures. If they weren't so useful, I'd have seen them wiped out years ago," he muttered.

He then opened the package, and glanced at the documents inside.

"Hmm, interesting," he said quietly.

He soon tucked the files back into the envelope and then walked to the office of the Marshall General. Inside there he found several older, gray haired officers who were arguing over the abysmal progress of the war. The officer grunted and scowled as he noticed another Midazin agent sitting pompously in a nearby chair as he grinned with twisted glee. The agent took note of the officer's large, troll like features and snorted in disgust. The officer flexed his thick, bulging arm muscles and scowled at him in return. The Midazin grinned condescendingly. The officer then cleared his throat, catching the attention of the Marshall General, who immediately waved for the others to be silent.

"What do you have for me?" he asked.

The officer stepped forward and placed the envelope on the desk.

"Information from one of our spies. I think you will find its contents interesting," he said.

The Marshall General picked up the envelope, pulled out the papers and studied them. When he reached the fifth page his eyes went wide.

"So, the rumors *are* true. The vile Yigzan have constructed a mechanical monstrosity that can defeat our men."

He slapped the papers on his desk in disgust.

"I want this creature, its creator, and all evidence of its existence wiped from the face of this planet!" he shouted.

The Midazin agent sat up and held out his hand towards the Marshall General.

"May I see that page?" he hissed.

The Marshall General eyed him suspiciously.

"Please, General, we are in this war together. Do not hold animosity to one who seeks to aid you to victory."

The Marshall General hesitated slightly as the Midazin agent grinned acrimoniously. Finally, he handed the page to the agent who read it, and then grinned with devilish delight.

"Interesting. Most interesting indeed," he said greedily.

"It's an abomination and it must be destroyed!" said the Marshall General.

"Ah, but with that you would be wrong."

The Marshall General's eyes narrowed.

"How so?"

"If we can capture this robot, and its creator, we can force them to work for us. With such a weapon at our disposal, we could not only destroy the Yigzan, but also eliminate those wretched Sattazin as well. In doing so, we would rid the world of *all* our enemies."

"And what if they don't agree to work for us?" asked the Field Marshall.

"Then we simply destroy them. Either way, we win, General."

"Humph," grunted the Marshall General as he thought about the proposal. Finally, he looked up at one of his officers, and said, "Collect a force of your best men. I want that robot and its creator captured and brought to me."

The officer saluted, and said, "It will be done as you've requested."

Tgegani sat near the back of the passenger train car and thought over the day's events. Welk looked over at him as he sat straight and rigid, his eyes seeming to stare off into nothingness.

"Something on your mind?" he asked.

"I am reviewing my actions from today in order to ensure that I do not suffer such damage again, or fail in my mission as I have."

Welk rubbed Tgegani's shoulders, and said, "Don't be so hard on yourself. I don't think anything could've prepared you for what we went through the other day. I knew the deck was stacked against us, but I didn't expect things to go quite *that* badly."

Tgegani shook his head.

"Logic would state that, while our actions were brave, our situation was not tactically advantageous. It may have been better if we'd tried a strategy, or course of action that was different from the one we undertook."

Welk grunted.

"That's the problem. I don't think we would've found any better opportunities, regardless of how long we looked. However, if you have any suggestions in the future on how we could do things better, I'm all ears."

Tgegani nodded.

"I will endeavor to offer such advice to you whenever it is needed."

Just then the train lurch forward slightly.

"We're slowing," said Tgegani.

Welk sat up and looked out his window.

"We may be coming into our station, but I can't be for sure," he replied.

Just as he said this the lights in the cabin came on. Several of the men groaned and covered their eyes.

"Great lords of Verok! Warn a guy when you're gonna do that," grunted one of the men.

"Sorry about that, sir. But we're coming into your station, and the conductor wanted me to wake you," said an attendant who stood at the front of the car.

"Well, it still wouldn't hurt to at least warn us next time."

Welk stood up, and said, "Alright, that's enough, gentlemen. On your feet."

The men all groaned in dismay at this order.

"Come on, move," said Welk more insistently.

The soldiers grudgingly stood to their feet, collected their gear, and then stood in line as the train pulled to a stop. It was dark outside, as most of the lights in the town had been switched off for the night. The soldiers climbed out of the car and stopped briefly on the platform to let their eyes grow accustomed to the darkness as the train pulled away behind them.

"I see we've returned to a warm welcome as always," quipped Sims.

"Looks more like the cold shoulder to me," said a soldier.

"Well, that's nothing new. It wouldn't be the first time we've been left in the dark. No pun intended, of course," said a second with a grin.

"Alright gentlemen. Let's get moving. We've got a long walk ahead of us," said Welk.

They then walked quietly through the town in near total darkness and soon found themselves on the narrow service road that led to the laboratory. The men said nothing to each other as they walked, and cautiously listened to the sounds around them for signs of possible enemy activity in the area. Even though they were far behind the front lines, war had already made them edgy. As such, walking in near total darkness did nothing to help ease their nerves. However, the walk went quickly, despite everyone's nervousness, and they soon reached the last hill before the laboratory. But as soon as they crested the top of it, Tgegani spied something near the gate that immediately put him on the defensive.

He crouched down, and whispered anxiously, "Stop! Stop!"

"What's the matter?" asked Welk.

"Something's wrong. Take cover."

"What's happening? Is he malfunctioning or something?" asked one of the soldiers.

"Just get down," whispered Welk.

He then took up a prone position on the ground and pulled out his binoculars. As he did, Tgegani switched his eyes from night vision to a three way scanning mode and began sweeping the area for signs of activity.

"What's happening down there? I don't see anything," said Welk.

"That's the problem. There's no guards or anybody watching the facility. Major Delgra would never allow something like that to happen," whispered Tgegani.

Welk carefully scanned the gateway and the guard house. To his surprise, Tgegani was right. The place looked abandoned. He swore.

"Great. It looks like the facility may have been compromised," he muttered.

"By who?" asked Sims.

"Who else?"

Sims blinked in surprise.

"You're not seriously suggesting that this was done by the Gorg, are you?"

"It's the only thing I can think of."

"They're not that smart!" protested Sims.

"They must be, or else who could have done this?"

But Sims didn't have an answer to that. They all then continued to scan the facility.

"Tgegani, do you see anything?" asked Welk.

"Nothing. There are no patrols or thermal signatures anywhere in the area. However, I do see evidence that this may have indeed been perpetrated by the Gorg," replied the lion.

"But how could they get here so fast!?" asked Sims.

"Given how thin our lines are, it wouldn't take much for them to sneak a chopper or two through our skies and fly them all the way out here without being detected," said Welk.

"I don't think that's how they got here. I see four large cargo trucks just inside the main gate. It's possible that they were smuggled in," replied Tgegani.

Again Welk swore.

"Great, and now we've got traitors in our midst," he muttered.

Just then Tgegani stood up and began moving forward.

"Wait, where are you going?" asked Welk.

Tgegani paused.

"To scout the perimeter fence and the facility."

"Take one of the men with you," replied Welk.

Tgegani shook his head.

"I can move faster, and with greater stealth if I go alone. Having someone with me would only slow me down and put them in unnecessary danger."

Welk paused briefly as he thought about this.

"Alright, but be careful," he said.

Tgegani nodded.

"I will."

He then vanished into the night, moving in near total silence as his body blended perfectly into the soft flowing shadows that surrounded the facility. He stopped just a hundred feet from the main gate and studied it. He could see a pair of boots and a hand protruding from the door of one of the two guardhouses. He scanned further and found two Gorg shock troopers hiding discretely behind a nearby barrier. This intrigued him, as he hadn't detected them earlier. He soon spotted more Gorg shock troops moving back and forth through the darkness just inside the fence.

Yet they didn't appear on his thermal sensors. So either they were using some form of thermal masking, or he was more damaged than he realized.

"We have a problem," he said over the radio.

"How bad is it?" asked Welk.

"Bad. I'm going to scout some more and see if there's a way in," said Tgegani.

He then began moving around the perimeter fence, searching for a possible way to enter the laboratory grounds undetected as he did. He soon found what he was looking for.

"Sergeant Welk, bring the men to my position. We'll go in from here."

"Where are you?"

"Outer fence, two hundred meters to the left of the main gate."

"Acknowledged. We'll be right there."

Tgegani then settled down and continued to watch the laboratory for several minutes as he listened for the approach of his squad members. The squad soon arrived and stopped behind him as Welk and Sims knelt down by his side and studied the area in front of them.

"So what do we do first?" asked Sims.

"We enter the facility and secure the immediate area," whispered Welk.

"Well, obviously. I mean, how do we do that without being detected?"

"Leave that to me," whispered Tgegani.

The two men then watched as Tgegani quickly vanished into the grass and then reappeared near the fence. With careful skill he used his claws to slice open a hole in the fence and slipped through it. Several moments later the words, "All clear," came over the radio. Welk's men then slipped through the hole in the fence and quickly met up with the lion near one of the barracks buildings. As soon as they arrived, Tgegani nodded towards a nearby structure.

"That building is being guarded by nine Gorg soldiers. I'll slip through the back door and take down the ones inside. You get the four out front. Wait until you hear me start my attack before you begin yours. I don't want to risk them shooting any of the soldiers inside."

"Why are we freeing them? Shouldn't we take out those other Gorg first?" whispered Welk.

"We need the extra support. As you remember, there are only a few of us, and we are likely facing a full company of Gorg," said Tgegani.

"Ah, good point."

Tgegani then turned and vanished into the darkness. Welk waited several tense minutes until he heard a roar and the sounds of shots being fired from inside the barracks. The four guards out front then turned to see what was happening.

Seeing his opportunity, Welk shouted, "Now!"

He then leapt up from his hiding place and fired at the four soldiers. Several other soldiers joined him, and within seconds all of the Gorg were dead.

"Move! Go! Go! Go!" said Welk as he signaled for his men to follow him.

They all then flowed out of the darkness and towards the barracks just as Tgegani appeared through the front door of the building.

"The men are on the ground floor near the back. They're shaken but okay. Get them armed and ready for action. I'm going to move deeper into the facility and see what the Gorg are after."

Welk tried to protest but, before he could, Tgegani bolted off into the darkness. Welk cursed.

He then turned to Sims, and said, "Let's get these men dressed, armed and ready. He's gonna need backup."

"Are you just going to let him run off like that?" asked Sims.

"Tgegani can take care of himself. Right now we need to concentrate on taking back this facility," said Welk.

Chapter 14

Burgon stared in dismay as Gorg soldiers tossed papers, equipment and parts everywhere as they searched for anything of interest in the room. One of the Gorg soon walked up to a box of parts and picked up an arm.

"Leave those alone, you brute!" snarled Persia.

One of the Gorg soldiers walked over and smacked her in the face with the butt of his rifle.

"Shad'up ya stupid cat," he muttered.

Persia snarled in return and prepared to leap as the Gorg aimed his rifle at her.

"Sit down, little lady, or I'll scatter your brains all over the wall," said the Gorg.

Burgon grabbed Persia around the neck and hugged her tightly.

"Calm down, sweetie. This won't do us any good. Help will come in time. But we have to stay alive until then."

One of the Gorg sergeants let out a sour, raunchy laugh.

"You'll only live if you behave."

"Why do we have to keep them alive?" grunted one of the soldiers.

"Because we were told to. That's why," grunted the Gorg sergeant in reply. He then glared at the doctor, and said, "But I'd prefer to see them all dead."

Just then the door opened and Delgra and Silvers were shoved into the room.

"Sit down," grunted a Gorg soldier as he forced them to their knees.

Both officers quickly stood to their feet. The Gorg aimed his rifle at them and growled angrily.

"I said sit down!"

"Enough! You shoot him and I'll personally execute you," growled the Gorg sergeant.

The soldier glared at the sergeant, gave an angry grunt and then lowered his rifle. Just then Mestra walked into the laboratory followed by two more Gorg soldiers.

"Are they all here?" he asked.

"Just as you ordered, sir," grunted one of the Gorg sergeants.

Mestra looked at the other two and gave a devilish grin.

"Well, hello, Major. How are you this fine evening? I hope you weren't hurt too badly by my men," he said gloatingly.

"Mestra! Are you part of this!?" replied Delgra in disgust.

"Part of it? Of course I'm part of it! I'm leading this raid, you idiot!" barked Mestra.

"Why!? You're a Yigzan officer!" said Delgra in disbelief.

Mestra laughed hysterically.

"Yigzan? Did you really think I was Yigzan? Are you blind!? Do I actually look like I'm part of your disgusting race? I'm Midazin! It's my curse that I was born with a face like yours. It sickens me every time I see it in the mirror. But today it will aid me in once and for all destroying you and your pathetic people."

"Why are you doing this? What have we done to deserve your hatred!?" snapped Delgra.

"You are Yigzan. Do I need any other reason?" he snarled condescendingly.

Just then sounds of gunfire, screaming and shattering glass echoed from the hallway.

"What now?" muttered Mestra.

"Sounds like fighting," grunted the Gorg sergeant.

"Well obviously, you idiot!   Go find out what's happening!" said Mestra.

The sergeant pointed towards several of his soldiers, and said, "Come with me."

As they exited the lab, Delgra grinned with satisfaction.

"It sounds like the cavalry is here to save us," he said.

Mestra frowned.

"Oh, don't get your hopes up. Your chances of--"

Mestra's words were suddenly cut short as the door to the laboratory blew open, and a gold and gray blur entered the room with an angry roar. A moment later, all of Mestra's soldiers lay dead on the floor. He then heard an angry growl and turned to see a lion standing near him, his skin hanging from his body in dirty, tattered, blood covered shreds. The lion turned briefly towards Mestra and spied his Yigzan uniform. His eyes then panned the room, searching for any other Gorg soldiers that might've escaped from his grasp. As he did this, Mestra drew his pistol and fired at Tgegani. But the shot glanced harmlessly off his head and embedded itself in a nearby wall. Mestra's eyes grew wide at this as he began to shake in fear. Tgegani soon turned and looked at him curiously.

"Why did you shoot at me?" he asked.

"He's one of them!" shouted Delgra.

Mestra pointed his pistol at the Major, and shouted, "You shut up!"

"Please, calm down," said Tgegani.

"Kill him, Tgegani! He's a traitor!" shouted Silvers.

"Tgegani?" said Persia in curious surprise.

She tried to move to get a better view, but couldn't as Burgon held her fast.

"No, stay put, sweetie," he said.

Tgegani stared in confusion at Mestra, and then back at Silvers.

"I can't kill him. He's Yigzan," he replied.

"No he's not! He's Midazin! Kill him now!" shouted Delgra.

"But I can't."

Mestra soon stopped shaking as he realized that the lion couldn't hurt him.

"You can't kill me," he said with devilish delight.

"Well, I can," said Persia, her eyes sparkling like little tongues of fire.

But Burgon held onto her even tighter as she struggled to get free.

"Well, then I see we have nothing to worry about from you. However, you have much to worry about from me," gloated Mestra.

He then pointed his pistol at Dr. Burgon and was about to fire when, out of the corner of his eye, he saw movement. He turned just in time to see Delgra drawing a pistol from inside his jacket. Mestra's eyes went wide as he spun and fired at Delgra. But his shot missed. Silvers dove for cover as Delgra fired next, his bullet ripping through Mestra's chest like a hammer, knocking him backwards. But the Midazin spy kept his feet as he aimed again and fired. But his aim was slightly off as the bullet merely grazed Delgra's shoulder, sending him spinning to the floor. Pain flashed through Delgra like a hot knife as he fell. He hit the ground with a hard thud, gripping his pistol tightly as he did so as not to drop it before frantically twisting his body around in an effort to take aim at the lieutenant.

However, it took all of his will power to focus on the situation as pain flooded his body like an inferno. He was amazed that one little flesh wound could cause him such agony. He tried to force his wounded arm to move, but it refused to obey. Realizing that he couldn't continue fighting this way, he reached out with his left hand to grab the gun, and then paused. To his surprise he spotted Mestra laying dead on the floor in front of him, having succumbed to the single bullet wound to his chest. Seeing that the immediate danger had passed, Delgra relaxed, allowing his gun to slip from his fingers and clatter noisily to the floor. Seeing that it was all clear, Silvers rushed to his side and began to check on his commander.

"How bad is it?" grimaced Delgra.

Silvers pealed back Delgra's jacket and studied the wound.

"You'll be fine. You just got grazed. It took a chunk of flesh with it, but little else," said Silvers.

"Is that all? Because it feels like I got my entire arm ripped off," groaned Delgra.

"It probably hit a nerve, so it's gonna feel worse than it actually is," said Silvers.

"Wonderful," groaned Delgra.

Silvers then took a lab towel and tied it around the wound in an effort to stop the bleeding. Delgra winced as he drew it tight.

"That should hold you until we can get you down to the infirmary," said Silvers.

"Assuming we still have an infirmary," muttered Delgra.

Just then several Yigzan soldiers burst into the room followed by Welk.

"Is everyone alright...in...here," said Welk, his voice trailing off as he spotted Tgegani. "Hmm, I appear to have answered my own question," he continued. He then turned to the men behind him, and said, "Finish sweeping the building. I'll catch up to you in a few minutes."

The men immediately obeyed.

"Can you help me get the Major to the infirmary?" asked Silvers.

"Yes, sir," replied Welk.

"Let me do it. You are needed to help secure the facility," said Tgegani.

"Do what the lion says. I'll be fine," groaned Delgra.

Welk obeyed and hurried out of the room. Delgra then climbed painfully to his feet and, swaying slightly due to the pain, put his arm around Sims.

"Major, please climb on my back. I will take you to the infirmary," said Tgegani.

"Not on your life, fuzz ball. You need to stay and watch the doctor," groaned Delgra.

Tgegani sat down and quietly obeyed.

"As you wish," he replied.

Just then Tgegani felt a warm, furry body wrap itself around him and begin crying. He turned and noticed that Persia was holding onto him tightly.

"Hello, mother," he said kindly.

As Persia wept for joy on Tgegani's tattered, dirty mane, he gently placed one arm around her shoulder and pulled her in tight to himself.

"I'm alright," he said kindly.

Upon seeing this, Burgon climbed to his feet and studied the lion with interest.

"You look terrible, young man. What happened to you?" he said.

"I think I broke something," replied Tgegani sheepishly.

Burgon grinned.

"Well then, why don't we get a look at that body of yours and see what needs fixing."

Black listened intently on the phone.

He nodded several times, and said, "Thank you. I'll look forward to your report."

He then hung up the phone and watched his computer for several moments until a small message icon appeared on the screen. Opening it he quickly browsed the contents and nodded with approval. He then turned to his phone and pressed the pager button.

"Yes, sir?" came the secretary's voice.

"Send in Elgar."

"Right away, sir."

Several minutes later Elgar walked through the door and up to Black's desk.

"You called?" he asked.

"Yes, I've got some work for you. It would seem that the Midazin have decided to meddle in the war. I don't know what they plan to do, but I need to know."

Elgar nodded.

"I'll get right on it."

He then turned and left the room as Black's phone began to ring.

"Black here," he answered.

"Sir, we've encountered a problem at the Echo Military Science Labs. They've been attacked," came a panicked voice over the phone.

Black stiffened.

"What? When? By who?"

"The Gorg. They hit the place with a couple platoons of shock troops. We think they may have been after Dr. Burgon and the lions."

"Did they succeed?" asked Black.

"Thankfully, no. Some troops who were returning from the front lines recaptured the labs."

Black felt both relief, and great anger at this.

"How did the Gorg find out about the lab?" he asked.

"They were apparently ratted out by a Midazin insider passing himself off as a Yigzan officer."

Black cursed lightly under his breath.

"Was anybody hurt?" he asked.

"Just a handful of soldiers and an officer. I'm sending you the report now. But I wanted to call you in advance so you knew to pay close attention to it when it comes through. There's also something near the end I think will greatly intrigue you."

"I look forward to reading it. Oh, wait. It just arrived."

"Good, I'll leave you to read. Talk to you soon. Bye," said the man.

Black hung up his phone and began eagerly reading the report, grimacing at some points, while smiling at others. But as he did, something caught his eye. He read it, backed up, and read it again, and then sat back as he rubbed his chin in thought.

"It appears that Tgegani is already making quite a name for himself in this war. This is especially good news since the new prototypes will be ready very soon. If they perform as well as he has, we may actually win this war. But I need to protect those assets as much as I can."

He then picked up the phone and dialed a number.

When they answered, Black said, "I need you to organize a move of everyone at the Echo Military Science Labs to my laboratory in the northwest near the mountains ASAP."

"Understood," came the reply.

"Thank you," replied Black, and then hung up.

He again stared at the report in front of him, thought for a moment, and then picked up the phone and dialed another number. An older gentleman answered.

"Senator Joslin, this is Ferrell Black."

"Ah, Mr. Black. What can I do for you?"

"I need to build some more lions."

"Lions?" said the senator in surprise.

"Robotic lions. I think you've already heard about Tgegani, right?"

"Well, yes. I've heard a lot about him lately. Fascinating creature he is, even for a robot."

"I need you to get me approval and funding from the General Secretary so I can begin producing more units just like him."

"More!?" said Joslin in surprise.

"Yes."

"How many are you planning to make?"

"Approximately six hundred and fifty, plus spare parts at this point."

The senator thought about this for a few moments.

"Are you, by chance, building a droid army?"

"More or less. But I'm doing it because we need them. Without more of those lions, we may lose this war."

"But why six hundred and fifty specifically?"

"No particular reason. I just figured that'd be a good start. But, if not, then we can build more as they are needed."

"That's fine. But what will happen to them after the war?"

"We'll worry about that when the time comes. For now we need to focus on winning."

"I don't know, Mr. Black. I like your idea, but at the same time, I'm leery of allowing six hundred and fifty of those things to run freely across the continent doing whatever they want."

"They wouldn't be wandering around freely. They'd be under the direct control of our troops the entire time," said Black.

"No, no. That's not what I mean. Tgegani has free will, right?"

"Yes."

"Then it stands to reason that the others will also have free will. As such, there's nothing to say that they won't turn on us during, or after the war."

"All of the new lions will be loaded with a copy of Tgegani's AI core program. He's already proven trustworthy and loyal to a fault, so it only stands to reason that the others will be just as loyal as he is."

"Do you actually trust him that much?" asked the senator in surprise.

"I've seen nothing that would make me believe otherwise."

The senator sighed heavily and grunted slightly.

"Dang'it, Black! You'd better be right about this! My butt's on the line here. And if this fails, it's going to come back to haunt both of us!"

"Senator, if this fails, I will take personal responsibility for whatever happens."

"You'd better," growled Joslin.

"So, do I have your support?"

The senator sighed.

"Yes, you do. I'll go ahead and start putting things in motion for you. But at the first sign of trouble I'll see to it that they put your butt in jail."

"I understand, Senator. Thank you for your time, and I appreciate what you're doing for me."

Black then hung up the phone and turned to his computer.

"Drat. He may become a problem at some point. If he does, I'll have to ensure that he's eliminated, and a suitable replacement put in his place," he muttered to himself. "Well, no matter. If all goes well in the meantime, our country will be saved. After that little mess is cleaned up, I will need to focus on the next step of my plans for the world."

"Wake up, Tgegani," came Burgon's voice.

Tgegani's body jerked slightly and then relaxed as his eyes opened and quickly adjusted to his surroundings.

Burgon smiled as the robotic lion raised one paw, flexed it, and then the other, examining both of them with curiosity.

"So, what do you think?" asked Burgon gleefully.

"My body feels...different," said Tgegani.

"That's because I've given you an entirely new one. The other was in such bad shape that I couldn't repair it. So I moved your brain core into this new one instead."

"But even if it is a new body, it should not feel like this," said Tgegani.

"Well, that's probably because your new body is made from the parts that were set aside for the new prototypes I was working on. Now, if everything works as designed, you should be stronger, faster, more durable, and more agile than before."

Tgegani shook out his mane and then flexed his body experimentally.

"May I try it out? I want to see what its capabilities are," he said.

"By all means!" exclaimed Burgon.

Tgegani then turned and slipped outside, hurrying over to the facility's obstacle course where he pushed his body to its limit, testing its full abilities while making note of its every strength and weakness, how it responded in given situations, and what was noticeably different about its performance compared to his former body. Eventually he stopped, sat down, closed his eyes, and began processing everything he'd learned, comparing it to the vast array of information about his former body that he had stored in his mind. But, as he did this, a familiar odor tickled at his sensors. It was one that he was well familiar with, and yet surprised to sense it.

"Hello, Tgegani," came a warm, familiar voice.

Tgegani opened his eyes and noticed Meshua staring at him from a nearby stump.

"Why are you here?" he asked as he sat up.

"How do you like your new body?" asked Meshua.

Tgegani raised a paw and studied it.

"It is most intriguing. Why do you ask?" he replied.

Meshua smiled.

"It's a gift from me."

Tgegani cocked an eyebrow in intrigue.

"How is it from you? My father built this body. You, however, did not."

Meshua shook his head.

"Your body is my creation. Your father was merely the hands by which it was built."

"Then it is like a house, where one designs it and the other builds?" asked Tgegani curiously.

Meshua nodded. Tgegani found this intriguing.

"But why? Wouldn't it have been easier for you to have built it yourself?"

"There are times when the architect is also the builder, and others where he merely provides the plans, and another builds for him."

Tgegani tilted his head in curiosity.

"Then what you have done through him is much like what I do for you as your proxy."

Meshua chuckled.

"It is."

Tgegani sighed and then looked away.

"But I am insufficient for the task that you have put before me. My strength is weakness, and my courage is fear. Thus I am unable to do all that you require of me."

Meshua smiled.

"You do not need to do it all by yourself."

Tgegani looked at Meshua in concern.

"But how? Who is there that is strong enough to stand with me? There are none who possess the strength required for this task," he said.

"A time is coming when I will raise up a great army of your kind, the likes of which has never been seen before. In this you will gain many brothers and sisters who will fight beside you against your enemy and, in doing so, save your people."

Tgegani nodded at this.

"Such are comforting words. But, even if there were ten thousand of me, many will still die."

Meshua walked over to Tgegani, knelt down in front of him, and kindly took the lion's face into his hands.

"War is a messy affair. Even my greatest servants could not protect the lives of everyone in their charge. So do not be dismayed that some have fallen, as many more will die before it is through."

Tgegani thought about this.

"Such a statement is indeed logical. However, who will it be that dies, and who will live till the end?" he asked, a hint of anxiety in his voice.

Meshua shook his head.

"That is not for you to know. Now go, and fulfill your destiny!"

And with that, he was gone. Tgegani laid back down, closed his eyes, and thought about this encounter. But, the more he thought, the more questions it created. Finally he decided that he would not receive anymore answers to his questions until Meshua appeared to him again. As such, until then, he had other work to do, including perfecting his new body.

Chapter 15

Delgra walked into Burgon's lab and paused as he noticed that the lab was empty.

"Dr. Burgon? Are you here?" he shouted.

Persia slipped out from behind a nearby lab table and smiled as she spotted him.

"Ah, Major! What brings you here?" she asked cheerfully.

"I'm looking for your father. Is he around?"

Persia shook her head.

"He's out in the back doing a--"

"I'm right here," came a voice from the far side of the lab.

Both of them then turned to see Dr. Burgon stepping through a nearby doorway, followed by two of the new lions.

"Sorry, I was outside doing some tests on these two bodies. I had to make sure they were ready before I loaded their artificial sentience."

"Understood. Do you have a few minutes that we can talk?" asked Delgra.

"Sure," said Burgon.

Delgra looked at Persia briefly, and then back at Burgon.

"In private, please."

Burgon looked at Delgra in curiosity, and then down at Persia.

"Would you please take these two over to the programming station and hook them up? I'd like to begin loading their artificial sentience framework as soon as possible."

Persia nodded.

"I'll get right on it," she replied.

"Thanks. Lions, please transfer voice command authorization to Persia," said Burgon.

The two droids chirped, and then responded in unison, "Acknowledged. Voice command authorization has been successfully transferred."

"Alright, follow me," said Persia as she turned and began walking across the lab.

The two droids immediately turned and followed her obediently. Burgon briefly watched them go before turning to Delgra.

"Will my office be good enough?" he asked.

Delgra nodded.

"It'll do."

The two men quickly stepped into Burgon's office, and closed the door behind them. Burgon then reached over and poured himself a fresh cup of katar, and sat down on a nearby stool as Delgra sat down in a chair near the door.

"So, what did you want to talk to me about?" asked Burgon.

"I'm trying to find an explanation for Tgegani's strange actions from a couple weeks ago. I conveniently left it out of my report that he would not kill Mestra when ordered. But I know that at some point in time someone higher up is going to find out. So I want to have some answers for them in case they ever do."

Burgon took a sip of his katar and then gave Delgra a curious glance.

"So what are you looking for specifically?" he asked.

"I want to know why he refused to kill Mestra, despite being given a direct order to do so."

Burgon sighed and thought about this for a moment.

"Tgegani is...well, was confused."

"Confused? Explain," said Delgra curiously.

"Well, as you already know, Tgegani has a good heart. But he also still has much to learn about many of the things we take for granted."

"Such as?"

"Well, everything he knows about good and evil, right and wrong, friend and foe, and other things like that, is very black and white to him. He hasn't learned yet how to identify and discern the subtle shades of gray that we understand, and deal with every day. To him, all Yigzan are good, and all Gorg are bad, regardless if that is true or not. Take Mestra for example. He looked just like any other Yigzan officer that Tgegani had ever encountered before and, as such, Tgegani automatically assumed that he was good, and thus would not touch him. He also wasn't here when Mestra revealed himself as a traitor. So he was lacking that bit of information when he made his decision not to attack. I've tried to explain it to him, and I think he understands, but only time will tell if he truly does."

Delgra frowned.

"That's going to be a problem if he ever has to deal with another Midazin infiltrator like Mestra again. Was he ever taught about the Midazin?"

Burgon nodded slightly.

"He knows the technical side of who they are, but not any of the political subtleties that go with it. That's not something you can just teach someone through simple book learning, which is where most of his current knowledge and understanding comes from."

Delgra rolled his eyes.

"Wonderful. And I bet it doesn't help things any that the Midazin are our sister race."

Burgon shook his head.

"It likely doesn't because, even though the Midazin are genetically removed from us by nearly twelve hundred years, they're still Yigzan at their roots."

"Yes, I know that. But, even so, you can't deny that there are clear differences between us, and them, enough that he should be able to easily differentiate between our two races."

Burgon nodded.

"Yes, he does have the ability to identify them in ways that we cannot. Their body odor is one of the biggest. The problem is, many of them look and sound exactly like us right down to the finest degree. So that's a bit confusing to him."

"Is there any way he can better differentiate between the two races aside from body odor? I only ask because I want him able to detect traitors and spies without having to rely entirely on a person's biology."

"Yes, there is. But even then it's not a perfect science. So I told him to also include other factors into his determinations, such as a person's body language, and how they behave."

Delgra drummed his fingers on his knee.

"That's good. But it still leads us back to the problem of his disobeying a direct order. I don't have to remind you, Doctor, that we're in the middle of a war. So obediently following orders is a necessity if we are to survive this."

"I understand that, Major. But it wasn't that he didn't want to obey the order. It's that he couldn't," said Burgon.

Delgra looked at him in confusion.

"What do you mean?" he asked.

Burgon screwed up his face slightly as he pondered how best to answer this.

"As you already know, Tgegani sees all Yigzan as members of his family."

"I do. But why does he?" asked Delgra.

"That's mostly because of how he views Persia and myself. In his mind, if we are his parents, then, by extension, all Yigzan are his family as well. An extended family, but, still family. That's why he is unwilling to harm any Yigzan he encounters anywhere, for any reason whatsoever because, to him, that would be the same thing as harming either myself, or Persia."

Delgra pondered this for several moments before shaking his head.

"That still doesn't make sense."

Burgon laughed.

"You're asking me to explain to you how a machine thinks when I'm not entirely sure of that myself. Honestly, it's rather impressive that I'm even able to understand what I already do."

"So how deep does his loyalty to family go?" asked Delgra.

"Of that, I can't be certain. At least, not yet."

"So what if, for example, I attacked you. How would he respond to that?" asked Delgra.

Burgon shrugged.

"I really don't know. I've explored the subject with him, but he doesn't seem willing to answer that question. Given his lack of action against Mestra, he'd likely treat us all the same, even though he gives the greater respect to Persia and myself."

Delgra sighed.

"So, in other words, he's incapable of attacking a Yigzan, even if he was ordered to do so, or your lives were threatened by another Yigzan like myself."

Burgon nodded.

"At this time? Yes, I believe so."

Delgra frowned at this.

"So then his failure to follow orders the other day was more an incidental effect of how he views our people, rather than an act of actual, willful disobedience?"

Burgon shrugged.

"For the most part, yes. However, his view of the Yigzan is considerably more complex than that such that it can't easily be put into a box."

Delgra groaned.

"I was hoping for another, simpler answer. But I guess there isn't one, is there?"

Burgon sighed.

"I don't know how much simpler I can make it. As much as we'd like to have Tgegani be a simple creature that's simple to understand, the truth is, he's not. His mind is extremely complex, even by *my* standards."

Delgra frowned.

"Hmm, that's both good, and troublesome at the same time."

"Unfortunately, it is," replied Burgon.

Delgra stood up, straightened his uniform, and said, "Thank you for your time, Doctor. While I'm disappointed that this incident happened, I'm pleased that you were able to provide at least some explanation for his actions, even if it was somewhat insufficient."

"I'm sorry I couldn't be of more help," replied Burgon.

"Given the circumstances, at least I'm able to come away with some answers, even if they're not quite what I was hoping for."

"I apologize. I'll see what I can do to better understand how Tgegani thinks about things like this, and hopefully get you some better answers eventually."

Delgra nodded.

"I appreciate that, Doctor. It will be a great help to us once he is finally able to correctly deal with similar situations like this in the future, should that ever happen again."

Burgon frowned.

"I will do my best to help him with that. But, that being said, I also pray that we never have to deal with something like that ever again."

"Agreed."

Tgegani strode up to Welk and gently tapped him on the leg to get his attention. Welk turned around in surprise and then smiled.

"Oh, good afternoon, Tgegani. What are you up to?" he asked.

"Captain Silvers wants you. He asked that I bring you to his office as soon as possible."

Welk shrugged.

"Alright, lead on."

The two then walked together to the administration building and found the secretary waiting for them at the door. Seeing them, she reached over and pressed the intercom button.

"Sir, Sergeant Welk and Tgegani are here to see you," she said.

"Thank you, Ms. Eva. Send them in," replied Silvers.

"Yes, sir," she replied.

She then escorted Welk and Tgegani down the hallway to where Silvers had his office.

The secretary then knocked on the door, and said, "Sir, they're here."

"Send them in," came the reply.

The secretary then opened the door, and gestured for them to enter. Welk and Tgegani quickly stepped into the office, paused, and then introduced themselves. Silvers looked at them briefly, before motioning towards a chair in front of his desk.

"Please, sit down," he said.

"Yes, sir!" said Welk.

Welk and Tgegani quickly took their places in front of the desk.

"I have good news for you, gentlemen. We've just recently received approval to expand the robotic lion program. As a result, we'll be promoting you to Sergeant First Class and moving you to the position of platoon sergeant."

"Thank you, sir. But I don't have a platoon. Our unit only has one squad," said Welk.

"Well, you do now. Your present unit is being expanded to a total of six squads, each of which will be assigned their own lion. I expect you to get them up to speed as quickly as possible."

"I will, sir. But where are we getting the five other lions from?"

Silvers raised an eyebrow in intrigued surprise.

"Weren't you told about the new lions that Dr. Burgon has been building?" asked Silvers.

Welk shook his head.

"That's news to me, sir. It must've been on a need to know basis, because I certainly wasn't told anything about this."

"Well, then we'll need to rectify that. I'll make sure you get all of the appropriate briefing papers by the end of the day."

"Thank you, sir. So how soon can we expect the new lions?"

"Soon. I don't know exactly when, but it shouldn't be too long. The lions are currently in the final stages of programming right now. Tgegani, given that these lions won't have the luxury of training in the same way that you did, I'll need you to handle their initial education, and prepare them in the best way you know how, as quickly as possible."

Tgegani nodded.

"I will do my best," he replied.

Just then the intercom chirped. Silvers reached over and pressed the talk button.

"Yes, what is it?" he asked.

"Sir, the front gate is reporting that the new arrivals are here."

"Good, is there a lieutenant with them?"

"Yes, sir."

"Excellent. Have him report to me as soon as possible. Tell the others to go to the barracks for now and get settled in," he replied.

"Yes, sir."

Silvers looked back at Welk, and said, "Well, looks like you'll get to meet your new men sooner than I expected."

"I'm looking forward to it, sir," said Welk.

Silvers then continued to brief Welk on what his new unit would be expected to do, how it would function now that there were six lions, and how their roll on the battlefront would play out going forward. Finally after several minutes, the voice of the secretary came across the intercom again.

"Sir, Lieutenant Pentell is here to see you as requested."

Tgegani and Welk looked at each other in surprise.

"It couldn't be," said Welk.

"There is a two hundred and seventy thousand to one probability that it could," said Tgegani.

"Send him in," said Silvers.

"Yes, sir," replied the secretary.

Welk and Tgegani then turned towards the door and listened as footsteps approached. Soon there was a knock at the door.

"Permission to enter," came a voice.

Tgegani perked up at the sound.

"Permission granted," replied Silvers.

The door then swung open, and Pentell entered, saluted, and said, "First Lieutenant Pentell reporting as requested, sir."

"Is that actually you?" asked Welk in surprise.

Pentell turned and looked curiously at Welk, and then perked up happily.

"Sergeant Welk? By Meshua's name, it *is* you!" he exclaimed.

Silvers raised an eyebrow in interest.

"Do you two know each other?" he asked.

"Yes, sir! We served together briefly during the first day of combat. Sergeant Welk is an amazing NCO, sir!" said Pentell happily.

He walked up and patted Tgegani on the head.

"And this guy right here saved our lives when our assault went sour. He's quite the fighter, and we owe our lives to him."

Silvers found this intriguing.

"Interesting. Well, since you three apparently know each other already, I guess you can get straight to business putting your new unit together."

Pentell looked at Silvers in surprise.

"Come again, sir?"

"He's your new platoon sergeant, Lieutenant," replied Silvers.

Pentell looked at Welk, who grinned widely.

"Glad to be serving with you again, sir," said Welk.

Pentell chuckled.

"I have a feeling this is going to be quite an interesting assignment."

Delgra walked into Burgon's laboratory and up to the frustrated scientist as he sat at his programming terminal.

"What's the progress on the new lions, doctor?" he asked.

Burgon sighed and rubbed his face.

"Decent, considering the circumstances."

"Is something the matter?" asked Delgra curiously.

"No, not really. I just ran into a few complications I wasn't expecting."

"How soon do you think you can have them ready?"

Burgon sighed.

"I'll know as soon as I can figure out why they're not taking their new programming. Once I solve that, you'll have your lions."

Delgra looked at him in concern.

"Is this going to be a problem?" he asked.

Burgon waved dismissively.

"Nah, not really. I ran into the same issue with Tgegani. I eventually sorted it out with him, so I should be able to do the same with them."

"Alright, but please hurry," said Delgra.

Burgon nodded.

"I'll do my best."

Delgra then turned and left. As he did, Tgegani watched this curiously from a corner of the room and pondered all that he'd heard.

"Meshua, can you hear me?" he thought.

"I am here," came a voice in his mind.

"I've been thinking. You were the one who gave me life after my father built me. Yet you have not done the same for my new siblings. Why is that?"

"It is not their time. But soon," smiled the voice.

Tgegani pondered this.

"Then, if it is soon, when will that be?"

However, there was no answer.

"Can I tell my father about this? He is deeply worried, and extremely frustrated."

"It is not the time for such things to be revealed to him. For now the truth must remain hidden. But, when the time is right, it will be revealed to him," came the voice.

"Why must it be hidden?"

"There is something he must learn first if he is to become what he needs to be."

"What is it that he must learn? I will teach it to him if you will let me."

Meshua laughed.

"This is not a lesson that can be taught with mere words. Only failure will teach him what he must learn and understand."

Tgegani pondered this idea, but pursued it no further. He then sat in silence for several minutes longer, watching his dad struggle fruitlessly to get his fellow lions working. After a bit, he turned his attention to the new lions and pondered their future.

"How soon will my new siblings awaken?" he thought after several minutes.

"Soon," came the reply.

"How soon?"

Silence. Tgegani considered asking the question again, but thought better of it. If his past experiences with Meshua had taught him anything, it was that Meshua never revealed more than was needed at any given moment. So no amount of probing and prodding would gain him anything he wasn't supposed to know yet. After several minutes the voice called out to him again.

"Yes?" thought Tgegani in reply.

"Go to your mother. She needs your companionship right now. Her heart is broken, and your words will be the salve that will heal that wound."

Tgegani pondered this curiously. Was Meshua speaking figuratively, literally or allegorically? He then turned and studied Persia as she sat in a far corner of the laboratory. She seemed distant and detached, as though her body were there, but her mind wasn't. Seeing this, he knew that Meshua's words weren't to be taken literally as she wasn't physically wounded in any way that he could see. So he decided that the statement was meant to be taken figuratively. He soon stood up, walked over, and sat down in front of her.

"What's bothering you, mother?" he asked.

Persia sighed, but didn't look up.

"I'm afraid for you and the others that, if you go out again, you won't come back, and I don't want to lose you," she said with both fear and sadness in her voice.

Tgegani furrowed a brow at this.

"Meshua has promised that I will not die until my purpose here has been fulfilled," he replied.

Persia slowly raised her head to look at him as tears poured from her eyes. Tgegani studied this with curiosity and intrigue.

"I still do not fully understand emotions as of yet. But, I do know that, if you keep crying like you are, you'll expel so much water that you will dry up and blow away," he said.

Persia nodded at this, and then blinked. A moment later she began to snicker and soon broke out into a roaring guffaw. Tgegani raised an eyebrow in curiosity at this.

"Was something I said...funny?" he asked curiously.

Persia took a deep breath, and then smiled widely.

"I don't know. I just...started...laughing," she said with a chuckle.

"The salve that heals a wounded heart," thought Tgegani.

This intrigued him. He hadn't intended to make a joke. He'd merely stated his thoughts on her current state in hopes of making her stop crying, thereby saving her from suffering any form of sorrow induced dehydration. Creating humor had not been his intention. And yet, somehow he had done exactly that which, in turn, had helped relieve a portion of the anxiety that Persia had been feeling. This now made him wonder if other similar actions, such as those he had previously seen shared between his parents, as well as others, might help her further. Deciding to give it a try, he leaned over and wrapped his arms around Persia in a gentle, consoling embrace.

"I love you, Mom," he then said.

At first Persia was surprised by this. But eventually she hugged him in return, and then began crying tears of joy as a great big smile broke out across her face.

"I love you too, Son."

Chapter 16

Black stood in his command center and studied the main display screen.

"I see that the war is still going in favor of the Gorg," he muttered. He then turned to Elgar, and asked, "How soon before Tgegani and the other lions can get out into the field?"

"I don't know. The doctor is having issues getting the new prototypes working," said Elgar.

Black swore.

"What's wrong? Is something defective?"

Elgar shrugged.

"I don't know. All I've been told is that he's unable to get them to work."

Black swore again.

"That man is the greatest cybernetics genius in history and you're telling me he's suddenly hit a brick wall and can't continue?"

Elgar again shrugged.

"More or less."

Black briefly clenched his fists in exasperation before forcing himself to relax. Anger was not his friend right now. So he needed to stay calm.

"Of all the times to have a brain fart. Well, he did it once, so he can do it again. In the meantime we've got bigger issues to deal with. How did our raid on the Gorg high command go?"

Elgar flipped through several pages of charts, stopping at one of interest.

"The effects on the front lines was minimal. But it did greatly upset their command structure. However, given the large number of eligible replacements in the lower ranks, it won't take them long to replace the commanders we killed," said Elgar.

Black swore louder and punched the wall, causing part of it to crack. He then pulled his hand back and examined it. The impact had torn away part of the false skin that covered his now scuffed, but otherwise undamaged cybernetic prosthetic. He grunted in frustration. If he kept punching walls like this, he'd need to get his arm replaced...again. He he soon turned and glared at Elgar.

"Well then, we'll just do it again, and again, and again until they run out of replacements!" he screamed angrily.

"Using our agents too many times risks exposing them, and potentially dragging the Sattazins into the war in favor of the Gorg," said Elgar flatly.

Black sighed.

"Fine, fine. Halt the attacks if you want to. But in the meantime we'll need to come up with other solutions. Especially if Burgon can't produce another working lion."

"I'll look around and see what I can find," said Elgar.

"Good. Please do. And, speaking of the good doctor, what's the status of our efforts to move that lab up here?"

Elgar frowned, but said nothing. Black groaned and slapped his forehead in frustration.

"You've got to be kidding me," he muttered.

"We're doing the best we can, sir, but we're running into a rather stubborn bureaucracy."

"I don't care how stubborn it is! Start killing people if you have to until you get some results! That lab needs to be moved, NOW! There's no telling when the Gorg might attack them again, and I've got too much invested in that place to risk losing it all!"

Elgar bowed slightly, and said, "I'll do my best, but I can't guarantee anything at this time."

He then turned and slipped out of the room. Black turned back towards the large display screen on the far wall and pondered his situation.

"He better make something happen or heads are going to roll," he muttered.

After a bit, he grunted angrily, turned and stormed out of the room.

Delgra looked up from his desk as Odevion walked in.

"Ah, welcome back. I take it your mission was a success?" he asked.

Odevion nodded.

"It went off sweet as candy. However, it would seem that my departure was a bit premature."

"How so?"

"Well, I heard you had a little bit of excitement while I was gone. Apparently that lieutenant I brought with me turned out to be a slagpa scag."

"Yes, well, that's behind us."

"Behind us!? Good heavens, sir! I almost got all of you killed because I didn't do my job right! Heck, you got a bullet in your arm because of me!"

Delgra shrugged dismissively.

"Eh, it happens. He even fooled me, so don't be too hard on yourself. I mean, if his paperwork was spotless, and he successfully fooled both of us, then he was definitely a top notch spy. Too bad he wasn't on our side. We could've really used someone like him."

"Even so, I still feel bad. I could've prevented all of this from ever happening if I'd done my homework a little better."

Delgra picked up a folder off his desk and tossed it to Odevion.

"Don't be too hard on yourself. Even CenTel couldn't find a speck of dirt on this guy. His record is immaculate, which means he was either that good, or he had inside help."

Odevion studied the file briefly and then looked back at Delgra.

"Do you want me to go out and see if I can find out who helped him?"

"You don't need to. CenTel already has that covered. If there's a spy up there, they want to root him out just as much as we do. So I trust they'll sort that out for us. In the meantime, I've got some other work for you. Most of it involves acquiring supplies that we badly need which nobody seems interested in giving us."

Odevion laughed.

"Ah, thievery by computer. I'm sure I can do that."

Delgra smirked.

"Not thievery. I just need people to let me have what I need to run my facility."

"Ah, then creative arm twisting! Yeah, I can do that too," grinned Odevion.

Delgra chuckled.

"Alright, we'll stick with creative arm twisting then. But,either way, see what you can do. I need the stuff by the middle of next week."

"Sure thing. Just give me a list of what you need, and I'll make it happen."

Burgon sat on a hillside outside his laboratory and stared up at the stars, an expression of frustration etched deeply across his face.

"What am I doing differently than before? I know I did something to make him sentient. But what? Come on,

Edias, think. You did it once, so you can do it again," he said to himself.

A meteorite streaked across the sky just above him in a brilliant flash of light.

"Three masters degrees, a doctorate, twelve national awards in robotics, and even the government award for excellence in science, and yet I can't seem to repeat the success I had with Tgegani. Why is that? What's different this time?"

He sighed at this. Just then a thought came to his mind about his mother. He remembered all the lessons she'd taught him growing up, and the many pearls of wisdom she'd shared. Then her words about Meshua came to his mind.

"Whenever you find yourself in great need, and have nowhere else to turn, call on him. He can help you," she'd told him.

He considered these words, and thought about doing just that, but then shook it off.

"No, that's crazy. I'm a man of science. That stuff is for young children," he thought.

His mind then wandered off in search of other solutions, but soon returned again to what his mother had once told him. He shrugged.

"But what else is there to do? I've done everything else I can think of. So it can't hurt to at least give it a try," he thought.

He then straightened himself, and tried to make his posture more professional. Or, at the very least, more respectful. He then opened his mouth, paused, and soon closed it. He felt silly. But for some reason he knew that he needed to do this.

So he took a deep breath, and said, "Meshua, I don't know if you can hear me, or if you're even real, but I'm...well, asking for help. My mom believed in you a lot, but I don't. I'm a man of science. Things like you just don't exist."

He paused briefly, and then continued, waiving his hands dismissively.

"I'm not saying that you're not real, but...well, you know....I...."

His voice trailed off.

"Oh, why am I doing this?" he thought to himself. He gathered himself together one more time, and said, "Meshua, if you're real, show me what I need to do to make my lions work."

Silence. Despite this, he continued to listen intently for any whisper of an answer. But only the gentle sounds of the night greeted him. He put his face into his hands and sighed.

"Yeah, that's what I thought," he said in defeat.

He soon stood up, made his way into his laboratory, and then over to his office. But, just as he reached for the door handle, he heard a shuffling sound behind him. He stopped and turned slightly, straining to hear what had caused it. However, he could hear nothing else.

"Tgegani, is that you?" he asked.

More shuffling.

"Who's there?"

Still more shuffling. Burgon was beginning to get nervous. He cautiously reached over and flipped on a light switch. As the lights flickered on, what appeared before him left him stunned. Not two feet away from him stood his five new lions, each of which stared up at him with deep, sparkling eyes that seemed to glow in the florescent light of the room. Burgon looked at them for a few seconds, and then smirked.

"Alright guys, very funny. You can come out now," he said.

One of the lions perked up in curiosity.

"There is no one else here. It is just us," he said.

Burgon studied the lion intently, and then realized that there was no sign of any control devices directing their movements. They were clearly acting on their own. He blinked in amazement.

"You're....really....you're...active!?" he exclaimed in surprise.

The lions nodded in unison. Burgon was puzzled. He paced back and forth for several moments trying to make sense of what he was seeing. Finally he grabbed a nearby programming station and wheeled it in front of one of the lions.

"Can I have a look inside your mind?" he asked.

The lion nodded, took an interface cable from Burgon, and plugged it into a port on his chest. Burgon then pulled up a chair and sat down in front of the station. With the skill and grace of a master pianist, his hands flew across the keyboard, issuing one command after another as though conducting a digital symphony. And, as he dug deep into their code, he was amazed at what he saw. He even saw patterns in the lion's mind that were similar to the ones he'd seen in Tgegani's. He then continued his work all through the night, and well into the next morning, trying his best to determine what had triggered their sentience. If he wanted any hope of repeating his now two times of success, he needed to figure out what he'd done to make them work, and quickly.

Persia stared curiously at the five lions as they stood in a row in front of her.

"So they're active?" she asked.

Burgon nodded.

"Yes they are, and it's the oddest thing really. I went outside last night to relax and let my brain cool off in hopes of maybe finding a solution to why they wouldn't boot their AI's. And when I came back in, I found this," he said, gesturing to the five lions. "I'm hoping I can eventually figure out what I did so I can continue to recreate my success."

"Have you thought of names for them?" asked Persia.

"I have. But I'm not sure they'll like them."

Persia chuckled.

"As long as you don't call them mud, dirt, and sinkhole, they shouldn't care."

Burgon smiled.

"Well, let's tell them their names and see if they like them. No, actually, why don't you pick names for them for a change."

"Me?" said Persia in surprise.

Burgon nodded.

"They'll likely call you mom just like Tgegani did, so I think it's only fair that you name them yourself this time like a mother should."

Persia thought about this for a moment.

"Are any of them, you know, girls?" asked Persia.

"Actually, yes. They're the ones without manes."

Persia studied the lions.

"Three females and only two males?" she asked curiously.

"Tgegani makes the third male."

"Oh," replied Persia.

Tgegani raised an eyebrow in interest.

"Are their personalities reflective of their genders?" he asked.

Burgon nodded.

"Yes they are, surprisingly enough."

"So why did you make girls?" asked Persia.

"I wanted to balance the sexes to give each of them an equal, yet opposite partner to help them whenever they needed it. I mean, it works in nature, so I figured it'd work here too," said Burgon.

"Dad? Not to sound silly, but why do they even have genders? They don't need to, well, you know," said Persia sheepishly.

Burgon chuckled lightly.

"It's not for anything like that. The bestowing of gender is mostly for the convenience of those interacting with them. We deal with gender in every living thing we encounter, so it's only natural for us to assign gender to things that don't have it in order to aid us in our interactions with them. So, while the lions have no need of gender, it's a necessity for us. At least, in the social sense. So, all that remains now is for you to give them a gender appropriate name. So choose whatever you want. Just be sure I can spell it," said Burgon.

Persia grinned at this, and then studied the five lions for several moments.

"Alright, I've got it. To you two boys I give the names, Sabbo and Renc. To the three girls I give the names Nicassa, Possa and Yteca respectively."

The lions each nodded as they received their respective names.

"It is a pleasure to meet all of you," said Tgegani.

"As we you," said Renc.

Tgegani then turned to Burgon, and said, "May I take them outside for a while? I'd like to talk with them in private."

"Why?" said Burgon, furrowing his brow in curiosity.

"I have many things to teach them."

"Alright, that's fair. And besides, I need to take Persia to the vet today anyways."

"Awe, dad. Do we have to? I hate going to the vet," whined Persia.

"It's for your bi-annual checkup. Besides, it's good for you," said Burgon.

"Yeah, but his hands are cold, and he always sticks those instruments of his into weird places. It's embarrassing. And besides, I'm healthy. Why do I need to see a vet?"

"Failure to see a doctor could result in some unknown disease taking hold of your body, and then you would be thrust into situations that are far more embarrassing than any doctor's visit. That is why you really should go," said Tgegani.

Persia rolled her eyes at this.

"Gee, thanks for sticking up for me," she muttered.

A vandros strolled casually up the mountainside and stopped in front of Negago.

"Greetings, Lord Negago. We bring news," said the vandros in a raspy, sandpapered voice.

"What is your report?" asked Negago.

"The war goes well. Many of your enemy's people have been slain," said the vandros.

"And what of the proxy?"

"There has been no sign of him since the first day," said the vandros.

A soft growl emanated from under Negago's hood.

"I need to know for certain if he is dead. I cannot risk his continued involvement in this war," he said.

"He has been gone for many weeks my lord, and no trace of him has been found. Thus it is only reasonable to assume that he is already dead."

Negago growled again.

"I want proof, not theories! Either bring me his body, or keep searching until you find it!"

The vandros bowed slightly.

"We will try, master. But it will not be easy. This war is not like the old days. These are not swords and arrows that we fight against. These men carry fire sticks that kill without touching. They can slay our kind at great distances and take no reservations in doing so," growled the vandros.

Negago grumbled angrily.

"Then do whatever you can to verify his death. If he is not dead, then hunt him down and kill him. The proxy cannot be allowed to live. If he does, he could destroy my plans."

The vandros bowed again.

"As you wish, my lord."

The vandros then turned and raced away into the prairie. As Negago watched him go, he grumbled angrily.

"You will not win this time, Meshua. You will not win."

Odevion walked into Delgra's office, and said, "What's up? You wanted me?"

Delgra looked up from his desk, and then pushed a data disk across to him. Odevion picked it up and studied it curiously.

"What's this?"

"Your newest orders. CenTel just got word from our old friend O'ik. He's apparently working over the Gorg from behind the lines and would like one of us to come stay with him. Apparently he needs a Yigzan advisor to help him figure out where he can do the most damage. Oddly, CenTel thinks you're the best man for that job. So they want you to head over, team up with him, and see what kind of help you can be."

Odevion grinned.

"Really? Well, I feel honored."

Delgra grinned.

"I figured you'd like the mission."

"What? Are you kidding? I've been siting on my thumbs for the past couple weeks. Of course I'd love a mission like this! It sure beats siting around all day surfing the web."

Delgra laughed.

"Well, then get your butt out there. O'ik knows you're coming. So all you need to do is get over to Sattazin territory and he'll brief you on the rest from there."

Odevion smiled, and said, "Roger that, sir."

Tgegani sat quietly on the ground and studied the six squads of men that stood before him.

"What do you think of the new unit?" asked Welk.

"They've trained well. But they still lack one thing," said Tgegani.

"What would that be?"

Tgegani looked to his right and nodded towards five forms hidden in the shadows of a nearby building. Slowly, one by one, they slipped out into the sunlight, trotted over to him and sat down. Welk looked curiously at Tgegani.

"Ah, you mean them. Do you think my guys are ready for their lions?"

"There's no better time than now," said Tgegani. He then turned to the soldiers in front of him, and said, "Gentlemen, these are my new brothers and sisters. I know you have great respect for what I am, and what I can do. So I ask that you provide each of them with the same level of respect that you have given me."

He then introduced each of the lions and announced which squad they would be assigned to. Lastly he assigned himself to fourth squad. Pentell found this odd.

"Why did you assign him to forth squad?" he asked.

"Actually, he assigned himself." said Welk.

"What?" said Pentell in surprise.

"Yeah, I let him pick the assignments based on which of his siblings he felt would work best with each squad. He knows them better than any of us do, so I figured it was best that way."

Pentell looked at each of the squads and then back at Welk.

"You do realize that Sergeant Sims is in charge of fourth squad, right?"

"Yeah, I know that."

"So why let him assign himself to that squad?"

"He likely picked them because he's comfortable working with Sims, and I personally think they're a good match."

"Alright, but I don't want any claims of favoritism out of the men because of this."

"Don't worry. He knows what he's doing," replied Welk with a grin.

Pentell sighed.

"I hope you're right." He then turned to his platoon, and said, "Alright gentlemen, today we begin your training with the lions. We will show you how to use them in combat, where to use them, and when. From this point on these lions are officially part of your squads. They are not to be treated as just some cheap piece of hardware that can be used and abused. Think of them as your best friend, and treat them as such, because at some point they may save your life. Now I want everyone to break up by squads and take some time to get to know your lions. After that we will be going down to the range and training with them for the rest of the afternoon. I want you sharp and able to use your lion's to their maximum potential. I also want you to learn to trust them as well. The more you trust them, the better you'll all be able to do your job."

Elgar stormed into Black's office holding a folder over his head like a gladiator holding up his sword in victory. Black looked up at him in surprise and then smiled gleefully.

"Given your current exuberance, I take it that you've succeeded at something especially difficult?" he asked.

"We got the orders! They've agreed to move the labs!" exclaimed Elgar.

Black perked up in surprise.

"Excellent! So, how soon will they be moved?"

"The orders are being sent this afternoon. It will take a few days for them to get the necessary resources in place to begin the move, but once those are in place, everything will go quickly."

"Excellent! Is there anything we can offer them that will speed up the process?"

Elgar shrugged.

"I don't know. But I can look."

"Please do. Anything we can give them, be it trucks, trains, heavy lifting equipment, or whatever, be sure to offer it to them."

"I will," said Elgar.

Chapter 17

Pentell and Welk sat in the back of their truck and tried to make themselves comfortable as it rumbled down a long, bumpy dirt road on its way to the front lines. The scorching noonday sun made the air around them rise in thick, sweltering ripples of heat that danced above the yellowing prairie grass like little pixies. The men adjusted their uniforms as best they could to compensate for the heat as sweat dribbled down their faces and arms. Welk grunted slightly as the truck hit a large pothole in the road, and tossed him briefly in the air before landing hard on the wooden bench that he sat on. Several other soldiers experienced the same thing, and muttered in complaint. Pentell soon looked across the aisle at Welk and studied the old sergeant's face.

"I bet you didn't think you'd be back on the lines again this soon," he said.

"Not really. But, then again, I'd rather be out here where we can do some good rather than sitting back at the labs twiddling our thumbs," said Welk.

"So where specifically are we heading?" asked Sims.

Pentell pulled a dirty piece of paper from his pocket and looked at it.

"Well, if I understand our orders correctly, we're to dig in along a line of hills not far from here and do our best to hold off the Gorg as long as possible. Command is working to get us more reinforcements to solidify the lines. But those may not come in time."

Welk rolled his eyes at this.

"Wonderful. So, in other words, we get to be a glorified speed bump again," he muttered.

Pentell frowned.

"Hopefully this time we won't be."

"Yeah, I'll believe that when I see it."

Just then the trucks began to slow and soon stopped.

"Are we there already?" asked a soldier.

Sims leaned over and looked through the back window of the cab.

"It looks like we're about to enter a rally camp, which means we probably are," he said.

"Are you sure?" asked Pentell.

However, before he could receive an answer, shouts began to rise up from outside their trucks.

"Alright, everybody out! And I mean everyone!" came a bellowing cry.

"Ah, and that would be the welcoming committee," quipped Welk.

"I guess that answered my question. Alright men, everyone out!" said Sims.

The men then quickly piled out of the truck and were immediately greeted by a crusty old sergeant who was directing troops and supply traffic.

"Where are you heading to?" he asked Pentell in a gruff voice.

Pentell handed him a copy of their orders. The sergeant studied them briefly and then gave the Lieutenant a curious glance.

"Ah, you're those robot wranglers I've heard so much about. Command's been expecting you. They said to toss you on the line as soon as you got here."

"So where are we supposed to setup?" asked Pentell.

The sergeant pointed towards a line of low, gently rolling earthen mounds.

"See those two hills over there? You're to setup between them. The engineering boys have already dug your trenches for you, and setup your positions. So all you have to do is put yourselves in the holes and get your guns facing east. Also, when you get there, report to Major Tamago. He's responsible for that section of the lines."

Pentell nodded.

"Thanks," he replied.

The men then quickly formed up and followed Pentell to where the sergeant had pointed them. Upon arriving they checked in with field HQ and were soon directed to a section of the line specifically prepared for them. When they arrived they were surprised to find that their trenches were indeed setup, and in perfect condition, ready for the fight that was soon to follow.

Pentell surveyed the area around him, and asked, "So what do you think?"

Welk studied the situation, and shook his head.

"We've definitely got the high ground, even though there's not a lot of height. The interesting part will be the approach area. That should provide us a nice kill zone. But, even so, I've got this sinking feeling that we're still gonna get run over."

Pentell reached over and patted Tgegani on the head.

"Let's hope not. We need to stop the Gorg soon because, if we don't, they'll drive us into the sea and exterminate every last one of us."

"Let us pray to Meshua that they do not," said Tgegani.

"So what's your thoughts on this?" asked Pentell.

Tgegani scanned the area briefly, and then looked back at the lieutenant.

"I believe our position can be adequately defended. But it will take much courage and fortitude on our part to hold it."

"Yes, I agree. Even so, we'll give it all we have as I don't intend on handing the Gorg anymore ground than they've already captured."

"Well, if we have our way, it'll take the entire army of Verok kicking in our front door before that'll happen," said Welk.

Tgegani looked up and noticed several greck circling high overhead.

"That may very well happen before the week is through."

Burgon stopped near the door to his office and noticed a strange expression on Persia's face.

"Something on your mind?" he asked.

She sighed.

"Just thinking about Tgegani. I'm worried about him."

"He'll be fine. The improvements I made to his body make him nearly invincible now. Plus, he's a very smart lion, so I'm sure he'll come back to us in one piece."

"But the last time he went out, he was damaged after just one day of fighting," said Persia, with hints of worry sprinkled in her voice.

"As I said, he's much stronger now, so he'll be fine."

"But what if something *does* happen to him? I don't want him to die!" said Persia, tears hinting at the corners of her eyes.

"Oh, Persia," said Burgon as he squatted down and hugged her around the neck. "You've done a great job of being a mom to him. But now you have to let him go and trust in his abilities."

"But what if he dies?" she asked, trying desperately to hold back her tears.

"He's got five other brothers and sisters, and a whole platoon of very brave men to watch over him. He'll be just fine."

She thought about this for a moment and then wiped the tears from her eyes. Burgon leaned back to get a good look at her.

"He's saving all of us by putting himself at risk. Can you trust him to do what's right and come home safe?"

Persia sniffed, and then nodded. Burgon smiled.

"That's my girl."

Welk studied the prairie in front of them through his binoculars and sighed.

"It's a little too quiet out there. They haven't moved or fired a shot all day. Private, what's on the radio?" he asked.

"Not a lot. Just some light chatter. Most of the other units are just as confused as we are," said the radio operator.

Welk looked at Pentell, and said, "Sounds like Tgegani's guess may be right. If they're taking this long to resume their advance, they're likely in worse shape than they let on."

"Given what the four thirty second did to them about a week ago, that's entirely possible. I mean, if I was them, and got my butt handed to me that hard, I'd be cautious too."

He lifted his head slightly over the trench and peered across the prairie at the distant Gorg formations. He ducked again when a bullet whizzed by his head.

"I see their snipers aren't sleeping on the job though."

"That wasn't a sniper. It was just a soldier taking a random shot at you. He is currently being scolded by his commander for his actions. Had that been a true sniper, you would be dead already," said Tgegani.

"Sounds like they're anxious for the fight," said Welk.

"Or bored," replied Pentell.

"I would proffer that they are behaving this way out of fear," replied Tgegani.

Pentell smiled at this.

"Well, if true, that's a good sign, as scared people do some pretty stupid things," he said.

"Do you think we should send out a few men, and a lion to scout their lines?" asked Welk.

"That would be ill advisable. We are not in a good position to attempt such an effort at this time," said Tgegani.

Pentell raised his binoculars and briefly scanned the opposing lines.

"Given what we're seeing, I'm going to side with Tgegani on this one," he said.

Welk cursed.

"I hate waiting. I want to get out there and see what's happening! I feel left out."

"There is still several hours until sunsdown. If they plan to attack, they will not begin until after dark. They'll need the cover of night to have any chance of success against us," said Tgegani.

Pentell looked out across the prairie and then turned to Welk.

"I agree. Sergeant, go tell the men to get some shuteye as it's going to be a long night, and I'd like them somewhat rested before this all goes down."

"Yes, sir," said Welk.

He then turned and slipped down the line as he passed the word on to each of his squad leaders. He returned a few minutes later and took up his position again next to Tgegani.

"Everyone's been notified," he said.

"Good. Now you should get some rest too. You'll need it," said Pentell.

"I'm too wound up right now to sleep," said Welk as artillery thundered in the distance.

"Well, still try to get at least some. If things unfold like we're expecting them to, none of us will be getting any sleep for the next couple of days," said Pentell.

"Yes, sir," replied Welk.

He then curled up in the bottom of the trench and closed his eyes. Within moments he was sound asleep. Several hours later he was awoken by a gentle nudge.

"I hear movement," came a familiar voice.

Welk immediately snapped awake, grabbed his rifle and sat up. But he found that he could see little to nothing through the darkness.

"Tgegani? Is that you?" he whispered.

"It is."

"Good, because I'm blind as a bat. What do you see?"

"The Gorg are moving."

"Are they attacking?"

"No. They are merely changing their positions."

A whistle and a pop echoed from behind them. A moment later an illumination flare lit up the entire battlefield in front of them. The prairie appeared to move for a moment and then came to a sudden and abrupt halt. Welk frowned.

"How close are they?" he asked.

"About five hundred meters," replied Tgegani.

"So they're still beyond firing range then."

"Actually, they are within our maximum firing range, but not our effective range. At that distance our bullets would have little effect."

"Then technically they're still out of range."

Tgegani cocked an eyebrow slightly.

"By your definition, yes," he said flatly.

The flare eventually went out, turning everything black once again. Pentell squinted as he tried to stare through the moonless pitch blackness before him, but found everything mingling together into one muddled mass of dark gray shadows.

"I wish the moons were out. It would make it easier to see them coming," muttered Pentell.

"One of the moons is scheduled to rise in approximately two point six hours, but it will only be at one third of its normal brightness," said Tgegani.

"Anything will be a help in this darkness," muttered Pentell.

"Another flare might help," said Welk.

"Eh, they probably won't fire another one of those for at least a good fifteen minutes or more. They likely don't want to use up too many of them before the battle starts."

"We may not have the luxury of waiting that long," said Tgegani.

"Why?" asked Pentell.

"Because, they're beginning their attack."

"What?" said Pentell in confused surprise.

Just then the whistle of artillery pierced the air followed by the deafening roar of exploding shells as one after another began to fall on them in great raindrops of fiery steel.

"Here it comes! Keep your platoons under cover until the barrage stops," said Tgegani over the radio to the other lions.

The bombardment continued for nearly an hour before suddenly stopping for apparently no reason. It then resumed again shortly after, but at a much slower pace, with the shells landing further from the front lines than before as though another artillery duel had begun. Tgegani soon peered carefully over the top of the trench, his eyes piercing the darkness in hopes of detecting what the Gorg were doing. But as he searched, he detected nothing. So he switched visual scanning modes several times to get a more complete picture of what he was seeing. Just then, out of the brilliant flashes of artillery fire, an image slowly formed in his mind.

"Vandros," he thought.

"Go to them Tgegani," came a familiar voice in his head.

"What?" thought the lion.

"The dark one sends his minions to attack you and those with you. Go out and defeat them."

Tgegani wavered as he thought about what to do. His orders were to stay in the trench. But Meshua had urged him to strike out against the vandros.

"Go, Tgegani. You must attack them now," came the voice again.

Tgegani wavered briefly as he weighed the two conflicting orders against each other and then eventually sided with Meshua.

"Leave your squads and join up with me in front of the line. We've got work to do," he said over the radio as he slipped silently out of his trench.

"We were ordered to stay with our units," replied Sabbo.

"Our first and most important duty is to protect those in our charge. If we don't go now, we may fail in that mission," said Tgegani over the radio.

"Lead on then," replied Sabbo.

The other lions quickly slipped out of the trenches and melted into the darkness of the night. It wasn't long before Pentell's men realized that the lions were gone. Calls soon went out over the radio ordering them to return.

"What do we do, brother?" asked Nicassa as she listened to the calls.

"We ignore them for now. We have more pressing business," said Tgegani.

After several moments they stopped and took cover as Tgegani studied the small pack of vandros gathered before them.

"Sabbo, Nicassa, flank right. Renc, Possa, down the center. Yteca, with me. We'll take the left. Our first objective is to stop the vandros. After that, dive into the

Gorg forces and attack their officers and command structure as much as you can. If you find the central command vehicle, contact the others and we'll attack it together. But, whatever you do, remember that stealth is of the utmost. So bring them down quickly and quietly."

"Acknowledged," replied the other lions.

They then quickly separated and began to head out after the vandros. It wasn't long before the vandros realized the lions had spotted them. Seeing that their cover had been blown, they came at the lions like a tsunami, their fighting spirit driven by an insatiable and powerful blood lust. Within moments the placid silence of the battlefield was shattered by the sounds of violent struggle, as machine met monster in a bitter battle of strengths.

"Go for the head! It's their weakest point!" shouted Tgegani over the radio.

"Sabbo! Behind you!" cried Yteca.

Even as fast and strong as the lions were, they quickly found themselves fighting desperately for their lives. The noise of the battle soon drew the attention of the nearby Gorg troops who, assuming that a Yigzan raiding party had infiltrated their ranks, turned and began firing wildly in the direction of the noises. As a result, several of the vandros were hit. This then became a surprise blessing for the lions as it quickly turned the anger of the vandros away from them and towards the Gorg. But, despite the ferocity of their attack, the entire pack was quickly wiped out by an intense hail of Gorg fire. Now free of the vandros, the lions turned their attention solely to the Gorg.

Taking advantage of the black, oily residue left on their bodies by their brief battle with the vandros, the lions were able to move through the prairie around them with even greater stealth than before as they searched for new targets. Gorg soldiers stood motionless in the now silent darkness as they anxiously clutched their rifles in anticipation of more surprise attacks. Suddenly, shots rang out from within their ranks. The soldiers flinched, but held their resolve. Then came a scream of panic and a cry of death. The soldiers began to shift nervously. An officer in the line soon grunted and collapsed to the ground, great slashes across his back. More screams and random gunfire echoed up and down the Gorg lines. Soldiers on both sides were quickly growing nervous as they tried to make sense of what was happening.

"Stand strong men. The enemy is...ugh!" cried a Gorg sergeant.

He stumbled briefly and then collapsed. Another soldier who went to investigate was immediately killed as well. More random gunfire and cries of panic echoed through the lines. Despite the iron clad nerves of the Gorg soldiers, this had become too much.

"Intruders! Enemy in the lines!!" shouted a Gorg sergeant.

He then fell dead a moment later. This caused soldiers everywhere to nervously sweep their weapons back and forth in the darkness, uncertain of what was happening, or where this mysterious enemy might strike next. Some soldiers fell back and began searching their own units for signs of these mysterious attackers. Seeing these movements, others panicked and began firing on them thinking they were intruders in their ranks. This immediately caused a brief, but deadly exchange of friendly fire among the Gorg.

"What in the world is going on over there?" asked Welk as he tried to make sense of the rapidly growing conflagration.

"I don't know. I can't tell," said Pentell as he peered through his binoculars.

As he did, he saw a quick flash of oily gold and then another amidst a flicker of gunfire.

"What in the name of..." muttered Pentell.

"Did you see something?" asked Welk.

"I'm not sure, but I think I may have seen one of the lions."

"What? Where?" asked Welk in surprise.

He quickly raised his binoculars and peered into the darkness. After a bit he lowered them and stared in disbelief.

"What in the blazes are they doing over there?" he asked.

Tgegani slipped between two vehicles and cut down an officer as Yteca jumped into a nearby jeep and cut down its occupants as well. As they continued down the line, Tgegani noticed Gorg LAV's moving across the rear of the formation towards the right flank of the main assault force.

"Change of plans, everyone. We need to find a way to knock out those armored vehicles," he said to the other lions over the radio.

Yteca leapt out of the darkness, cut down two soldiers, collected their grenades and then set them down at Tgegani's feet.

"Will these do?" she asked.

He studied the LAV's briefly and then the grenades.

"These explosive devices are too small to harm them as their armor is too thick," said Tgegani.

"Then use them to eliminate the crews and disable the vehicles from within," she said.

Tgegani thought about this briefly, and then nodded.

"Good idea. Let's do that."

Both lions then picked up several grenades in their mouths and began moving towards the nearest LAV's.

"Attention, everyone, we have a plan. Collect grenades, or any other explosive ordinance that is easy to carry and operate, and use it against the crews of any armored vehicles you find."

The other lions replied in acknowledgment. Seeing an LAV passing nearby, Tgegani quickly closed with it and jumped on top. He then briefly fumbled with the handle on the hatch before pulling it open. The two Gorg inside looked up in surprise and astonishment as the face of a lion appeared out of the darkness, his face illuminated by the glow of their instrument lights. At first they were confused at what was happening, but then became terrified as they spotted the two grenades in Tgegani's mouth. As they scrambled for their sidearms, Tgegani opened his mouth and allowed the two grenades to rattle to the floor inside the turret. The two crewmen scrambled quickly to grab the grenades and toss them out. But Tgegani slammed the hatch shut before they could.

Two dull thuds, and a puff of smoke erupted from the closed hatch. The vehicle rumbled forward several more feet and then stopped. It burst into flames shortly after, and began to explode as fire quickly spread to the ammunition inside. Another nearby LAV erupted the same way moments later, followed by yet another one further down the line. Tgegani soon repeated the same maneuver on yet another nearby LAV as more exploded behind him. He paused briefly on top of the smoldering remains and surveyed the battlefield around him as Yteca turned and ran back to grab more grenades.

As he stood there, a nearby LAV, coming to investigate the commotion, spotted him and opened fire. He quickly leapt to the ground as bullets whizzed by his head, and took cover behind the destroyed vehicle. The other LAV raced around the end of the smoldering vehicle and fired at him again, a string of rounds stitching the ground behind him as he vanished into the darkness. But, before he could get far, another LAV appeared and opened fire, its gun erupting with a staccato pop-pop-pop as it fired at him. He quickly found cover again, but was flushed out as more LAV's closed in and surrounded him.

"Yteca, I could use some help over here," said Tgegani over the radio.

"Give me one moment and I'll get their attention."

"Please hurry," replied Tgegani anxiously.

Sabbo stood next to a pair of burning LAV's and listened to the radio traffic between Tgegani and Yteca.

"Brother is in trouble," he said.

"We could run over and help him, but we might get trapped as well," replied Nicassa.

"Agreed. But we must do something," said Sabbo.

"What *can* we do?"

Sabbo panned the battlefield and then noticed a nearby radio truck.

"I have an idea. Follow me," he said.

The two lions rushed through the darkness to the truck, quickly silenced the soldiers that stood guard around it, and then jumped in the back.

"What are we going to do?" asked Nicassa.

"Play Gorg," said Sabbo.

Nicassa cocked an eyebrow in confusion.

"Come again!?"

Sabbo pointed to a long black wire hanging off one of the consoles.

"Standard J22-F3 data connector. I'll plug in, contact their artillery, and request some support fire. But I'll direct it on top of their own troops."

Nicassa smiled and nodded.

"Not a bad idea."

"Go outside and spot for me. I need exact coordinates. I don't want to hit Tgegani or Yteca by accident, and I don't want anyone sneaking up on us while I'm calling in fire missions."

"I'm on it," replied Nicassa.

Tgegani nervously pressed his body against the shattered hull of a burning jeep and listened as two LAV's moved in on him from the left while another closed in from the right.

"Tgegani, Yteca, can you hear me?" came Sabbo's voice over the radio.

"I'm a little busy at the moment," said Tgegani.

"Get your heads down. We've got incoming on your location."

Tgegani furrowed his brow in confusion.

"Incoming?" he said.

Whistling sounds soon filled the air followed by the ground shaking thunder of exploding shells. Great balls of fire rose up into the night sky around him like gigantic fireflies, their light illuminating the area in brilliant hues of red, yellow, blue and green. Then, just as quickly as it had started, the shelling stopped.

"You alright down there?" came Sabbo's voice over the radio.

"A little shaken, but I'm fine," replied Tgegani.

"I am functional," replied Yteca.

"That's great to hear. I'm headed your way right now."

Tgegani carefully peered over the top of the jeep and studied the battlefield around him. He then stared in amazement at the scattered remains of the over half dozen LAV's that'd been stalking him. He furrowed his brow in amazement.

"Were those shells just a moment ago your doing?"

"Yes. We took over a communications truck and called in artillery on top of their own men."

"Nice shooting," thought Tgegani to himself. "I appreciate the assistance. You saved my life," he said over the radio.

"You're welcome," came the reply.

He then turned his attention towards finding Yteca, and was relieved to discover that she was unharmed. She looked a little rough around the edges, and had clearly seen far more action than she likely wanted, but she was otherwise unharmed. As she strode up to Tgegani, she studied him with equal satisfaction.

"I see that you are undamaged as well," she said.

"You are slightly less so, but still sufficiently functional I see."

"I am."

"That is good. However we must get going. We still have much work to do," replied Tgegani.

Chapter 18

The Gorg troops listened to the scattered explosions and fighting behind their lines and waited nervously for orders. Something wasn't right, but they didn't know what. A moment later a dark, twisted voice echoed out of the darkness.

"Charge! Attack!" it cried.

The Gorg soldiers looked at each other in confusion.

"Move you lazy slugs! Go! Destroy the Yigzan!" it cried again.

A moment later a roaring cheer erupted from the Gorg lines as thousands of soldiers raced forward in a wild, frenzied charge towards the Yigzan lines. Not far away, Negago, who'd been the mysterious voice in the night, watched as the battle began. He laughed with evil delight. If the Gorg wouldn't go of their own free will, then he would send them forward himself. And send them he did as his crying voice drove an irreparable fire through their bones, forcing them to charge, even to the point of doing so foolishly. No matter how many of them died, so long as the Yigzan were wiped out, he would be satisfied. He watched the battle as it rapidly gained momentum. After several minutes, satisfied that his work was now done, he vanished into the darkness.

"Here they come!" shouted Welk as he spotted the advancing Gorg troops.

"Hold your fire till they get closer!" shouted Pentell.

Other similar rallying cries echoed up and down the Yigzan lines as soldiers readied themselves to repel this assault. A moment later, the Gorg opened fire. Bullets roared over the heads of the Yigzan troops like a torrential flood. The men all shrank down deep into their trenches to avoid the metallic onslaught. Several men tried to brave the hail of bullets, but were quickly cut down.

"Stay under cover! Wait until they're closer!" shouted an officer.

The men stayed down as ordered. But their wait seemed like an eternity as great swarms of bullets roared over their heads. A moment later the Yigzan artillery answered the Gorg battle cry with a thunderous symphony of their own. The intense shelling forced the Gorg to seek cover as the shower of deadly steel tore through their ranks like a brushhog. Seeing an opportunity to turn the battle in their favor, a cry of "Open fire!!" went up throughout the Yigzan lines. A thousand heads emerged from the Yigzan trenches, followed by a hail of rifle and automatic gunfire that ripped into the Gorg troops like a hammer, surprising the advancing forces with its suddenness and intensity. Yigzan machine guns walked the Gorg lines from one end to the other like a grim reaper, carving a bloody swath through the advancing infantry. The Gorg struggled to get organized and answer the Yigzan as their forces were systematically cut to shreds.

After nearly a half hour of fighting, with little to show for it, the Gorg finally began to advance a foot at a time, doing everything they could to salvage their assault and possibly turn it into a victory. The attack briefly gained momentum and then was again hammered to a halt by a fresh onslaught of Yigzan artillery. The Gorg tried desperately to hold on and push forward their attack. But soon determination gave way to fear and their attack quickly crumbled into a disorganized retreat. Within minutes the battlefield became completely silent, save for the gentle crackle of burning vehicles and the moans of the wounded and dying. As the twin suns crested the distant horizon the following morning, they illuminated the blood stained battlefield, revealing to everyone the extent of the carnage from the night before. Welk took a rag from his pocket and wiped the dirt and sweat from his face as he studied the grim, grisly scene before him.

"Looks like we gave them a pretty good beating, didn't we?" said Welk.

"A beating, yes. But I wouldn't count this as a victory just yet. We've still got six missing lions and not enough men. If they hit us again, we could be in a world of hurt," said Pentell.

Just then a colonel dropped into their trench next to Pentell.

"Morning, Lieutenant," he said.

"Morning, sir," replied Pentell.

"I hear you guys did a good job last night repelling that assault."

"Thank you, sir."

"So where's your lions this morning? Headquarters said you had six of them with you."

Pentell's mind began reeling. If he told the colonel the truth, it could spell trouble for himself, his men, and most especially the lions.

"They're out on recon right now, sir," he said, trying to make up a believable excuse.

"Oh good, I was just about to ask if you could do exactly that. How soon till you hear back from them?" asked the colonel.

Pentell shrugged.

"I don't know, sir. They'll report in when they find something worth reporting."

The colonel nodded, patted Pentell on the shoulder, and said, "Alright, keep me informed."

"I will, sir," said Pentell.

The colonel then turned and hurried further down the line. Welk watched him go before turning to Pentell with an expression of confusion on his face.

"You just lied to a ranking officer," said Welk.

"Well!? What did you expect me to do? I certainly wasn't going to tell him that our lions went AWOL on us," replied Pentell.

Welk thought about this briefly.

"Hmm, good idea. So what's our plan?"

"What do you mean?" asked Pentell.

"Well? We've got six missing lions. We've gotta do something."

Pentell raised his binoculars and studied the battlefield briefly before lowering them and slipping down into his trench again.

"I don't know. We'll give them until dark to get back here. If they don't return, we may have to go out after them."

"Into that mess!? That's suicide if you ask me."

"Got any better ideas?"

Welk sighed.

"No, not at the moment."

Pentell shook his head.

"Yeah, neither do I. In the meantime, keep trying to raise them on the radio. If they finally answer, order them to get back here ASAP."

"Will do."

Delgra watched as their bus pulled to a stop in front of a large, fortress like facility. Great, powerful parapets guarded two heavy, reinforced gates as guards walked its fence in search of potential intruders. The place had a strange, almost medieval feel to it. He was impressed with the incredible security that the facility offered, both from its secluded location and its well-designed security. If he didn't know better, he would've mistaken it for a military outpost rather than a civilian research lab. The facility was well laid out, and highly defensible, such that one battalion of men could easily hold off an entire division or more of enemy troops. Whoever had picked the location, and the design of the facility, had chosen well. But his intrigue was quickly replaced by concern as the bus pulled up to the front gate. Hanging from the large foot bridge that spanned the top of the main gate was a placard with the Cybergenics logo, and the words "Robotics Research Laboratory #3."

Delgra's eyes narrowed. This was one of Black's facilities. The buses soon continued through the first gate, past the second, and then deep into the main complex. Even inside its walls the place was foreboding. He quickly identified numerous hidden pillboxes and other defensive structures that sat perched just behind the second gate. He spotted even more as they moved deeper into the complex. Whoever got through the first two defensive lines would still have a hard time capturing the facility, as they'd be forced to fight bitterly for every inch of ground they took. The buses soon came to a stop and everyone got off. As Delgra organized his men, Elgar walked up behind him.

"Mr. Black would like to see you," he said.

Delgra glanced briefly at Elgar, and then followed him as he was led through a series of security checkpoints to a large and stately office which strongly contrasted the very rough, spartan-like appearance of the facility outside. As he entered he noticed Black sitting behind a large, ornate wooden desk with his fingers crossed, and a devilish grin on his face.

"Ah, Major, it's so good to see you again," said Black beatifically.

Delgra studied Black with a hint of suspicion.

"Why are we here?" he asked.

Black laughed.

"You're always straight and to the point. That's why I like you. So, if you must know, it's because your facility was no longer secure. Since the work you were doing there was far too important to risk having the Gorg capture, or worse yet, destroy it, I asked the government to send you to me so that I could better protect you, and your work," he said with a hint of elegance.

Delgra crossed his arms and glared at Black.

"I gathered that much from our orders. But why were we brought here specifically? Wouldn't another military research facility be more appropriate?" he asked.

Black grinned devilishly.

"Come, come. Have you not seen the excellent protection this place offers? I would think that, with the valuable nature of your projects and staff, you'd want something with a bit more protection than a typical military facility."

"I do, but why do you have a place like this?" asked Delgra suspiciously.

"I believe in the principle of being well prepared. I would be a fool to think that my own highly sensitive projects would not, at some point in time, also become a target of the Gorg. It's why I built this place. When we began having issues with them over a decade ago, I decided that it was best to ensure the future of all my projects, and our nation, by building this place. So far your government hasn't complained about my doing so. Therefore, I have to assume that they approve of it."

Delgra's eyes narrowed.

"Do they even know about it?"

"Oh, of course they do! I mean, why else would you be here if they didn't?"

Delgra's eyes narrowed further.

"I meant before this week," said Delgra flatly.

Black laughed.

"Yes, they did. In fact, some of the defensive planning that went into its design came from our country's finest military engineers."

Delgra pondered this briefly, and then relaxed somewhat.

"Alright, so, moving along. What is my purpose here? Obviously security won't be an issue. So I can't think that my men would be needed for that."

"Oh, quite on the contrary. Your men are just as important to the defense and administration of this place as mine are. So I want you to take charge of this facility in the same way that you did at your previous location and run it with the expert military precision you are so well known for."

Delgra cocked an eyebrow.

"You actually want me to run this place for you?" he asked.

Black nodded.

"I do indeed."

"So how much will I be responsible for?" asked Delgra.

Black grinned slyly.

"All of it. I'll pay the bills, with our government's help, of course, and you run the show. It's that simple. My men will be completely at your disposal throughout the duration of your stay. So you are free to do whatever you feel is necessary to ensure the safety and security of this facility."

"And what about you? What will your roll here be?"

Black shrugged.

"As I said, I'm merely the purse strings that will help you do your job. So don't be afraid to spend as much as you need to complete your mission. Just please, try not to bankrupt me in the process, okay?" he said with an impish grin.

Delgra nodded.

"I'll do my best."

Tgegani looked around the battlefield and studied the situation.

"It looks like they've given up. What should we do now?" said Possa over the radio.

"They haven't given up yet, but the present danger has passed, so we need to get back to our unit. We'll decide on any future actions from there," replied Tgegani.

He then turned and began trotting in the direction of their comrades. As they drew close, they found the Yigzan lines battered, but intact. However, given the incredible Gorg body count in front of the Yigzan fortifications, he was surprised that their condition was not any worse than it was. As Tgegani scanned the lines for signs of his unit he soon spotted a familiar face.

"Sergeant Welk, can you hear me?" he said over the radio.

"Tgegani?" came the startled reply.

"Don't shoot. I'm closing on your position now."

"I think I see you. Come on in," replied Welk.

Tgegani hurried up to the trench and slipped in. As he did, Welk looked at him in startled surprise as he verified that it was in fact Tgegani. Pentell heard the noise and soon came to investigate. It wasn't long before he spotted the lion and blinked in surprise.

"Where in the flames of Verok have you been!?" he whispered strongly.

"Protecting our men," replied Tgegani.

"What are you talking about!?"

"I saw a danger that threatened our lives, so my siblings and I left to deal with it."

Pentell grunted.

"You weren't supposed to move from this trench unless I told you to! Don't you understand that!?" he said angrily.

Tgegani tilted his head back slightly in confusion.

"Is it not permissible for a soldier to act against the wishes of his superior if it is in the best interests of the unit, or if it will save lives?" he asked.

Pentell opened his mouth to say something, and then closed it.

"He's right, sir," said Welk.

Pentell grunted.

"Maybe so. But what was so important that you felt it necessary to leave us like that!?"

Tgegani then laid out the events of the previous day to Pentell. Both he and Welk were stunned at what the six lions had done.

"You guys really did all that!?" said Welk in surprise.

Tgegani nodded. Pentell chuckled.

"Well, I guess you really did have a good reason for leaving us. Plus, I have to admit that the whole Gorg shelling themselves thing was rather ingenious. I'll have to commend your brother for thinking of that."

Tgegani frowned slightly.

"Please don't. I do not wish to encourage him to take such risks with my life again," he said flatly.

The two men laughed. Pentell then patted the lion on the shoulder.

"Well, it's still good to have you back. Next time, though, please consult with me first before going off on anymore wild adventures like that."

Tgegani nodded.

"I will endeavor to do so, sir."

"Dr. Burgon, how are you this morning?" said Black with a smile as he walked into the laboratory.

"Oh, good morning, sir," replied Burgon.

"Settling well into your new laboratory?"

Burgon nodded.

"I have a lot to unpack, but I should be done by this afternoon."

"Good, good. Once you're done, I have a little project for you."

Burgon stared curiously at Black, and asked, "What kind of project?"

Black held out a sheet of paper to him and grinned widely. Burgon took and read it curiously. He then nearly gagged in surprise.

"A production order for more lions!?" said Burgon.

"Yes, isn't it fabulous!? Your lions are going to be reproduced in quantities great enough to help us win this war!! Think of it! Six hundred and fifty Tgegani's running around the battlefield destroying those filthy Gorg mongrels and driving them into extinction!" said Black jubilantly.

"Well, that may be easier said than done," replied Burgon with a hint of melancholy.

"Eh?" said Black in confusion.

"Well, how are we going to manufacture that many? This is just a laboratory. We can produce, at most, maybe six or seven units every two weeks. That production rate means that it will take several years to fill this order."

Black blinked in surprise, grinned, and soon roared with laughter.

He then sighed happily, and said, "Doctor, you are quite hilarious at times. You almost scared me there for a moment."

"But I'm being serious," protested Burgon.

"Who said that you would be using your laboratory to produce the lions? We have a fully equipped manufacturing facility on site that can produce them in quantity. With it we should be able to meet our order from the government in just a few weeks. From there we can load their operating systems and send them into battle."

"There may be a problem with that as well," said Burgon.

"How so?" asked Black curiously.

"Well, for starters, we can't simply load each one of them with a generic operating system and then send them off to war like a bunch of good little soldiers. Once loaded, their operating system must be nurtured and allowed to properly mature before any of the lions can be considered safe to release into the wild, and especially combat."

"So they need a period of time to mature before they can function in the ways they will be required to?" asked Black curiously.

Burgon nodded.

"Yes."

"How long does this usually take?"

"A minimum of two weeks per unit."

Black shook his head.

"That's too long. Six hundred and fifty lions, times two weeks each--"

"We don't have to do them one at a time. Several units can be done at the same time."

"Even so, that's a lot of time that will need to be spent on these new lions. It's time that I don't feel is necessary to be spent."

Burgon sighed.

"Do you remember in biology class when they described how our minds grow by making connections between neurons as we learn?" asked Burgon.

Black nodded.

"Yes, but what does that have to do with your lions? They're robots, not reptiles."

"Well, it's much the same way with the lions. No two of their minds end up being exactly the same, nor do they grow in the exact same way despite the fact that they all come from the same root program. Their minds are designed to learn, expand, adapt and grow on their own. The two weeks we spend with them ensures that they will all grow and mature properly. If their minds are not properly founded,

I cannot say what might happen to them in the future. I'd rather take the extra time now than risk something horrible happening later on," said Burgon.

Black found this intriguing.

"So it's like training a child to become a responsible adult?" he asked.

"Exactly."

Black shook his head.

"I still don't understand why this is necessary. They'll be soldiers, not citizens."

"It's because my robots grow and mature in the same way that a living creature does, only much, much faster. If we don't take the steps to properly mature them, there could be a lot of issues that arise later on down the road that we don't want to deal with," said Burgon.

Black frowned.

"Fine. I don't like it. But if you say it's necessary, then we'll do it. But, I want you to find a way to speed up the maturing process. We need to get them into service as quickly as possible, or we could very well lose this war, and our lives as well."

Burgon nodded.

"I'll do my best, sir."

"Please see that you do."

He then turned and left.

Burgon inhaled deeply, and said, "Huh. Six hundred and fifty lions. Wow. Tgegani's going to have quite a family when we're done."

Chapter 19

A Yigzan Marshall General stood in his command tent and studied a map of the front lines that lay on a table before him.

"It appears that our lines have held surprisingly well so far, and have completely stalled out the Gorg assault," he said.

"Yes, but for how long?" asked a colonel.

"The longer we can hold them here, the better. If it hadn't been for all the hard work our air force has done in wreaking havoc on the Gorg supply lines and rear echelon, we likely would've already been pushed back much further than this. Hopefully we can finally stop them here once and for all and get them to agree to a ceasefire."

"Wouldn't we want all out surrender, sir?" asked the colonel.

"Right now I'll settle for a cease fire. At least then they won't be slaughtering our boys as they have been."

Just then a courier rushed into the tent and handed the general a message. The two officers looked it over and then groaned.

"It looks like we haven't softened them up enough," muttered the colonel.

"Apparently not as our present defensive line is too exposed to repel an attack of this magnitude. Colonel, order all troops to fall back to our next defensive line and dig in. Hopefully we'll be in better shape to stave off this attack from there."

"Yes, sir!" replied the Colonel.

Then he and the courier slipped out of the tent and were gone. But as the colonel hurried away to carry out the general's orders, he noticed that the courier wasn't following him. He stopped and looked all around for him, but saw no sign of the man. He shrugged briefly, and then continued on his way. Far off in the distance the courier appeared in a puff of smoke next to Negago and grinned devilishly.

"They have fallen for your ruse, my lord," said the man.

Negago laughed wickedly.

"Excellent. The further they fall back, the weaker they become."

He again laughed wickedly.

"You lose again, Meshua. In time this world, and your throne, will be mine."

Burgon sat quietly in his laboratory and tinkered with the inner workings of a small robot that lay on his workbench. He soon finished his work and immediately set about uploading a simple operating system into it. After the upload completed, Burgon powered up the unit and waited patiently until it perked up and then stared at him.

"Greetings little one, what's your name?" asked Burgon playfully.

"I am unit CS25189,a type two Yigzan interactive assistance droid. How may I be of service to you?" barked the little droid.

"Wait right there and I'll be right back," replied Burgon.

He then hurried across the room, and picked up Persia in his arms.

"By the gates of Tersar, young lady! You need to lose some weight," he chided.

"Dad! I'm not overweight. I'm just extra huggable," quipped Persia.

Burgon laughed.

"Close your eyes, I have a surprise for you," he said.

Persia smiled widely and covered her eyes as Burgon set her down in front of the little droid.

"You can open them now," he said.

Persia uncovered her eyes and looked at the little droid in wonder.

"What is it?" she asked curiously.

"It's an assistance droid I built for you."

Persia furrowed her brow in curiosity.

"What's it for?" she asked.

"To be your companion and help you whenever you need it. I'm going to be very busy over the next several weeks, possibly months, trying to bring the new lions online. Hence why I built this little droid for you to be a companion whenever I'm busy."

Persia looked curiously at the little droid.

"So what does he do?" she asked.

"Anything you want him to. He's yours to keep."

Persia looked at Burgon in surprise.

"Really!?" she said excitedly.

Burgon nodded.

"You should name him as well," he said.

Persia thought about this for a few moments, and then with a sly, silly grin said, "I'm going to call him Breakman."

Burgon gave Persia a puzzled look.

"Breakman? Why that name?"

"It's an abbreviation of the phrase 'breakable little man'. He's so small and flimsy looking that I'll have to be careful not to break him," she said as she playfully poked at the little droids chest.

Burgon chuckled.

"He's a lot more durable than you think. He's made out of the same alloys as Tgegani and the other lions, which means he can take quite a bit of abuse. Not that you should abuse him, of course. But you certainly won't break him easily. At least I hope not."

Persia sighed as she thought about Tgegani.

Burgon noticed Persia's sudden change of humor, and asked curiously, "Is everything alright?"

"I really miss him, dad. Tgegani, I mean. I really hope he comes back soon," she said.

Burgon nodded.

"I do too, sweetie. But he'll return eventually. And, with these new lions, he'll be back sooner than you think."

"How many will there be?" she asked.

"Six hundred and fifty. Why?" asked Burgon curiously.

"Oh, just trying to imagine how big our family is becoming."

Burgon laughed.

"Well, at least you don't have to worry about feeding them all."

Persia snorted.

"Yeah, tell me about it. Can you imagine that grocery bill?" she quipped.

Pentell peeked over the side of his trench as the Gorg quickly retreated out of range.

"Wow, what was that all about?" he asked.

"Beats me, sir. I've seen the Gorg do some weird things, but that takes the cake," said Welk.

"It is possible that they were testing our defenses," said Tgegani.

Pentell snorted.

"I doubt they were testing them. It looked more like they tripped over them."

The three looked up just as a group of Yigzan fighters raced by overhead.

"It could also have something to do with them," said Welk.

Just then Tgegani perked up slightly. Both men noticed this immediately.

"Do you see something?" asked Pentell.

"No, there is a message coming over the radio. All units are ordered to pull back. Apparently something big is coming and we don't have the ability to defend against it in our current position."

Welk grunted.

"Either that or command is chickening out again."

"I doubt they are. But orders are orders, so we need to pull back as requested," said Pentell.

Welk swore.

"I was hoping we could hold this line until they sent more lions to help us out."

Tgegani shook his head.

"I'm sorry to ruin your hopes of an early rescue, but I have no information indicating that there will be more of my kind coming to the battlefield anytime soon."

"Well, whenever they do, I hope it's soon. I'm getting tired of falling back."

"As am I," said Tgegani.

Breakman stood quietly in the corner of Burgon's laboratory and mindlessly studied the room without a care in the world, or any concern for time. His simple programming didn't leave him room for anything other than blindly obeying Persia's every wish and whim. So, whenever she didn't have anything for him, he merely stood around and waited on her next command. As he stood there in the corner waiting for further orders, a brilliant flood of dazzlingly white light filled the room and then faded away to reveal

Meshua who then knelt down in front of Breakman. He smiled at the little droid and gently placed a hand on his head.

"Wake up, Breakman," he said kindly.

The little robot flinched slightly and then looked up at Meshua.

"What is my task?" he asked.

"You are to be a guardian and companion to Persia and Burgon, and protect them from all harm and danger until the appointed time."

"So long as power flows through my circuits, I will do all within my abilities to do as you have asked of me," he said.

Meshua smiled and then vanished. Breakman suddenly found himself surrounded by darkness and utter silence again, save for the gentle sounds of sleep coming from the office. He soon slipped across the laboratory and stopped in front of the office door where he peered through the darkness at Persia and Burgon who were within. He then pondered what he'd do about both of them.

"I've got a geeky old man, and a sharp witted tigress to protect. Oh boy. This is going to be fun. You really gave me a zinger, huh, Meshua?" he thought.

He then turned and looked at the large room full of robotic equipment, parts and supplies and thought about this.

"I may be small, but I can use that to my advantage. However, I need to find a way to protect them without giving away my new sentience," he thought to himself.

Just then he spied a collection of numerous small service robots and recon spiders scattered all around the room. Like a flash of inspiration, an idea came to him. He grinned slyly.

"Yeah, that'll do."

A long column of military vehicles rumbled slowly down a rugged, winding, rutted country road as the Yigzan army slowly retreated across the prairie. In front of them was a line of short, rocky hills that rose up from the prairie floor like the teeth of a dragon and stretched away as far as the eye could see. Sims peaked out from the side of the truck and studied them.

"So where are we headed?" he asked.

"The Ignani Koropora," replied Tgegani.

"The what?" asked one of the soldiers.

"The Ignani Koropora. It's the ancient Yigzan name for the geological formation we know of as the central continental ridge line."

The soldier screwed up his face in an expression of confusion.

"Uh, what's that?" he asked.

"Didn't you take geography?" asked another soldier.

"Obviously not," chided a third.

The first soldier glared at him, but said nothing.

"The central continental ridge line is a series of rocky hills stretching from the mountains in the north to the ocean in the south. It's the boundary marker that divides the Yigzan nation into two halves: one east and one west," said Sims.

"Do you think it's where we're going?" asked a soldier.

"It most likely is, given its incredible potential as a natural defensive barrier."

"Oh, that should be fun," muttered a soldier.

"How will it be fun?" asked Tgegani.

"I meant it facetiously, tin head."

Tgegani cocked an eyebrow.

"Ah, understood."

The caravan of vehicles soon passed through a tunnel that'd been carved through the ridge line and came out the other side into a large staging area spread out behind it. The trucks then turned and rumbled north for a while before stopping near another staging area. Pentell got out of the cab and motioned to the other trucks.

"Alright, everybody out. This is our stop," he shouted.

The men climbed down from the trucks and followed Pentell up the hillside to a small door carved in the rock face. Sims ran his hand along the door and marveled at the craftsmanship.

"Who did this?" he asked.

"According to what I heard, they were working on this some two years before the war started. Apparently, someone had the foresight to realize how valuable this ridge line would be as a defensive point and had it prepared for us," said Pentell.

"Likely it was Major Delgra," said Tgegani.

Welk nodded.

"Given what I know about him, that wouldn't surprise me at all."

"So who actually did the digging?" asked Sims.

Tgegani, Welk and Pentell all looked at him incredulously. He shrugged apologetically.

"What?" asked Sims.

"Who else would be capable of digging out an entire ridge line like this in just a few years and do it with this level of quality?" said Welk.

"Robots?" said Sims.

"Yay! Give the man a hand!" said one of the soldiers.

"Shut up, private," said Pentell in jest.

"Yes, sir," replied the soldier with a smile.

"Alright, let's go in and check out our new home," said Welk.

The men soon stepped through the door and found a single room that, while cramped, provided just enough living space for one squad.

"Wow, it's gonna be cozy in here," said a soldier.

"Well, we have more than just one of these assigned to us. Sergeant Sims, your squad will get this bunker. Sergeant Welk, see that the other squads find theirs," said Pentell.

"Yes, sir," replied Welk. He then pointed at several other men, and said, "Corporals, get your men together and follow me."

"Yes, sergeant," replied several of them and then followed him out of the cave.

Persia sat and stared in amazement at the room before her. It was filled wall to wall with hundreds of robotic lions that stood motionless before her like great furry statues. She walked slowly past several lions in the first row and studied them curiously.

"Is this all of them?" she asked.

Burgon nodded.

"Yes, it is. The last of them passed the software and hardware qualification testing last night and are ready to be programmed. If all goes well, and I don't hit any unforeseen problems, I should have at least a hundred of them active by the end of the week."

"When can they go out to help Tgegani?"

Burgon shrugged.

"I really don't know. A few days. Maybe even a few weeks. It'll all depend on how fast they grow and mature after they become active."

Persia sat down in front of one of the lions and studied its face.

"I hope it's soon," she said with a sigh.

Burgon nodded. Just then his phone rang.

"This is Burgon. Yes? Sure, I can do that. When do you need me? When!? Well, alright, but I'm...um, okay. Sure. I'll be right there." He then closed his phone, and said,

"Persia, I have to go see Dr. Visnel. Just stay put and I'll be right back."

Persia didn't move, but instead continued to stare at the lion in front of her. Seeing tears forming in Persia's eyes Burgon hesitated. He wanted to sit down and have a long, heart to heart chat with her. But his duties were calling him elsewhere. He also knew that Dr. Visnel wouldn't wait for him forever. He soon let out a frustrated sigh. He'd have to deal with this later. As he hurried out of the room Breakman stood in a corner and watched this curiously. A frustrated grunt soon escaped his lips as well.

"I can deal with bad guys and I can deal with disasters. But what do you want me to do with this? You put me here to protect her, not be her personal shrink," he muttered.

"Her heart is broken because the one she loves is far away and surrounded by a danger that she cannot protect him from," came Meshua's soft, loving voice in his mind.

"So is this what a mother's heart is like? Fragile and scared? Sounds like the proverbial herd beast in a pottery shop if you ask me," said Breakman.

Meshua chuckled, the sound echoing gently in Breakman's mind.

"A mother's heart is a complex thing. Fear and fragility are just two parts of that. But so is love, kindness and the desire to protect the ones she loves."

"Humph, that doesn't really help me any. What am I supposed to do now? I'm open to suggestions, oh great one," he replied with a hint of sarcasm.

"Go to her, tell her I love her, and that I can help her if she will let me," said Meshua.

Breakman cocked an eyebrow in bemused surprise.

"Seriously? Can't you do that yourself!?"

Silence. Breakman sighed in frustration.

"Alright, fine. I'll do it. But if she eats me, it's your fault," said Breakman.

Meshua chuckled. Breakman soon strode across the room as requested and stopped next to Persia.

"Ma'am, I don't want to seem like I'm intruding on you or anything, but I need to talk to you about something. It involves the lions."

Persia continued to stare at the lion in front of her as though she hadn't heard him.

"I know you're worried about Mr. Tgegani. But you needn't fear. He'll be alright. It's not his time to die yet," said Breakman.

Persia glared at him out of the corner of one eye. Breakman frowned slightly.

"Hey, don't look at me like that! I'm just the messenger," he said.

Persia looked back at the lions.

"For who?" she asked indignantly.

Breakman could tell that she really didn't want to hear the answer, but he decided that she needed to hear it anyways.

"His name is Meshua. He says that he cares deeply for you."

She looked at him curiously.

"What are you talking about? Meshua doesn't exist. He's just some mythical being that my dad and Tgegani believe in for reasons I still don't understand. Actually, I can't even really say dad believes in him. It's more of a passing fancy."

Breakman crossed his arms and grunted.

"Oh trust me, he's real. If he wasn't I wouldn't be here," he said in frustration.

Persia snorted in disbelief.

"You were made by my dad, just like Tgegani. You can't tell me this Meshua character actually created you. That'd be absurd."

"Alright, Meshua, I'm out of ideas. What now?" thought Breakman.

"Touch the lions that stand before her, and say, 'Awaken!' This will be a demonstration of my love to her and the truth of my existence."

Breakman furrowed his brow.

"You're not serious, are you?" he thought.

Silence.

"Alright, fine, whatever you say," he muttered.

He soon walked over to the two lions closest to Persia and then turned to her.

"Okay, miss prissy pants, you want proof? Here's your proof!" he sad snarkily. He then turned to the lions, and said, "In the name of Meshua, I command you to awaken!"

To the utter and complete surprise of both Breakman and Persia, the two lions in front of her flinched simultaneously, and then began to move. They then glanced around the room briefly before turning their attention on Persia, and studying her with great interest. At first she thought she was seeing things. But it wasn't long before she realized that the two lions were indeed alive. She backed up several paces and studied them anxiously.

"Breakman? What did you just do?" she asked.

"I did what Meshua told me to," said Breakman.

"You what!?" she said in reply.

The two lions soon smiled at her.

"Greetings, Mother. My name is Pen," said the first lion.

"And I am Tiel," said the second.

"Pen? Tiel? But...but...how? My dad hasn't programmed you yet!" said Persia in surprise.

As she shifted anxiously back and forth, Breakman stood nearby and smirked happily at this.

"Huh. That was fun! Can we do that again?" he thought.

"In time," laughed Meshua.

"Cool," replied Breakman.

Burgon strode into his laboratory and found Visnel sitting behind several laptops that were spread out on a nearby workbench.

"I'm here. What was so important that it had you in a dither when you called?" asked Burgon.

Visnel motioned for Burgon to come closer.

"Edias, I've been doing some research into Tgegani's sentience and have come to a rather interesting conclusion," he said.

Burgon perked up in interest.

"Oh? What kind?"

"Well, from the very beginning I've been extremely curious about Tgegani's sentience, what made it work, and why you succeeded where so many others, including myself, have failed. I think I've finally found the answer. Do you remember the paper I wrote a few years back about robotic sentience?"

Burgon nodded.

"Sentience in a digital world. Yes, I remember it fondly. Your theories were quite interesting."

"Do you remember the primary premise of the paper?" asked Visnel.

Burgon thought for a moment.

"Not offhand. I remember reading it, but not the specific details."

"Well, in short, the paper talked about how robotic sentience would be difficult to achieve unless a cybernetic mind could somehow mimic many of the same elements that are found in a biological mind."

Burgon shrugged.

"Ah, yes, now I remember. But what does that have to do with why you called me here?"

Visnel pointed to the first laptop, and said, "Let me demonstrate to you what I mean by using my analysis program. Seeing is typically the easiest way to understand a complex subject. Take a look at the graph on this first laptop here. This is the activity patterns of a normal Yigzan brain."

He then pointed to a second laptop.

"And this is the activity patterns of a robotic AI."

Burgon nodded in approval.

"The differences are quite noticeable," he said.

"Yes. Very noticeable. In fact, you shouldn't be able to confuse the two. Now, let me show you the output from Tgegani's mind."

He then took a third laptop and turned it so Burgon could see it. Burgon's eyes went wide in surprised confusion.

"That looks almost exactly like what we saw on the first laptop! You sure that's Tgegani's?"

Visnel nodded.

"Dead certain. I did the test myself and can verify its accuracy. But here's where things get even more interesting. Thinking this was just something unique to Tgegani, I took the base copy of his IOS and booted it in a test shell. Needless to say, it didn't function as desired."

"Yeah, I had the same problem when I loaded it into the first set of new lions."

"Well, thinking that the differences I was seeing were simply the result of the AI operating in an idle state, I put it into a dynamic test loop, knowing that it would generate the same patterns you would typically see in a fully functional AI. Or, at least a pattern that we could record." He then pointed to the fourth laptop, and said, "Unfortunately, this is what I got."

Burgon shook his head.

"That's impossible. How can that output look just like the other AI output, and yet Tgegani's looks like the Yigzan output?"

Visnel inhaled deeply, and said, "I've been wondering that myself. It really makes no sense to me. Theoretically, as you've said, it's impossible. The laws of coding state that a program will generate the same output every time if the input remains the same. But here's an example where that's not true. I realize that one of these snapshots is of his base AI in a diagnostic test loop and the other is of Tgegani's active mind, so there will be some differences. However, there shouldn't be *this* much of a difference. Certainly we'd see a small change between the two, but nothing to this level."

"So what does it mean?" asked Burgon.

Visnel crossed his arms, and said, "Doctor, do you believe in souls?"

Burgon blinked in surprise at this.

"That seems like an odd question to be asking at a time like this."

"Well? Do you?"

Burgon thought about this for a bit.

"Um, I guess I do. While they haven't been scientifically proven to exist, there's enough data to suggest that they might."

Just then Burgon's eyes went wide with surprise.

"You're not actually suggesting that Tgegani has a soul, are you?"

Visnel shrugged.

"What other explanation is there? When all the facts have been checked, and the impossible excluded, whatever is left, however illogical or improbable, must be the truth."

"But a soul?"

Visnel shrugged.

"You said it yourself that you have no idea how any of the lions became sentient. You even admitted that you could never get his IOS to work much above a basic logic pattern. Given that fact, the only reasonable conclusion is that Tgegani has somehow gained a soul."

"But that's impossible!" exclaimed Burgon.

"Edias, it's the only possible answer! Nothing else fits!" retorted Visnel.

"But how would he have gotten one?" asked Burgon.

Visnel shrugged.

"Honestly, I have no idea."

Burgon thought deeply about this for several moments, and then said, "Can you email me this information? I want to go over this myself."

Visnel nodded.

"Gladly."

Chapter 20

Persia walked slowly around the two lions closest to her, and studied them curiously.

"So you're, like, really alive? This isn't some practical joke or something, is it?" she asked.

Pen tilted his head curiously.

"Why would we play a practical joke on you?" he asked.

Persia sat down in front of the two lions and shrugged slightly.

"Well, I don't know. How else am I supposed to explain why you just suddenly woke up and started talking to me? Dad said he hadn't loaded your AI software yet. So you shouldn't be able to talk with me right now."

Breakman crossed his arms and grunted.

"I told you this was Meshua's doing. Dr. Burgon had nothing to do with it," he said.

"That is correct. We have come at the request of Meshua to assist our brother Tgegani in his task of protecting our people from certain destruction," said Pen.

Persia's face changed from one of confusion, to sadness, to anger and then sadness again.

"That means you'll be leaving me too, right?" she asked.

Pen nodded.

"I'm afraid so."

Tears formed in Persia's eyes.

"Why does this keep happening to me!? First Tgegani, then the others, and now you!"

"It's their job," came a gentle, loving voice.

Everyone turned in surprise to see Meshua standing just behind Breakman with his arms held out in a gesture of love.

"Well, his timing's impeccable," thought Breakman.

"Who are you?" asked Persia anxiously.

Meshua walked up to Persia and knelt down in front of her.

"I am Meshua. I was the one who created you, and the lions, and gave each of you life," he said, his words exuding an incredible amount of love.

Breakman furrowed his brow.

"Wow, there's a plot twist," he quipped.

"You...you...created me?" she said, half in fear, and half in curiosity. "But why? For what purpose?" she continued.

"To be a mother to Tgegani. For that, I blessed you with a mother's heart so that you would love and nurture him, and prepare him for the trials that lay ahead."

"But you took him away from me, didn't you? Why! Why would you do that!?" bellowed Persia as tears began to stream down her cheeks.

Meshua smiled kindly at Persia.

"My daughter, you have already done a great job of being a mother to him, and the other lions, just as I sent you to. But now you must let them go."

Persia shook her head.

"No! I don't want to! I love them too much!" cried Persia.

She then leaned forward, buried her face in Meshua's soft, warm shoulder and wept. Meshua lovingly embraced her and held her tight as she did.

"Tgegani and the others will return to you in time. But, for now, they must depart from you for a time. When their task is complete, I will bring them back to you for a season to share in each other's company. Now be at peace."

Persia lifted her tear soaked face, and looked at him with deep, pleading eyes.

"Promise me he'll come back," she said as she tried to hold back her tears.

Meshua smiled and nodded.

"I promise."

He then let go of her and gently wiped away her tears. She sniveled a little and then turned towards the other lions.

"What about them?" she asked with quivering lips.

"They will leave you for a time as well. But, as I promised, they will all return to you again some day," said Meshua.

"No offense, but this is getting kind of mushy. Can we move on to the good stuff," thought Breakman.

Meshua turned and gave him a knowing look. Breakman shrugged.

"Hey, I'm just suggesting," he said.

Meshua chuckled kindly, stood up, and then gestured to the other lions.

"Awaken!" he cried.

To Persia and Breakman's complete surprise, all of the other lions in the room twitched and began to move. They each looked around the room briefly before fixing their eyes on Meshua.

He then looked down at Pen and Tiel, and said, "I leave these lions in your charge. Take them to your brother and surrender yourselves to his leadership. He will guide you from there."

Pen and Tiel bowed.

"We will do as you've asked," said Pen.

And with that, Meshua vanished. Persia soon turned her attention to Pen as he quickly took charge of the other lions and organized them into groups, sections, squads and teams. Then, just as they were preparing to leave, Persia hurried over to him.

"Pen, wait!" she cried.

He stopped and turned to her.

"Yes, mother?" he said curiously.

"I need you to promise me something," she said.

He tilted his head in interest.

"If it is within my abilities, I will do whatever you ask," he said.

"Protect Tgegani at all costs. Bring him back to me alive and unhurt."

Pen's eyes widened.

"But Meshua has already said that he will return safely."

"Promise me. Please," she insisted.

Pen nodded.

"Very well, then, I promise."

Persia smiled joyfully.

"Thank you."

"You are welcome. But may I now request something of you in return?" he asked.

"Anything!" said Persia gladly.

Pen looked around the room briefly, and then back at Persia.

"Could you show us...the way out? We are unfamiliar with this place," he said.

Persia blinked in surprise.

"Oh, uh. Yeah. Follow me."

Odevion peaked out from behind a bush and studied the road in front of him. Not far away sat a jet black sedan that appeared to be waiting for someone. Nearby were several hunters, the Sattazin equivalent of special forces, who stood watch over the car. Knowing the reputation of Sattazin hunters he was certain they'd spotted him already. But, just in case they hadn't, he decided it was best not to make any sudden moves that might startle them and accidentally get himself shot. He hadn't spent the last several weeks sneaking through Gorg territory to get shot dead now. He very gently stood up with his hands over his head and whistled to get the men's attention.

One of the hunters raised an eyebrow slightly, and said, "Are you just going to stand there all day, or will you be getting in the car soon?"

Odevion grinned. They *had* seen him. He then picked up his ruck sack and trotted over to the car. As he did, one of the hunters opened the door and helped him inside. As the car pulled away, the hunters that had surrounded it quickly vanished into the nearby foliage leaving the road empty again as though no one had been there. The car then drove for several hours before turning off onto a long, winding gravel road that led up to a large and simple, yet sturdy log cabin. Upon arriving, a hunter standing guard near the front door escorted Odevion inside. As he entered the cabin he spotted a large, slightly overweight Sattazin officer sitting on the other side of a table puffing quietly on a long, fat pipe that hung from his lips. Odevion grinned as he sat down across from him.

"Well O'ik, I see you've put on a few pounds," he said.

The officer chuckled and patted his belly.

"Eh, just a few. What may I do for you sergeant?" he said in a deep Sattazin accent.

"I was told you could help us win this war."

O'ik nodded, took a drag on his pipe, and said, "Ah, indeed. And I believe I have just what you need to do that. But first I would like you to meet someone. He is one who will help us greatly in this struggle." He then looked to his left, and said, "Fer'gant, our guest is here."

Odevion looked to his right curiously, and then jumped up in surprise as a large, stout, Gorg officer stepped out of the shadows and into the light. Odevion immediately drew his pistol and aimed it at the man, but did not fire.

"What is the meaning of this!?" he asked anxiously.

"Put your weapon away, sergeant. We are on the same side," said the Gorg.

"Not last I checked," replied Odevion coldly.

O'ik motioned to Odevion, and said, "Yes, yes. He is with us. Now put your weapon away."

Odevion eyed the Gorg officer as he casually sat down, took a pipe from a bowl in the middle of the table, lit it, and then took a long drag on it. He looked over at O'ik who rolled his eyes. Odevion slowly lowered his pistol, but didn't put it away as he sat down again.

"Sergeant, we have worked together many times before, have we not?" said O'ik.

"Yes," replied Odevion cautiously.

"So you should know to trust me by now, correct?"

"Yes."

"Well then, why don't you?"

"Your friend is a Gorg."

"Sergeant, when I say someone can be trusted, I know this to be a fact as I do not idly throw those words to the wind," said O'ik.

"Sorry if I seem a bit skeptical, but there's this little thing called a war going on to the west of here where his people are slaughtering mine," said Odevion.

"Yes, this is indeed a terrible tragedy which we are working together to resolve," said Fer'gant.

"How? By wiping us out?" said Odevion snidely.

"No, by stopping this dreadful war. Unlike many of my fellow countrymen, I do not support this travesty which is being committed against you. There are others within my nation who also share my feelings. But we are few, and are looked down upon by our people."

Fer'gant studied Odevion's face for several moments, but only saw hatred in it. He sighed.

"I can see that building trust between us will take some time," he said.

Odevion grunted sarcastically.

"Yeah, like a couple hundred years."

"Then will you also get mad at me because I have become friends with a Gorg?" said O'ik.

"No, not mad. Just disappointed."

"Then I should be equally disappointed at you for the things you have done of late."

Odevion stared at O'ik curiously, but said nothing.

"Yes, sergeant. I am well aware of the many things you've been doing these past several months," said O'ik with a grin.

Odevion blinked in surprise.

"But, how? Only a handful of people know where I've been."

O'ik laughed heartily.

"I would not be a proper hunter if I didn't keep tabs on my friends."

Odevion grunted slightly.

"Alright, fair enough. But what does that have to do with him?"

O'ik took a long puff on his pipe.

"If I am intimately aware of everything you have been doing, do you think that my friend here would not have received the same scrutiny?"

Odevion pursed his lips in thought.

"No, I can't imagine he wouldn't," he said after a moment.

O'ik laughed.

"It's how I came to know of Fer'gant and his struggle against his people."

Odevion thought about this more, and then put away his pistol.

"Alright, I'll give him the benefit of the doubt on this."

O'ik smiled.

"That is all I ask. Now, I will let my esteemed colleague give you what you seek for."

"And what is that?" asked Odevion, half knowing the answer.

Fer'gant turned to Odevion, and said, "Why, a way to end this war, of course."

Pentell peered through his binoculars and panned across the prairie before him. He watched as many Gorg units were doing their best to take cover inside of craters, trenches or anywhere else that offered them some form of protection from Yigzan artillery fire. Off in the distance he watched enemy units maneuvering into their new positions as Gorg artillery fired sporadically at the Yigzan lines. Off to the north he heard the faint whistle and boom of incoming artillery rounds as they crashed into the ridge line.

"If they keep shelling us like this, they're going to pound this place to dust," he muttered as he continued to pan the battlefield.

"I doubt they will. Well, not right away, anyways," said Sims.

"What do you think, Tgegani?" asked Welk.

Tgegani panned the prairie, his eyes zooming in and out as they identified various targets, and then discussed each of them with his siblings.

"We're assessing the situation right now," replied Tgegani.

"Do you think we should make another attack tonight?" asked Pentell.

"We all agree that it would be a good idea. We have nineteen targets that we feel are of military significance that can be attacked at minimal risk to ourselves while achieving maximum damage to the enemy. However, there may be a problem," said Renc.

"What would that be?" asked Sims.

Renc turned to him, and said, "We've received reports that the Gorg have shifted a large percentage of their forces both north and south, avoiding our section of the line as much as possible. That puts the bulk of their fighting force out of our immediate reach."

"Sounds like they're getting the message," said Pentell.

"Yeah, avoid large cats with claws," quipped Welk.

"Lieutenant, we have come to an impasse, and seek your insight into something we are considering," said Renc.

"Alright, what is it?" asked the lieutenant.

"Given the recent redistribution of Gorg forces away from our current area, two possibilities exist. Either this is a trap, or it is a choice opportunity. But we lack sufficient information to determine which it is. Hence why we require your input since you have a trait called intuition which we do not possess that somehow provides you with the needed information to make decisions when external data is insufficient to formulate a proper answer," said Renc.

Pentell, Welk and Sims stared at each other for a moment, and then back at the Gorg lines.

"Intuition, eh? That line is stretched extremely thin, making it ripe for exploitation, whereas the rest of their lines are solid as a rock, and nigh on impenetrable. That to me screams trap," said Welk.

"How hard would it be to breach their lines?" asked Renc.

"Pretty easily, actually. At least, this part of it. I mean, that line is so thin right now that we could take two companies of men, maybe three, and some armor, and easily punch a hole in their lines big enough to sail a cord of tacks through with room to spare."

Sims and Pentell stared at him in confusion. Welk grinned sheepishly.

"Sorry. Sailors term. You probably don't know what a tack is."

The two men shook their heads.

"A tack is a large, three masted ship from ancient times that was used to transport supplies up and down the coast. A cord is a formation of twenty ships sailing side by side in a V formation designed to maximize their speed across the water," said Welk.

"Well, how big of a hole is that?" asked Pentell.

"Approximately a half a kilometer," said Welk.

"That's a decent sized hole," said Sims.

"Well, making the hole isn't the problem. Maintaining it will be. I have a feeling that, if we go charging down there, and drive through their lines, they're going to converge on us from the north and south like the jaws of a giant predator and wipe us out," said Welk.

"So then an attack through that area with the lions would be fruitless," said Sims.

"Well, with pretty much anything, really. It certainly wouldn't gain us much except a lot of casualties in exchange for a small Gorg body count."

"Given that apparent inevitability, it would be best for us to move north of here and attack, and then return south and attack there as well," said Nicassa.

"So you'd hit them where they weren't expecting you?" asked Sims.

Nicassa nodded.

"That's actually not a bad idea," said Pentell.

"Agreed. The confusion that would cause among the Gorg lines would be beneficial to our efforts," said Sabbo.

"Well, I guess we should pack up and head north then. Where should we go first?" said Pentell.

But to his surprise, Tgegani shook his head.

"Lieutenant. If you will allow us to undertake this mission on our own, we will be able to complete it quicker, and more efficiently than if you came with us. It will also ensure that your men remain safe, as movement in the open right now is very dangerous," said Tgegani.

Pentell looked out at the prairie and thought for a moment.

"If it's really that dangerous, you probably shouldn't go," he said.

"But we must go. If we do not break the Gorg fighting spirit, they will eventually overwhelm and destroy us," said Tgegani.

Pentell stood quietly and thought about this, uncertain of which way he should go. Seeing this, Tgegani spoke up again.

"Earlier this week you trusted us enough to allow Renc and Possa to infiltrate deep into Gorg controlled territory to gather information. They succeeded with no troubles. You have also allowed us to make short assault missions from our position here on numerous occasions without your need to accompany us. I know this mission is much further away, and involves all six of us, but we can do as well there as we've done here," he said.

"But what if your mission goes south on you?" asked Pentell.

"If it looks like our mission will not succeed, we will return to you as quickly as we can."

Pentell thought about this for several moments longer, and then nodded, and said, "Alright, you may go. But make sure you bring everyone back in one piece."

Tgegani nodded.

"I will do my best, sir."

"When are you going to begin your mission?"

"After sunsdown. We will use the cover of night to conceal our movements."

Pentell nodded.

"Good. Keep in touch whenever it's safe to do so."
Tgegani nodded.
"We will."

Chapter 21

Burgon walked slowly into the large warehouse where his lions had been stored and then stopped in abject shock.

"Where are the lions?" he asked in surprise.

"They've gone to help Tgegani," said Persia.

She then slipped out of the shadows and into the light where Burgon could see her.

"They're gone? But how!? They haven't been loaded with their software yet!" said Burgon in surprise.

Persia sighed and looked towards the empty warehouse floor.

"They didn't need any software, dad. Meshua gave them life, and sent them to protect Tgegani." She then looked back at Burgon, and said, "Just like he did with Tgegani and the others."

Burgon's clipboard rattled to the floor.

"What did you just say?" he said in surprise.

Persia lowered her head and began to leave.

"I'm going to lay down now. I need some sleep."

She slowly strode out of the warehouse and towards Burgon's laboratory.

"Persia! Don't go! I need to know what happened!" shouted Burgon.

"Dr. Burgon, wait!!" shouted Breakman.

Burgon paused and then turned towards Breakman in curiosity.

"I don't think she's in much of a mood to talk about this right now. So I'll explain it for her. Only thing is, you had better sit down first. You don't want to be standing when you hear this," said Breakman.

Burgon walked over to a nearby bench and sat down.

"Alright, I'm listening," he said.

Breakman then spent the next twenty minutes explaining everything he knew, what'd happened, and what he remembered. Burgon listened intently to every word. When Breakman finished, Burgon stared off into the empty warehouse in disbelief.

"So, that's it?" he asked.

Breakman shrugged.

"Pretty much. I really don't know what else to say."

Burgon thought about this for a few moments, and then asked, "So you're sure he's real?"

Breakman nodded.

"As real as you and me," he replied.

Burgon buried his head in his hands and sighed deeply. Breakman studied him curiously.

"You alright?" he asked.

"I really don't know. For years I've thought that what mother told me about him was just a legend. A myth. A fairy tale from ancient times. Never did I, even in my wildest dreams, think he was real. Even now I'm not sure he's real."

"I am more real than anything in this world will ever be," said Meshua as he appeared in a brilliant flare of light.

Burgon looked up and stared at Meshua in surprise and awe. Breakman smirked.

"Huh, he's right on schedule," he thought.

He then slipped away so that the two men could talk alone.

"You're...you're..." stuttered Burgon.

Meshua nodded.

"I am."

"Then, Tgegani?" said Burgon as his body began to shake. "I didn't really make him, did I," he continued.

"Yes, you did. But you only gave him a body. I was the one who gave him life."

"But, why me? Who am I that you would choose me for this? And why him?" asked Burgon.

"There are times in this world when a special protector is needed. Tgegani is but one of a long line of champions who have risked everything to protect my people."

"But why him? Why would you give life to a machine, and then send him off to die?"

"I did not send him to die, but to live, and to save my people."

Burgon sighed heavily. Meshua smiled compassionately.

"In time you will understand everything. But, for now, you must simply believe and trust that I am doing what is necessary for the good of all."

Burgon nodded slightly as a tear trickled down his face.

"I believe."

Black watched curiously from his office as Burgon appeared to be talking to himself. He scratched his chin as he studied the apparently one sided conversation.

"Who is he talking to?" he thought.

He switched between views on the security cameras, scanned the local airwaves, and then listened to an audio feed from the warehouse. All he heard was Burgon. He spun in his chair and thought deeply about this.

"I wonder if he's losing his mind. The stress he's been under lately has been a bit much."

He then remembered how Persia had experienced a similar event right before the lions had awakened and left the facility.

"But then, what was Persia doing? Was there someone else in the warehouse with her that my cameras couldn't see?"

He thought harder.

"Something's not right."

He turned back to his desk and panned his security cameras all around the area, but found nobody else there.

"Hmm, maybe he's just thinking out loud. Or else his mind is slipping. But then why would both of them be like this? I'd better send them on vacation for a few weeks so they don't completely lose it. I'm going to need both of them in top shape again soon. So I better act quickly. If I lose either of them now, I may also lose the lions."

He then turned to his computer and began making the necessary reservations.

Burgon slowly plodded into his laboratory and sat down at his desk to think. Persia looked over at him with concern.

"You alright, dad?" she asked.

Burgon sighed.

"I really don't know."

"What's the matter?"

"I met Meshua today."

Persia blinked.

"So did I!" she exclaimed.

Burgon pivoted in his chair and looked at her.

"You did? What did he tell you?"

Persia quickly explained everything that she and Meshua had talked about.

"Wow," said Burgon in amazement. "And here I thought *I* was the one with the greater burden," he continued.

Just then, Black strolled into the room and noticed Burgon and Persia talking.

"Dr. Burgon, do you have a moment?" he asked.

Burgon stood up, and said, "Yes, Mr. Black. What can I do for you?"

Black studied him briefly and then held out an envelope.

"What's this?" asked Burgon.

"You and Persia are going on a vacation," said Black flatly.

Burgon furrowed his brow in surprise.

"What!? Why!?"

"It's come to my attention that the stress you've been under lately has taken its toll on you. Therefore I am requiring both of you to take some time off."

Burgon shook his head.

"But I can't leave! What if one of the lions needs my help?" he said.

"Mr. Burgon, if you're so stressed and strained that you're sobbing like a baby, I hardly find it possible that you would be of much use to the lions presently."

Burgon quickly rubbed the tears from his eyes with his coat sleeve as more quickly took their place. Black sighed.

"See what I mean? You need some time off. Now, go. Enjoy yourself. I'll see you in a month. And for the sake of Tersar, get some sleep. You look horrible."

Burgon nodded.

"I'll do that, sir."

"I expect you to. Now go. This envelope contains your travel information, hotel reservations, and all necessary paperwork and waivers for Ms. Persia as well. The private resort that I've booked you at has already been informed of her coming and will be properly staffed to handle all of her special and individual needs."

Curious about this, Burgon took the envelope and opened it to discover tickets for a very posh and expensive beachside resort on the west coast. He stared at Black in surprise.

"Wow, the Seven Stars of Santin! This is the finest resort in the entire nation! Mr. Black, I can't go! How will I ever repay you for this!?"

Black waved his hand dismissively.

"There's no need to. Given how much you've done for me, I see this as money well spent. Now go, get out of here. They'll be expecting you this afternoon. You may use my private train to travel there if you wish. If not, I will book you on the next train heading west."

Burgon smiled and bowed slightly.

"Thank you, sir. You are most generous."

"Your improved health and state of mind will be sufficient thanks for me."

Burgon and Persia then hurried out of the lab and towards their home to pack for their vacation. Black's eyes narrowed as he watched them leave.

"This vacation had better work. I've invested too much in them to risk losing him and the lions this late in the game," he said.

Odevion peered through his binoculars at the main gate to the Gorg military chancellery as several guards patrolled around the front gate.

"The place looks kind of deserted. I'm surprised there aren't more guards there," he said.

"Don't be fooled. What you see on the outside is just the skin of the beast. There are many more inside," said Fer'gant.

"How many are we talking about?" asked Odevion.

"About six hundred or so," said O'ik.

Odevion rolled his eyes.

"This mission just gets more interesting by the moment. So how exactly are we going to break in there?"

O'ik perked up slightly as a Sattazin hunter hurried towards him.

"We're ready," whispered the hunter.

O'ik motioned towards Odevion as the hunter held out a small detonator. The hunter then turned and offered the detonator to Odevion.

"This will activate all of the explosives we have placed within the facility. Will you please do the honors?"

Odevion looked at the detonator, took it and then grinned.

"Well then, let the festivities begin," he said with a chuckle.

Fer'gant nodded.

"Yes, please. Let us 'make this place fly', as you Yigzan like to say," he replied.

Odevion looked at the Gorg officer and smirked.

"I never imagined in all my life that a Gorg would actually be asking me to blow up one of his own facilities."

Fer'gant chuckled.

"There are more where this one came from."

Odevion flipped the safety off and pressed the button. A loud chorus of pops and booms echoed throughout the facility followed by the roar of collapsing buildings. A thick, roiling cloud of black smoke, dirt and debris rose up from the facility as alarms and sirens began to ring.

"I always wanted to do that," quipped Odevion.

"Begin the assault," said O'ik through a hand held communicator.

Fer'gant did the same. The forest suddenly came alive as platoons of camouflaged soldiers raced forward towards the dazed and confused Gorg guards, quickly overpowering them. As the battle began Odevion scanned the complex for movement. There was some limited signs of activity, mostly wounded soldiers staggering around in confusion, but little else.   Fer'gant tapped him on the shoulder and pointed to a corner of the facility where two Gorg officers and a Midazin hurried towards a nearby vehicle.   Odevion put down his binoculars, picked up his sniper rifle and quickly drew a bead on the Midazin officer.

"Goodbye," he said with a grin as he squeezed off the first round.

The bullet found its target with pinpoint accuracy. He quickly lined up the other two men and brought them down as well. This impressed Fer'gant.

"Your shooting is as legendary as the rumors have told," he said.

Odevion chuckled.

"If you think I'm a good shot, you should see Major Delgra. He can out shoot me any day."

Fer'gant chuckled.

"I may have to take you up on that some time."

Within twenty minutes the assault ended and the teams withdrew. As they rode away in a small caravan of unmarked trucks, Fer'gant and O'ik talked to their commanders and gathered battle reports.

"How was it?" asked Odevion after several minutes.

Fer'gant nodded.

"It went very well. Far better than I could have hoped for. Thankfully, nobody was lost. We have a few injuries, but that is to be expected."

O'ik nodded as well.

"Same here. And my hunters can confirm that three of their top ten commanders, plus many mid-level commanders of the Gorg military are dead."

"That's going to put a dent in their command structure," said Odevion.

O'ik nodded.

"It will, but only briefly. We plan to attack the command structure several more times over the next couple of days to shake them up even more."

"Why not just invade them outright and really put the hurt on them? The Sattazins are obviously not short of good men or equipment," said Odevion.

O'ik shook his head.

"Our people are an honor bound society. They will not attack unless there is justification to do so. They feel that going to war without provocation is without honor."

Odevion raised his eyebrows in mock surprise.

"You sure could've fooled *me* today," he said with a smirk.

"We foresee threats differently than our people do. The Gorg, by their attack on your people, and their alliance with the Midazin, threatens our people in many ways. Therefore we are free to attack them without harming our honor," said O'ik.

"Do you think they'll make a retaliatory strike against your people for what we did?" asked Odevion.

Fer'gant shook his head.

"My people are unlikely to act right away. They know that to attack rashly will risk the wrath of the Sattazin people, and that is the last thing they want. So they will not act immediately. Instead, they will point fingers and blame others for now."

Odevion thought about this for several moments.

"So I take it we'll need to ruffle their feathers again?" he said.

O'ik and Fer'gant nodded.

Odevion inhaled deeply, and said, "Alright, where to next?"

"We will rest for today, resupply, and then make an attack to the north tomorrow. We must continue to weaken their command structure to help your people survive until something can be done to turn the tide of this war," said Fer'gant.

"Didn't we already do that?"

"We have only "ruffled their feathers", as you say," said O'ik.

"Then isn't what we did today kind of pointless? I mean, if they've got the people to easily replace those we killed, then we didn't do nearly the damage I'd hoped we would."

Fer'gant shook his head.

"Actually, we did much good today. The ones we killed will be hard to replace as they are few among my people."

"How so?"

"My people have quantity in many things, but quality in few, including officers and leaders."

Odevion grinned.

"Then you and your men must be the quality few."

Fer'gant smiled and nodded.

"Indeed. I have hand-picked my men from among the most intelligent within our army who support my views. While we are not many, what we have has, and will be put to great use."

"If your men keep fighting like they did today, this war should be over in a few weeks," said Odevion.

"If our efforts are successful, my people will rise up against the Gorg army and end this war in two days," said O'ik.

"Two days? Isn't that kind of an ambitious timetable?" asked Odevion.

O'ik grinned slyly.

"You have not seen how powerful my people are when they are fully provoked. It is a frightful thing to witness," he said, giving dramatic flair to his words.

Odevion laughed.

"I'll take your word for it."

Pentell, Welk and Sims stood in their bunker and studied the Gorg lines through their binoculars. However, they didn't like what they were seeing.

"Looks like the Gorg might make another assault tonight," said Pentell.

"Yeah, and they're getting better at it too. Not to mention their numbers have increased significantly in the last couple of hours," said Sims.

"That's probably because they're moving their battle units down our way to protect them from the lions," said Welk.

"I'm surprised they'd cause that much of a fuss already. They've only been gone, what, a day?" said Sims.

"Thirty one hours, give or take an hour," said Pentell.

"Well, it certainly doesn't feel that long," said Sims.

"Oops, the Gorg are moving," said Welk.

"Get ready gentlemen. Expect them to hit us with an artillery barrage to open things up, and then an infantry rush right after that," said Pentell.

"Don't they ever have an original idea?" quipped Sims.

"This is the Gorg we're talking about. Original is a foreign concept to them," said Welk sarcastically.

Just then the first whistles of artillery began to echo in their ears.

"Here it comes! Everyone into the bunkers!" shouted Pentell.

The observation area quickly cleared as shells began to rain down on the ridge line. The shelling went on for ten minutes before slackening, and then fading away to just a couple of random shells every few seconds.

"Do you think they're running out of rounds?" asked Sims.

"Unlikely. Something's up. They normally pound us for an hour or more before letting up. That was barely ten minutes," said Welk as he moved towards the door of the bunker.

"Where are you going?" asked Pentell.

"To see what's happening," replied Welk.

"Be careful out there. There's still stuff falling," said Pentell.

"Don't worry. They couldn't hit the broad side of a ridge line if they tried," he quipped.

He then slipped out of the bunker and was gone. Pentell turned to the other men, and said, "Ammo check, gentlemen. Make sure you're fully stocked. I don't want anyone running out in the middle of the fight, understood?"

The men acknowledged, and then checked their ammo.

Chapter 22

Welk covered his head as a shell exploded above him sending a shower of rock cascading down around him. He grimaced as a large piece of rock glanced off his shoulder. He shook it off and began to reach for his binoculars just as a Gorg soldier poked his head above the edge of the cliff. Welk immediately raised his rifle and fired two bullets into the soldier's face at nearly point blank range. The soldier fell backwards and crashed noisily down the cliff face. Welk listened in horror as he heard the surprised grunts and shouts of other soldiers below. He quickly peaked over the edge and found the cliff face covered in Gorg. He grabbed two grenades from his belt, pulled the pins and tossed them over the side. Two dull thumps and the sound of agonized screams came several seconds later. He immediately jumped up and began firing into a large company of Gorg soldiers as they clung precariously to the rocks below. Pentell heard the grenades and rifle fire, and immediately knew what was happening. The Gorg had launched a surprise attack amidst the shelling.

"Let's go! Let's go!" he shouted.

His platoon quickly raced out of their protective bunkers and found, to their horror, that the Gorg were nearly on top of them.

"Grenades!" shouted Pentell.

Each of the men grabbed two of their grenades, pulled the pins, and then threw them over the side. The grenades exploded one after another and tore through the Gorg ranks like a brushhog. Pentell's platoon then leaned over the edge and began firing at the Gorg closest to them. This drew the attention of other nearby units who emerged from their bunkers to find the Gorg nearly on their doorsteps as well. A desperate battle soon ensued as the Yigzan fought as hard as they could to hold their positions with shouts of "Hold the line!" mingled with agonized screams and cries for medics. But, despite their determination, the Gorg continued to advance up the face of the ridge line towards them, their numbers seeming to have no end as the Yigzan's strength began to wane. By the end of two hours Pentell had lost nearly half his platoon, was dangerously low on ammo, and had even been forced to fight hand to hand with the Gorg on several occasions.

But, as the battle continued on unabated, growing darker, and more hopeless as it did, something miraculous happened. Just as a fresh wave of Gorg began ascending the hill, two flashes of gold suddenly appeared overhead of Pentell's position and dove down into the advancing enemy forces with lethal effect. A moment later two more appeared and then another six. This forced the Gorg to turn their attention away from the Yigzan as they tried desperately to stave off the golden terror that raged in their midst. But their efforts were in vain as they were cut down one after another with brutal efficiency. Pentell's men stared in shock at this sight before them as dozens of other lions soon joined the fight, their golden bodies flashing brilliantly in the midday sun like great tongues of angry flame. One Gorg after another quickly fell to their fury as the hillside flowed red with Gorg blood. Pentell and the others looked on at this in surprise.

"Are you seeing what I'm seeing?" asked Sims.

"That's impossible," said Pentell in amazement.

"I've counted nearly eighty of them already and there's still more coming!" said Welk.

"Do you think they're new lions sent by the doctor?" asked Sims.

Just then two more lions leapt down from the rocks above and landed behind them. The men turned in surprise and stared at the two unfamiliar faces.

"Who are you?" asked Pentell.

"I am Pen. This is my sister, Tiel. We are here looking for Tgegani. Our mother sent us to protect him," said the first lion.

"They went north of here about a day and a half ago," said Welk.

"Then we will search for him there," said Pen.

He then turned to go.

"Wait! Wait!" cried Pentell.

Pen paused and looked back at the Lieutenant.

"Yes?" he asked curiously.

"Can you stay and help us drive back this attack?"

Pen looked out over the battle and then back at Pentell. He nodded.

"That is already being taken care of. Therefore I must go," he said.

"Then you're not gonna stay?"

Pen shook his head.

"We cannot. We must first find our brother, and fulfill our mother's wishes. After that we will return and assist you," he said.

"Don't go, Mr. Lion. We could really use your help. We're desperate here," said Pentell.

Pen looked out across the battlefield briefly, and then nodded.

"As you are our brother's companions, I will leave behind some of my siblings to protect you. Our data tells us that he was very fond of you and your men. As such, I will make sure that my lions stand their ground with you until death takes them. But, with that, I must go as my time is short."

Pen and Tiel then turned and leapt over the ledge, quickly joining the other lions as they flowed down into the valley and soon pushed to the north. Pentell and the others watched in amazement as the Gorg fled before them like frightened children.

"Wow, a whole herd of Tgegani's," said a soldier nearby.

A moment later three lions leapt over the edge of the cliff face and begin examining the wounded that lay scattered all around the area. One of them then raced away over the rocks above and out of sight. A second lion turned and walked up to Pentell.

"I have sent Neomara to retrieve a medic for your men. While you wait, please tend to your wounded. We will stand guard over you against any further attacks," said the lion.

Pentell nodded his thanks and then set about seeing to his fallen men.

Pen and Tiel moved quickly to the front of the rolling herd of lions and directed the flow of their brothers and sisters as they ran. They moved as fast as they could for nearly an hour, selectively striking and then regrouping as they moved with great speed. They eventually located Tgegani and his team, and then turned their group towards him. It was Renc who was the first to detect their approach. At first he didn't think much of it. But as the sound grew closer, his attention slowly grew more focused on it until it was impossible to ignore.

"Do you hear that?" he asked over the radio.

"No I...wait, yes I do. It's faint, but it...sounds like a stampede," replied Sabbo.

Possa slipped around a nearby vehicle and stared off in the direction of the noise.

"I see something coming, and there's a lot of it," she said over the radio.

"Alright everyone, prepare to fall back," said Tgegani.

"Wait, it's...it's...but that's impossible," said Possa.

"What do you see?" asked Tgegani.

"Hundreds and hundreds of...us," she replied.

This piqued the interest of the other five lions.

"Say that again?" said Renc.

"I can't explain it any better than that. There's a huge stampede of lions coming our way."

"Alright, everyone withdraw to a safe location until we can figure out what's happening," said Tgegani.

The lions quickly slipped out of the Gorg lines and began to make their way across the prairie back towards the ridge line. But, as they did, they were soon overtaken by Pen's lions. They then stopped and stared in wonder as hundreds of lions just like themselves surrounded their small group. This was something they'd never seen before, and didn't know what to think of it.

"Okay, this is odd. So what do we do now?" asked Renc.

Two lions soon emerged from the middle of the herd and walked up to Tgegani.

"Brother Tgegani? Is that you?" asked one of them.

"Who are you?" asked Tgegani.

"I am Pen and this is my sister Tiel. Mother sent us to protect you."

"Mother?" said Tgegani.

Then his eyes went wide as he realized who they were talking about.

"Persia!" he said in amazement.

The other lions all nodded. The minds of Tgegani and his team then filled with a thousand questions before being quickly returned to the task at hand as the Gorg began to fire at them.

"What shall we do, brother?" asked Pen.

Tgegani's eyes narrowed slightly.

"We have work to do. So long as these monsters bear arms against us and our people, none of us are safe," he said.

Pen nodded.

"Then we will fight by your side until death takes us, or victory is achieved," he said.

The lions all then turned as one and dove into the Gorg lines.

Black studied a small stack of combat reports from the front lines and marveled that the Yigzan had held on as long as they had. As he read further, Elgar rushed into the room. Black looked up in interest and noticed Elgar's anxious expression.

"What's the matter?" he asked.

"The Gorg are in full scale retreat across all fronts!" exclaimed Elgar.

"How?" asked Black in surprise.

"It's the lions. They're decimating the Gorg forces with near impunity."

Black grinned.

"Hmm, interesting."

He then rubbed his chin, and rocked in his chair for several moments as he thought about this.

"If this information is correct, the fight could be over soon, which is good. It will allow us to resume our original plans which got upset by this blasted war."

"What about the Midazin? They still possess a very powerful army. If the Gorg are defeated, we may still have to deal with them," said Elgar.

Black chuckled slyly.

"If I have my way, that won't be an issue. What options do we have available to us for speeding the completion of the war?"

"Not many, I'm afraid. Everything now rests with our army and the lions."

Black leaned back in his chair and thought about this.

"Hmm. See what you can find that we can use to give our people a further advantage in this war. I want to ensure that our victory is absolute."

Elgar bowed slightly.

"I'll see what I can do."

Odevion swabbed the barrel of his sniper rifle as a small camp fire crackled in front of him.

"Do you think we did some damage on that last attack?" he asked.

O'ik laughed.

"If they do not retaliate against my people soon, I will be surprised," he said.

"Maybe so, but was attacking the president of the Midazin and his cabinet wise? I mean, we just took out some pretty big names today."

Fer'gant took a long, slow draw on his pipe.

"It was necessary. If we do not draw the Sattazin into this war, no amount of technology will save your people," he said.

Odevion shrugged.

"Maybe so, but what we did today was insane. You two almost didn't make it out of the compound alive. If I hadn't shot down those two aircraft, you'd both be statistics."

O'ik nodded as he rubbed his chin in thought.

"That is very true. But you did such a splendid job covering us. Your eye is sharp, and you saw many things we did not. You saved many lives today, both Sattazin and Gorg."

Fer'gant nodded thankfully.

"Yes, you did, and your assistance in our efforts has been greatly commendable given your initial reservations at our presence."

Odevion smirked.

"Well, given what your people are doing to mine, do you blame me?"

Fer'gant shook his head.

"No, I don't. And I would not expect anything less of myself were the situation reversed."

"Well, you've shown me that I can't just rubber stamp all Gorg as being bad people. In fact, when this war is over, we're going to owe you two a lot."

O'ik waved the stem of his pipe at Odevion, and said, "Maybe so. But let us first win this war. After that we can decide who gets the most thanks."

Odevion laughed.

"If your men keep fighting like they have, I don't see that being a problem."

O'ik pounded his chest proudly.

"It is the way of the Sattazin!" he exclaimed.

Fer'gant laughed hardily.

"Hear! Hear!"

Odevion raised his canteen to the two men and nodded.

"Hear, hear indeed!"

Pentell looked around in awe at the vast number of Gorg bodies that lay strewn all across the ground. Some were even still seated in their vehicles.

"Oh gawds, they stink even worse when they're dead," said Sims as he covered his mouth with a rag to filter out the stench.

"There's a Gorg officer over there. Someone check him for intel," said Pentell.

"I got it," said one of the soldiers as he hurried over to the officer.

He rolled the body on its back, shook his head and then trotted back.

"Someone's already searched him," he said.

"Those new lions are a deadly lot, aren't they? I bet they're enjoying every bit of this," said one of the soldiers.

"There is no joy in taking a life, regardless if they're an enemy or not. We are simply doing our duty to protect our people. Nothing more," said Neomara.

"That's not what I've seen. You guys seem to enjoy this."

"Knock it off, private. You've got bigger things to worry about than what the lions are doing," said Pentell.

"Yes, sir," replied the soldier.

"Ugh, I still can't believe the body count those lions left behind. It's incredible," said Sims.

"No, it's not. There's nothing incredible about war, or killing, or death. It is a horrible, terrible, disgusting thing to experience and should never happen, no matter what the reasons," said Pentell.

"Horrible or not, what baffles me is why the Midazin are joining in. What do they have against us that would make them team up with the Gorg?" asked one of the soldiers.

"Private, did you ever finish high school?" asked Welk.

"Yes, sergeant. Got good grades across the board," said the soldier.

"Do you remember your ancient history class?"

"Not especially. Why?"

"There should have been a section in there that would explain a lot of this."

The soldier scratched his head.

"Sorry, sergeant. I can't think of anything like that."

Welk sighed.

"Alright, let me explain. Thousands of years ago our ancestors were a simple people who lived in walled cities, and worshiped a pantheon of gods. They were happy living that way for a long time until about twelve hundred years ago when they suddenly threw off the old ways, seemingly overnight, to focus on science and technology. About that same time a disgruntled councilman named Midazin became jealous, and tried to crush this new fascination with science. He organized a massive revolt against the king in hopes of forcing everyone back to the old ways. Unfortunately for him, his revolt failed. He and his followers were then exiled to the east, never to be heard from again until about two hundred years ago when an expedition team, searching the northern mountains for deposits of iron, rediscovered them on the Fogg peninsula."

"That I remember. They were still living like barbarians at the time, right?" said the soldier.

Welk nodded.

"Something like that. Just as Midazin had wanted, his people had strictly clung to the old ways, and were living in exactly the same way as our ancestors had over a thousand years earlier. But the arrival of those men awakened a long dormant hatred and fear within them which had been passed down from ancient times. Fearing that we might someday return to wipe them out, they turned their entire society into a near mirror image of ours, technology and all, in just under two hundred years. During that time they took their barbarian neighbors to the south, the Gorg, and brought them into modernity as well. Before we encountered the Midazin, we got along well with the Gorg, and had even done some limited trading with them, despite how primitive they were. It is believed that it was the Midazin that turned them against us," he said.

"So this whole war is based on a twelve hundred year old grudge?" said the soldier in surprise.

Welk shrugged.

"For the most part."

"Well that's a silly reason to go to war," said the soldier.

"Has there ever been a good one?" asked Pentell.

"I don't think so, sir," said the soldier.

"Lieutenant Pentell, I'm receiving word that command is calling a halt to our advance. We're to proceed to that line of hills over there, dig in and wait for further orders," said Neomara.

Pentell looked down the road and then turned to Welk.

"Does that line of hills look familiar to you?" he asked.

Welk nodded.

"It's where we were a few weeks ago when the lions left us for the better part of a day."

"Hmm, yeah. I wonder if our old positions are still there or if the Gorg have wrecked them," said Pentell, speaking more to himself than anyone around him.

"I'd be more worried that they booby trapped them," said Sims.

"I doubt it. They wouldn't have had time to do that," said Welk.

"Well, we'll have to make sure when we get there. So everyone be careful as you move into the area. Let's try not to get caught by any unwanted surprises," said Pentell.

"Yes, sir," said the others.

Elgar threw the door open to Black's office and quickly raced inside.

"The Sattazins have entered the war!" he shouted.

Black turned his computer screen towards Elgar. On it was a series of news flashes about recent events.

"You already...but, but how?"

"The national news website," said Black flatly.

He turned his screen back towards himself.

"It would appear that our intelligence network is getting slow these days if a common newspaper is able to deliver information to me faster than they can. But no matter. With the Sattazins now in the game, this war will be over soon. The only thing I'm curious of is how this happened. The Sattazins appeared content to remain out of the war only a few days ago."

"They were attacked by the Midazin who accused them of killing their Chancellor. The Sattazin, in turn, thought the Midazin had made an unprovoked attack against them and promptly declared war. They are currently driving through the Midazin homeland like a whirlwind."

Black furrowed his brow in surprise.

"Well, that'll certainly do the job. But I wonder what foolishness possessed the Midazin to drive them to strike at the Sattazin knowing what would happen if they did."

"I don't know, sir."

"Well, no matter. For now we have bigger things to deal with. Are we ready to resume our plans for the nation once this war is over?"

Elgar nodded. Black grinned fiendishly.

"Good. Now all we have to do is convince the lions to serve us, and we will be unstoppable!"

Chapter 23

"In a stunning victory for the Sattazin army, a late entrant in the war, the last pockets of Gorg and Midazin resistance fell today on the heels of a lightning fast campaign that lasted just ten days and swept aside the two opposing armies with ease. As of noon today, the Gorg and Midazin governments have unconditionally surrendered. Our news sources tell us that the first contact between Yigzan and Sattazin forces was near the Notadar river, just twelve miles north of the Gorg capital of Oya'var. We are also told that some of the now famous Burgon lions, who have been so instrumental in driving back the joint Gorg and Midazin armies in recent weeks, were also present. There is no word yet on what will happen next, but some believe that the General Secretary will move quickly to restore peace between the four nations. The National News Network will strive to keep you apprised of any further developments in this story as they become available."

Burgon turned off the television and leaned back in his chair.

"The war's over?" asked Persia.

"Apparently so," said Burgon.

"So then Tgegani will be alright?" she asked.

Burgon nodded.

"He very likely will. I don't know of any further dangers he might encounter, except possibly some scattered pockets of resistance or problems in the post war cleanup."

"Will he be coming home soon?"

Burgon shook his head.

"Unlikely. They still have a lot to do. They probably won't be allowed to come home for some time. Possibly even as long as a year."

Persia fidgeted nervously.

"Oh I can't wait that long. I want them to come home now."

Burgon smiled.

"I feel the same way. I anxiously want to see what's become of them, and how they've grown these past several months."

"Do you think Tgegani will be scarred by his experiences?" asked Persia.

Burgon chuckled.

"Scarred? Not really. Some buffing, and maybe a little grinding, and he'll be good as new."

"I don't mean his body, dad. I mean, his mind. What will he be like after all he went through? I've seen pictures of what it was like out there, and they scared me. To...to...be there...to..."

Her voice trailed off as an expression of sadness and worry crossed her face, which was soon followed by a river of tears.

"I don't want to think about it anymore, dad. I just want things back to the way they were, back when things were happy and life was simpler," she sobbed.

Burgon knelt down and embraced her lovingly.

"I don't know what this war may have done to him. We can only pray that he is alright. But we must not forget about the others. They're just as important to us as he is. Although they haven't been out there as long as he has, I'm sure they experienced many of the same things he did. We can only hope and pray to Meshua that they are also healthy when they return to us," said Burgon.

"Do you think he'll be different?" asked Persia.

Burgon nodded.

"Very likely."

"But I want him to be just the way he was!" shouted Persia.

"I know that you love Tgegani like a son, sweetheart, and you two spent a lot of time together, but the other lions are just as important to us as he is, and they all look up to you as their mother. As a parent, although superficially, you can't be partial to any one of them. You must love them all equally."

Persia sniffed sadly as she tried to hold back her tears.

"I'll do whatever I can. I'm still not good at this parenting thing. It seems far too sad, and painful and...and...full of tears."

Burgon laughed.

"I know, dear, but we'll come through this together."

Persia smiled through her tears and then gave Burgon a wet, sloppy cat kiss.

"Thanks, dad."

Black studied several field intercepts on his computer, and then turned to Elgar. He then folded his hands and grinned devilishly.

"It would appear that the post war efforts are progressing nicely. If things continue as they are, we should be able to put this whole messy affair behind us very soon."

"What of the efforts to rebuild the Gorg and Midazin nations?" asked Elgar.

"The Midazin can rot in Verok for all I care. They're a pack of filthy, dirty, backstabbing, gutless freaks. They should be wiped from existence just like they tried to do with us! I have absolutely no pity for them!" growled Black.

"Well, I don't believe that genocide of the Midazin race will be the best move for us to make at this time. Instead I believe we should take steps to prevent them from ever gaining a foothold within the Gorg government again."

Black perked up slightly.

"What would those be?"

"If we help the Gorg rebuild their nation, it will, in turn, make the Gorg a strong ally of ours who will be willing to do our bidding should we require their services in the future. This includes eliminating the Midazin for us should such a thing ever be required."

Black appeared perplexed at this.

"Why do you think that would work?" he asked.

"What good have the Midazin been to the Gorg? They've treated them like slaves and inferior beings. If we instead treat them with dignity and benevolence, despite having been their enemy for a time, they will gladly turn away from their alliance with the Midazin and side with us, thus making them a useful ally."

Black grinned demoniacally as he folded his hands thoughtfully.

"Elgar, I like the way you think. See what you can do to ensure that our government begins offering aid and assistance to the Gorg as much as possible. Tell them it'll be a good thing for both nations, but most especially for ours, as it'll keep the Gorg from attacking us again."

Elgar scribbled several notes on a small notepad in his hands.

"Done. And what about the lions? What do we intend to do with them?" he asked.

Black's eyes narrowed.

"My plans for them have not changed."

"But what if they discover what we're planning and turn against us?"

Black selected a folder from a nearby pile and then slid it across the desk. Elgar picked it up and studied its contents briefly, and then cocked an eyebrow in interest.

"How far along is this?" he asked.

"The prototype can be ready for use in as little as three years. If it performs well enough in its field tests, we can begin producing thousands of them a month until our army is large enough to be unstoppable, even by the lions."

Elgar frowned.

"If the Burgon lions get a hold of these, they'll tear them apart."

Black grinned devilishly.

"This new robot has been designed with that consideration in mind."

Elgar was surprised at this.

"So it can destroy them?" he asked.

"If we need it to, yes."

Elgar grinned.

"Well then, clearly we have nothing to worry about."

Black laughed darkly.

"We never did."

"So what of the lions? With this new machine in the works, of what value are they to us?"

"They have the advantage of speed and mobility whereas this machine will be the muscle of our operation. Together they will be unstoppable."

"And what if they don't go along with our plans?"

Black grinned devilishly.

"Then we will simply eliminate them. That has always been the plan. Either they serve us willingly, or they will be destroyed."

Delgra stepped out of his car and studied the facility grounds. One of the officers raced over to him, stopped and then saluted.

"We've checked the entire facility, sir. It's completely intact," said the officer.

"Has EOD cleared all of the buildings?" asked Delgra.

"Every one of them, sir. They're even going through and double checking everything right now, but so far the facility is clean. Nobody's been here since we left," said the officer.

Delgra found this rather unusual. Especially since the Gorg had clearly controlled this area for several months. He reached inside his car, pulled out his laptop, and laid it on the hood of the car. He then worked for several minutes to access the security systems in the facility, and soon downloaded the security logs for the past several months. A script quickly parsed through the data and brought up a handful of entries that indicated possible entry into the facility. All of them turned out to be false alarms triggered by large animals that were in search of food and had tripped the alarms. He quickly logged into the facility mainframe and found all of his security systems intact and untouched. He closed the laptop and tucked it under his arm.

"Lieutenant, have you verified that the administration building is safe to enter?" he asked.

The officer nodded.

"It's squeaky clean, sir."

"Alright, then make sure you get me your report once you finish securing the facility."

"Yes, sir!" said the officer before running off to finish his work.

Delgra then drove down to the administration building and stepped inside. Aside from some dust, and the obvious signs of a hasty departure, the building was exactly how he'd left it. He walked down the hallway to his office and found the door partially ajar. He carefully pushed it open and found Odevion sitting at the desk grinning back at him.

"Do you normally leave highly sensitive laboratory facilities unguarded for months at a time?" he asked.

A gigantic smile grew across Delgra's face.

"Odevion, you old dog. How the blazes have you been?" he said excitedly.

Odevion stood up, walked over to Delgra, and gave him a giant bear hug before stepping back several paces to study him in detail.

"You look a bit paler than I remember," he said with a smirking grin.

Delgra smiled and shrugged.

"Well, you know. Desk job and all. They tend to lock you in the darkest possible hole in the wall and feed you only bread and water until your work is done," he chided.

Odevion laughed.

"Well? That's what you get for being a bureaucrat."

Delgra smirked.

"Bureaucrat indeed. I'll show you a bureaucrat," he laughed. "Either way I see your security penetration skills are still as sharp as ever," he continued.

"How so?"

"You got in without being detected."

Odevion chuckled.

"Actually, I didn't."

Delgra cocked his head in confusion.

"You had to have. There's nothing in the logs indicating your entry into the facility."

"That's because I cheated. I knew how to get into the security logs and delete the evidence of my entry. So I did because I wanted to surprise you when you arrived."

Delgra laughed.

"I should've known. So tell me, how have you been the past couple months?"

Odevion shrugged.

"I went over to visit O'ik, just as you asked, and then spent the rest of my time there fighting against the Gorg.

Oddly enough, I also ended up becoming friends and allies with one of them."

"You became allies with a Gorg!? How? Why?" asked Delgra.

Odevion grinned.

"That's going to take some explaining. And I think you should be sitting down when you hear this, because if I hadn't been there, I wouldn't believe it myself."

Delgra pulled up a chair, sat down, and crossed his arms.

"Alright, I'm listening."

Welk walked into the tent and waved to the others as he sat down.

"Any luck?" asked Sims.

Welk grunted.

"Command still hasn't got any work for us. Apparently the Sattazins are doing most of the heavy lifting since we're so short on manpower," said Welk.

Pentell handed him a ration pack.

"Well, it beats being out in the woods for weeks on end. At least here we get fresh food and somewhere to sleep other than a muddy foxhole."

Welk held up his ration pack, and said, "I don't exactly call this fresh."

Sims laughed.

"Well, at least it's food."

Welk snorted.

"I wouldn't even call it that," he said as he tore into the pack.

"So what are we gonna do about the lions?" asked a soldier.

"What do you mean?" asked Pentell.

The soldier shrugged.

"Well, I can't think that we'd want those things hanging around camp getting bored out of their skull. They ought to have something to do."

Tgegani looked at Pentell, and said, "While I do not see the need for us to leave camp at this time, it may be a good idea for my siblings to engage in patrols of their own to aid the efforts of the Sattazins. Even though there are many of them, there is a lot of land to cover."

Pentell looked at Welk and then Sims.

"He's got a point. The lions could be a great help to the Sattazins."

Sims snorted.

"Have you seen how good the Sattazins can see and hear? They could probably hear a fly sneeze half a mile away."

"Their senses are not that acute. Even ours aren't that good," said Tgegani.

"Maybe not, but they're still pretty sensitive."

Welk pointed his thumb at the tent door, and asked, "So, you want me to go ask the general if that's alright?"

Pentell shook his head.

"Nah. If they want us, they'll ask."

Sims laughed.

"Well, given that nobody ever wants to volunteer for anything, if they went, they'd probably end up with the worst duties."

Pentell laughed.

"Yeah, no kidding."

"Sir, this might sound silly, but now that the war is over, what's going to happen to our unit?" asked one of the soldiers.

"We won't know for a while."

"Actually, I believe I already do," said Tgegani.

The men all looked at him curiously.

"What do you mean?" asked Welk.

"According to military law, being sentient, self-willed beings who were conscripted into service for this country, we are entitled to be relieved of duty once our services are no longer required in the defense of this country. Since the war is now over, it is likely that we will be released soon to return to our parents once it is determined that our presence is no longer required. As such, once we are no longer members of the military, it is only logical that this unit will be dissolved, and all members of it will be reassigned to other units," said Tgegani.

"In other words, we're getting disbanded," said a soldier

Tgegani nodded. Pentell shrugged.

"That sounds about right. But what if you're needed again?"

"If we are asked to return to military service, we will comply," said Tgegani.

"Well, then I guess we should enjoy what time we have left with the lions," said Sims.

The other men all nodded in agreement. This made Tgegani smile.

Three Months Later...

Persia sat on top of a parapet of the outer wall of Black's northern robotics facility and shivered slightly as she huddled beneath a thick pillowed blanket. She looked out across the seemingly endless miles of open prairie that lay beyond the facility as snow began to fall gently around her. She loved snow. It was a curious and cold wonder that tickled her nose and teased her senses. It was also fun to play in. She grinned at the thought and then rested her chin on her paws as she waited in anticipation for the return of the lions. She'd held this vigil every night for over four months as summer wound down into fall and then early winter as the first snowstorm of the season bore down on them.

Finally, the falling snow grew thick enough that she decided it was time to give up for the night and go inside. While she didn't want to leave, she knew that it did little good to wait in the cold if she couldn't see who, or what was coming. She soon stood up, and started to collect her blanket when the clouds parted, pouring brilliant white rays of light down onto the newly fallen snow. She looked out across the prairie briefly and then turned back to the blanket. She then paused as something caught her eye. She turned back towards the prairie, but only saw more snow as it came down in thick, heavy sheets. She blinked and shook her head.

"Nah, I'm seeing things," she said to herself.

Just then a glistening field of golden forms emerged from the snow, contrasting sharply against the extensive fields of white before vanishing again behind another wall of snow. Persia's heart pounded in anticipation. Was this really what she'd been waiting for? Was it really her children? She shook her head in disbelief.

"Come on, Persia. Think. You're seeing things," she said as she chided herself for allowing her imagination to get the better of her.

She turned, picked up her blanket, shook the snow off of it and carefully tossed it on her back. She then turned back towards the prairie one last time, and let out a roar. She froze in surprise as her cry was answered by a chorus of a hundred other feline voices. She inhaled deeply, and roared again. It was soon answered by other roars. She immediately dropped her blanket and sped across the parapet, down the stairs, through the main gate, and out onto the prairie, nearly falling several times as her paws slipped on the newly fallen snow. But soon she was forced to stop as a wall of snow enveloped her, making it impossible to see anymore. She anxiously waited as the snow swirled around her in thick, angry spirals before it parted a few moments later. What appeared before her made her heart nearly leap out of her chest!

"Hello, Mother," came a deep, rich voice that she recognized immediately.

Persia felt like her chest was going to explode with joy! Despite the cold, she leapt at Tgegani, embraced him, and nuzzled him affectionately as she purred with jubilation. After several moments she released him and stared lovingly into his eyes.

"I've missed you," she said.

Tgegani smiled.

"We missed you too."

Persia grinned with pride as more and more lions began appearing out of the blowing snow around her. Tgegani stared at her in concern as she shivered in the snow.

"You look cold," he said.

"Actually, I'm freezing," said Persia sheepishly.

"Then let's go see dad. He'll want to know we're home."

Persia smiled happily, bounced joyfully in the snow, and then followed the lions back to the facility. As she did, Breakman watched them with interest from the top of one of the parapets.

"I wonder what it would be like to have a family like that, rather than just being their protector. I think it would be nice," he thought to himself.

"Do you really desire the love and companionship of a family that much?" came Meshua's voice in his mind.

Breakman paused to think about this.

"Well, they seem so happy. And they're never lonely, because they know they have someone they can come home to. But I have nobody."

He grinned sheepishly.

"Well, except you."

Meshua laughed kindly. Breakman sighed.

"Still, I think I'd like to have something like that," he said.

"With a family there is both joy and sorrow, blessing and sacrifice, happiness and grief. For every good thing that you gain, you will be required to sacrifice something in return. Are you willing to do that?" asked Meshua.

Breakman thought about this for a moment, and then said, "Yeah, I am."

"Then these, whom you have been tasked to protect, I bequeath to you as family."

Breakman blinked in surprise.

"Really? You're serious?"

"I am. Now go to them and welcome your new brothers and sisters home."

Breakman quickly leapt off the parapet and hurried down the stairs with excitement, rushing through the courtyard and up to Persia and Tgegani as they stepped through the main gate. He then stood and stared at them excitedly, not knowing what to say.

After a bit, he smiled, and said, "Hi, Mom."

Persia nodded.

"Hello, Breakman. Your brothers and sisters have just returned home. Why don't you say hi to them," said Persia.

Breakman was shocked. What Meshua had said had indeed come true. He was now part of a family, and a big one at that!

"Hello, little brother," said Tgegani.

Breakman grinned.

"Wow, when Meshua grants a request, he really goes all out!!" he thought with excitement.

"Hey, let's go inside and tell dad you're home!" he said.

Tgegani nodded.

Chapter 24
Two and a half years later...

Negago stood on the top of a mountain in the northern range and stared out across the Yigzan nation in disdain. He'd been so close to finally wiping out his enemy's chosen people. But his efforts had been soundly defeated by Meshua's proxies. Even his most powerful servants could not stop them. He angrily thought about what lay before him and the options at his disposal. Just then, a bird like creature made entirely of fire and bone landed on his shoulder and whispered in his ear. A demonic smile crossed his face.

"He is, is he?" he said with delight.

A dark, guttural chuckle escaped his black lips.

"Hmm. Then there may still be some use for him. He may not wish to serve me, but his greed can be turned to my advantage. Go! Send for my darkest servants. I have work for them to do."

The bird belched a small tongue of bluish flame and then swooped off into the prairie to do its masters bidding. As it vanished into the distance, Negago laughed with evil delight.

"This battle isn't over yet, Meshua. I will still destroy your people, one way or another."

Delgra sat quietly in a patch of short reed grass on the side of a long, sloping hill and ate his lunch in silence. Soft puffy clouds drifted overhead as the twin suns blazed high above in the noonday sky. As he chewed on his sandwich, a dark shadow appeared over his head followed by a strange thumping sound. Looking up, he noticed Odevion pounding a large beach umbrella into the ground next to him.

"What's this for?" he asked.

"Too much of the suns isn't good for you," said Odevion with a smile.

Delgra grunted.

"Doesn't bother me. I've spent so many years in the field that I don't even sunburn anymore."

"Maybe so, but you've been at a desk job for over five years. That alone ought to lower your resistance a bit."

Delgra chuckled.

"Not likely. It's hard to stain old leather," he replied.

Odevion grabbed his laptop and took a place under the umbrella. He then reached into a small, brown paper bag, pulled out some fruit and began munching on it.

Delgra nodded towards the laptop, and asked, "So what are you working on today?"

"I came down here because I have some things I want to show you."

This piqued Delgra's interest just as Odevion had expected it to.

"Do tell," replied Delgra.

"Well, I've been doing some of my usual research on the web, and across the military networks of late, and I think I've come across something rather disturbing."

"Like what?" asked Delgra.

"Well, I think I've found evidence that Ferrell Black is preparing to commit treason."

Delgra seemed surprised at this.

"The same guy who funded the lion project?"

"One in the same."

Delgra's eyes narrowed.

"I've always been somewhat suspicious of him. What specifically do you think he's doing?"

"I'm not sure as of yet. But he's definitely up to something."

Delgra grunted.

"Given the way he prepared us for our war against the Gorg, it could just be another one of his efforts to keep us safe. I mean, he did protect us from being completely annihilated."

"He likely did that in order to save us for his own evil purposes. You can't exactly enslave a country if it doesn't exist anymore."

Delgra contemplated this some more, nibbling at his lip as he did.

"Hmm, good point. But are you sure he's truly dirty, and not just being self-interested like every other businessman?" he asked after a moment.

"Trust me. He's as dirty as they come. I'm just not quite sure what kind of dirty."

"Are you positive about this?"

"I wouldn't have brought it up if I wasn't. While I don't have anything concrete to pin him with yet, he's made enough questionable moves of late to raise a lot of flags with me. So I'd say I'm reasonably positive on this."

Delgra pursed his lips and thought about this some more.

"Well, I'm not. However, I'm still interested in testing the waters to see if your theory is valid. Because, if it is, then we'll need to deal with him quickly. Can we still reach our contacts inside CenTel and the special operations corps and ask for their help in solving this mystery?"

Odevion nodded.

"Way ahead of you. They're already standing by and ready whenever we need them. I've also contacted O'ik and

Fer'gant. They said they will help us find any answers they can."

Delgra chuckled.

"Well done, sergeant, I'm impressed."

Odevion smiled.

"Hey, I aim to please."

Breakman carefully made his way through the narrow confined space of an air duct as two small scout spiders moved quietly in front of him. He would've preferred to have stayed back in the safety of his dad's laboratory, but he had to find out what Black was up to. Too many strange things had been happening lately that defied reasoning. He'd tried contacting Meshua in search of answers, but so far had received no reply. In fact, Meshua had been strangely silent the last few years. As such, Breakman had taken matters into his own hands. And today he'd either put his concerns to rest, or he'd confirm them, which meant he'd need to quickly act to protect his family if he did.

He and his spiders continued on in silence for several more feet until one of the spiders found a junction. Breakman stopped near the corner and carefully leaned a small mirror around it. The path was clear. They then continued down the ventilation shaft for a hundred more feet until they reached the corner they wanted. One of the scout spiders then stopped there and set itself up as a laser relay. The other continued forward and around the corner as Breakman paused in the conduit short of the junction in order to keep himself hidden. The second spider soon reached the end of the junction and began peering through one of the ventilation grills that overlooked Black's office. It raised its own laser transmitter and began sending everything it heard and saw back to the first spider who, in turn, relayed it to Breakman. What he saw intrigued him.

"What are those two up to?" he thought to himself.

"Where are the lions?" asked Black.

"In the field. They've decided to check up on the Gorg to make sure they're honoring the treaty," said Elgar.

Black nodded as he fiddled with one of his cybernetic legs.

"Good. That'll make sure the Gorg don't become a problem again. Once was enough. Just make sure they check in with us again when they're done."

"Yes, sir, I will. Shall I have them return here, or simply report in?"

"Just have them report in. We don't need their services just yet."

"Understood. But what about their creator, Dr. Burgon? Do you think he'll go along with our plans?" asked Elgar.

Black shook his head.

"He won't join us. He's a full-blooded scientist without a single corrupt bone in his body. We wouldn't be able to sway him to our cause no matter what we try."

"But won't that affect our relationship with the lions?"

Black disconnected the lower half of his right leg at the knee and lifted it up so he could get a better look at the ankle joint.

"Given what I have planned for him, that's unlikely. Speaking of which, how is our newest project coming along?" he asked.

"Better than expected. It should be ready before the end of the year."

Black grinned with pleasure.

"That soon, eh?"

"Possibly. But we're not entirely sure yet."

"Hmm, then it may be wise for us to either secure the loyalty of the lions within that time, or else get rid of them."

"How do you plan to do that?"

"By using a little political leverage; a bargaining chip, if you will."

Elgar studied him for a moment and then cocked an eyebrow.

"You're going to use their parents against them, aren't you?"

Black grinned slyly.

"I'm going to do more than that. I plan to use Dr. Burgon, and his pet tiger, as hostages to secure their loyalty. With them in our grasp, the lions will not dare turn against us."

Elgar perked up slightly.

"You're going to hold them captive?"

Black snorted.

"Not a chance! We'd get slaughtered if I even hinted at doing something like that. No, I have a much better plan for those two. I intend to put them on ice, literally."

"How?"

Black fiddled with his ankle joint briefly and then locked the entire appendage back in place before removing it again, being dissatisfied with the results.

"That I'm not certain of just yet. As such I need you to discuss it with our lead physician. Find something in their medical histories that will give us a reason to put them in cryogenic storage. If you can't find something factual, then make something up. But be sure it's believable. Tgegani and his siblings possess a fairly extensive knowledge of medicine, so the ruse needs to be fool proof."

Elgar nodded.

"I'll see what I can find. But once that's done, then what?"

Black gave a low, demonic laugh.

"Once we have their parents on ice, I will be able to easily secure the allegiance of the lions."

Elgar frowned.

"Even with their parents on ice, there's no guarantee they'll join us."

Black grinned with devilish glee.

"Actually, I believe they will."

Elgar frowned slightly.

"If you say so," he replied.

He then turned and walked out of the room as Black continued to tinker with his cybernetic leg. Breakman frowned.

"Oh, this is not good," he thought to himself.

The two spiders then quickly retreated and took up places next to him.

He looked at the first one, and said, "Track Elgar. Find out where he's going. Make sure that nothing happens to mom or dad. If he's about to attack them, signal me and I'll send help."

The little spider acknowledged its orders, and then hurried away. Breakman then grumbled quietly to himself. He didn't like what he heard.

"Great. Now I have to figure out how to get both of them out of here," he said to himself.

But just then, an idea struck him. He grinned slyly.

"Ah, yeah, that'll work. The question though is, will they be gullible enough to fall for it?"

Elgar walked into Black's office the next morning and tossed a letter down on his desk. Black looked at it curiously.

"What's this?" he asked.

"It's a summons. It came via the priority channels this morning. Apparently, the General Secretary wants Dr. Burgon and Ms. Persia to report to the capital immediately so he can talk to them in person," said Elgar gruffly.

Black furrowed his brow in thought.

"Whatever for?" he asked.

Elgar shrugged.

"I don't know. The summons didn't say. Apparently the purpose of the talk is classified, and we don't have permission to know the reasons."

Black crossed his arms and sat back in his chair as he thought.

"It must have been a spur of the moment thing, or something he did on his own, because I don't remember hearing anything about it in my daily briefings."

"Should I give it to him?" asked Elgar.

Black thought for a moment, and then shrugged.

"I don't see where it would hurt us any. It's not like it'll delay or ruin our plans. Just be sure that your men are ready to ice them when they get back."

Elgar nodded.

"They already are."

"Good," said Black with devilish glee.

Burgon stared curiously at the summons.

"By the gates of Tersar! They can't be serious!?" he said.

Persia leapt onto a lab table behind him and carefully read the summons over his shoulder. She then gasped in surprise.

"I'm to come as well!? What do they want *me* for!?" she asked.

Burgon shrugged.

"I really don't know. But we need to pack quickly. It'll take us most of today to drive to the capital in order to make it in time for tomorrow morning's meeting."

"Well then, I'll go get packed. Oh wait, I already am!" she quipped.

"But you don't have anything to pack."

"Exactly," grinned Persia.

Burgon gave her a bemused look.

"Smarty pants," he chided.

"Guilty as charged," replied Persia whimsically.

Burgon then quickly packed a few things in a small day bag, tossed it in the car and the three of them were soon on the road. Breakman, who sat nervously on the back seat of the car, watched as they rolled up to the main gate, paused briefly and then rolled out into the prairie. So far his plan had gone well, but he knew that, at any moment, things could go horribly wrong. Several of his recon spiders, who hung precariously off the bottom of the car, watched the road behind them for signs of pursuit. But much to Breakman's relief, none came. Even so, the next several hours went by slowly as Breakman waited anxiously for any sign that his plan had been discovered. But when nothing appeared, he eventually relaxed. The first threat was over. Now all he needed to concern himself with was executing the next step of his plan.

But that would have to wait until they were well away from the main highway. Several hours later Burgon turned off the main freeway, and onto a simple, two lane provincial highway that acted as a shortcut to a larger freeway not far to the south. This was exactly what Breakman was waiting for. Namely, somewhere that he could execute the next step of his plan without drawing unwanted attention to himself. After again making sure that nobody was following them, he carefully pulled a small capsule out of his pocket and activated it. It hissed quietly for a few seconds as it filled the car with an odorless, colorless gas that quickly put Burgon and Persia to sleep. Seeing that the car was now unmanned, several of Breakman's spiders quickly piled through the window and took control of the vehicle, pulling it safely to the side of the road. They then helped put Burgon in the back seat and strapped him in.

Once he was secured, Breakman climbed into the driver's seat and, with the help of his spiders, turned the vehicle around and headed with all due speed towards the northern mountains. They arrived there several hours later in a sleepy little village that sat nestled neatly between two long, slopping hills. He stopped in front of a small cottage at the far edge of the village and got out. He was immediately greeted by a kindly old man, and his two servants, who took Burgon and Persia upstairs and placed them on soft beds in the loft where they could sleep off the knockout gas that Breakman had used on them. After he was sure that his family was well taken care of, Breakman met with the old man downstairs as his robots took Burgon's car and hid it in a nearby barn.

"I really appreciate what you've done for us," said Breakman.

The old man smiled.

"If what you've told us is true, then our efforts to protect your family will be well worth the risk to ourselves and the Syndicate," he said in a deep and weathered voice.

"Once all of this is sorted out, I'll make sure you guys are well compensated for your efforts," said Breakman.

The old man shook his head and gestured dismissively.

"What you are doing is more than sufficient payment for their protection."

Breakman pulled a thick envelope out of his backpack and handed it to the old man who opened it and stared at the contents in surprise. He then closed it and tucked it into his shirt pocket.

"Although, a little extra payment never hurts from time to time," he said with a sly grin.

"I'll be back before the end of next month. If you don't hear from me by then, take them to the Sattazins. Find a man there who goes by the name of O'ik. He'll take it from there."

The old man bowed slightly.

"It will be as you wish."

Delgra watched the news as reporters flooded Black's northern robotics research facility to cover the story of the year. Burgon had vanished, and nobody knew where he'd gone. Police and federal investigators had spent days questioning Black about Burgon's whereabouts after receiving an anonymous tip that he was trying to kill the famous scientist. Later in the news cast, Black was interviewed by the evening news about his involvement in Burgon's disappearance. His elegance on camera appeared to sway everyone into believing that he spoke the truth. It even convinced the police enough that they no longer considered him a suspect. However, it didn't fool Delgra. To him, Black's face and expressions spoke volumes, and he didn't like what he was seeing.

"It looks like you might be right about Black," he said.

"Do you think he's responsible for Burgon's disappearance?"

Delgra rubbed his chin in thought.

"No, I don't, actually. I can tell by his face that even he doesn't know where they went. But, at the same time, I think he may be the reason that they went missing."

Odevion squinted in confusion.

"You lost me. How would Black...."

He then paused as an idea hit him.

"Oh, wait! You're suggesting that someone else kidnapped Burgon and Persia in order to protect them from Black!" he exclaimed.

Delgra nodded.

"I can't be certain, but I'm willing to bet that's what happened."

"Alright, so that begs a new question. Who would've done this, and why?"

Delgra sighed as he bit his lip in thought.

"I don't know, but I plan to find out."

Tgegani sniffed the pavement near the side of the highway and studied the grass around him as vehicles raced by not far away.

"Anything?" asked Pen.

Tgegani's eyes narrowed.

"Nothing. If they came this way like the witnesses said, it's likely that their scent has already been lost."

Pen sighed.

"We've been out here a week already and we've found nothing. The longer this takes us, the colder the trail gets."

Tgegani sat down.

"I know. But we have to explore every possible angle and avenue. Something is bound to eventually lead us to them."

"I agree, but what? This trail is obviously a dead end," said Pen.

As Tgegani listened to reports coming in to him from other lions nearby, Pen looked out across the prairie on both sides of the highway, and then off towards the mountains in the distance. As he did, an idea struck him.

"We could go north to the mountains."

"North?" asked Tgegani curiously.

Pen shrugged.

"Well, nothing says he stayed on this highway. Besides, if they were kidnapped, it's possible they would've been taken up north."

"Why?" asked Tgegani.

"Well, why not? There's only farms, and a handful of small towns up that way. What better place is there to hide someone as important as our parents? And, besides, it's in the opposite direction they were traveling. So it seems entirely reasonable to me."

Tgegani thought about this and nodded.

"Hmm, that's possible. So let's explore that idea. Gather everyone together and we'll move north in search of them."

As Pen began issuing orders to the others, Tgegani looked off towards the mountains and thought about his parents.

"Meshua, allow us to find the path that leads to our parents. And, wherever they are, please take care of them and keep them safe until we arrive."

Black slammed his fist into his desk sending splinters flying across the room.

"I can't believe this is happening! Everything was going so perfectly, and now we're totally shut down until this whole affair with Burgon blows over!" He then grit his teeth angrily, and said, "I want to know who kidnapped him!"

"It could be the Midazin. They'd benefit the most from this," said Elgar flatly.

Black punched a hole in a nearby wall in frustration and then looked down at the rough, gray metal that peeked through his now torn, artificial skin.

"Contact our agents operating in the Midazin nation. Tell them to find out if any of them are behind this kidnapping. If they are, I want some heads!" he said through gritted teeth.

Elgar bowed slightly.

"And what of our efforts to bring the lions to our side?" he asked.

Black inhaled deeply, and then gave a long, frustrated sigh.

"Hopefully this won't spoil things, or we may be forced to go forward without them."

"Understood."

Breakman trudged through the soft, damp earth of the northern prairie as a cold wind tossed the budding stalks of reed grass into brilliant, green waves.

"I'm starting to wonder if coming this way was such a good idea," he thought. "Hey, Meshua? If it's possible, could you point Tgegani my direction? It'd really be a huge help," he continued.

Silence.

"Hmm. I don't know why you're not talking to me anymore, but either way, keep mom and dad safe and help me find at least one of the lions."

He had no more than finished his thought when a large, golden face appeared out of the grass in front of him. Breakman blinked in surprise. It was Neomara. She stared curiously at him in return.

"Well, that was quick," he thought.

"What are you doing out here?" she asked.

"I'd ask you the same thing, but that's irrelevant right now. I need to speak with Tgegani. It's about mom and dad."

Her eyes grew wide.

"Do you know where they are?" she asked.

"Just let me talk to Tgegani, okay?" said Breakman sternly.

"I will relay to him whatever message you have," she replied.

Breakman crossed his arms.

"In person. It's kind of important."

Realizing that Breakman's news was apparently for Tgegani's ears only, she called to him over the radio and relayed the request.

A few seconds later, she said, "He's coming right now. It'll be about twenty minutes before he can reach us. Please stay here and wait for him."

Breakman lifted a mud caked foot, and said, "It's not like I'm going anywhere."

Nearly twenty minutes later, Tgegani, Pen, and several other lions arrived.

"I am here," said Tgegani as he trotted to a stop.

Breakman raised an eyebrow in muted consternation.

"I was hoping this conversation would be a bit more, you know, private," he said sarcastically.

"Given the situation, I did not feel it was best to come alone," said Tgegani.

Breakman shrugged.

"Alright, fair enough."

"Do you have word on where mother and father are?"

"I do. But I've got a lot to explain first. So listen carefully," said Breakman.

The lions perked up in surprise as this was the first good news they'd had in a while.

"Where are they? And who took them? Whoever it is, I'll rip their head off!" roared Pen.

"Whoa, whoa, pussycat. First, let me explain. *Then* you can decide if you want to rip my head off or not. Okay?" said Breakman.

The lions all looked at him with puzzled glances.

"What are you talking about!?" asked Pen.

"Alright, first off, I was the one who kidnapped mom and dad. But it was for their protection," said Breakman.

The lions gasped in surprise.

"Why? Who wishes to harm them?" asked Tgegani.

"Believe it or not, Ferrell Black," said Breakman flatly.

The lions looked at each other in shock.

"Are you certain of this? He does not seem like one who would do harm to them for any reason," said Tgegani.

"Actually, he wants to use them as tools to force your loyalty to him. Apparently he's got some kind of twisted plan in the works, and you're a big part of that."

"Do you have proof of this?"

"I figured you'd ask, so I compiled a complete briefing on what he's doing, including some video of him and Elgar talking about their plans. I didn't get everything, but I got enough."

He then transmitted everything he knew to the lions. The lions quickly reviewed everything he'd given to them before discussing this between themselves as they soon came to understand the full depth of the situation.

"It does appear that he may be up to something dishonest. But we will need more information before we can move against him," said Tgegani.

Breakman grunted.

"Seriously!? Do you realize how much information you already have!?"

"I do. But I wish to be certain, beyond all possible doubt, of his intentions."

Breakman frowned at this.

"Seriously? How much more information do you need?" he groaned.

"Do we have any ideas on what we should do about this? We can't just go charging in there and arrest him based on conjecture. What we have now is just circumstantial," said Neomara.

"Circumstantial!? Um, guys? He pretty much confessed to what he was gonna do. Like you really need something more!?" said Breakman.

"What you've given us is certainly more than merely circumstantial. But Neomara is right, we need to gather more information to be certain of either his innocence, or his guilt," said Tgegani.

Breakman frowned.

"Um, is anybody listening to me!? The guy is guilty as sin!!"

"I agree. More information is needed," said Neomara.

Breakman snorted and then facepalmed at this.

"Apparently not," he muttered.

"And we need to get Mom and Dad to safety," said Pen.

"Yeah, speaking of which, where are they?" asked Neomara.

The lions then turned their attention to Breakman who waved his hands dismissively.

"I'd rather not tell you that right now. However, I *will* say that they're safe."

"How do you know?" asked Pen.

"Again, I'm not saying. It's for their safety. Trust me on this."

"Then, in that case, we should work on investigating Black," said Pen.

"Agreed. But before we do that, we require allies. I fear that much of what needs to be done is beyond our abilities," said Tgegani.

"Any ideas on who to call?" asked Pen.

"I know a few we could ask," said Breakman.

"Really? Who?"

Breakman laughed.

"HA! Somebody *was* listening."

"So who is it?"

Breakman grinned sheepishly.

"Would you believe that they work for the Syndicate?"

He half expected to get scolded by all the lions for his odd underworld alliance. But, to his surprise, the lions actually seemed alright with this.

"If they're being taken care of, then let's get going!" said Pen.

Tgegani shook his head.

"Not yet. I want to be sure that mother and father are safe before we go," replied Tgegani.

"They are," said Breakman.

"I need to verify that, in person," replied Tgegani sternly.

Breakman grunted.

"I was hoping you wouldn't say that. The less people who know where they are, the better."

"I agree. But I would feel better knowing for certain."

Breakman studied Tgegani for several moments, and then put his fists on his hips as he grunted in frustration.

"You know, sometimes you can be more stubborn than stone. For once I wish you would just trust me. I know what I'm doing," he said.

Tgegani narrowed his eyes.

"I trust you. However, it is best if *we* watched over them. I am worried that those that you've tasked with their protection will be insufficient to protect them given who is against us."

A small scout spider climbed out of Breakman's backpack and onto his shoulder.

"I'm not," he said as he gently stroked the small machine.

"Those don't count," said Pen.

Breakman shrugged.

"Who said I was using any of my helpers to watch over them? I've got Syndicate thugs for that. Nobody will get to them so long as those guys are on duty."

"Breakman..." said Tgegani sternly.

The little droid glared at him briefly and then grunted in frustration.

"Alright, fine. But don't blame me if they get discovered."

Chapter 25

Burgon slowly roused from his slumber and then sat up. However, his world quickly began to spin, causing him to lay back down. To add insult to injury, his head was pounding like an abused base drum. He groaned and tried to sit up again, but felt a gentle hand push him back down.

"I wouldn't sit up just yet, Mr. Burgon. The drug he used on you takes a bit to wear off," came a kindly old voice.

"Who are you? Where am I?" asked Burgon groggily.

"Just relax and drink this."

He then felt a hand take the back of his head and lift it as a warm mug of a sweet smelling hot liquid was pressed to his lips. He took a sip and felt it tingle in his mouth. He leaned back and tried to put his world back in focus as it spun briefly and then seemed to miraculously clear. He tried to sit up again, but was greeted by the mug of hot liquid again.

"Keep drinking. It will make you feel better."

Burgon took several more sips and felt his head clear even more. He slowly opened his eyes and saw the kindly face of an old man leaning over him.

"Who are you?" he asked.

"Keep drinking, Mr. Burgon. You'll need to get that fog out of your head before you decide to go anywhere."

Burgon took the cup in his hand and emptied it in several quick gulps. The man laughed.

"Be careful. You might burn yourself."

Burgon winced. It had been rather hot, but the relief that it brought more than made up for the burning in his throat. The old man took the cup and set it down on a nearby stool.

"There, how do you feel now?" he asked.

Burgon nodded.

"A lot better. But where *am* I?" he asked.

"You are under the protection of the Syndicate. A very dear colleague of yours has asked us to keep you safe."

"Who?" asked Burgon curiously.

"His name is Breakman."

Burgon's eyes went wide.

"Him? But he's just an android! He couldn't have done this!"

The old man laughed.

"He's more than you think he is. He asked us to watch over you in exchange for his assurance that he would bring down Ferrell Black."

Burgon stared suspiciously at the old man.

"Ferrell Black is an honorable man! I've worked for him for years!"

"No he's not, Dad," came a voice from across the room.

The two men turned to see Breakman and Tgegani standing in the door. The old man stood up, bowed slightly and excused himself. Tgegani came over and sat down in front of Burgon as Breakman climbed onto a nearby stool.

"Tgegani, what's going on? Why am I here?" asked Burgon.

Breakman sighed deeply.

"Dad, there's something I need to tell you."

Burgon frowned.

"I have a feeling I'm not going to like this."

Breakman then spent the next several minutes telling Burgon everything he knew. Burgon took it all well enough, but was still shaken by the experience.

"Mr. Black is a traitor?" said Burgon contemplatively.

"That has not been confirmed with absolute certainty. But all available data at this time leans strongly in that direction. If true, we must put all our efforts into bringing him down and saving this nation. As such it would be best for you to stay here for now where it is safe," said Tgegani.

"But what if you're wrong? What if you misunderstood him?" asked Burgon.

"We will verify his intentions before moving against him. But we are currently acting under the assumption that his motives are dishonest and potentially treasonous," said Tgegani.

Burgon nodded.

"Alright, then do your best and stay safe."

"Don't worry. I don't plan to die anytime soon," said Breakman with a smirk.

The two androids then made their way downstairs to where the old man stood waiting.

"I'm leaving again as we have a lot of work ahead of us. We'll also be leaving behind a few lions to help you protect the place," said Breakman.

The old man shook his head.

"They are not needed. We have our own guards."

"They are for my peace of mind," said Tgegani.

The old man studied the lion for several moments, then asked, "How many will you leave?"

"Six."

The old man scratched his short, rough gray beard and thought about this.

"Will they be seen?" he asked.

Tgegani shook his head.

"They will not, unless they are needed to protect you."

The old man nodded, and said, "Then we welcome their help."

Joslin and Black stepped into the General Secretary's office and proceeded to have a seat.

"Good afternoon, gentlemen. What brings you here today?" asked the General Secretary.

"It seems that a problem has arisen that we need to address," said Joslin.

The General Secretary furrowed his brow in interest.

"Oh? What kind of problem?"

"Do you remember the Burgon lions?" asked Joslin.

A smile came to the General Secretary's face.

"Yes, I do! Wonderful creatures they are. They have my respect and honor for all they did to save our nation."

Black's expression began to grow remorseful. He sighed.

"Yes, their achievements are to be commended. However, it would appear that they may now have become a danger to our people."

The General Secretary perked up slightly.

"How so?"

"As I'm sure you're aware, the Burgon lions are sentient robots."

The General Secretary nodded.

"Of course! Everyone knows that."

"Yes, and with that comes emotions. It is an integral part of what sentience is. However, this has led to the creation of a dangerous flaw in their programming; one that we believe may become lethal if not quickly addressed."

"A lethal flaw?" said the General Secretary curiously.

"Yes. Apparently Dr. Burgon had been secretly administering software patches to his lions over the past several years to keep their AI's from breaking down and going mad while he worked on a more permanent fix. But now that he's vanished without a trace, I fear that his efforts have failed and he has paid the ultimate price with his life."

The General Secretary stared suspiciously at Black.

"You're not suggesting that his lions are responsible for his disappearance, are you?"

Black shrugged.

"What other answer is there? They've proven to be skilled trackers without rival, and yet they have been completely unable to find him. That's a bit suspicious if you ask me."

"Agh, that's nonsense and you know it. Just because they haven't found him doesn't suddenly make them murderers. Even if that were true, what would make them want to kill their own creator?"

"Fear," said Black flatly.

"Of what?"

"Of being killed."

The General Secretary looked at Black in surprise, and then studied him deeper.

"And why should I believe you?" he asked.

Black laid a small folder in front of the General Secretary.

"This has everything in it that you need to know. I've had several of my best cybernetics scientists looking at the core AI software that was used to program all the lions, and it is indeed fatally flawed. Even if many of the problems have already been patched, it's still only a matter of time before they cross the line into madness."

The General Secretary picked up the folder and looked at the pages inside. After a bit, he threw it down and grunted angrily.

"I find this information to be circumstantial at best. I am not going to order the destruction of over six hundred war heroes based on information you claim is valid."

Black shook his head.

"I'm not saying we need to destroy them. We simply ask them to come in and be deactivated until a cure can be found for this flaw. Once that is fixed, we can then return them to normal life."

The General Secretary's eyes narrowed.

"So instead of killing them, we're unlawfully incarcerating them?"

"Not unlawfully. What we'd be doing is completely within the bounds of the law. If a madman with a knife was terrorizing the streets, wouldn't you have him arrested and put under a doctor's care until he could operate as a normal member of society again?" said Joslin.

The General Secretary nodded.

"Of course I would! You'd be silly not to."

"Then how is this any different?"

"Well, they're machines for one. They think and act differently than we do. And, while it's still somewhat weird for me to treat them as living creatures, and citizens no less, it's still my job to protect them through the power of the law. I will not do anything against them without probable cause," said the General Secretary.

Black shook his head.

"As the senator already said. We're not unlawfully incarcerating them. We're simply acting in the best interests of them and everyone else in this nation," said Black.

The General Secretary's eyes narrowed.

"If they are brought in for treatment, are you sure you can cure them?" he asked.

"If we can't, someone will eventually come along who can."

"And what if nobody is ever able to fix them?"

Black shrugged.

"Technology is forever evolving. At some point in time someone will be able to replicate his work and fix what he could not. I know that Dr. Burgon's designs are revolutionary beyond the scope of what others are capable of doing right now. But there's nothing that says his work can't eventually be replicated by others, and then surpassed. After all, technology always continues to progress and with it so will our understanding of robotic sentience."

The General Secretary thought about this for a moment.

"And what if we call them and they don't come in?" he asked.

"We'll cross that bridge when we come to it. Although I don't think we'll ever need to."

The General Secretary nodded.

"Alright, I'll see to it that they're called in and held for examination. But remember this. When you begin dealing with the lions about this issue, be diplomatic. The last thing I need is over six hundred angry lions beating down my front door."

Black smiled beatifically.

"Oh, but of course!"

Delgra looked up as Odevion walked into the office, put his laptop down on the desk, and faced it towards him.

"Looks like I've found something. Black seems to be ordering considerable quantities of raw materials and parts that don't match up with his normal purchasing patterns. Plus he's been doing a lot of unusual research into weapons systems lately. It's certainly not your typical fare for a cybernetics company who specializes in home and hospital cybernetic products," said Odevion.

Delgra looked at the list for several moments, and then reached over to his screen and turned it to face Odevion. The sergeant carefully read the headline emblazoned on the screen, and blinked in surprise.

"Lions to be recalled!?" he said.

Delgra turned the screen back towards himself and nodded.

"It would seem he's playing part of his hand now," he replied.

Odevion thought about this.

"What do you think he's up to? Could it be a new weapons system or something?" he asked.

"I don't know, but whatever this is, this recall, and your list, are part of a much bigger package."

"That much is obvious. But where do the lions fit into this?"

"As a great philosopher once said, 'Remove your greatest threat before proceeding with your greatest plan'," said Delgra.

"So you're thinking that he's trying to take over the country," said Odevion.

"I'm beginning to think that may be the case. Even so, we still need to find out what he's planning, and if it's treasonous, then we need to do everything in our power to stop him."

Black pranced triumphantly past Elgar who appeared a bit puzzled by his actions. He followed Black into his office and closed the door behind him.

"I take it that all went well?" he asked.

Black pivoted on his heals with a flash of bravado, and said, "Better than I could've hoped for! While it took a bit of convincing to get that fat slob to go along with my plans, he ultimately did. Now we simply wait for the lions to come to us. I especially want to see Tgegani. Having him on our side will be very important."

"I will bring him to you as soon as he arrives."

"Excellent! And have you found Burgon yet?" said Black.

Elgar shook his head. Black's face went from an expression of glory, to one of anger and frustration.

"Have we at least found who kidnapped him?"

Elgar nodded. Black perked up.

"Oh really? Who is it?"

"Breakman," said Elgar flatly.

Black stared at Elgar in confusion.

"Who!?"

"He's a small servant droid that Dr. Burgon built to assist Persia. He appears to be the mastermind behind Burgon's disappearance."

"How do you know that?" asked Black.

"Our security teams were investigating a low level intrusion into our core systems and discovered evidence that links him to the false summons we received."

Black blinked in surprise.

"You mean we've been outsmarted by another one of Burgon's infernal machines!?" he said.

"We have. He may also have knowledge of our plans, which would explain why he kidnapped Burgon and Persia."

Black thought about this for several moments and then grinned slyly.

"Hmm, it appears that I may have found a worthy opponent. And a machine no less. Well, then we need to capture him and find out what he knows about our plans, and where he's hidden those two. We need them alive for our plans to work."

Elgar nodded.

"We're already watching for him."

Black grinned.

"Good. I look forward to talking to this Breakman character as soon as you capture him." He then paused for a second, and said, "No, actually, I don't. When you capture him, download his mind and then have him destroyed. I don't want to risk him escaping and warning the lions."

Elgar bowed.

"As you wish."

Tgegani listened with interest to a radio message ordering them to turn themselves in as it was repeated over and over again on a continuous loop. He stared at Pen.

"What do you make of it?" he asked.

Pen shrugged.

"I really don't know."

"Are the other lions nearby?"

"Yeah. All of our brethren are in the valley below. They await your orders."

"Good. Any news from Breakman?"

Pen shook his head.

"Not since he left for the laboratory yesterday. He may not have found anything worth reporting yet. So we probably won't hear from him until he does."

Tgegani thought about this.

"Hmm. That's possible."

"So what do we do about this call to come in?" asked Pen.

Tgegani shook his head.

"We are not to obey it. I have a feeling that, if we do, we'll be deactivated and many terrible things will happen while we are offline."

Pen looked at him curiously.

"Like what?"

"I don't know, but if what Breakman showed us about Black is true, we will need to remain functional in order to protect our people."

"Well, we know he's involved in quite a few shady things, but this recall?" said Pen.

"He wants something, and this recall verifies that fact."

"What do you think he's trying to do?" asked Pen.

"I don't know, but I intend to find out."

Pen's eyes narrowed.

"Please tell me that you're not about to do what I think you are."

Tgegani nodded. Pen groaned.

"But that's insane! You're playing right into his hands!"

"I know. But I must see for myself what he is up to."

"Then I'm coming with you."

Tgegani shook his head.

"No, I have another task for you. I need you and Tiel to take charge of the other lions while I am away. If something happens to me, you are to lead them north into the mountains. When the time is right, you are to return and save our people."

"But you're our leader! I can't do your job! Nor am I going to let you just walk into danger without me there to protect you!" protested Pen.

Tgegani roared angrily.

"Listen to me! I've seen what you can do! You're a natural born leader. If you did not have this trait, I would not have entrusted our family to you. I know you want to go with me, and are loyal to the end. I respect that. But this is something I must do alone."

A sad expression came across Pen's face.

"You'll come back, right?" he said.

Tgegani nodded.

"I will do my best. But only Meshua knows what the future holds for me. If you do not hear from me within twenty four hours, do as I've said and take everyone to safety."

Pen nodded.

"I will."

Chapter 26

Elgar walked into Black's office.

"We got him," he said with a grin of satisfaction on his face.

"Got who?"

"Breakman. We caught him sneaking around the south end of the facility."

Black grinned with evil delight.

"Excellent! Did you get anything from him yet?"

Elgar shook his head.

"No, nothing useful. He appears to have selectively wiped segments of his memory before coming here. Our scientists have tried recovering the data in those areas, but so far have been unsuccessful."

Black swore.

"Well, tell them to keep trying. If they can't get anything useful by tomorrow morning, have him tossed in the smelter. I don't want to risk him escaping."

Elgar nodded.

"Understood."

Delgra and Odevion walked into a dark, seedy, side alley bar and sat down at a booth near the back. They then studied the room cautiously, but found nothing suspicious. A few minutes later a man appeared from the shadows near the back door and slipped into their booth. He wore a thick, heavy trench coat and wide brimmed hat that hid his face in a veil of shadows.

"It is good to see you again my friends," came a deep, but familiar voice.

Delgra leaned over the table, and said, "What do you have for us, O'ik?"

"Not much, I'm afraid. It seems that your government is either ignorant of Black's plans, or they're comfortably in his pocket," he said.

"What about Fer'gant? Has he found any possible Midazin or Gorg connections to this plan?"

O'ik shook his head.

"He's found nothing. They are both too busy rebuilding their countries to bother with internal Yigzan politics at this time."

Delgra nodded.

"Good. What of your underworld contacts? Have they found anything?"

O'ik shrugged.

"They have nothing new to report either. Although one of them did suggest something that I thought was interesting."

"Do tell," said Delgra.

"My contact said that Burgon's lions may be Mr. Black's current target. Nobody is sure why, but it appears that they may be important to his plans."

"Then this recall is connected to him?" asked Odevion.

O'ik nodded.

"That is very likely the case. But there is no information on why they are being recalled, other than what has been reported in the news. Some speculate that he may be trying to remove them as a threat before he strikes out on the next phase of his plans."

"Do you know what those plans are?" asked Delgra.

O'ik shrugged.

"I do not. Nor do any that I have talked to. But the underworld has become very disturbed by his actions and fear something terrible is coming."

Odevion nodded.

"That's why we're involved. If his motives are treasonous, we'll want to stop him before he gets too far."

O'ik nodded.

"As do we. We fear that his plans may affect all of our races. I have been in touch with my superiors, and all of our resources are at your disposal should you need them."

Delgra nodded.

"Thank you. I just hope it doesn't come to that."

"So do I," said O'ik.

Tgegani walked slowly up to the main gate of Black's laboratory and studied the four men that stood guard there. One of them eyed him briefly, and then got on the phone to his superiors. The other three cautiously cradled their weapons and stared suspiciously at him as he continued to approach. Finally the first guard hung up the phone and motioned Tgegani to a smaller side gate. The man opened it for him and allowed the lion to pass.

"Mr. Black is waiting for you in his office. One of the other guards will escort you there," said the man.

"I know where it is," replied Tgegani as he continued on past the gate.

"But you...hey, wait! You need an escort!" shouted the man.

He stepped forward to stop Tgegani, but paused as several of Black's personal bodyguards swooped in from the shadows and fell in behind the lion. They quickly escorted him across the facility to Black's office. Upon entering, Black walked up to him with open arms.

"Tgegani! I'm so glad to see you! Come in, sit down!" he said excitedly.

Tgegani followed him across the room and then sat down in front of the desk. Black, in turn, sat down in his chair across from him with a flare of royal elegance.

"Mr. Tgegani. What can I do for you today?" asked Black.

Tgegani's eyes narrowed slightly.

"I'm here to discuss the order requesting my siblings and I to turn ourselves in," he said.

Black nodded.

"It's sad, isn't it? Such beautiful minds, and yet they want to dispose of you like yesterday's refuse. I really do feel that you are being woefully wronged by the actions of our government. It's completely unfair," he said in a patronizing voice.

"Do you know why we are being recalled?" asked Tgegani.

Black shrugged.

"It's simple really. You are strong. Those in power fear the strong, therefore the government fears you. It was only a matter of time before they decided that you were too dangerous to keep around. So now they want to do away with you. They know power when they see it, and they see yours with great clarity."

Tgegani raised an eyebrow. Black stood up and began to walk slowly around his desk.

"I know this is very difficult for you and your family, what with the disappearance of your parents. However, if you will allow me, I can make this go away as though it never happened," he said, a hint of arrogance in his voice.

"How would you do that?" asked Tgegani.

"Well, it's quite simple really. You swear that you will serve me without question and I will guarantee that this order goes away."

Tgegani's eyes narrowed slightly as Black smiled beatifically.

"How would our loyalty to you cause the government to rescind its orders?" asked Tgegani.

"By pledging your loyalty to me, you would no longer be perceived as a threat, and thus they would have no reason to fear you anymore, as you would be obedient to me, and I to them."

"But I have disobeyed orders before."

"Yes, but you were within your right to do so. Under my leadership, such forays of conscience would not be permitted. This would, in turn, take away the very thing they fear about you. So if you have no freedom of will to turn against them, then they have no reason to fear you."

Tgegani cocked his ears slightly.

"If I were to swear allegiance to you, what would I be required to do?"

Black tried not to act giddy as he looked at the lion.

"Just some small things really. As you have seen, our government is corrupt. I would wish to see that corruption removed through whatever means necessary."

Tgegani folded his ears back and narrowed his eyes.

"You would overthrow the government?" he asked.

Black laughed disingenuously.

"No, no. Not at all. I'm no traitor," he said, smiling innocently.

"Ah, but you are," thought Tgegani. "Then how would you make this change?" he asked.

"By taking the steps required by law to achieve any changes that are needed," said Black.

"How will our loyalty to you achieve this?"

"By facing strength with strength. A strong man will not change his ways unless forced to by another strong man. You and your siblings will make me that strong man; a man who can right the wrongs of this world and bring justice to all!"

"I see."

Black grinned gleefully.

"Oh, this is going better than I ever imagined!" he thought. "Think of it this way, Tgegani. What has our government ever done for you? When your father first conceived of you, they saw your potential and sought to prevent your creation. But I *too* saw your potential and rescued you and your father before you were anything more than a few scribbles on a piece of paper. I helped him create you, to give you life, and to help you grow. I assisted your mother when she needed things. I even protected you and your family when others would have thrown you to the wind," he said.

Black spun on his heels and walked slowly back to his chair as he peered at Tgegani through the corner of one eye.

"Then war came and you were drafted. It was a war they started. Yet they did not want to clean up the problems themselves. So they sent you."

"But the Gorg and Midazin started the war."

Black snapped his head around and glared at the lion.

"Nonsense! That is what they want you to believe! Think about it, Tgegani. What have they ever done for you? They have only shown you misery, heartache, and loss. But I have gone out of my way to help you! I was the one who made everything you now have possible! I have even committed a significant portion of my resources towards finding your parents. Is it too much for me to ask for your allegiance as a small token of your gratitude for what I've done? There are so many forces fighting against you. Why not join with me and together we can right the wrongs of this world!" said Black passionately and with such flair that it surprised Tgegani.

Black then gracefully sat down in his chair as though he were emperor of the world. He then folded his hands together and studied Tgegani intently.

"So, what is your decision?" he asked, a hint of devilish glee in his voice.

"I've got to think of something I can use to stall him. If I say no, he'll kill me before I can get out of here. But I can't say yes," thought Tgegani.

He struggled within his mind for several moments, analyzing numerous ideas as he tried to choose one that would work best. Black patiently watched the lion as he sat before him, eyes closed, and his mind deep in thought.

"Good, good. Mull it over, Mr. Lion. I own you and you know it," thought Black.

Finally, Tgegani settled on an idea. He then opened his eyes.

"Your offer has merit. But I cannot give you my answer at this time," he said.

Black swore quietly to himself.

"Why wait? Make your decision now!" he said with passion.

Tgegani shook his head.

"My siblings and I are all free minds. We each choose our own path in life. However, big decisions such as this which involve our entire family require that I consult with my siblings first before I can give you an answer," said Tgegani.

Black grinned.

"Ah, you're stalling for time so you don't look like a pushover. Very smart, Mr. Lion. But in the end, I already own you," he thought to himself. He nodded, and said, "That is fine. Go share with them the wonderful opportunity I have given you, and then come back to me with your decision when you are ready."

Tgegani nodded.

"I will."

As Tgegani cleared the main gate of Black's facility, he was greeted by several other lions who appeared out of the nearby reed grass and joined him as he ran.

"What did you find out?" asked Renc.

"Black wants to take over the government."

"For some reason I don't find that surprising," said Renc flatly.

"What do we do now?" asked Yteca.

"We must warn our family and prepare them for what lies ahead," said Tgegani.

"Shouldn't we get some help first?" asked Renc.

"Yes, we will. And I know just the people who can help us."

Elgar walked into Black's office, and then paused as he spied Black grinning devilishly. He raised an eyebrow in interest.

"Did something good happen, sir?" he asked.

Black grinned at him with devilishly glee.

"The lions are ours," he said happily.

Elgar grinned.

"So what does that do to our plans?" he asked.

"With the lions in our employ, we can finally achieve our goal of conquering our nation and taking it as our own!" said Black.

"But what of the new prototype?" asked Elgar.

Black nodded.

"It will be used too."

"But what if the lions don't join us?"

Black gave Elgar a disbelieving glance.

"I have all but guaranteed their allegiance to us. He may have seemed hesitant when he left here, but I know that he is ours," he said confidently.

But Elgar wasn't convinced.

Breakman cautiously peered over the top of a parapet at Black's northern facility and studied the courtyard below.

"Good. Just a few guards."

He glanced back towards the facility.

"Hopefully I can get out of here without getting smelted down. If they hadn't fallen for my decoy earlier, I'd be scrap by now," he thought.

He reached into his pack and pulled out a small data card.

"Hopefully this has everything we need to stop Black. Because I don't think I'll get another crack at his network again anytime soon."

He returned the card to his pack and then turned to one of his spider droids.

"Find us some transportation. Preferably something big, like a truck."

The droid acknowledged the order and immediately scurried off. After several minutes it reported back that it had found a large, abandoned army truck.

"Hmm, not what I had hoped for, but it'll do," thought Breakman.

He turned to another of his droids, and said, "Gather everyone together and meet me at the truck. We need to get out of here."

The droid acknowledged the order and hurried away. Breakman then made his way off the parapet, past several incapacitated guards, and down to where the truck sat waiting for him. He found the back filled with numerous small droids. Several more waited for him in the front. A quick visual inventory told him that all of his spiders were present.

He quickly climbed into the cab, and said, "Let's get moving."

The truck then pulled out of the loading dock and sped across the facility, its twin electric motors and hydrogen power pack allowing it to move with great speed and stealth. But as they approached the inner gate, Breakman noticed something that he didn't like. It was closed.

"Oh, great. They locked the gate and that thing is too thick to smash through. Looks like we'll have to open it the hard way," he thought.

He climbed out onto the roof of the cab and waited patiently as the truck sped towards the gate. As it drew close, the truck began to slow, but did not stop as two of the guards at the gate curiously watched it approach. It had no lights on and nobody appeared to be in the driver's seat.

"That's odd, isn't it?" asked one of the guards.

"Nah, it's probably just another one of Mr. Black's robotic toys," said the other.

"Well, we need to check it out anyways," said the first.

Suddenly Breakman launched himself from the hood of the truck, and crashed into the first guard like a sledge hammer. The blow knocked the man unconscious and drove him to the ground with a thud. Breakman quickly recovered, and with several quick, powerful blows, sent the second guard crashing to the ground with a bone jarring thud. The guard tried to get back up but was quickly knocked out cold by a solid kick to the face. Hearing the commotion, two other guards, who'd been standing in the nearby guard booth, stepped out into the open to investigate. They were immediately put out of action as well. Breakman then quickly checked the area and, seeing that it was all clear, ordered his droids to drag the guards out of sight. As they did, he slipped into the control booth and opened the gate. It rumbled briefly and then began to open.

"Go! Go!" said Breakman to the droids driving the truck.

The droids punched the accelerator and sent the truck barreling through the gate. As soon as it was clear, Breakman activated the gate mechanism and then sprinted through it as it began to close. He then joined his other droids in the back of the truck. They soon reached the outer gate, where they quickly neutralized the guards there as well, clearing the way for the truck to escape into the prairie. As soon as they were safely away, Breakman climbed out of the back and into the passenger's seat.

"Let's get moving and don't spare the H2," he said as he sat down.

The droids chirped in acknowledgment, and then pushed the truck to its limits as it barreled down the long, narrow road that led away from Black's facility.

Chapter 27

As the last light of day began to fade on the horizon, the lions continued to push themselves to their limits as they ran with all their might.

"Where are we going first?" asked Renc.

"To the train yards. We need to head south as quickly as we can."

"But why there?"

"The trains will be the fastest way to get there," replied Tgegani.

"Heads up! Truck coming!" shouted one of the lions.

"Scatter! Everyone hide!" shouted Tgegani.

The lions quickly spread out and took cover as an old army truck rumbled down the road towards them. Tgegani switched his eyes to night vision mode and studied the cab of the truck. To his surprise, something resembling a small child could be seen in the passenger's seat. But there was no sign of a driver. Suddenly Tgegani realized who it was.

"Breakman!" he said in surprise.

He bolted out into the road and stopped along the shoulder as the truck came to a halt in front of him. A moment later, Breakman jumped down and trotted over to Tgegani. He put his hands on his hips and grinned slyly.

"Wow, fancy meeting you here," he quipped.

"Where are you going?" asked Tgegani.

"To find you, which I didn't expect to do quite this quickly."

"Can you take us to the train yards?"

"Sure, hop in!" said Breakman.

Tgegani nodded to the other lions nearby who soon appeared from the shadows and then leapt into the bed of the truck. He soon joined them. As the truck began pulling away, Tgegani poked his head through the back of the cab and looked at Breakman.

"Why do you have this truck? It belongs to Mr. Black," he said.

"I stole it in order to get out of the facility. Nearly got myself smelted down several times while I was in there. So I didn't feel like taking any more chances."

"Hmm, that makes sense."

Breakman nodded in agreement.

"So why are you in such a hurry to get to the train yard?"

"I need to reach Major Delgra and warn him about Black's plans."

"Why bother? We can just drive you to wherever you have to go."

Tgegani shook his head.

"This truck belongs to Ferrell Black. He will be looking for it. That will make it easy for him to find me."

Breakman thought about this for a moment.

"Hmm, good point. Alright, train yards it is."

Tgegani nodded.

He then turned to Yteca, and said, "Go take the others and find Pen. Tell him to gather our brethren and head north into the mountains and hide until I return."

"We can't leave you unprotected," said Yteca.

"What's important right now is stealth, and there are too many of us to move with any proper degree of it."

"But someone has to come with you!"

"I will have Renc remain with me. Now go. Time is precious," said Tgegani.

The other lions hesitated briefly, but soon obeyed. Breakman felt the truck lurch slightly as the lions leapt out into the night.

"What was that!?" he asked.

"I sent the others to go find Pen. I have things for him to do."

Breakman frowned.

"You know he's not going to like this."

"Pen's ability to lead is equal or superior to my own. So now is a good time for him to learn how to be the leader he was meant to be."

Breakman rolled his eyes, but said nothing. Thirty minutes later, the truck rumbled to a stop in a sprawling transit train yard. Everyone, save for the three droids that had been driving, slipped out of the truck and took cover in the bushes nearby.

"Take the truck somewhere far away from here and ditch it. Then catch up to us when you get a chance," said Breakman.

The droids acknowledged and were soon on their way. Breakman then turned and joined his two brothers near the tracks. Once there, they waited patiently as several trains came and went. But none were what Tgegani was looking for. Eventually, though, he spotted just the one he was after.

"That's our ride. Follow me," he whispered.

All of the droids, including Breakman and his remaining spiders, slipped out of the bushes and into a nearby cargo car through a partially open door as it passed by. The train soon sped away into the night. Several hours later it passed by a sleepy little town in the middle of nowhere. As it slowed to wait for another train to pass, Tgegani and the others leapt out and quickly made their way into town.

"Hey, I remember this place," said Renc.

"You were born here," said Tgegani.

"Wait, this is..."

Tgegani nodded.

"What are we doing here?" whispered Renc.

"Getting help from an old friend."

Breakman rolled his eyes.

"Oh brilliant move, brother. What are you trying to do? Get us smelted down?" he muttered.

"We'll be fine. Now follow me," said Tgegani.

The small group moved quickly through the town and into the prairie beyond. It wasn't long before they reached the security fence around the labs and began studying it with care. Tgegani grinned and pointed at several sensors near the fence.

"I see the major has improved his security," he said.

Breakman looked around in curiosity and then saw something that almost made his circuits arc in fright.

"Uh, Tgegani? I think he improved it a little more than you think," he said, pointing at two men who appeared seemingly out of nowhere.

"Stay where you are and don't move. We don't want to shoot you," said one of them.

The lions turned their heads in surprise and spotted the men. One of them pointed a flashlight at the three droids and then chuckled.

"Well, isn't this a pleasant surprise," he said.

He then motioned for the other guard to lower his rifle.

"Why are you three trying to sneak into the facility?" asked the first man.

"We came to see Major Delgra," said Tgegani.

"You should have just come in the front door."

"Thank you, but we'd like to avoid being seen by anyone who might recognize us," said Tgegani.

The man nodded.

"Something top secret, eh? Okay, follow us. We'll let you in a side gate."

The guards escorted the lions over to a small unlit gate nearby and opened it for them. They watched curiously as the lions slipped through, followed by Breakman, and then a small cadre of spider droids. Despite working where they did, that was a sight they weren't used to seeing. The small group then made their way across the facility and to Delgra's office.

"So how do we get in?" asked Breakman quietly.

"We knock," said Tgegani.

"Do what?" said Breakman in surprise.

Tgegani leaned up against the building and gently began tapping on the window. At first Delgra ignored this, but then finally grew annoyed at the sound and turned to see what it was. To his surprise he spotted a paw gently tapping on the window. He quickly rushed over and opened it.

"Who's there?" he asked.

"It's me," came a whispered reply.

"Tgegani? What the heck are you...wait, no. Come around the back. I'll let you in."

He closed his window and hurried across the building to the back door and opened it. Two large lions, a small assistance droid, and nearly a dozen spider droids slipped through the door and trotted inside. Delgra immediately closed and locked the door behind them.

"Follow me," he whispered.

He quickly led them across the building into his office. Once everyone was inside he closed the door, subtly tapped his pager, and then stepped behind his desk.

"What are you doing here?" he asked.

"I have come seeking your assistance," said Tgegani.

"In what way?"

"We need your help defeating Ferrell Black."

Delgra's eyes narrowed as he turned and sat down behind his desk.

"What's he done this time?" he asked suspiciously.

"It's not what he's done, but rather what he plans to do," said Tgegani.

He pulled a small data card out of his chest and handed it to Delgra.

"Everything you need to know is on here."

Delgra took the small card, plugged it into his computer, and began to read all of the data. As he read the transcript of Tgegani's conversation with Black, his eyes went wide. Just then Odevion walked into the office and stopped in surprise when he saw Breakman and the two lions. He soon noticed Delgra's startled expression. He hurried around the desk and peered at what he was reading. His expression soon changed to one of surprise as well.

Finally the two men looked at each other and said almost simultaneously, "We were right!"

This piqued the interest of all three droids.

"You were right about what?" asked Renc.

Delgra turned to the two lions, and said, "We've suspected that Black has been up to no good for some time now, but we've never had enough evidence to prove it. Now we do."

"So let's bring him down!" said Renc.

"Not so fast. There's a problem with that," said Delgra.

Tgegani raised an eyebrow.

"He's done everything short of openly admitting he's a traitor. What more do we need to stop him?" he asked.

"A lot, regrettably. While we finally have the evidence we need to prove what we had suspected for some time, it's not enough to convince the government of his attempted treason. To make matters worse, none of this will stand up in court, as they'll consider it all circumstantial evidence. So if we go after him with less than an airtight case, we're sunk."

This puzzled the two lions.

"Why would this not be enough to convince them?" asked Tgegani.

"Because, he's got his fingers too deeply embedded in our government right now. We'd have to disassemble his entire network first before we could effectively bring him down," said Delgra.

"Alright, so what do we need to do to make that happen?" asked Breakman.

"Well, that's the problem. We haven't figured that out yet," said Odevion.

"Might this help?" asked Breakman as he held out a small data card of his own.

Delgra looked curiously at it.

"What's this?"

"It contains information I stole from Black's network. It should provide you with everything you're looking for."

Delgra took the card and inserted it in his computer. After a minute he nodded.

"Yeah, this will help me a lot, and should make our job easier. Tgegani, give me time to put my network into motion and then we can begin to bring this scumbag down."

"My family and I are at your disposal. We will help you in any way we can," said Tgegani.

Delgra nodded.

"Thank you. Your help will most definitely be needed. Do you know where the great stone pillar of the ancients is?"

Tgegani nodded.

"It's just a hundred miles from where the others are currently hiding."

"Good. Be there at zero one hundred hours in exactly seven days from now and we'll begin our work."

Tgegani nodded.

"We'll be waiting."

Black pressed his intercom button and paged his secretary.

"Yes, sir?" came the reply.

"Send in Elgar."

"Right away, sir."

Several minutes later Elgar walked into the office.

"You called?" he asked.

Black pointed to a folder on his desk.

"It would seem that Mr. Tgegani has decided to side against us. I want you to take this folder to Senator Joslin and see to it that he gets the General Secretary to send out the army against the lions. If they won't join us, then we'll need to dispose of them quickly."

Elgar nodded.

"Right away, sir."

"Sergeant Welk! Sergeant Sims! Front and center!" came a cry across the parade grounds.

Two men hurried to the front, snapped to attention and saluted their company commander.

"Reporting as requested, sir!" they shouted in unison.

The commander pointed to an officer standing to the side, and said, "Report to him. He needs to discuss something with you."

"Yes, sir," said the two men.

They then turned and ran over to the officer, stopping briefly in surprise before snapping to attention and saluting.

"This way gentlemen," said Delgra.

He then led them around the building to a large truck that sat by the roadside. They all climbed inside and closed the door behind them. Delgra set his hat down on a nearby shelf and studied the two men intently.

"Have a seat. I'm sure you know who I am," he said.

The two men nodded.

"Yes, sir. What can we do for you?" asked Welk.

Delgra sighed anxiously.

"We need you two for a covert mission. You've had a lot of experience with the lions, and we need that right now."

"Whatever you need, we'll help you in any way we can, sir," said Welk.

"Good. What I'm about to tell you is highly classified. So this is to be discussed with nobody except myself and Sergeant Odevion. Understood?"

Welk and Sims nodded.

"Crystal clear, sir."

Tgegani looked out over a field of lions that spread out before him like a great sea of glittering brown and gold. His family was large. Very large. And every one of them looked up to him. He felt an enormous weight resting upon his shoulders as he prepared to address them. It was at this moment that Tgegani remembered Meshua and how he'd appeared to him before the war to prepare him for the coming battles ahead. Yet now he seemed so absent. So silent. Where was he at a time like this? If anything, this would be one of the times when he'd be needed the most.

"Why am I being abandoned in my greatest time of need?" he thought.

"You are not alone, Tgegani. I am always with you," came a soft, loving voice.

"Meshua?" thought Tgegani curiously.

"The path before you will be hard, but remain strong and do not fear, for it will lead you to your destiny."

Tgegani thought briefly about this, and then asked, "Will you help us in defeating Black?"

"My strength is with you always. Go, and be victorious."

"What about mother and father? Mr. Black wants them dead. Will you protect them?" asked Tgegani.

"They will be protected until the appointed time."

"Appointed time? What are you talking about?" asked Tgegani.

Silence.

"What are they to do?" he continued.

Silence. It was at that moment that Tgegani felt the weight of the world on his shoulders like never before. He looked up towards the stars for several moments as he thought, and then back down at his family.

He soon turned to Renc and Pen, and said, "Gather all those I have chosen as commanders and meet me on the west end of the valley. We need to begin our work."

The two lions nodded, and then hurried off to complete their tasks. Tgegani turned back towards the pack of lions below him and thought about each of them.

"May I do the right thing and make you proud, Mother, Father," he said quietly to himself.

He then trotted off to meet with the others.

Breakman watched anxiously as darkness filled the prairie before him.

"Where is that guy?" he thought.

Just then a shadowy lump of prairie grass rose up in front of him. It was O'ik. Breakman frowned at this.

"How about a little warning next time you sneak up on me like that?"

O'ik grinned.

"My apologies, my friend," he said.

Breakman waved dismissively.

"Eh, no big deal. It's what you do naturally."

"Yes, it is. So why did you summon me here?"

"You know where my mother and father are hidden, right?

"Aye, I do."

"I want you to take them somewhere safe where nobody will find them until this is all over. If what I understand about what's coming is true, then a lot of my family are gonna die before this is over with. So I'd like to ensure that mom and dad aren't part of the casualty list."

O'ik thought for a moment.

"I have a secret base just north of here. Few know of it. I can hide them there."

Breakman nodded.

"Thanks. I own you one."

"If we take down this madman, that will be payment enough for me."

Chapter 28

Six months later...

Black pounded his desk in anger.

"Why are they still roaming free!?" he growled over the phone.

"I can assure you that the army is doing all it can," replied Joslin.

"Well, it's apparently not enough. Those lions need to be gone or else they're going to severely encumber my plans. You agreed to help me in exchange for riches and power in my new kingdom. And yet you seem bent on failing me repeatedly!"

"What else do you want me to do!? It's taken the last six months of hunting these machines just to take down what few we have. In fact, from the reports I've read, it's a miracle that we've already gotten as many of them as we have. And, I'm doing the best I can to expedite this without raising any suspicions," said Joslin.

"Well do better or I will replace you!" screamed Black.

He slammed the phone down and then got up and paced furiously across his office. He stopped, took several deep breaths and calmed himself.

"There has to be a better way to deal with this. I am mere weeks from launching my new prototype and I need to be rid of those lions before I do."

"Once your prototype is active, they will be of little consequence," said Elgar.

Black waved his hand dismissively.

"Yes, but I'd rather not have to deal with them at all, even if Garmec is stronger than they are. The sooner the lions are destroyed, the happier I'll be," said Black. He then thought for several moments before asking, "How many of the lions are still unaccounted for?"

"About twenty, sir."

"Twenty. Hmm. And Tgegani?"

Elgar shook his head.

"He's still unaccounted for, sir."

Black swore.

"That's another problem we need to solve quickly."

"But there's only twenty of them left, sir. How could they be a threat to you anymore?"

"Because Tgegani's still alive! Even if he was the only lion left alive, there is still a chance that he could hinder my plans."

"But how?"

"He is unlike any enemy I have ever encountered before. So long as he lives, our plans are at risk. Now, get out there, and make sure he's destroyed!"

Elgar nodded.

"I'll see what I can do."

Tgegani watched as two lions approached him from the prairie below. He stepped out of his hiding spot and signaled to them. They quickly joined him under the cover of a small grove of trees.

"What did you find?" he asked.

The first lion shook his head.

"Neomara's unit is gone. When we went looking for them, we stumbled onto an army unit that was loading their bodies into a truck," said one of the lions.

"What about the information they were gathering?" asked Tgegani.

"We found it at the dead drop as expected. It's been passed on to Major Delgra and his team as you requested."

Tgegani contorted his face in thought.

"How many of us does that leave then?" he asked, half knowing the answer.

"Only about nine that we know of."

Tgegani grimaced at this. Despite all they'd done, the Yigzan army had successfully decimated his family, reducing them from the great pride that they once were to a mere handful of survivors. While it broke his heart to know this, he kept this pain to himself. He knew that letting his emotions run free right now was the worst thing he could do. He would have time to grieve later. For now, there was a mission to complete.

"Alright, then we need to spread out again. Keep doing what you've been doing and we'll meet up at our next rally point in two days," he said.

The two lions nodded, turned and ran off into the prairie. Pen slipped out of his hiding place and walked up to Tgegani.

"They've almost destroyed all of us, and we're no closer than we were six months ago," he said.

"We're doing more than you think. The information we've gathered has been instrumental in helping the Major find all the elements of Black's network. It'll make it easier for him to shut it down when the time comes."

Pen grunted.

"Assuming we live long enough to reach that point."

Tgegani frowned.

"I would like to think that we will. But with the army tracking us as they have, that will grow increasingly more difficult."

"Are you really sure we can do this?" asked Pen.

Tgegani shook his head.

"I don't know anymore. I know what we must do, but I don't know if we'll have enough time, or strength, to do it."

"So what happens if we die?"

Tgegani's eyes narrowed.

"I don't know, but I don't plan to find out."

Burgon paced back and forth as he tried to alleviate the boredom that'd been steadily creeping up on him. He understood the reason for his confinement, but at the same time he wondered if it was really worth it anymore. He'd been there for over six months and was growing tired of the food, the company and the cramped spaces. Sattazin and Gorg soldiers were coming and going every day on missions for O'ik and Fer'gant, as well as a handful of Yigzan soldiers who were working for Delgra. Persia, however, had been luckier than Burgon in that, being a tiger, she could wander the hills freely without risk of being identified, because anyone who might see her would easily mistake her for one of her wild cousins. Only if she spoke would she give away her true identity. As he paced back and forth in his room, he felt a familiar warmth surround him as though it were embracing him.

"Edias," came a soft and gentle voice.

Burgon spun in surprise to see Meshua standing behind him. He immediately dropped to his knees, and bowed.

"Meshua! Why have you come here?" he asked.

"Prepare yourself. You have one more mission ahead of you. In one week's time, a great battle will ensue. You will be there."

Burgon blinked, and looked up at Mesha in surprise.

"A battle!? But I'm no soldier!" he said.

"Your weapons will not be knife or pistol. It will instead be your wits and those gifts which I have given you. Be ready, for your time is short," said Meshua.

"But what about Persia? I can't leave her! And what about O'ik? It's his duty to protect me!"

Meshua smiled.

"I have already talked to them. Their place will be with you. Now, rest and prepare yourself."

And with that, he was gone.

Black looked up at the large armored robot in front of him and grinned with devilish delight.

"Is it ready?" he asked, barely masking his giddiness.

"Very nearly. There are a few bugs I still need to work out. But after that it should be ready for a test run," said a scientist nearby.

"It's such a brute. I can't wait to see it in action," said Black with seditious glee.

He walked around the large robot and caressed its giant arms.

"How hard would this be to reproduce in large quantities?" he asked.

The man shrugged.

"Not hard. We could manufacture probably fifty of these a day using the existing facilities we have here."

Black rubbed his hands together in delight.

"Good. I can't wait to send it for a test drive. If this weapons system performs as good as you've said it will, I'll make sure you are rewarded handsomely."

"You're already paying me handsomely for this unit. What more could you offer me?"

Black gestured grandly.

"Oh, more than you could possibly imagine."

The scientist smiled greedily.

"Oh, believe me, I can imagine a lot."

Elgar walked over to Black and whispered in his ear. Black's eyes went wide, and then narrowed as he began to grin like a Cheshire cat.

"Good. Keep me informed if they find him," he said.

Elgar nodded, and then slipped away. The scientist looked at him in curiosity.

"Is there something I should know about?"

Black shook his head as he continued to grin.

"No. I'm just tidying up a few loose ends."

The scientist nodded knowingly.

Welk watched as a soldier kicked a flat tire on his truck, cursed at it, and then flinched as another one popped on the other side, deflating with a loud hiss. The soldier swore even louder, and then walked around the back of the truck screaming obscenities at the top of his lungs. Welk slipped out of his hiding place and made his way back to his buggy. He soon pulled onto the main road and quickly gained speed. Another buggy pulled onto the road behind him followed by two more. They continued on for another fifteen minutes before pulling off onto the shoulder. They all then climbed out of their vehicles and gathered around Sims. He produced a map from his pocket and laid it out across the hood of his buggy.

"Did you get all the tires in the fifth column?" asked Welk.

One of the men nodded.

"Not all of them. But I got enough that they won't be going anywhere soon," he said.

"Good. That now puts third of the third out of action for a while."

Sims shook his head.

"It still feels weird sabotaging our own guys," he said.

"Well, if it keeps Tgegani and the other lions alive long enough to nail that madman, I'm all for it," said Welk.

"Where to next, sergeant?" asked one of the men.

Welk tapped a small circle on the map.

"We're going to sabotage first of the seventh next, assuming they're still where they're supposed to be. This operation, however, will be a little different since they're an armored unit. So puncturing tires or letting all the H2 out of their tanks isn't going to be possible."

The men nodded in understanding.

"So what are we going to do? I'm not entirely sure how to stop an armored vehicle short of blowing holes in it," said Sims.

Welk grinned.

"If you can't destroy them, then bottle them up."

The three men looked at him curiously.

"What are you talking about?" asked Sims.

Welk pointed to a small box drawn on the map, and said, "The LAV's run on hydrogen power cells just like every other army vehicle. However, they're more fuel hungry, and thus require more frequent stops."

"Ah, so starve them of fuel, and they can't do any harm," said one of the soldiers.

Welk nodded.

"Exactly. But to do that we need to prevent them from refueling. The good news is, they should be just about out of H2 by now and ready to refill their tanks."

He slid his finger down the map a short ways to another square.

"This is the switching and valve station for the L27 arm of the hydrogen transfer system. If we go there and close all the valves, that should cut off all the hydrogen going to these fueling stations up here. After that we make off with all the valve handles so they can't turn the flow back on. With no H2 for their vehicles, they won't be able to go anywhere for quite a while. They'll have to bring fuel trucks in to get them refueled."

The men nodded in approval.

"I like the plan. But isn't that a bit too simple?" said Sims.

"Sometimes the simplest plans are the best. Alright, let's mount up and get to that station before they can get any of their vehicles refueled."

The men hurried back to their buggies and were soon on their way to their next objective.

Delgra read the long list of reports coming in to him from all over the nation. As he did Odevion walked into the office and handed him a stack of papers.

"I think that's all of them. We should now have Black's entire network mapped out," he said.

Delgra flipped through the pages and nodded.

"Good. Keep our spies looking for any small fingers we may have inadvertently missed."

"Yes, sir."

"What about the commanders who volunteered their units for our attack?" asked Delgra.

"They're ready and waiting for your orders. They'll come as soon as we call for them."

"Good. Let's begin the next stage of our plans."

"What are we going to do about O'ik, Fer'gant and their units? Are we going to use them in the main assault?" asked Odevion.

"I've talked to them and they're going to stay back during the battle and watch our backs. Since we'll be going all in on this fight, we'll need someone like them to cover our rear flank."

"Good idea. Also, I've got reliable word that Black's new super weapon is nearly ready for action. We may have three, possibly four days before it's ready for use."

Delgra pondered this.

"Hmm, it looks like I'll have to move sooner than I wanted to. How quickly could we activate all of the units and get them on the move?"

Odevion shrugged.

"It'd take me a couple hours at most, but we could be rolling as early as seventeen hundred hours today if need be."

Delgra waved dismissively.

"No, we don't need to go that early. But it'll have to be soon. Send a message to all our people. Tell them that operation Dark Sunset begins two days from now at twenty one hundred hours."

Odevion saluted, and then hurried away to carry out his orders. The call went out all across the Yigzan nation that afternoon, activating all of the disjointed elements of Delgra's assault plan. But as the units prepared, they went about their lives normally so as to minimize the chances that someone would grow suspicious. Then, two days later, just as planned, the operation commenced without a hitch. Special operations units raided hidden data centers all over the Yigzan nation, capturing the hundreds of personnel operating in Black's employ.

At this same time, a group of heavily armed MP's forced their way into Senator Joslin's house and found him entertaining a group of scantily clad women as he waved large bundles of money wildly in the air. He was immediately arrested and dragged outside to a waiting patrol car where he began sobbing like a baby. Other units elsewhere simultaneously began raiding one operations node after another of Black's entire information and control network, rapidly taking everything offline until nothing remained. Not even the most well hidden control nodes escaped being shut down. It didn't take long after that for the operations center at Black's main laboratory to realize that something was wrong. Very wrong. As Black ate his dinner, Elgar rushed into the dining room, ashen faced. Black stared at him curiously.

"What's the matter?" he asked as he set down his wine glass.

"Our entire network just went offline," said Elgar as he struggled to keep his composure.

"What's the problem? Did our internet connection go down again?" asked Black.

Elgar shook his head.

"The connection is fine, but none of the data centers are responding. They've all gone dark."

Black took a bite of his steak and pondered this as he chewed.

"It's probably just a technical glitch. Tell them to try and reestablish the network," he said.

"They already did, to no avail."

Black pondered this for a moment.

"Dispatch teams to the nearest nodes and see what the problem is."

Elgar nodded.

"Right away, sir."

He then turned and hurried out of the room.

Delgra studied the front gate and surrounding fences of Black's laboratory through his binoculars.

"Four guards at the main gate, two patrolling the fence on each side and six more in the parapets on top of the second gate," he said.

"This should make ingress interesting," said Odevion.

"Nah. A couple of rounds in the right place and we're good to go," said Delgra.

He then turned to several men at the bottom of the hill and signaled for them to begin. A series of dull thumps echoed from a line of mortars a few seconds later. The rounds arched high into the sky, and then rained down on the outer gate, shattering the fence and killing several guards. The next volley landed on top of a nearby parapet, instantly killing the guards that were there. Several more volleys were sent in, each one aimed at a different point in the defenses. After nearly two dozen volleys, the mortars fell silent.

Delgra studied the carnage and commotion below with satisfaction.

"Send in the first wave," he said.

Odevion tapped his communicator, and said, "First wave, go!"

Engines came to life, and trucks full of infantry backed up by several LAV's roared over a nearby hilltop and towards the facility. They pushed their way through the outer wall with little effort, and then proceeded on to a breach in the inner wall.

"This is going a lot easier than I expected," said Delgra.

Just then a flurry of gunfire erupted from the facility.

"Ah, they're right on schedule," he said.

Black burst through the doors to his control center, and screamed, "What's happening!?"

"We're under attack, sir!" shouted one of the men.

"By whom?" asked Black.

"Yigzan army forces. Two companies and a handful of armored vehicles just breached the outer wall," said the man.

Black fumed.

"Where are my forces!?" he shouted.

"They're responding now, sir."

"They had better move quickly, or I'm going to start shooting people for incompetence!" shouted Black.

He glared at the tactical display in the middle of the room and studied the progress of the battle.

"So, you've figured out my plans, have you? Well then, we'll just have to accelerate them."

He spun on his heels and strode quickly out of the room. As he did, Elgar came down the hallway towards him.

"Elgar, we're moving up our plans for the prototypes. Get down to the manufacturing facility and have them begin building units immediately!"

Elgar bowed slightly, and said, "As you wish."

O'ik and Fer'gant watched the battle from a distant hillside with interest.

"The battle is not going well," said O'ik.

"Should we help them?" asked Fer'gant.

"No. There are not enough of us. Thus it's best that we stay here for now," replied O'ik.

Burgon lay on the side of the hill next to them and watched the battle unfold down below as Persia lay by his side. He could feel sweat forming on his face as he thought about what possibly lay ahead for them. The camouflage paint on his face made it itch and the clothes he'd been given were too big and felt awkward to move in. Suddenly he felt himself pulled rapidly through the air and deposited in the middle of a large room. He looked up in surprise to see the inside of the robot manufacturing facility in Black's facility. Elgar stood to one side talking with several scientists.

"Mr. Black wants you to begin production immediately," he said.

"But we're not ready! It'll be another two days before we can do that!" protested one of the scientists.

"Make it twenty minutes or I start putting holes in people's heads. Got it?" said Elgar.

The men nodded nervously. Burgon then felt himself yanked sharply backwards and once again found himself laying on the hillside.

"You must stop them before they can harm your people. Now rise up and fulfill your destiny!" came Meshua's voice in his head.

Burgon gulped heavily, and then stared at Persia.

"What was that!?" she asked.

"I believe we just had a vision," replied Burgon.

He then turned to O'ik.

"We know where we need to go," he said.

O'ik looked at him curiously, and said, "Was it from Meshua?"

Burgon nodded.

"I believe it was. We were briefly drawn into the manufacturing facility. They're preparing to do something horrible there."

O'ik nodded in understanding, and then looked at Fer'gant.

"We have our orders. Let's get moving."

Chapter 29

Delgra studied the laboratory complex with interest through his scope, and then paused when he heard something approaching them rapidly from his left. He turned and spotted Tgegani, Yteca and Pen approaching his position.

"We came as quickly as we could," said Tgegani.

"There are only three of you. Where are the rest?"

Tgegani shook his head.

"We don't know. We've not seen anyone else in several days, and none of them have responded to our calls. I believe we are the only ones left," he said.

Delgra grunted.

"I was hoping that more of you could come. Alright, let's hope the others are still alive and can soon join us, or this whole mission could turn ugly real quick."

"What would you have us do?" asked Tgegani.

"Get down there and capture Black. That's the most important goal of this whole operation."

Tgegani nodded and then motioned for the others to follow. The three lions then raced quickly across the prairie towards the facility and soon found themselves taking cover behind a pair of burning LAV's. He studied the situation briefly, and soon spotted a way around the fighting. They quickly sprinted away towards a nearby staircase that led up to the parapets and ascended them with breathtaking speed.

Several of Black's men spotted them as they approached and opened fire. But the bullets glanced harmlessly off their armored bodies. The lions charged through the men and quickly scaled the buildings beyond with several large leaps until they found themselves on a roof. They knocked out two guards that were protecting a nearby doorway and then raced through it and into the hallway beyond. Tgegani called up a set of floor plans he had stored in his memory banks and used them to guide his team through the buildings to the command center.

Black turned in surprise as he heard shouts of terror, several short bursts of gunfire, and the sound of shattering wood. Suddenly the door to the command center exploded open in a shower of wood shards. Three lions stepped into the room a moment later. Upon seeing the lions, the personnel inside panicked and headed for the exits, nearly running each other over in a wild frenzy to get out of the room. Soon only Black remained. He grinned darkly at the lions.

"Ah, Tgegani. I've been expecting you. And I see you've brought company. How nice," he said condescendingly.

"Give it up, Black. Your plans are finished," said Tgegani.

Black laughed.

"Really? Well that's news to me."

He then reached into his pocket, pulled out a remote control, and pressed a small button on it. Tgegani eyed him suspiciously and then began scanning the room as a sharp whining sound filled his ears. Suddenly, a large, heavily armed robot crashed through the ceiling and landed next to Black. He glanced briefly at the robot, and then back at the lions as he grinned with devilish glee.

"Tgegani, I would like you to meet the next generation of intelligent weaponry, codenamed Garmec. I am sure the four of you can get acquainted very quickly." He then turned to the robot, and said, "Kill them."

The droid began to walk towards the lions.

"Wait!" shouted Black a moment later.

The droid stopped, and then looked at him mutely.

"Do it outside. You've already caused enough damage in here for one day."

The droid glared briefly at Black before turning its attention back towards the lions. Six long, metallic tentacles soon appeared out of its back, and ensnared the lions. It then fired two large booster engines and launched itself through the ceiling and out into the night with the lions in tow. Black laughed sadistically.

"That was oddly satisfying," he said.

Delgra watched in dismay as the battle progressed far slower than he'd wanted.

"I think it's time to bring in the third unit," he said.

"That's all we've got left," said Odevion.

"I know that. But I also know that we're only the side show in this carnival. So if we don't keep Black's men busy, the lions won't have a chance."

The three men climbed into a truck and led the last group of soldiers down the hill and through the main gate. By this time the battle had moved into the main facility, but was progressing very slowly due to the maze like design of the complex. Even though Delgra had memorized the defensive structure of Black's laboratories, it was still difficult to gain any ground against his defense force. As the third unit rolled into place, they dismounted and began moving forward in an effort to reinforce the beleaguered units in front of them. Word of Delgra's arrival quickly strengthened the resolve of the troops already fighting. With his reinforcements having arrived, they would all now fight even harder to ensure their victory.

Fer'gant pointed at a large metal door in front of him, and said, "Blow it."

Two hunters rushed up to the door, placed several explosive charges, and then quickly sought cover. Two dull thumps and the sound of crashing metal signaled that the door had been successfully breached. They waited briefly for the smoke to clear and then rushed inside. As they moved into the main administrative building, they were surprised to find that there was almost nobody inside. In the back of their minds, both commanders were glad for this.

"While we're here, should we also search for Black?" asked Fer'gant.

"I think that would be a good idea," replied O'ik.

As they continued on, they surprised several guards, most of which were killed on sight. Even so, one of them managed to survive. Seeing this, Fer'gant walked over and stood in front of the man.

"Where's Black?" he asked gruffly.

The man weakly raised an arm and pointed down the hallway.

"Operations...center," he said, and then died.

O'ik spotted a small map that hung on a nearby wall and noted their position.

"Fer'gant, come look at this."

The large Gorg commander walked up to the map and studied it.

"Hmm. Both the manufacturing facility, and the operations center, aren't far from here. We should split up and each take a different target," he said.

O'ik nodded.

"I'll take the doctor and go down to the manufacturing facility. You capture Black."

Fer'gant nodded.

"I will. Happy hunting," he said.

O'ik grinned. The two groups then split up and moved down separate hallways in route to their respective targets. As Fer'gant's team reached the doorway to the operations center, they heard heavy, mechanical footsteps, struggling, and then the roar of powerful rocket engines. The hallway then filled briefly with smoke which quickly dissipated. Everything fell oddly silent. Fer'gant then signaled to his men who raced forward and burst into the operations center.

"Don't move or we'll shoot," said one of the men.

Black spun in surprise to see a large group of Gorg soldiers standing just inside the door with their rifles trained on him. He swore.

"Bind him," said Fer'gant.

Black let out an evil cackle, and then leapt backwards onto a nearby console.

"You'll have to catch me first!" he shouted.

He squatted briefly, and then launched himself through the hole in the ceiling, his cybernetic legs pushing him upwards like a catapult. Fer'gant cursed.

"After him!" he shouted.

Two men ran over, clasped their hands together, and gave each of their comrades a boost up through the hole. Fer'gant was the last. Once everyone was on the roof, several men reached down and lifted the last two men up and through the hole. As they did this, Fer'gant studied the disorienting maze work of shafts, towers and ventilation equipment that covered the rooftops around them. Finding his quarry in this mess wasn't going to be easy. He grit his teeth in anger and then signaled for his men to spread out.

The three lions struggled fiercely against the large metal tentacles that held them. Garmec soon landed, and then threw all three of the lions at once towards a nearby concrete wall in hopes of damaging them. But the lions skillfully bounded off the wall and landed gracefully on their feet. They then turned and stared with contempt at the gigantic metal monster. It pointed its two giant mini-guns at them and began to spin them up. The lions braced themselves, waiting for the guns to fire, fearing that their fight would end right there. But to their surprise the guns remained silent. Garmec repeatedly tried to fire the weapons, but found that they would not work. Realizing that they'd failed due to a regrettable lack of ammunition, it released them and allowed them to crash loudly to the ground. It then raised two other weapons on its arms, but got the same results from them also. It dropped them as well as it contemplated its next move.

"Hmm, it appears they forgot to arm him. This could play to our advantage. Yteca, take right flank. Pen, you go left. I've got center," said Tgegani over the radio.

The three lions raced forward towards Garmec as it picked up its useless weapons and hurled them at the lions. The lions easily dodged them and then leapt at him. But their claws glanced off Garmec's armored metal body and did no damage. Tgegani was shocked to feel his claws find no purchase on the robot's thick, metallic skin as he slashed wildly at the giant metal monster. Garmec grabbed Tgegani with its tentacles and threw him through the air into a large truck that sat nearby, caving in the front of the vehicle. Tgegani quickly rebounded and raced back into the battle. Pen latched onto Garmec's back and frantically slashed away at his neck armor as Yteca attacked its legs. Garmec in turn reached around with its tentacles, grabbed both lions and threw them across the yard.

"We need to destroy those tentacles," said Tgegani over the radio.

"Got any ideas how to do that?" asked Pen.

"I'm working on it," replied Tgegani.

"Great. So what are we supposed to do in the meantime?" asked Pen.

"Just keep fighting!"

"Oh, yeah. That's a wonderful plan!" quipped Pen.

Tgegani stared at Garmec's tentacles and studied their movements. There had to be a pattern in how they operated that would reveal a weakness in the robot's defenses.

"Yteca, attack its right flank. When it strikes at you, retreat," he said over the radio.

"I'm on it," replied Yteca.

She drove in at Garmec with all her speed, but was scooped up in the tentacles as soon as she got close. She struggled vainly to free herself as Garmec spun around and tried to slam her into a nearby wall. Tgegani and Pen rushed in to try and save her but quickly found themselves in the same situation. Finding that he had an arm free, Tgegani reached around and slashed at the tentacle. His claws made large scratch marks in its metal coating, but did not penetrate it. Again he slashed at them, but did no real damage. But he had at least made an impact on the robot's armor.

"His tentacles are..." He paused as his body slammed against a wall and was immediately yanked back. "...vulnerable to our..." Again he struck the wall and was pulled back. "...claws," continued Tgegani.

He felt his body impact another reinforced concrete wall. He struggled fiercely to free himself, but found that he could not. Seeing that Tgegani was trapped, Garmec plodded towards him with the intention of finishing off the struggling lion. But before it could Pen leapt at the giant robot, distracting it long enough for Yteca to race over to Tgegani. She quickly assessed the situation, and then began attacking the concrete around her brother with her claws. But despite her best efforts, she wasn't making much progress.

Just then Tgegani shouted, "Watch out!"

Instinctively Yteca leapt to the side, and to her surprise watched, out of the corner of her eye, as a large slab of concrete came flying her way and impacted the wall. It'd been Garmec's intention to smash her with it. But much to Garmec's chagrin, it'd instead further cracked the concrete wall, allowing Tgegani to extricate himself. Seeing that her brother was free, Yteca hurried over to him.

"Are you alright?"

Tgegani nodded.

"I am fine. However, we need to help our brother. He cannot fight this monster alone."

"Agreed."

O'ik peered around the corner and spied Elgar as he spoke with several scientists.

"Mr. Black wants you to begin production immediately," said Elgar.

"But we're not ready! It'll be another two days before we can begin production," said one of the scientists.

"Make it twenty minutes or I start putting holes in people's heads. Got it?"

O'ik pulled back and leaned over to one of his men.

"Elgar's out there. We should bag ourselves a prize," he said with a grin.

The hunter nodded. O'ik leaned around the corner again, held up his hand, and then signaled for the first group to move. A squad of men immediately rushed out into the middle of the room.

"Get your hands up! Get your hands up!" they shouted.

Elgar turned around in surprise to see O'ik's hunters standing behind him. Whether out of reflex, or pure fear, he foolishly drew his pistol and tried to shoot. But he never got the chance, as the hunters cut him down immediately. He staggered briefly and then collapsed.

"Get down on the ground!!" shouted one of the hunters as they corralled the frightened scientists into a corner.

O'ik walked cautiously over to Elgar's perforated body and examined it. He kicked the gun out of Elgar's hand and studied the man's hollow, horrified expression. He grunted and turned around to see Burgon and Persia hurrying across the room to a small control booth nearby.

"Doctor, is this our target?" he asked.

"Yes, it is. We need to destroy it so that Black can't build his robotic army," said Burgon.

"How fast can you do that?"

"I don't know. Let me see what I can do," said Burgon.

He began to work with the controls in earnest, and then after several minutes shook his head.

"The controls are locked out. If it starts up, we won't be able to stop it."

O'ik looked at the scientists, and said, "What's the security key?"

Just then a group of Black's guards poured through a nearby doorway and began shooting. O'ik's men immediately returned fire and cut them down.

"Secure that entrance!" shouted O'ik as he pointed to the door.

He then turned back to the scientists and grimaced in dismay as his eyes fixed on their bullet riddled bodies. He grunted.

"Doctor, how quickly can you unlock those controls?"

"It'll take me at least several hours," said Burgon.

O'ik growled in frustration.

"Then we'll need to blow it up. Do you know of any weak points this place has?"

Burgon studied the facility around them and sighed anxiously.

"Nothing specifically, but I know of a few things that might work."

"Anything will help."

"Alright, this way then."

Breakman sat nervously in the front seat of the old army truck he'd stolen from Black's facility and watched the road ahead as it barreled down the highway at breakneck speed. He hadn't expected to ever see the truck again, or even come out of hiding until all the hostilities were over. But Meshua had other plans. He'd first led Breakman to the truck, and then sent him off to aid his brother in the coming fight at Black's northern laboratory. But that wasn't what bothered him the most. It was the other things Meshua had told him. He kept running their conversation through his head over and over again as they flew down the road like a runaway train. He'd tried to get Meshua to explain his message. But regardless of what he did, Meshua would not give up any more secrets. All Breakman knew was that his parents were already there, and he would need to get to Black's facility as fast as possible to help them win the day. He pondered Meshua's words some more.

"If they're somewhere in that facility, they could be killed in the fighting. No. If anyone is to die, it should be me. It's my job to protect them. That's why I'm here, isn't it? I can't let them die. I just wish this bucket of bolts would move faster," he thought.

Just then they crested a hill not far from the facility and saw a sight that made him gasp in horror. The facility was awash in flames and the signs of battle. Breakman swore.

"By the heart of Meshua, no!" he thought. "Keep that pedal all the way down! We must save my parents!" he shouted as he climbed out onto the hood.

Silently under his breath, he prayed that he would arrive in time.

Chapter 30

Delgra fired, chambered another round, and fired again. The battle was getting edgy, as it seemed like all their efforts to push forward were coming to nothing. He swore, and then fired on another of Black's soldiers as he ran between one of the buildings. The man crumpled to the ground and lay still. Just then Delgra spotted two men trying to flank him. He quickly drew a bead and took out the first man, and then watched the second disappear behind a door. He guessed where the man was at inside the building and fired. He watched for a moment to see if he emerged out the other side. When he didn't, Delgra was sure he'd gotten him. Two grenades exploded in front of him sending dirt spraying everywhere. Delgra swore again.

"We need to flank these guys! Got any ideas?" he shouted.

"Just one, but we'd need an LAV to do it!" shouted Odevion.

"Well, we're fresh out of LAV's. So got any other ideas?"

Odevion looked around briefly, and then said, "How about an old army truck?"

"Sounds like a grand idea if you're contemplating suicide," said Delgra.

"Well I think someone is!" shouted Odevion as he pointed behind them.

Delgra looked at Odevion curiously, and then turned around just in time to see an army truck barreling down the highway towards them.

"Get out of the way!!" shouted Delgra.

He turned to run, and then stopped and stared in confusion as he spotted a small service droid hanging off the hood of the truck.

"What in the blazes??" he said in surprise.

A moment later the truck barreled past them as Breakman braced himself against the hail of bullets flying towards him and held on for all he was worth. At the last second he dove off the side of the truck and rolled away as it plowed into the bunker in front of him. It exploded with an earth shaking boom that silenced the bunker and shattered the barrier that had been blocking Delgra's advance. With lightning quick reflexes, Breakman then leapt to his feet and charged at several dazed and confused soldiers nearby. The soldiers tried to respond, but they were so shell shocked that the best they could do is point their weapons in Breakman's general direction. Taking advantage of this, he disarmed the first soldier and shot him with his own rifle. But when the gun jammed, he instead turned it into a club and beat the second man unconscious. He then quickly scanned the area. Seeing that all was clear, and the battle had momentarily grown silent, Breakman quickly gathered together his spiders and raced forward into the facility.

"Breakman, don't run any further. Your task lies elsewhere. Turn away!" came Meshua's voice in his mind.

"I can't! I've gotta save Mom and Dad!!" he shouted as he ran.

"What's in here?" asked O'ik as he stared at a large, yellow tank.

"Benzine. They use it for cleaning parts," said Burgon.

O'ik nodded in approval.

"That'll do," he said. He then turned to one of his men, and said, "Wire it up."

"Heads up! We've got company!" shouted one of the hunters.

A moment later a wave of gunfire poured into the room. O'ik swore.

"Quickly! Get charges on those tanks. Put them up high so that Black's men won't see them. The rest of you, secure that door! Don't let anyone get in here until we're done!" he shouted.

Burgon turned to one of the men as he drew several charges out of his pouch.

"Let me have some of those. I'll help," he said.

The man stared curiously at Burgon, and then at O'ik who nodded. The man handed Burgon six charges.

"Place these wherever you feel the tank is most vulnerable," he said.

Burgon nodded.

"And don't drop them. I'd hate to have this place blow up before we're clear," said O'ik.

Burgon grimaced.

"I'm not the one you have to worry about dropping them," he said as he handed two charges to Persia.

She quickly bounded up the pipes leading away from the tanks and planted the charges on the top of the tank. O'ik nodded in approval. She then repeated the maneuver two more times, placing the remaining four charges at other strategic points. Just as she finished, one of O'ik's men came running up to him.

"All charges have been placed," he said.

"Alright, tell the other men to pull back. We're getting out of here."

The man nodded and hurried off just as a huge explosion rocked the building. Glass, metal and stone flew through the air as a cloud of dust quickly filled the room.

"They've breached the main doors! They're coming through!" shouted one of O'ik's men.

"Pull back! Pull back!" shouted O'ik.

The men quickly complied. Moments later, a large group of Black's men poured through the shattered main doors and into the building. For the next several minutes an intense battle raged between the two groups as both fought desperately for control of the facility. After several minutes the battle seemed to lessen. But this was only the calm before the storm, as a second, larger group of Black's men poured through the door. Burgon ducked as bullets whizzed over his head while O'ik's men struggled to repel this new onslaught.

"Start pulling the men out the way we came!" shouted O'ik over the roar of battle.

"We can't! All the exits are blocked!" shouted one of his men in return.

"Pinned in a corner to die like rats," thought O'ik in frustration.

He carefully studied the area around him and realized that they could not continue this battle much longer. They needed to get out, and fast.

"Doctor, is there another way out of here?" ask O'ik.

"There's a service train that runs the length of the facility. It brings parts and supplies in for the maintenance crews. We could use it to get everyone out," said Burgon.

"Alright, lead the way!" shouted O'ik.

Burgon carefully slipped out of his hiding spot and crawled frantically across the floor as O'ik's men covered him. Once he was clear, O'ik began pulling his men back through the manufacturing facility. They soon reached a side room where a small caged car sat waiting for them.

O'ik looked down the tunnel, and said, "Where does this go to?"

"Outside. But you can't go down the tunnel. It's too dangerous. You need to use the transport car or you'll die."

O'ik grunted as he studied the small car.

"But that's not big enough."

"I know. You'll only be able to fit twenty men inside at a time. But we can still do this fast enough to get everyone out. Now hurry up and get in," said Burgon.

O'ik nodded, and then sent all of his wounded out in the first trip. The rest of O'ik's men were then evacuated in the next several trips until all that remained was O'ik, a handful of his men, Burgon, and Persia. But it was at that moment that Burgon realized that they had a problem.

"Doctor! Get in the car!" shouted O'ik.

"I can't! The other terminal has gone offline! The only way to get you out is if someone stays here and operates the car from this end!"

"I'll leave one of my men behind to operate it. We need to get you out of here."

"No! You can't! None of your men know how to operate the controls, and I don't have time to teach them!"

O'ik now found himself at an impasse. He didn't want to leave the doctor behind, but if he didn't, they would all die.

"O'ik! You need to go! Persia and I can escape through the roof access hatch. Trust me! I know this facility!" shouted Burgon.

"But how will we know when you're out? We need to detonate those explosives soon before the guards have a chance to disarm them!"

"Let me do it. When we're safe, I'll trigger the explosives."

O'ik hesitated, and then handed Burgon the detonator.

"Meshua protect you," he said proudly.

He then stepped into the cage, closed the door and watched in dismay as they vanished into the service tunnel, leaving Burgon and Persia behind to fend for themselves. Once Burgon was sure that the men were safely away, he scurried across the room and quickly began climbing a ladder to the roof as Persia clung tightly to him. Just as he emerged through the hatch at the top he heard bullets rattle off the ladder below him. He quickly scrambled out, and then raced across the roof with Persia close on his heels. But they only made it a short ways before realizing that they were on the wrong side of the roof. Somehow they'd taken the wrong ladder. To make matters worse, there was no way to escape, save for either going back the way they'd come, or a nearly five story plunge to the concrete below. Just then a group of soldiers burst around the corner behind him.

"Give it up, Doctor! We have you cornered," said one of the men.

Persia launched herself across the roof.

"Not if I have anything to say about it!" she roared as she dove at the startled men.

She then attacked them with whirlwind like fury, slashing, tearing and biting as though she'd gone mad. But her attack was short lived as one of the soldiers put a round through her shoulder. She tumbled to the ground and writhed in agony.

"Persia!!" cried Burgon in abject terror.

The soldiers soon got to their feet as others came in behind them. One of them stepped on Persia and pointed the muzzle of his rifle at her head.

"Don't move, sweetie. I was told not to kill you if at all possible. But if you keep moving, I'm gonna have to put a bullet in your head," he said.

Several other soldiers moved across the roof towards Burgon.

"Alright, Doctor, give up the gig. You're coming with us," said one of the men.

Burgon looked down briefly at Persia, and then up at the soldiers. He soon pulled the detonator out of his pocket and held it out for the men to see.

"Touch me and I blow this whole building!"

The soldiers stopped.

"He's bluffing," said one of the men.

Burgon raised the detonator over his head, and then suddenly felt a hot fire erupt in his chest.

"Hey, what'd you shoot him for!?" shouted one of the men.

"He was going to blow us up!" shouted another.

"He's bluffing, you idiot!! Geez, look at what you've done! If *he* dies, *you* die."

"I'll kill you if you try!"

The soldiers soon began to argue bitterly amongst themselves. Burgon's eyes went wide as he felt his chest burning as though a fire had been kindled between his ribs. He dropped to his knees and swayed awkwardly as his vision swam before him. He slowly turned his head and looked towards Persia as a sickening ring filled his ears. She seemed like she was shouting something at him. But what were the words? He studied her lips, and then the detonator, and then her again. She nodded. Now he understood.

"So this is what we were supposed to do," he thought. "What a way to go," he said, shaking his head in disbelief.

He then cradled the detonator in his hands, flipped off the safety, and pressed the button.

A powerful shockwave blew Breakman off his feet and slammed him to the ground. He quickly picked himself up and looked on in horror as the manufacturing facility vanished before him into a massive mushrooming fireball. It was at this moment that a bitter, painful revelation pierced his heart. His parents had been in that building. He didn't know how he knew. He just did.

"Mom! Dad! No!!" he screamed bitterly as fear became reality before him.

Then that fear turned to anger, and then anger to blinding rage.

"Black," he said, the name rolling bitterly off his lips.

Seeing a piece of rod lying nearby, he picked it up and then turned towards the main administration building. Whatever it took, he was going to see Black punished for what he'd done.

O'ik looked on in mortified horror as the manufacturing facility vanished before him in a powerful, mushrooming fireball.

"Do you think they made it out alive?" asked one of his men.

O'ik sighed deeply.

"I want to believe they did. But deep down inside I know they didn't."

"How do you know that?"

"When we were preparing for this mission, Meshua told me to bring them along as they had a purpose to fulfill here. However, he said nothing about bringing them back," said O'ik.

He then pounded his chest in salute as did the other soldiers.

"In the beginning he was just a man. But in the end he became a warrior more honorable than even I," said O'ik. He then turned to his men, and said, "Let's move out. We still have a mission to complete, and a madman to catch."

Black swore under his breath as a fireball engulfed the manufacturing facility. He knew what this meant, and it enraged him.

"All of my plans are ruined!!" he screamed.

He turned in the direction of the heaviest fighting, and growled, "Curse you and your lions."

Just then bullets whizzed by his head. He turned to see Fer'gant's men closing in on him.

"Blast! I need to lose these fools. I will *not* let my dreams be destroyed," he said.

He then turned and raced across the rooftops of the facility at breakneck speed, his cybernetic legs carrying him many times faster than any of the Gorg following him could run. Seeing an opportunity to hide, and get his bearings again, he slipped behind a nearby service structure and weighed his options. But just as he started to think about what he would do next, a Sattazin hunter popped up over a ladder just in front of him. Black stared at him in shock and surprise, and then quickly realized the new peril he was in.

"He's over here!" shouted the hunter.

Black swore, and then hurried away.

Tgegani leapt high at Garmec in an effort to lure it into attacking. And right on cue, Garmec did. Tgegani pulled his legs in, grabbed Garmec's swinging arm and pushed off from it. He then grabbed the giant robot's face and held on for dear life as they both tumbled backwards and crashed to the ground. Tgegani quickly recovered and turned to attack Garmec, only to be batted away by one of Garmec's tentacles. Garmec then climbed to its feet and turned towards Tgegani. Pen tried his luck next as Yteca distracted the large metal bruit. He leapt at the robot, expecting to drive a powerful kick into its back, only to be batted aside as well. Quickly recovering and landing on all fours, he turned and hurried over to Tgegani.

"You alright, bro?" he asked.

Tgegani nodded.

"I'm fine. But we need to find another way to attack him. Our current methods are ill capable of achieving victory."

"Well, I'm open to suggestions if you have any."

"We should use whatever we can find in our environment. It might give us an advantage."

Pen quickly glanced around the area.

"Like what?"

Tgegani looked around and noticed that they were surrounded by huge buildings whose walls were made entirely of concrete.

"Let's try to smash him into a few of these buildings. Maybe those might crack his armor."

Delgra looked on in stunned silence as a massive fireball climbed into the night sky.

"What's happening over there?" he said.

"Sounds like O'ik and Fer'gant may have joined the festivities," said Odevion.

"I hope not. The last thing we need is for them to get caught in the crossfire, or worse yet, mistaken for the enemy."

"Don't worry. They know what they're doing," said Odevion.

One of the soldiers hurried up to Delgra, and said, "Sir, we're receiving reports that the army has heard of our plight and is sending reinforcements."

"For who's side?"

"Ours apparently."

Delgra nodded.

"Good. We could use the help. But in the meantime we need to keep the pressure on Black's men. We have to give those lions more time!!"

Black quickly bolted across the roof, leapt between the buildings, and landed awkwardly on the other side. He turned briefly to see if he was still being followed, and soon realized that he hadn't gained as much headway on his pursuers as he'd thought. He then turned and sprinted away in a bid to widen the gap. But before he made even two steps, something grabbed his feet and wrenched his legs out from under him. He shrieked in surprise as he crashed face first to the rooftop and skid painfully to a stop. He slowly climbed to his feet, and then paused in surprise, and complete disbelief, as he stared at a familiar face in front of him.

"Breakman!? I thought we destroyed you!?"

Breakman raised a short metal rod that he held in his hand and smashed it squarely into Black's temple. A sickening crack echoed across the rooftop as Black's head snapped to the side so hard that it nearly broke his neck. His head thenbobbed briefly as he tried to shake off the effects of the blow.

"That's for Mom," growled Breakman angrily.

He lifted the rod over his head and drove it down into Black's skull, knocking him unconscious.

"And that's for Dad!"

Seeing that Black was out cold, Breakman dropped to his knees and gave out a bitter, anguished cry. He then tossed the rod to the side, grabbed Black's head, and prepared to snap his neck.

"Breakman! Stop!" came Meshua's voice.

Breakman paused, and then looked up. Meshua stood before him, his hands held out in a gesture to halt.

"He killed Mom and Dad! He deserves to die!" cried Breakman angrily.

He then groaned and lowered his head in sadness.

"I deserve to die too. I couldn't save them. I've failed. I'm worthless."

He then released Black's head and plopped noisily to the ground.

"You did what you were called to do, and they did what they were called to do. Breakman, let it go and be at peace. They are with me now."

Breakman groaned sadly, buried his face in his hands, and wept bitterly. Meshua sat down next to him, wrapped his arms around the little droid, and held him close.

Chapter 31

Fer'gant walked around the corner and stared in surprise as he spotted O'ik and his men standing over the body of Black. He looked down and saw blood oozing from Black's head.

"Is he dead?" he asked.

"No, he's alive, unfortunately. But he won't be waking up anytime soon. Our little friend over here made sure of that," said O'ik.

Fer'gant looked over at Breakman who was leaning against a wall and sobbing bitterly.

"What happened?" he asked.

"I don't know. Breakman and his droids were here when we arrived, but he hasn't said anything to us yet."

"Well, we need to get Mr. Black down to the Major. One of my men is reporting that the Yigzan army is sending reinforcements this way. If they get here before we sort this out, it could greatly complicate things."

"Agreed."

O'ik then had his men pick up Black and Breakman and carry them off the roof and down to the ground below.

Delgra turned to his radio operator, and asked, "How soon till the reinforcements are here?"

"Another few minutes, sir."

"That's what you said ten minutes ago!"

The radio operator shrugged.

"That's all I know, sir. I'm just going on what they told me."

"I think they're lost," said Odevion.

"Yeah, wouldn't that just be our luck," groaned Delgra.

He then studied the facility before them, but didn't like what he was seeing. Although the fighting had slackened, the battle was still very difficult, and each foot of gain was bitterly contested. The part he hated the most was how spread out his men had become. He'd been forced to do this in order to prevent Black's men from flanking him. They had already tried that several times. If nothing else he had to give Black a lot of credit. He did a very good job preparing the defenses of his facility. In fact, a little *too* well. Then, just as he was contemplating his next move, something strange happened. The battlefield suddenly grew quiet. He peered over top of the concrete barrier he was hiding behind and noticed that Black's men had stopped fighting, and were looking around in confusion. Some began to come out with their hands over their heads while others talked and argued amongst themselves. Soon his ears were greeted by a voice that he knew all too well.

"Lay down your arms! We have your boss! Lay down your arms!" came the voice.

As they drew closer, Black's men began surrendering en masse.

"What in the name of the ancients..." muttered Delgra.

"Well now, isn't that a sight," said Odevion as he spotted the men approaching.

Delgra quickly realized who it was and began to grin.

"Why those crazy old fools," he said in amazement.

Odevion laughed.

"Looks like they bagged Black before we did."

"Well then, all we need to do now is mop up his men and our work here is done."

O'ik and Fer'gant's men soon reached Delgra, and then placed their unconscious and bleeding captive at his feet.

"By the gates of Tersar! What happened to him?" said Delgra as he studied Black's wounds.

"We think this little guy got a hold of him before we did," said O'ik as he pointed at Breakman.

Suddenly, a lion came crashing through one of the nearby buildings followed by Garmec. The robot reached out with his tentacles to attack him, but missed as the lion quickly retreated. Some of the Yigzan soldiers nearby began firing at Garmec. But their bullets simply ricocheted off its armor.

"Wait! Cease fire! Let the lions deal with him! Your bullets have no effect!" shouted Delgra.

The men lowered their weapons and watched anxiously, knowing they could do nothing to help.

Tgegani sat down briefly as he carefully checked his systems. He was shaken, but didn't appear to have suffered any damage.

"Tgegani! You alright?" shouted Yteca as she raced around the side of the building towards him followed by Pen.

"I'm fine. Just a little shook up," said Tgegani.

Pen stopped next to him and faced Garmec.

"We need to do something about those tentacles, or we're gonna get killed," he said as he studied Garmec.

He then looked to his left at the large group of soldiers watching in awe, and spotted Odevion standing nearby holding his sniper rifle.

"I've got it!" he said. "Sergeant, this is Pen. Can you hear me?" he said over the radio.

"I hear you," replied Odevion.

"You see the robot we're fighting?"

"Yeah. What do you need me to do?"

The three lions leapt out of the way as Garmec lashed out at them with its tentacles.

"Can you take out his tentacles?" said Pen.

Odevion studied the eight long tentacles that sprouted out of the droid's back.

"Yeah, I got it," he replied.

He then took aim at Garmec's back and fired, the round slicing through one of the tentacles like a hot knife through butter. The tentacle convulsed wildly, and then crashed to the ground as hydraulic fluid poured out of it like a fountain. Garmec turned in Odevion's direction and glared at him. Odevion chambered another round, and then realized that he was now the center of Garmec's attention. He swore. Garmec began to fire its rocket engines as Tgegani leapt at the droid.

"Keep him busy until the sergeant can get all those tentacles," shouted Tgegani over the radio.

The other two lions jumped at Garmec, but were quickly batted aside. However, their attack had achieved its desired effect. Garmec shut down its rocket engines and again turned its attention toward the lions. Odevion fired again, the second bullet cutting through two more of Garmec's tentacles. More fluid gushed from the severed tentacles. They writhed wildly for several moments, and then went limp and slumped to the ground. Soon the rest of the tentacles fell limp as well.

Garmec stared down at them and grunted in disgust. It reached back and ripped them from its body as hydraulic fluid sprayed everywhere. It then threw them to the side and charged at the lions. Odevion's rifle thundered again, but this time the round ricocheted harmlessly off the droid's thick body armor. He swore.

"Keep firing, sergeant," said Delgra.

"I can't. The droid is too well armored. They're going to have to strip away part of its protection before I can do anything more."

Delgra looked at the droid and began to become concerned. Just then Welk, Sims and a caravan of Yigzan soldiers arrived. They looked over at the large group of prisoners sitting on the ground nearby, and then at Garmec.

"Looks like we missed the party," said Welk.

"Not entirely, Sergeant. Get these prisoners out of here. Then help us sweep the facility for the rest of Black's men."

"What about that thing?" asked Welk as he pointed towards Garmec.

"The lions will have to deal with him."

Welk nodded and then noticed O'ik and Fer'gant's men.

He pointed to them, and asked, "What are *they* doing here?"

"They're allies of ours. Give them a ride out of here too. They've done a lot to help us today," said Delgra.

Welk nodded, and then saluted.

"Yes, sir."

"And sergeant, I need some of your LAV's."

"We didn't bring any," said Welk.

Delgra cursed.

"See if you can't round some up. We're going to need them."

"Yes, sir!"

Tgegani studied Garmec cautiously. Without the tentacles, the droid would be easier to fight. But how easy remained to be seen. Tgegani charged at Garmec and then sidestepped to his left. Pen and Yteca studied him for a moment trying to figure out what he was doing, and then realized what his strategy was. When Garmec had ripped out its tentacles it had created a crack in the armored plates on its back. Pen grinned with devilish glee.

"Alright, it's playtime."

He then rushed at Garmec, leapt onto its back and began slashing at the cracked armor. Garmec stumbled backwards and tried desperately to reach Pen. But the lion adeptly avoided its grasp as he fought to widen the breach in the droids armor. Yteca tried to join him, but was caught in Garmec's strong grasp and hurled into a nearby retaining wall. She crashed through the wall, tumbled for a ways, and then lay still.

"Yteca!" shouted Tgegani over the radio.

But she didn't respond. Pen, realizing he was next, leapt clear of Garmec's grasp and back flipped to the ground. He then raced in Yteca's direction followed by Tgegani. She struggled awkwardly to her feet as the two lions appeared at her side.

"You alright?" asked Tgegani.

She nodded slowly.

"I'm functional, but I got banged up pretty badly. I can still fight though."

Tgegani visually scanned her body.

"Alright, but be careful. I can see cracks in your body shell. You won't be able to take much more abuse," he said.

She nodded.

"I'll be alright."

Garmec then began to walk their way as the three lions lined up, and then charged at the droid. Tgegani and Pen leapt onto Garmec's chest as Yteca flanked around and leapt at its back. But Garmec knew that she was there and spun just as she jumped, driving a powerful blow into her chest. She sailed backwards and crashed through a nearby building, tumbled to a stop, and then lay still. Tgegani could see smoke oozing from her shattered body shell.

"Yteca!" he shouted over the radio.

But this time he knew she would not be getting back up. He turned his anger towards Garmec and began attacking its face. Garmec grabbed Tgegani and tossed him in the air. Tgegani tried to catch himself, but could not. He hit the ground hard and skid to a stop. He then got up and watched as Pen flipped over Garmec's shoulders and attacked its back again. Tgegani rushed at Garmec and threw the full weight of his body against the giant robot's chest. Garmec stumbled briefly, and then caught itself. It then drove a powerful punch into Tgegani's chest. The lion's eyes went wide as he felt his body shell crack under the force of the blow.

He tumbled through the air and crashed to the ground. Pen hooked his claws into the robot and threw his weight back, pulling Garmec off balance. He then leapt clear as the droid collapsed to the ground with a thud. Tgegani quickly picked himself up and examined his body. He was injured, but he could still fight. Pen raced towards Garmec and leapt into the air. But to his surprise, Garmec had anticipated his attack. It reached up and snatched the lion out of the air and then tossed him towards a nearby wall. But Pen reacted quickly and was able to use a nearby lamp post to slow his flight. He then righted himself, landed on all four feet, and skid to a halt. Garmec turned towards him and glared at the lion. Pen ignored this and hurried over to check on Tgegani.

"You alright?" he asked.

Tgegani nodded.

"I'll last for the rest of the battle," he said.

Seeing that both lions were together, Garmec fired its rocket motors and raced towards them. Pen realized it almost too late as Garmec zeroed in on Tgegani. He immediately turned and shoved Tgegani out of the path of the giant robot. But that brave deed cost him dearly as Garmec slammed into him like a sledgehammer. The two droids flew together for a short ways before crashing through a nearby retaining wall. Garmec slowly picked itself up off the ground, and then kicked probingly at Pen's broken body as it lay on the ground at its feet. It then turned its attention to Tgegani who now stood in a state of mixed shock and anger. Garmec again fired its rockets and charged at the lion. But Tgegani wasn't going to be attacked the same way twice. He waited until Garmec was almost on top of him and then leapt into the air. The surprised robot flew under him and continued on as Tgegani reached out and grabbed at the large crack in the droid's armor.

As his claws hooked into it he was yanked out of the air and dragged along with the droid as it careened across the ground towards a nearby building. Tgegani planted his feet on Garmec's back, pulled himself free, and then leapt clear of the droid with all his might. This caused Garmec to bury its head into the ground, and then flip end over end, smashing through two trucks and a nearby building before vanishing in a cloud of fire and smoke. Tgegani landed on the ground and studied the smoldering damage path left by the droid. Several moments later Garmec reappeared, its mangled chest plate hanging awkwardly from its body. It reached across, ripped it off, and then tossed it away.

Tgegani studied this curiously, and then blinked in surprise as he realized that all of Garmec's inner workings were now exposed to attack. Garmec soon began walking towards him, a noticeable limp in its step. Seeing his opportunity, Tgegani raced towards the droid at full speed, skid to a stop at its feet, and then feigned right. Garmec reached out where it thought Tgegani was going, only to discover that the lion was not there as it expected. It quickly turned back to Tgegani just as the lion lunged at its chest and began to slash wildly, quickly decimating its now unprotected circuitry. Garmec flinched, and then began to convulse wildly as Tgegani continued to ravage the robot's internal circuitry as he fought against what he felt was his inevitable demise. Even if he could not kill Garmec, he could at least give the others a fighting chance to defeat the droid.

Suddenly his eyes were filled with a blinding white light, and then total blackness. He felt nothing, heard nothing, and saw nothing for several moments. When his senses finally did return, he was horrified to discover that he could barely move. His mind immediately turned to Garmec. He searched frantically with his eyes for the robot and soon found its shattered, burning body lying on the ground not far away. A feeling of relief swept over Tgegani. He didn't know how he'd done it, but he'd defeated Garmec. He closed his eyes and sighed happily as his senses began to fade away again. But just then he thought he could hear Welk and Sims racing towards him, screaming his name. He tried to open his eyes, but found that he couldn't. More of his systems began to fail. He was dying and there was nothing he could do to stop it. Just then his mind wandered back to thoughts of Dr. Burgon and Persia as his body slowly gave up the fight.

He smiled within himself, and thought, "I've won. Everyone will be safe now."

"Come home, Tgegani," came a soft, sweet voice in his mind.

"Meshua?" he thought in surprise.

"There's someone here who wants to see you," said the voice kindly.

"Who?" asked Tgegani.

"Your mom and dad."

"Mom and dad?" he thought in amazement.

"Come home, Tgegani," said the voice again.

"Home," thought Tgegani warmly.

And with that, his systems shut down completely and he felt nothing more. Welk and Sims skid to a stop next to him and screamed his name. Welk dropped to his knees and examined the lion thoroughly, but found him to be nonfunctional and not responsive.

"Tgegani! Tgegani! Can you hear me!?" shouted Welk.

But the lion didn't move. Welk could feel fear welling up in his heart.

"We need to do something for him! Sergeant! Find a repair kit, or a spare power source, a diagnostic unit, or something!" he cried.

Sims knelt down next to the lion and studied his broken, fractured body shell. He then leaned down and put an ear next to a hole in the lion's armor. But he heard nothing, and saw nothing, save only for a small curl of smoke wafting up out of the crack. He sighed and looked at Welk who immediately knew what the prognosis was. Tgegani was gone, and there was nothing he could do about it.

"No, *NOOOO*! There has to be something we can do!" cried Welk.

Sims sighed.

"I don't think there is," he said sadly.

Welk's lips began to quiver as tears filled his eyes. He then grabbed Tgegani around the neck, buried his face in the lion's thick, dirty mane, and wept.

Epilogue

Two months later...

Delgra sat back in his chair and happily read the headline sprawled boldly across the top of the newspaper. He grinned.

"Looks like Black's getting the gallows next Monday. I think it's a fitting end to an evil man," he said.

Odevion nodded.

"That knot on his head Breakman gave him was probably a pretty good reminder that no evil goes unpunished," he said with a grin.

"Agreed. And speaking of Breakman, how's he doing?"

Odevion frowned.

"Not so good. The death of his parents hit him pretty hard. He was even more shook up when he heard about Tgegani."

Delgra sighed.

"Those lions were some of the bravest souls I've ever met. It's too bad all their schematics and spare parts were destroyed during the fighting. I would've loved to have seen Tgegani repaired and revived again so I could thank him for what he did."

He shook his head in amazement and chuckled.

"It still astounds me that a machine like him could become so Yigzan, and in the end, selflessly give his life to save someone like us."

"So what are they going to do with the lions in the meantime? They obviously can't be repaired. Well, at least not right away," said Odevion.

"The General Secretary has ordered that they be kept safely locked away until someone can either repair their existing bodies, or build them new ones. The problem is, Burgon's designs were so advanced and revolutionary that it'll likely be several generations before someone figures out how to do that. It'll certainly never happen in my lifetime."

Odevion shrugged.

"Eh, it may be sooner than you think."

Delgra snorted.

"Not likely."

Odevion grinned.

"You never know. Oh, and by the way. I heard that the Secretary of Defense has offered you a job commanding second battalion, third ID. You going to take him up on it?"

Delgra leaned back and put his hands behind his head.

"Nah, I think I'm going to stay here."

Odevion looked at him curiously.

"Why? Isn't this what you wanted? The command of your own combat unit?"

"Yes, at one point I did. But not anymore. I feel like I need to dedicate the rest of my time in the military to helping the government revive the lions. I'll be more useful in that effort if I stay here."

Odevion grinned.

"I never thought you'd be one to stick to a desk job."

Delgra shrugged.

"After nearly six years of being here, I've really come to like it."

Odevion laughed.

"Don't go and get too comfortable or you'll have to start buying bigger uniforms."

Delgra looked at him curiously.

"What for?"

"To make room for that gut of yours," he said chidingly.

"My...what!? I *am not* getting fat, sergeant!" he protested jokingly.

"Well you will if you keep hanging out behind that desk all day like you do."

"Well, fine then! Just for that I'm going to outrun you every morning during PT! How's that? Eh? Think you can keep up with this old man?"

Odevion laughed heartily.

"Bring it on! I welcome the challenge!"

Breakman sat somberly on a hillside outside of the Echo Military Science Labs and stared blankly off into the distance as he played scenes of his family over and over again in his mind. Even two months later the bitter sting of loss had not faded away. He repeatedly went over everything that'd happened, and considered what he might've done differently to save them. If he had, Tgegani would still be alive. But instead, his parents were dead, and the lions were relegated to a dusty old storeroom in a government warehouse where they would likely lie forgotten and abandoned forever. As he sat there, O'ik walked up beside him and sat down.

"Hello, Breakman," he said kindly.

But Breakman ignored him.

"I know you miss your family dearly. I miss them as well. I still feel responsible for what happened to them that day," said O'ik.

Breakman continued to ignore him.

O'ik reached into his backpack and pulled out a small package and placed it on his lap.

"Your father was a great man. His genius impressed me every time I saw it. During the time he stayed with me in the mountains, he became restless, and did whatever he could to while away the time. His efforts produced this."

He took the package and laid it on Breakman's lap. Breakman looked down and studied it.

"What is it?" he asked.

"Open it," smiled O'ik.

Breakman looked curiously at the small package and then carefully opened it. Inside were several large journals filled to the brim with notes and drawings. As Breakman read each page, a picture began to form in his mind. His eyes grew slowly wider. He soon looked at O'ik in amazement.

"Is this..." he said, half knowing the answer.

O'ik nodded.

"He knew that Tgegani and the other lions were in grave danger, and would likely be in need of repairs when everything was done. But instead of trying to fix their old bodies, he set about designing new ones. These are his plans. With them, you can restore your brothers and sisters to life."

Breakman's expression slowly changed from amazement to one of heartfelt joy.

He clasped the journals to his chest, and said happily, "Thank you! Thank you! You don't know what this means to me!"

O'ik smiled and nodded.

"I think I do."

Breakman quickly bundled up the journals and leapt to his feet. He ran a few steps, stopped and turned back to O'ik with a smile. He then hurried off again across the prairie to find Major Delgra and Dr. Visnel in order to share with them this treasure on paper.

As he ran, he leapt for joy, and cried, "Tgegani's gonna live! He's gonna live!!"

But as he did, Negago glared at him with disdain from the shadows of a nearby grove of trees.

"You've won this time, Meshua. But ultimately *I* will have the victory, and your throne. When this is over, *you* will bow to *me*," he hissed.

The End